By the same author

The Greatest Love Story of All Time
A Passionate Love Affair with a Total Stranger
The Unfinished Symphony of You and Me

The Day We Disappeared

LUCY ROBINSON

PENGUIN BOOKS

PENGUIN BOOKS

UK | USA | Canada | Ireland | Australia
India | New Zealand | South Africa

Penguin Books is part of the Penguin Random House group of companies
whose addresses can be found at global.penguinrandomhouse.com.

Penguin
Random House
UK

First published 2015

001

Copyright © Lucy Robinson, 2015

The moral right of the author has been asserted

This is a work of fiction. Names, characters, places and incidents are either the product
of the author's imagination or are used fictitiously, and any resemblance to actual persons,
living or dead, or to actual events or locales is entirely coincidental.

Set in 12.5/14.75pt Garamond MT by Palimpsest Book Production Limited, Falkirk, Stirlingshire
Printed in Great Britain by Clays Ltd, St Ives plc

A CIP catalogue record for this book is available from the British Library

ISBN: 978–1–405–91160–3

www.greenpenguin.co.uk

There's no freedom quite like a flat-out gallop
early on a summer morning.

This book is for my mum, Lyn, without whom
I might never have known.

A young girl sits at the edge of the field with long fronds of prairie grass tickling her chin. She can smell the daisies hung in chains around her neck; a sour, sappy sort of smell that reminds her of gone-off milk and thunder. She leans back against the dry-stone wall and watches a little bug wander up her shin. There are many bugs here; bugs and itches and brilliant green slashes of grass speckled with tiny hairs.

The sun climbs higher in the sky. She wants to go and sit under the ancient beeches across the field, their swaying green leaves overhead like kaleidoscopes, those gnarled roots that you can tuck yourself into during hide and seek.

Her mother is still in the woods. She wants to go and find her, insist that they resume their game. But she can't. Without fully understanding why, she knows she must stay by the wall, concealed by the long grass, until her mother reappears.

They are going to pick apples later and make an apple tart tartan, whatever that is.

She sniffs her forearm, which smells strange and hot and mallowy, and wonders how much longer it will be until something happens. She doesn't like this game.

Out in the centre of the meadow, where the grass is shorter, daisies form a vivid blanket that shimmers strangely in the unyielding heat of the day. The girl wishes she'd never suggested hide and seek.

She hears another sound from deep within the woods, a horrible, frightening sound, and she starts to cry.

Chapter One

Kate

I stared in confusion at the hayloft.

It was not a hayloft.

It was a square white room with a single bed and a sticker on the wardrobe saying, 'I ♥ PONIES!' Even more disappointing was an unironic poster of Mark Waverley, my new employer, staring into the camera with a horse at his side. Perhaps the photographer had told him to try to look mysterious and a bit smouldery, but it hadn't worked out. He looked like a twat. Handsome, but still a twat.

The girl who had shown me up the stairs was watching me with amusement and undeniable pity. She knows, I thought, embarrassed. She knows I expected this to be a hayloft.

'Everything okay, pet?' she asked, in the mother of all Geordie accents. A smile was gathering at the weather-bruised skin round her eyes.

'Yes! It's . . . It's a lovely room!'

'Aye,' she agreed insincerely. 'Beautifully done.'

I smiled. 'It's not quite on a par with the others.'

But it was at the top of the house. A busy house, at that. It would do.

'I'm Becca,' she said, pulling off a big furry headband

she'd been wearing outside. 'And I'm sorry you've got the worst room. The trainee always gets this one, I'm afraid! But at least you're at the top of the house, so less chance of Joe bursting in naked.'

'Joe?'

'He's one of the other grooms. Randy little bastard.' She saw my face pale. 'Ah, I'm only joking, pet. Joe's a filthy old whore but he always asks first.'

'Ha-ha-ha-ha,' I said weakly. 'Always asks first. Grand.'

I clawed together what I thought to be a bright smile – the kind of smile they'd call *effervescent* in a magazine – so Becca wouldn't realize I was close to hysteria.

'So, your first job in an equestrian yard?' Her eyes drifted down to my brand-new red Hunter wellies.

'It is. You can probably tell by my wellies.'

Becca, who seemed like too decent a person to laugh at anyone's footwear, just shrugged. She had cropped hair and a nose ring and a dead roll-up sticking out between tattooed fingers. It looked like a sickly old snout that had given up and died in her hand.

That was how I was beginning to feel. Like a sickly old snout who had given up and . . . *Sweet Jesus, will you stop it!* I told myself. I was Kate Brady, that chirpy little whatsit from Dublin! Kate Brady did not wallow around in the Bad Shit! Not now, not ever!

'First job it is,' I said, more stoutly. 'But I'm not a total stranger to a horse.'

'I'd hope not, pet!'

Christ. I wasn't far off.

Becca hugged my radiator for warmth; it wasn't balmy in there. 'We had a little posh kid in on work experience last week,' she told me. 'Eighteen, straight out of ag college . . . One of those kids who leans on the broom rather than sweeping, you know?'

'I do so,' I tutted, taking note.

'And you know what she said on her first day, the silly beggar?'

'What?'

'She said, "So this place is like those Jilly Cooper novels, right? I can't *wait* to meet Mark – he's gorgeous!" I thought, Kill me now.'

'No!' I made myself titter. 'She thought it was going to be all champagne and humping your man there?'

'Exactly.' Becca shook her head. 'She was here lookin' for Rupert Campbell-Black, the silly girl.'

'Rupert Campbell-Black!' I crowed. 'Oh, sweet Jesus!' I'd have said all of that.

Becca ran her hands through her hair, which was very tired and dirty. Although all of her was, really. Bits of hay stuck to the top of her long socks and her fleece was full of holes. She had tattoos poking out of every piece of clothing she wore, and muted trance music was playing from her room, across the landing from mine.

Becca was the antithesis of anyone I'd read about in a Jilly Cooper novel, although I liked her already. There was humour lurking in her features and she'd looked after me with a touching warmth since I'd slid into the communal kitchen half an hour ago, all shaking hands and wild eyes.

I hope she'll become my friend, I thought. I was in desperate need of an ally.

'Sex and parties and whatnot.' Becca was looking wistful. 'This must be the only eventing yard where that doesn't happen. If she wanted rock 'n' roll she should've have gone and worked down the road at Caroline's, eh?'

'Caroline?'

'Caroline Lexington-Morley!'

'Of *course*,' I murmured.

Becca seemed not to notice that I had no idea who she was talking about. 'Caroline and her grooms are always first at the bar the night before a competition opens, while we're stuck in Mark's lorry polishing his boots. A charmless arsehole, pet, and he's not even good-looking. Jilly Cooper'd never write a character like that.' She massaged her heel, scowling comically at Mark's poster. 'Someone did an article in *Elle* recently, about him being Team GBR's heart-throb. Mark bloody Waverley? She must have been on the 'shrooms! He's a toad!'

I turned back to the poster in surprise. In spite of the scowl, the man was unequivocally good-looking: tall, dark-haired, classically handsome. Quite similar to Colin Firth, I thought, but without the softness of his eyes. There was nothing toadish going on there. Then again, Becca didn't look like she was very interested in men. And the coldness in Mark's face – that slight sense of unmined anger – did not sit well with me either.

I'd seen Mark Waverley at the London Olympics in 2012 and had greatly admired his bottom and the calm, unflinching way he'd ridden that monstrous cross-country course. But I'd been a different person then. All I'd needed to worry about were matters like rain ponchos or the length of the burger queue. Had anyone told me that within a couple of years I'd have quit my life and started working for him deep in the West Country of

6

England I'd have laughed, then cried, then probably just ended it all.

'Well,' I said eventually, 'he doesn't look very comfortable in his own skin.'

Becca roared with laughter. 'Mark Waverley is more comfortable in his own skin than any other man I've met! Perhaps if he was a little less comfortable he wouldn't be such an arsehole, pet. You noticed that in your interview, I'd imagine?'

I frowned. 'Well, actually –'

Becca carried on: 'If I didn't get to look after such beautiful horses I'd have left years ago. He's not right in the head – this place is like an equestrian labour camp at times.'

I started to wilt, in spite of my fierce intention to remain perky. Had I managed to walk into a nightmare as big as the one I'd just exited? Was this, like everything else I'd done in recent memory, just another huge error of judgement?

You're grand, Kate Brady, I told myself determinedly. The Jilly Cooper thing was just a passing thought! You're not shallow, just a little bit mad at the moment. And if this place is going to involve hard work then so much the better, quite frankly. You need something else to think about.

'Well, your man didn't interview me,' I said. 'I only met Sandra, so I suppose I have the pleasure of Mark to come.'

Becca stopped massaging her heel. 'Sandra? *Sandra* hired you?' She began to grin.

'Yes. Is that unusual?'

'I'd fuckin' well say, pet!'

Sandra had been absolutely delightful: a cup of hot

chocolate in human form, who'd chatted happily with me about how nice horses smelt and about how desperately proud she was of her son. 'To have come from almost nowhere and end up in the World Class squad in just six years!' she'd said mistily, as if I knew the significance of this. 'Mark is a very special man; I'm sure you'll love working for him. If you'd like the job, dear?'

I'd said yes, absolutely, and suddenly we were shaking hands and she was telling me I could join the team as a live-in trainee yard assistant starting next week, if that was okay?

'That's perfect,' I'd whispered, cradling my first tiny scrap of hope in a very long time. This could be it. The one-way ticket out of my life that I'd so longed for, while never really believing such a thing could exist. It didn't matter that I wasn't getting paid. I'd have somewhere to live, food on the table and a lot of miles between me and trouble. I'd be safe here, folded into the Exmoor hills, surrounded by people yet screened off from the world.

Becca was still looking perplexed. 'Sandra interviewed you, eh? Well, Mark'd only have let his mam do it if he was already dead certain about you.'

Something wasn't right here. 'Really?'

'Sandra's away with the fairies, that's all, pet, and I've never known her to do the interviews. But Mark'll have gone through your CV with a fine-tooth comb. It'll all be groovy.'

'I told you so,' said the Bad Shit. 'Didn't I say it was all a bit too easy? Didn't I?'

I'd marvelled, upon finishing my interview, at how simple it had been just to waltz in and get a job at one of the most prestigious eventing yards in the country. I knew next to nothing about horses and even less about eventing but I was perfectly clear about who Mark Waverley was: he was about as good as it got, not just in Britain but in the world. How extraordinary that he'd been happy to have a total novice crashing round his yard! How lucky that all I'd had to do was agree with Sandra that her son was a great rider! It was all too good to be true!

From the sound of things, it was exactly that. *Please, no*, begged a frightened little voice inside me. *I need this job to work out.*

I sat down suddenly on the edge of my bed and the Bad Shit cackled. It had me back in its sights.

The Bad Shit referred to any and all things that made life less than splendid. 'Kate Brady's so good at being happy, isn't she now?' people always said. 'Look how chirpy she is!'

The trouble was that lately the Bad Shit had got out of hand. I had never been less chirpy. *Come on, Brady*, I pleaded. *Fight.*

'So . . . What sort of thing would Mark have been looking for on my CV?' I asked pathetically. Hot, hopeless tears built in my eyes, ready for the humiliation of her reply. I hadn't an ounce of fight in me.

Becca shrugged. 'Ah, you know, the usual stuff. Years hanging round horses, good stable management, decent riding skills – although you won't get on a horse any time soon. Just mad enthusiasm, you know!'

'And, erm, just to be clear, it *is* a trainee's job, right? Even though you'd still need to be really experienced to do it?'

'Jesus, yes! Can you imagine putting a complete novice in here? Under Mark?'

I tried everything to stop the tears falling. I tipped my head back and breathed hard, but there was no stopping them. A big bobble of shame and despair rolled fatly out of one eye, followed by another. And then they fell like pouring water, down my exhausted face and on to my crispy new Gore-tex coat.

This job was not the solution. It was not the solution at all. I would be sent packing in the morning. And then? Fear moved in my stomach, black and fast.

Becca came over. 'Is there a problem, pet?' she asked cheerfully. Then: 'Obviously there's a fuckin' problem. Tell Auntie Becca. We'll sort you right out.'

I cried until I had nothing left.

Becca dug around in her pockets and found a damp, balled-up tissue and a weird navy glove with pimples on it. 'You could blow your nose on one of these,' she offered. 'Although if I were you I'd use that nice new sleeve of yours.'

Slowly, sadly, I wiped my nose on my nice new sleeve. 'I'm going to be sacked,' I said eventually.

'Ah, we all think that. Especially when Hitler over there has a go at us,' she said, gesturing at Mark Waverley's poster. 'But you'll be just fine, my little duck. You're only shovelling shit after all.'

I wiped my hands on my jeans and smiled flatly. 'No, I really will get sacked. I don't know the first thing about horses,' I told her. 'I've never been in an equestrian yard in my life. Let alone one like this.'

Becca cocked her head to one side. It was not even comprehensible to her that I might be telling the truth.

I took a deep breath. 'Sandra and me basically had a big gossip about Mark and how nice he is, and she offered me the job on the spot.'

Becca frowned. 'But your CV, pet, I don't understand . . .'

'I didn't bother sending one. I just sent an email in response to the ad online, and said I loved horses and was willing to work hard and . . . I didn't know! It said it was a trainee job!'

'Right. But surely . . .'

'But surely nothing. I needed to get out of Dublin and there was a job in Somerset for an entry-level trainee. Boom.'

Becca thought for a bit. 'So you've never looked after horses? Like, never?'

I leaned down and opened my zipper case. Inside were a few pairs of Topshop jeans and a nice merino wool cardigan. Alongside sat a pair of brown suede ankle boots and a skirt. Plus a not immodest collection of facial skin-care products. 'Do you think,' I asked, 'that if I'd looked after horses, I'd have packed like this?'

Becca peered inside. 'Ah.'

I put my head into my hands and Becca sucked in her breath, pondering my situation. I wondered if they'd even let me stay the night, and with that thought, I started to cry again.

'Ah, don't go crying,' she said absently. 'All's not lost, like.'

'All is seriously lost,' I wept. 'And on top of everything else I've gone and messed you all around.'

Becca patted my arm. There was a tattoo of a little mouse on her hand. 'It's fine,' she soothed. 'We can just advertise for someone new, it's no big deal. Mark'll probably shout at his mam for a bit, she'll say she's sorry, we'll all have a good laugh about it and you can find another job. A better one!'

'There is no better job!' I muttered. '*This* was the one. I need this job more than I can tell you . . .'

Becca carried on patting my arm while I cried, watching me with a fascination that I'd otherwise have found funny. 'Pet,' she asked eventually. 'Have you got yourself into a spot of bother?'

A spot of bother. I almost smiled.

'Well, I know all about those,' she said kindly. 'And if you need to keep the job then I'll help you blag it. But you'll have to tell me what we're working with here.'

I felt so hopeless at that moment that I almost considered telling her the whole story. 'Well,' I began, after a sniffy pause. Best to stick with the headlines for now. 'I had a bit of a breakdown.'

Becca looked cheerful. 'Didn't we all?'

'I was after working for Google in Dublin but I'd to leave because I was suffering severe stress.'

Becca, rather to my surprise, started sniggering. 'Have you escaped the nuthouse?' she asked. 'Are there a load of psychiatric folk on your trail?'

'Erm, I hope not. I didn't go mad, just hit a wall quite badly. Executive stress, you know.'

Becca slapped her leg. 'Ha-HA! Executive stress! Whatever next?'

I smiled thinly. 'The job was fine, it was me that was the problem. I mean, they did everything they could to support me . . . But I'm just a fruitloop. Burned myself out, let everything get to me. You know.'

Becca nodded sympathetically but I could tell she was trying not to laugh.

I took a deep breath. 'I came here because I wanted – literally – some fresh air. I wanted to be somewhere I wouldn't have any cause to think about Dublin and the Bad Shit for a long time.'

Becca couldn't keep it up any longer. First she snorted, then she gave up and roared with laughter. 'Pet, you need a lobotomy! I can't believe you! You left your job suffering stress and you came to a *horse* yard to recover? Where you'd have to do manual labour twelve hours a day? What were you thinking?'

'Um . . .'

'Could you not have gone and worked in a kebab van or something, my little love? Oh, God, this is priceless.'

In spite of everything, of how exhausted and frightened I was, I smiled. Becca rolled across my bed with an imaginary rifle and took a stealth position at my window, lining someone up in her sights. With her cropped hair and dark eyes she was pretty authentic, I thought.

'Boom,' she whispered, into an imaginary mouthpiece. 'Both hostiles are down. This area is clear, I repeat this area is clear. All mental-health professionals chasing Kate Brady have been deleted.' She rolled back, removing an SAS helmet. 'You're going to be okay, pet. It was a tough call there, but I've got it under control.'

I was giggling, which was pretty rare, these days. 'It sounds ridiculous, doesn't it?'

'It does indeed, pet, but you've brightened up my day. A fugitive in our midst!'

We both laughed, and I felt very grateful that this

complete stranger was giving up her evening to listen to the Bad Shit. Or at least an approximation of it.

'My body is fine,' I insisted. 'It was my head that broke. I don't mind the hard work, Becca. I just need time out.'

Becca watched me, her brain ticking over. 'Okay, pet, let's talk about what we're going to do.' The smile had gone, although there was still warmth in her face. 'I can help you keep your job, if you want, but I need to know you're serious about it. If you've just run off to hang out on a pretty farm and play with the nice horsies, you've come to the wrong place.'

I shook my head. 'No way. I want a routine, I want physical work and I want to live somewhere that couldn't be more different from, well, from Dublin. I'm not here for the nice horsy games.'

Becca rested her chin on her fingertips, studying me. She had a sweet little snub nose, just like my mum's. 'This is one of the hardest jobs there is, Kate. Grooms only survive because they want it so badly. They never get enough sleep, they work in the snow and driving rain, they're never allowed to be ill or tired, and they don't really have control of their own lives. The horses always come first. Your family, for starters – you're not going to get time off to go over to Ireland any time soon. Are you okay with that?'

I took a deep breath. 'My family aren't expecting to see me for a very long time,' I said truthfully. 'They're not happy about it but – well, they'll survive.'

I smiled, because the guilt was overwhelming and I didn't know what else to do.

'Okay. Well, on top of that, Mark's an arsehole and

Tiggy – she's the Head Girl – she's only okay if you play her game. Oh, and Joe's a nice lad but he's also a dirty sex pest.'

'Grand.'

She smiled wryly. 'This is not an easy job. Are you sure you want it?'

'Absolutely,' I said.

Becca nodded, apparently satisfied. 'We'll forget we ever had this conversation, then. You're going to work your little peaches off and you'll have forgotten about Dublin and your "executive stress" in five minutes. Deal?'

'Deal. But what about all the stuff I'm meant to know about horses?'

'Once you've learned to shovel shit, love, we'll teach you the rest. Auntie Becca'll sort you out.'

'But if Mark Waverley's as bad as you say, you'll lose your job.'

'Very noble of you. But where are you going to go if I don't help you out, like?'

A good question. The world yawned emptily around me; the world that was no longer my friend. 'I'd sort something out.'

Becca grinned. 'Kate, love, it'll be okay. By the time Mark even bothers to ask your name you'll know enough to blag it.'

I breathed out slowly. This might just be the answer. 'Why are you doing this for me?' I asked her.

To my surprise, Becca blushed. 'Never you mind,' she muttered. 'Never you mind about that, pet. Anyways, do we have a deal?'

I held out my hand, soft, plump and white, and took

Becca's, rough, red and dirty. 'We have a deal,' I said softly. 'And whatever reason you have for helping me, Becca, thank you.'

'There's a lot to learn,' Becca said, still pink-cheeked. 'But we'll get there.' She pulled out a packet of tobacco and some Rizlas, rolling a fag with mesmerizing dexterity. I suddenly loved this crop-haired, nose-ringed Geordie woman. I wanted to grab her grubby fleece and hug her all night. I was so completely lost and alone, so totally disconnected from the entire universe, that my boundaries were shot. I'd have hugged a chicken, if it was nice to me.

'Get yourself settled, then come downstairs to meet the others. Later we'll do a tutorial.'

I forced my best smile. It was like a migraine. 'Grand! Thanks! I'll be down in a sec!'

'Cool. Later.'

'Oh! Becca?'

'Yeah?'

'What time do we start in the morning?'

'Seven.' She sounded casual, as if this were a reasonable time of day to be awake. Let alone working in the mud and cold.

I sank back on my very mediocre bed.

'Are you going to kill yourself, pet?'

'I am.'

'Right you are. I'll leave you to it.' She left, humming along to the trance music coming out of her bedroom.

I slid the bolt across my door and went over to shut my curtains. I glanced out beyond the floodlit horse yard to the silky blackness of the fields, feeling vaguely hopeful again. I'd just have to take it one day at a time and trust I was up to it. Because, really, it was that or return to my old life, which was an impossibility. Quite apart from the Dante-proportioned inferno I'd fled, I felt a horrible certainty that my family and friends would never forgive what I'd done.

No, *this* was my life now. It was 17 March and spring would officially begin in three days. Spring would inch slowly forward into summer, never back into winter, and if I knew what was good for me, I'd tag along.

As I turned away my eye was caught by a sudden movement at the edge of the blackness and my heart stopped. Muscles weakened by fear, I turned back to see what it was.

A big grey dog trotted in from the fields and across the yard towards Mark Waverley's house. A bright floodlight snapped on. Downstairs a door banged and laughter from the kitchen floated up the thirty-three stairs that lay between me and the world. 'Happy St Patrick's Day!' someone shouted.

I pulled the curtains closed and breathed.

In.

Out.

In.

Out.

Chapter Two

Annie

The four of us were in that French restaurant up the side of Clapham Common tube. None of us could remember its name.

We referred to it as Le Cloob – French(ish) for the Club – which was what the restaurant had become for us. It was absurd that we had to meet so far away from our homes: I lived in Lower Clapton, Tim lived in Bethnal Green, Claudine lived in Chiswick and Lizzy lived in Chelsea. But Claudine insisted that we met there, and people didn't argue with Claudine.

She was the fiercest and most terrifying woman any of us had known, yet she was also one of the funniest and most loyal. She loved us all ferociously and made us laugh until we cried, and as long as we kept on the right side of her the friendship worked. Certainly for me this beautiful little Rottweiler was a source of strength that my life otherwise lacked entirely. If I was to avoid drifting vaguely off the side of the earth and into space, I needed firm tethering and Claudine had stepped into that role ten years ago with neither consultation nor appointment. I had been, and remained, grateful. Tim and Lizzy couldn't carry on managing me for ever.

A couple of years ago Claudine had said she could only

live in 'this dreadful country' if she got to eat bona-fide confit duck or steak tartare when she dined out, so we'd agreed to meet only in French restaurants. It kept Claudine quiet and provided a wonderful excuse for me to eat bread and cheese and all the things I wasn't allowed. ('But I'm gluten-free and dairy-free!' I'd wail, shoving my baguette into a giant baked Camembert.)

After trying almost every French restaurant London had to offer, Claudine had announced, without sharing any reasons, that this was her favourite. So here we were once a month: Le Cloob.

The only problem: 'I '*ate* Clapham,' Claudine said, giving her chair a little kick as if it were Clapham. 'I must find another restaurant. My soul dies every time I come to this '*ole.*' Claudine spoke with a heavy French accent, in spite of being fully bilingual, because she didn't see the point in trying to sound English.

'Claudie, darling, do behave,' Lizzy said. She was beautiful tonight in orange lipstick and one of those padded skirts that trendy people were partial to. 'We only come here because of *you*, my little Froggie. Although I do rather hate Clapham myself.'

Tim was not the sort of person to hate anything or anyone, so he just smiled tolerantly. As did I, because I avoided discord at all costs. 'Happy St Patrick's Day!' I offered, raising my glass.

The waiter came to take our dessert orders and, as usual, spoke only in French. A few years ago, Claudine had gone on strike as our translator – 'You are an embarrassment to your country,' she'd muttered darkly, so Tim had done a year of French evening classes to rescue us.

That was the sort of man Tim Furniss was. Unimpeachably brilliant.

As usual I dithered agonizingly and Tim stepped in. 'I ordered you a crème brûlée. Apricot. Is that okay?' he asked, after the waiter had gone. 'What with you not eating sugar?' There was a little too much cheek in his smile.

'Ah, well. It's a one-off.'

He grinned.

'Sssh, Tim. And crème brûlée is perfect, thank you.'

Tim, like Claudine, was excellent at hoicking me out of paralysed indecision, only he, poor man, had been doing it since we were teenagers. Aged sixteen, I'd walked into that awful support group and found Tim lurking by the door, looking as depressed as I felt. Within days, we had become inseparable. He was my rock, Tim Furniss, my anchor. Tonight he'd brought me an article he'd read in some clever periodical about how many therapists and mental-health professionals – not just complementary therapists like me, but proper psychotherapists, psychologists and even psychiatrists, like him – were basically mad themselves. And how that was okay because we were all human beings, struggling through the boggy wilderness of life. It had made me feel so much better.

Sometimes I could feel quite sad about the fact that my mental health was so sketchy. I was thirty-two; it wasn't right. What kind of thirty-two-year-old was so scared of making decisions that her friend had to choose her dessert? What kind of thirty-two-year-old spent so much time worrying about things that she never actually did anything? Not to mention having been essentially boyfriendless her whole life. And having had sex only once.

Well, one and a half times. But half-sexings were a minor detail in that mess, really.

More wine was poured. St Patrick's Day was toasted several times and everyone became increasingly drunk. Dessert arrived and Claudine, with a ferocious look in her eye, started grilling Lizzy about her multiple lovers.

'I'm thirty-four, darling.' Lizzy shrugged. 'Two boy-friends at the same time is a simple matter of expediency.'

I watched my big sister curiously, wondering if this was how she really felt.

'But these are real relationships, you 'arlot!' Claudine cried. A few years ago Claudine had fallen in love with (and promptly married) one of her osteopathic clients, a hairy man from Melton Mowbray called Sylvester. Once or twice a month Sylvester gave people 'gong showers' for a tenner a pop but otherwise he sat around playing computer games and farting. Rather surprisingly, given the kind of formidable woman Claudine was, she adored this farter. She was unswervingly committed to the marriage and very severe with anyone who didn't take their own relationship seriously.

'Lizzy, my dirty little cabbage, these men think they are your boyfriend! They spend ze weekend wiz you! I am betting they do all that smiley pillow talking on a Saturday morning! *Merde*, you are the very worst!'

'You're right.' Lizzy giggled, digging into her *tarte au citron*. 'They both adore me! I do one weekend with Freddy and the next with Tom. They think I'm looking after Dad when it's their weekend off. Ha-ha!'

'Disgusting,' Claudine grumbled. 'Depraved.'

'Oh, Lizzy.' I sighed. 'Leave Dad out of it.'

'Oh, *Annie.*' Lizzy sighed back. 'Bugger off. I haven't said he's dying of cancer or anything, just that he's lonely and needs company. Which is true so don't go all pious on me.'

It was true. Lizzy and I frequently travelled to Bakewell to keep Dad company, separately so he'd receive more visits. We'd eat cake and listen to music, look at old photos and make plans for a redecoration of the house that would never happen. When I returned home on the train to St Pancras my heart would ache. He was so humble in his solitude, so uncomplaining.

'Do you think you might one day make one of these men your full-time boyfriend?' Tim asked.

Lizzy thought about it. 'Honestly? No. They're terribly precious, in their different ways, but I don't want either of them to father my children.'

'Then shouldn't you let them go?' Tim asked mildly.

'Listen to Tim,' Claudine hissed. 'You must set them free. You are being prostitute of the highest order.'

I didn't think Lizzy was being a prostitute of any order but I did worry about her technicolour love life. Quite apart from the fact that she was still repeating the same dysfunctional patterns she'd started as a teenager, I couldn't help worrying that one of her boyfriends would one day discover he was being cuckolded and kill her or something. A little scene played out in my head where I went round to her flat and found a raging ex-boyfriend leaving with a bloody hammer, and I had to organize a funeral while my organs collapsed with misery.

'Look, *I* don't think you're a filthy whore,' I began. 'But I do think it's a bit unhealthy, Lizzy Lou . . .'

'Butt out.' She grinned. 'You don't get to go around psychologizing me with a love life like yours!'

Claudine, who had no loyalty to anyone, agreed.

I blushed painfully. My outstandingly disordered relationship history was a textbook case for any psychologist, although I failed to agree that Lizzy's was any better. Mum had died when I was seven and Lizzy was nine, and since then we'd exhibited all the classics – fear of abandonment, terror of intimacy and a sturdy collection of unhelpful emotional defences and coping mechanisms. My pattern was to spend my time avoiding men, fantasizing safely about the ones I couldn't have, while Lizzy's was to have wild, often painful flings with hundreds while never really letting anyone get close to her.

It was annoying. I'd been seeing a shrink on and off for years. I had self-awareness coming out of my pores yet I didn't seem able to change. I longed for a Saturday cuddle with a nice boyfriend, all morning breath and semi-tumescent willies, but the reality of attempting anything like that left me in a white panic. Instead I 'enjoyed' pampering Friday nights behind my triple-locked front door, 'revelling' in the luxury of my homemade avocado face-masks and Buddhist-lite meditations, while a secret part of me stung bitterly as I imagined other people meeting their future partners in trendy bars that I was too scared to go into.

All the while Lizzy, with her glossy mane of wavy golden hair and her milky-skinned beauty, blazed through a trail of men who wouldn't give up and often died trying.

'Your love life, Annie.' Lizzy smiled. 'What was it Kate Brady said last time she was over?'

'That my love life is just fine,' I mumbled.

'No, darling. Kate said – and forgive me for quoting this directly, but it's rather special – she said your love life was like something from a provincial radio's Sunday-night phone-in. I thought that was outstanding.'

I blushed even harder. Kate Brady was a little bugger. We'd met a few years ago during one of my (many) backpacking trips to Asia and I had formed an enormous girl crush on her from the get-go. She was the sunniest, most carefree woman I'd ever met, with a mane of deep red hair, big green eyes and that beguiling Irish accent. Everyone loved Kate Brady, with her relentless cheerfulness and point-blank refusal to wallow in what she called the Bad Shit. Were it not for the fact that she lived in Dublin we'd have made her a full-time member of Le Cloob. As it was, she was the only civilian who was granted entry to our monthly meetings whenever she visited London.

'I'm joking, little one,' Lizzy said, touching my shoulder.

'I know.' I swallowed. 'But you're still right. You *and* Kate. It's not great.'

Lizzy tucked my hair behind my ear. 'You're doing fine,' she said gently. 'Just fine.'

I nodded.

'And anyway,' she turned to Tim, perhaps to take the spotlight off me, 'even if Annie's not getting any, we can at least be grateful that Tim is, eh, Timmy?' She cackled with deep Chaucerian filthiness as all eyes turned on him.

'Thanks,' Tim said, in his lovely soft Derbyshire accent. 'I assume you've been online stalking me?'

'Yes! Tell us everything!'

*** DUE DATE REMINDER ***

Library name: BSHO

Author: Thomas, Rosie.
Title: The illusionists
Item ID: 1805737341
Date due: 2/2/2019,23:59

Author: Trigiani, Adriana.
Title: The Supreme Macaroni
Company
Item ID: 1805256816
Date due: 2/2/2019,23:59

Author: Scott, Nikola,
Title: My mother's shadow
Item ID: 4102885839
Date due: 2/2/2019,23:59

Author: Robinson, Lucy.
Title: The day we
disappeared
Item ID: 1805737309
Date due: 2/2/2019,23:59

'It's early days,' he said. 'We've been on maybe half a dozen dates.'

Lizzy crowed and Claudine muttered choice French words. 'She's called Mel,' he said.

I picked at a bobble on my jumper.

'She's twenty-nine,' he continued, 'and she does yoga with my sister-in-law, Miranda. Miranda thought I'd like her.' Lizzy leaned in, waiting for his verdict. 'And I do.'

'Get in!' Lizzy shouted. 'Tim's back in the saddle!' When Lizzy got drunk she forgot to speak like a dandy.

Tim stared at Lizzy, perhaps in disgust, then smiled. 'I like her a lot, actually. But, as I said, it's early days.'

'*Fantastique*, my little koala,' Claudine muttered. 'I 'ope that *you* show your relationship the respect it deserves.' She scowled at Lizzy, who took no notice whatsoever.

Meanwhile I was having strong words with myself, because – as it always did when Tim met a girl – my heart had sunk ever so slightly at this news.

Tim and I were not meant to be: we'd tried it once, many years ago, and it had been horrible. A hot fumbly month 'together', beginning with the one and a half sexings and concluding in three months without contact, which was unheard of for us. When we did finally meet up and agree that it was not something we would ever try again, the relief was thundering.

But there was always a little astringent pain when he started going out with someone. A scratching sadness that it wasn't me; that we had never quite managed to solve the problem of our incompatibility. Tim would make a brilliant boyfriend, if only we fancied each other. I'd be safe with him.

'That's great news, Tim,' I said, smiling at my tall, hand-some, preppy friend, who wore nice ironed shirts and had lemony armpits. 'Well done, you.'

Lizzy ordered another bottle of wine. 'Time to cele-brate,' she shouted, far too loudly. 'Our Timmy is stepping out with a nubile yogi!'

Tim agreed to the bottle of Bordeaux that Lizzy couldn't afford and winked at me. 'But Annie has some news too,' he said.

'You're not seeing someone, are you?' Claudine whis-pered, horrified.

I couldn't help but laugh. 'No. But if I were, I'd have been very touched by your reaction.'

'*Désolée*, my little Jerusalem artichoke.' She grinned. 'I am 'orrible. Uneasy in the happiness of others, no? Tell us your news!'

'Um, well, I've got a new job!' I announced, happy again. Of course it would be okay if Tim fell madly in love. Everything was going to be fine because I had a sparkly new job and a glorious new boss with whom I could fall in safe, unreciprocated love.

'You sly dog!' Lizzy was scandalized. 'Tell us everything!'

It had all happened quite quickly. My private practice as a masseuse and reiki healer had dive-bombed during the recession, because most people had decided – quite sensi-bly, I had to admit – that healing was not top priority when they were at risk of losing their home. I'd been unable to keep my practice in London Fields and had had to start renting rooms by the hour at a host of complementary health centres across the city, only two of which were near my house in east London.

I practised in Balham, Marylebone, Farringdon and Dalston during the week, with fortnightly clinics in Bethnal Green and Wandsworth. At the weekend I worked in Kent and sometimes even Surrey. Three years into this punishing cross-town schedule I was exhausted and almost beaten, more useless than ever at maintaining my supposedly healthy lifestyle and looking increasingly like a fat old buffalo, as opposed to a sparkling and vital alternative practitioner.

I desperately missed my private treatment space, a beautiful old room on the easternmost tip of London Fields, a five-minute cycle from my house. I'd set up the practice with Claudine, who was an osteopath, and another girl called Tessa, who was a nutritional therapist. Our rooms overlooked vast lime trees which spread their rustling fingers far across the park, and I never had to deal with the tube or the centre of London, both of which roused anxiety in me that had become harder and harder to contain.

My workplace had been the Garden of Eden. There had even been a *receptionist*.

Now it was the fiery pit of Hell, a dismal tangle of tubes, trains and buses, packed with unsettlingly furious people and limitless opportunities for me to lose Oyster cards and train tickets. I hated it. It took all I had to force myself on to the tube each day; all of those people I neither knew nor trusted, all those smells and germs, possible terrorist attacks and cramped spaces.

These days, I could barely remember the steady determination to improve the lives of others that had driven me to train in the first place. It all just felt like a trauma.

Tim, Lizzy and Claudine all had other friends, of course; Le Cloob meetings were just a part of their calendar. And once upon a time I'd been the same. But these days Le Cloob was the sum total of my social life because I had lost the confidence and energy to reach further.

There had been discussions about my work situation. Lizzy counselled me to borrow from the bank and brave it out in private practice until the recession ended, but she had no real understanding of money. She had a freak scientific brain – the only one in our family – and spent her days designing crazily complicated algorithms that somehow translated themselves into smartphone software. The money was good but she lived as if she were the chief executive of Apple, rather than a tiny, tiny bite of its operations. Dad and I had bailed her out more than once.

Claudine usually went quiet when the subject came up because she'd had no trouble finding a new clinic and was now making buckets of money. She was excellent at shouty advice but poor at hand-holding. And Tim was great with suggestions for finding peace amid the madness but he was a bit stumped on the subject of how to get me a new job.

I'd written a rambly blog for a while – as if that was going to help anything – but had stopped because I felt uncomfortable putting myself out there into the world. The world knew too much about me already.

So, the dent of unhappiness and frustration in me had deepened, and with that had come a low-level rumbling of fear. I had by no means forgotten what I was capable of when I was really low.

Then the day before yesterday the end of the tunnel

had appeared, seemingly out of nowhere. An angel called Stephen Flint had walked into my Farringdon clinic and everything had changed, for ever.

As my penultimate massage had come to an end I'd been dimly aware of some sort of rumpus in the reception area. It had taken me quite a while to calm myself – I had initially decided we were being robbed, of course – but eventually I made it out to Reception where my next client, who appeared to be at the centre of the commotion – was waiting. Somehow he had reduced Dorota, our usually mute and evasive receptionist, to shrieking giggles.

Amazed, I turned back to look at him. He was a typical City client – moneyed, extremely well dressed, attractive. But the almost-palpable charm of the man, the powerful electrical field around him, was not so typical. Dorota was as shiny as a bauble.

'Oh dear.' He smiled. 'We've distracted you. It was her fault,' he said, in Dorota's direction.

Dorota screamed.

I took in the client's long legs in expensive tapered trousers and his pale, piercing blue eyes. Sandy hair styled neatly, and a cardboard espresso cup, even though it was nearly eight p.m. I wished I could go home now, rather than having to massage a caffeinated businessman who flirted with Slovakian receptionists while his wife was probably putting the kids to bed.

In time I would remember that moment. The moment before Stephen Flint meant anything to me. I was barefoot, my hair in a raggedy plait. I was wearing a long skirt I'd bought in India and I smelt of geranium oil. I was still

Annie Mulholland. I was still in the driving seat of my own life.

'Sorry,' he said, with a subversive grin. 'Best behaviour now.'

'No problem. Stephen Flint, yes? Come on through.'

'Thanks.' He was up already – surprisingly tall – and shaking my hand. 'And you must be Annabel. How are you?' He asked it as if he'd known me for years.

'Er, take a seat. Can I get you a glass of water?'

'Oh, go on, then. If I must.' He sat down, grinning at me with ice-bright eyes as I handed him the water and closed the door. It was lucky, I thought, that I could so comfortably welcome male clients into a treatment room when I hated being alone with men in any other situation. A little reminder that I really did love my job, in spite of all the trouble that was attached to it these days.

'So, is this your first time having massage therapy?' I began, noticing a hangnail on my thumb. The room smelt of massage oils and tiredness; I was relieved to be going home in an hour.

'It is,' Stephen said. 'I was ordered to get some massages by one of the wellbeing coaches we have at work. Fearsome woman. I can't say no to her, even though I pay her.'

I started to take notes. Stephen Flint was a founding director of FlintSpark, a massive global media agency. Whatever that was. As he rocketed on I remembered that one of their employees had visited me for some massages last year, a sweet Australian girl who'd been so distressed about her line manager that she'd ended up going back Down Under.

Stephen Flint looked like the sort of man who'd be devastated to learn that something like that had gone on in his company. 'The happiness of my workforce is an embarrassing obsession,' he explained eagerly. He had supplemented his award-winning workspace with every imaginable employee benefit, including – more recently – a wellbeing team. 'Everyone has to see a wellbeing coach once a month, whether they want to or not. If someone's not happy, the coach will find out. They'll send them for counselling, business coaching, a nutritionist, whatever, and we pay the first six sessions. All totally confidential, we never know who's been referred where. You're my coach's latest attempt at reducing my stress levels.' He giggled like a naughty schoolboy. 'She says my body is in peril. She wants me to eat kale, get massages and start yoga. Yoga!'

Stephen had founded FlintSpark in 2001 and now his company was one of the most successful in the industry, with offices popping up around the world. He worked a crazy schedule, under a great deal of pressure ('Entirely self-imposed,' he said cheerfully. 'But God never takes a day off so neither do I. I'm the Leader of the People, you see.') Nonetheless he had agreed to an occasional massage, given that this clinic was only a few doors down from his company's state-of-the-art glass headquarters in Farringdon.

'I'm only here to get the coach off my back,' he admitted. 'And that's no slight on you and your work – but, let's be honest, people like me are a total waste of your talents. I arrived with a double espresso, for starters.'

In spite of myself, I smiled. I felt little connection with

men like Stephen Flint but at least he was honest. 'Massage is wasted on nobody,' I said. 'Even if your investment in self-care only extends to one massage a week, it's a start. There's all sorts of research papers about the benefits of just thirty minutes.'

'Really?' Stephen rested his chin on his hands, watching me intently. He wore a fashionable narrow tie. 'Do you agree with that? Do you think massage really makes a difference?'

'Of course! I wouldn't do this job otherwise. Helping people feel good . . . relax . . . find a bit of peace . . . it's . . .' I blushed for no reason. 'It's everything to me,' I said, surprised by my honesty. It *was* everything to me. If I couldn't help myself find peace, I could at least help others.

'So.' Stephen seemed fascinated. 'This is your job simply because you want to help people?'

'Yes.'

He broke into a brilliant smile. 'How refreshing,' he said, after a long pause. 'How very refreshing to hear something like that. We need generous people like you in the world. I knew as soon as I found you that you'd be right.'

My face was red. I didn't know why. 'Well, I'm metres away from your office,' I mumbled.

'There is that too.' He chuckled. 'Well, Annabel, do your best. Feel free to crack out a mallet when you get to the knotty bits.'

Stephen was full of knots, of course. Which was a shame because he had a beautifully put-together body, smooth and brown and perfectly proportioned. He fell asleep quite soon into the massage, like so many men of his type, and at the end was like a swaddled baby, encased in towels, all drooping eyelids and soft edges. 'Oh, my God,' he groaned. 'Oh, my God, that was incredible! Annabel, I can't thank you enough.' He closed his eyes again, grinning sleepily. 'You're amazing . . .'

I went outside while he got back into his clothes. Rather embarrassingly, I heard my phone go off in my bag, which was still in the treatment room. I had to get better at remembering to turn it off. I'd have looked awful if it had gone off during his session – he could have reported me to the Association of Complementary Therapists, who might strike me off the register. And if I couldn't practise as a masseuse what else could I do? I had no other skills, I –

Sssh, I told myself. *Relax, Annie. You'll be home soon.*

Sometimes I could beat the Bad Shit, as Kate Brady would say. Mostly, though, I could not. I made a mental note to Skype her soon; it had been ages.

Dorota had gone home, leaving a soft lamp on in Reception. I was stunningly exhausted after a full morning in Marylebone, a full afternoon in Farringdon and a rushed lunch eaten on the Circle Line between the two. I popped my feet up on the sofa next to me, rubbing them gently with my still-oily hands, and closed my eyes.

'I'm afraid I'm going to have to wake you,' a voice said quietly. I panicked. A man was staring at me in the semi-darkness of a room I didn't know.

'I couldn't quite bring myself to sneak off without paying.' He smiled.

His eyes were sky-bright, even in the low light. Oh, God. Stephen. Client. Sleep. Silly, silly me. 'I'm so sorry,' I began, my face and neck staining red. 'I must have drifted off while you got dressed.' I hauled myself up to a sitting position, my heart still racing. Stephen sat down next to me. 'No, no, take a rest,' he said, as I tried to get up. My legs were still limp with shock so I did as I was told.

'Really, no need to apologize.' Stephen folded some crisp banknotes in his hand, watching me. His face was kindly, amused, almost tender, still marked by the massage table's face hole. 'You looked very sweet and peaceful there. Not to mention completely shattered.'

'I am shattered.' I didn't have the energy to lie.

'Long day?'

I nodded. He sounded so sympathetic that I somehow forgot about my normal client boundaries. 'Very long day. It's lovely work, but it's very physical.'

'Yes, I'd imagine. You guys must have to do all sorts of exercise to stay strong.'

'I don't really have time for exercise,' I said. 'Or to eat well! I used to cook everything from scratch.'

I cleared my throat and tried to straighten up a bit but there was something hypnotic about the sofa, the low light and that surprisingly compassionate man. Normally my conversations with clients were one-way affairs: long monologues about them and their problems punctuated by sympathetic comments from my corner. And I quite liked that. I enjoyed the focus being on someone else. Here, though, was someone who wanted to turn the lamp of kindness on me.

'It seems a shame,' Stephen offered, 'that someone who wants to help others doesn't have enough time to help herself.'

I'd never thought about that. He was right.

'Maybe instead of having my next massage I'll send you off for some yoga and an early night, and pay you anyway.'

I smiled tiredly. 'In all honesty I think I'd die if I tried to do yoga, these days! I'm so unfit . . . But it's a nice idea.'

'I know how you feel,' he said, surprising me again. 'I kind of don't really allow myself to stop because if I did I think I'd be so broken I'd never start again.'

I looked at him, at those twinkling eyes. Now he came to mention it, I could see the tiredness in them. And a warmth I didn't expect from his sort. 'You said it's all self-imposed, though,' I said, after a pause.

Stephen yawned and stretched, leaning back into the sofa. He popped his feet up on the coffee-table, just like that, and turned his face to the ceiling. 'It is entirely self-imposed,' he reflected. 'But it's just how I am. There aren't many people like me in business, people who can lead so effectively. I hope that doesn't sound arrogant. I just mean that to be a leader, a role model, a friend to your work-force, you have to sacrifice your own life a bit. Well, a lot. You have to be their mum, their dad, their brother and their annoying bossy old granddad.'

I stared at his monstrously expensive shoes, tickled by the idea of this extremely attractive man being a bossy old granddad. 'Do you have a private jet?' I asked, on a whim.

'The company does,' he admitted, 'and I find it embarrassing, but we basically have to have one, with offices in so many places. So I plant more bloody sustainable forests than farmers plant carrots. I'm the ultimate guilty capitalist.' He smiled at me suddenly, an intense sort of a smile that made me feel like he could see all of me. 'So much about my life must look ostentatious and gaudy,' he said, 'but I reckon that as long as I stay nice underneath, it's okay.'

'I reckon so too,' I said. We were still looking right at each other.

The moment passed. 'Right, well, I'd better take some money from you,' I said.

'What time are you back here tomorrow?' He handed me some banknotes and I got up to find him a receipt. 'Will you get a lie-in at all?'

I explained that I worked all over London and was only there two afternoons a week.

'Crikey. No wonder you're tired! Well, I hope someone's going to make you a lovely dinner and give you a nice massage all of your own.' He pulled on his coat, a wool affair in a grey herringbone.

'Um, not tonight.' I was unwilling to tell him that I lived alone.

'No?'

'No.'

'Oh dear! Well, Annie Mulholland, I demand that you get a very expensive takeaway. The sort that arrives with a bottle of Chablis and a bunch of flowers.'

Stephen looked as if he cared about my evening a great deal, possibly more than he cared about his own. And I was impressed that he'd not only remembered my name but been brave enough to call me Annie.

I wished for a second that *he* would be there when I got home, serving something wholesome in a nice rustic bowl, with that smile and those warm, penetrating eyes. Being all handsome and leaderish.

The reality was that I'd arrive at a lonely, dark house and probably eat two chocolate mousses before passing out.

'Can't you just work in one clinic?' he persisted. 'So you don't have to spend your life on the run?'

I explained, as briefly as I could, why my work situation was as it was.

'You poor thing,' he said. I handed him a receipt and shrugged.

'You're very talented at what you do, Annie. That was the nicest hour I can remember. Although you're substandard at the old admin, I'm afraid. You've made this receipt out for September and, unless I'm much mistaken, it's March the fifteenth.'

'Oh, God, sorry! I do this sort of thing all the time – it drives me mad!' I wrote him a new one, thinking that this was probably the longest conversation I'd had in years with a man who wasn't Tim or my dad.

'I'll have my wellbeing people get in touch,' Stephen said. 'If you're interested in becoming a supplier of services to the company, they can arrange direct payment, so you don't have to deal with physical money next time I come.'

'Oh! Yes, I'd love to talk to them about that!'

'Excellent.'

'Thank you,' I said suddenly. 'Thank you for being so concerned. It's very kind.'

'We men aren't all bad,' Stephen said, as I handed him the new receipt. 'Some of us are actually quite pleasant.'

I ducked my head, fussing around with the receipt book. *If only you knew*, I thought.

'I read a book once,' he continued, 'about a man who was stuck. His life had gone so far from the direction he wanted it to that he barely knew himself any more. He was sad, exhausted, and felt completely alone in the world.'

'Oh, yes?'

'This man didn't know what to do, so he began by hugging himself throughout the day. Telling himself that everything would work out fine.' He paused. 'It touched me. I tried it, and it was lovely. Maybe you could try it some time.'

After he'd gone I stood in the reception area for several minutes. I hadn't expected that at all.

I went home, ate two Gü chocolate mousses and passed out after fifteen minutes of a Jeremy Paxman documentary about the Great War. I didn't hug myself.

I received a call at eight fifteen the next morning.

'It's Stephen Flint,' said a vaguely familiar voice. 'How are you!'

The blue-eyed boy. He must have been back to my website. To my surprise, I rather liked that idea.

I watched the rammed Overground train pull into Homerton station, people squashed up against the doors like gherkins in a jar. My heart sank. The sky was filthy brown and if I didn't fight my way on I'd get soaked.

'Hi, Stephen,' I said, tensing anxiously as I prepared for the scrum.

'Would you like to come and work for us in-house?' Stephen asked, as casually as one might say, 'Would you like a packet of crisps?'

I had managed to lever myself into the train but my

worn Burmese bag was trapped between a pregnant belly and a briefcase. I tried to coax it out without squashing the belly.

'Hello?' Stephen sounded as if he'd just walked into a coffee bar. 'Double espresso, please,' he said, in the other direction. 'Can you hear me, Annie? I was asking if you'd like to come and work for us. That massage was top rate, and if I brought someone like you into the offices our wellbeing coaches would die happy. You don't want to carry on schlepping around London, do you? We could give you the treatment room of your dreams here. Soft lighting. Oxygenating plants. A man with pan pipes.'

The carriage, stuffed with people, was completely silent. I was shoved up against an old man with a bobble hat who smelt of death. He had done nothing at all other than smell bad but already my heart was thumping anxiously at his proximity.

'Erm?' I said. Was Stephen Flint seriously offering me a job? I arched my back to keep as far away from the bobble-hat man as possible.

'I could even try to get a little health-food shop installed.' I could hear him grinning. 'Hemp bars and beet-root juice and, er, other disgusting things.'

I wanted to laugh but I was scared someone on the train might actually kill me. The atmosphere was silently furious.

'Come in and see how we work,' Stephen invited. 'Our building will knock you out. We've got pool rooms, a gym with classes and a yoga studio, music spaces, kitchens run by some of the world's best chefs and even a little spa. Famous musicians come and gig here. There's three concierges, and two lovely office dogs that come in to de-stress anyone who's having a bad day. We're determined to wrestle Employer of the Year off Google this year.'

Kate Brady worked for Google in Dublin. The day we'd met, in one of the few travellers' bars in Bangladesh, she'd had my jaw on the floor with her tales of the offices there. We'd pondered our respective jobs one hot night while getting drunk on Bangladeshi rice beer and, even though I'd only ever wanted to practise alternative ther-apies, I'd felt strangely jealous. I'd found myself longing to work somewhere like Kate's office, where I'd have a routine and someone else organizing my day. Somewhere nice and safe where I could just sort of disappear among hundreds of other employees.

Now someone I'd met twelve hours ago was on the phone offering me just that, at a place I could cycle to in twenty-five minutes. *It's a blast, working in that office*, I remembered Kate saying. *It's nicer than my house, Annie! I'd live there if I could!*

'You gave me the best massage I've ever had,' Stephen was saying. 'If everyone on my team had access to one of those each fortnight they'd fly. We'll pay you very hand-somely indeed and you'll get all the employee benefits. At least come in for a visit.' He hesitated. 'I really hope you don't mind me saying this, but you did rather strike me as someone who could do with a break.'

'CAN YOU MOVE YOUR FUCKING BAG, PLEASE?' shouted the owner of the pregnant belly. 'I'M PREGNANT.'

'Fat bitch,' muttered a man on the other side of me.

'Eat me,' whispered the old man with the bobble hat.

I could almost hear Kate Brady. *Are you MAD, woman? Go for it!*

'Yes,' I said, to the voice on the phone. 'I can come in tomorrow morning.'

'And he just hired you?' Lizzy breathed. 'Like, this morning?' She was pink with excitement.

'Yes. And for once I was actually capable of making a decision! I said yes on the spot!'

Lizzy screamed.

'It sounds like he is trying to get into your knickers,' Claudine muttered. 'He cannot just 'ire you like that! He knows nothing of you!'

'It's just insane, isn't it?' I beamed, ignoring Claudine. 'And get this, he offered me nearly TWENTY GRAND more than I make now! CAN YOU ACTUALLY BELIEVE IT? Then he showed me this incredible area on the top floor, where you can see all the way across London to the countryside, and he said they'd convert it into a bespoke Annie Kingdom. That was what really swung it. I mean, you couldn't have designed a better place for a treatment room. Spectacular views and yet total privacy, it's stunning!'

'He called it this?' Claudine asked. 'A bespoke Annie Kingdom?'

'Yes. Isn't that nice?'

'It is.' Claudine smiled reluctantly. 'It is very nice indeed. But I still do not think I like the sound of him. This is not the behaviour of a good businessman!'

I sighed. This sort of thing was not unusual with Claudine. 'Claudie, I'm a massage therapist, not a hedge-fund manager.

I showed him I'm great at massage, and he wanted to hire me because he's expanding his wellbeing service. Did you want him to interview me for five hours, or something?'

'Yes.' She humphed.

'Oh, Claudie, get over yourself, darling,' Lizzy told her affectionately, and Claudine couldn't help but laugh.

'Sorry,' she said, smiling apologetically at me. 'I am the worst.'

I loved my friends. When my therapist challenged me to socialize with more people, I often pointed out that Le Cloob contained the best people in the world, so why would I bother? She would say I was missing the point. I would pretend not to hear her.

'So, what are the offices like?' Lizzy asked. 'I've heard they're legendary.'

'They are. And, most importantly, the food is ALL FREE! Stephen took me for breakfast with organic eggs and mangoes and stuff, and I got so excited I stole a Danish pastry. Plus just as I was leaving I bumped into Stephen's wellbeing coach, who turned out to be Jamilla from next door to our old Hackney practice, Claudie. Remember her? It all seemed too good to be true. But maybe I've gone mad. I mean, it's a massive corporate company.'

'You mean, there'll be people there who have proper jobs?' Lizzy smiled. 'Darling, you'll have nothing to do with all that. You'll just shuffle around in your own private practice, like the strange old lady you are, only this time you'll have a stream of guaranteed clients.' She threw more wine at my glass. 'You'll be rich! You can buy some proper clothes!'

'Never.' I smiled.

'I *insist* that you buy proper clothes, my little mushroom,' Claudine said. 'I cannot have you working at a media consultancy in batik.'

'You really deserve this, Pumpkin,' Tim chipped in. 'You've not enjoyed the last few years.'

Thrilled to have the support of Le Cloob, I allowed myself to feel truly excited. I'd worried that a vague, forgetful, incense-burning recluse like me, who sometimes wore actual clogs, might never fit into a company like that, but they were right: I didn't need to. I would be up there in my lovely peaceful Annie Kingdom, a little oasis of healing and goodness far from the corporate crowd.

'Well, there you have it,' I muttered dazedly. 'This little hippie has got herself a big job in Posh London.'

'That's it?' Lizzy asked. 'That's all you have to say? You're not going to talk to us about – oh, I don't know – your fit new boss?'

I felt my face turn tomato-red. 'He's just my boss, Lizzy. Nothing to say.'

Stephen's hand had brushed mine as we'd stepped into the lift earlier, and I'd nearly had one of those spontaneous orgasms that you read about in magazines about weird people. It hadn't escaped my notice that I'd experienced none of my usual panic about male intimacy with Stephen. It hadn't escaped my notice either that I'd actually enjoyed, rather than felt stressed-out by, his company.

'Is he married? Girlfriended? Mentally sound?'

'I'm sure he'll be married. Probably has a family in Surrey. Or maybe one of the trendy bits of Essex. Where was that Essex village they had in the *Guardian*'s Let's

Move to . . . article last Saturday? With the Michelin-starred pub? That'd be the sort of place he'd live. With his wife, and his . . .' I trailed off.

'I can see you haven't been thinking about him much,' Lizzy remarked.

'Of course I've thought about him. He's been absolutely lovely. Like a knight in shining armour. But that doesn't mean I *fancy* him.'

Of course it meant I fancied him. Stephen had taken me out for lunch today to offer me the package personally. Rather than somewhere formal and starchy-tableclothed, where I would have been desperately uncomfortable, we had gone to a funny little wholefoods café where we had chatted about India, boy-bands and dogs.

He'd ordered us organic wine, which was a novelty, and I'd got a fraction drunk. When he offered me the most appealing working arrangement I'd ever heard of I'd been horrified to see two embarrassing tears of joy plopping into my glass.

'Ah, you see?' Stephen had grinned broadly. 'This is why I wanted to make the offer to you myself!'

'So you could watch me cry?'

'Ha-ha. Yes.' He rested his chin on his hands and looked straight at me. 'Obviously this is what my HR team are there for but – ah, I dunno. Don't tell anyone I said this but it means more to me than you can possibly imagine to see someone so happy at being invited to join this firm. *My* firm. Something I made. It makes it all worth while.' He glanced around furtively. 'Seriously, if you ever tell anyone I said that, I'll have to kill you. I'm meant to be a ball-breaker.'

Another two plops into the fruity Rioja below me. He was right. I *was* happy.

'Pull yourself together,' I said to myself. No man, other than my dad and Tim, had ever seen me cry: this was terrible! And yet there was something so normal about Stephen Flint, so *safe*. Warm and sexy and – 'STOP IT,' I hissed.

'Yes, stop it right now,' Stephen said sternly.

Briefly, shockingly, he touched my arm. 'From the conversation we had the other night, it sounds like you've had a rough time of it in recent years.'

I didn't trust myself to speak.

'And although it's completely unprofessional of me to tell you, Annie, I've had quite a rough time in my own life lately. It's left me quite wobbly. So I'm very happy to be able to help you.'

I was surprised. Men like him didn't have rough times. 'Men like me don't have rough times?' he asked, as if reading my mind. 'Everyone in the company would agree with you. They think I'm a corporate machine, the Big Strong Leader. I'm still a human being, though.' He smiled. 'Still not immune to bad times. I like a good cry into a glass of red wine as much as the next person.'

I wanted to ask him more, find out what could possibly go wrong for a man as gorgeous and successful as him, but I was tongue-tied. *I was having lunch with a man!* And although for most people a low-key lunch would be no big bananas – nothing was happening, after all, save some vague bonding over unspecified crappy times – it was an enormous step for me.

'How did you start FlintSpark?' I asked. 'You're very young to be a CEO.'

'How old do you think I am?'

I blushed hotly. 'I don't know. Please don't make me guess.'

'I'm thirty-eight. And it all happened quite easily, really. That's the thing about business. If you're a natural, it doesn't need to take half a lifetime to get to the top.'

I drank some more naughty lunchtime wine. The drunker I got the easier it felt to be here, doing this . . . this *thing*. I kept waiting for the usual thoughts to kick off – he's trying to trap me; he's probably going to write a hideous contract I'll never escape from; he's going to find out I'm a total waste of space and sack me – but none of them came. I just felt good.

'I started out on a graduate programme like everyone else,' Stephen explained, 'and I was sacked after six months for being "too good". That's what they told me and, by the way, I'm not being big-headed. I worked at a couple of other places but similar things happened – people felt threatened by me. I got fed up with it all and decided to set up on my own. Clients wanted to come with me, because they knew they were in good hands, and I persuaded a load of stinking-rich venture capitalists to invest. And boom. Here we are.'

'Wow.' Imagine being able to do that! 'How did you get the investors to give you so much money?'

'Oh, mostly I lied,' Stephen said airily. Then, catching sight of my face, he added, 'They expect you to lie, Annie – and they lie right back. As long as everyone makes money, everyone's happy. Those guys are laughing all the way to the bank now.'

I hated the sound of business.

'It's ugly,' Stephen admitted, 'very ugly at times, but it's what I was born to do. And I send literally millions of pounds to charities. We've built five schools in rural Cambodia and we've set up literacy projects across the world. We've dug wells, provided doctors and funded infrastructure in some of the very poorest countries. I go out and meet every single community we help. It's not all bad, you know. And, as I said, I'm still a fairly nice bloke. An average bloke who's never really got used to daytime drinking and who is currently a bit squiffy. Oops. Can we order lots of desserts, please?'

I looked at Stephen and had a thought that excited and terrified me: *I wonder what it would be like to kiss you.* That was when I stopped drinking.

Le Cloob were still looking as dazed as I felt.

'I need to see a picture of him,' Lizzy decided. Embarrassingly, there was already a Google image search on when I got my phone out. 'Ha! You've been stalking him!' She giggled as she took my phone. 'Oh, blimey,' she muttered. 'Kiddo, he is *hot*.'

Claudine coolly removed the phone from Lizzy's hands and took a look. Expecting her to say some sexy-sounding French words, I was a bit disappointed to see her brow knitting. 'Oh,' she said.

I took the phone back. 'What does that mean?'

She shrugged. 'I do not like him.'

'Why?' Lizzy asked. 'Did you go blind?'

Claudine frowned. 'I just do not like him. He looks . . . obvious.'

'Guys, he's not my boyfriend. He's just my new boss. Who I'm NOT INTERESTED IN.'

Claudine studied my face for a few moments. 'Okay. Okay.'

Claudine never approved of any of my crushes. It was like she actually wanted me to be single. It was like she wanted me to reach thirty-three in May and have had sex only one and a half times. 'Even Kate likes him,' I lied. She definitely would like him – she'd love him, but I wanted to call and tell her my news tomorrow.

Tim gave me a sideways hug, which Lizzy watched from across the table with interest. She was convinced we were secretly in love with each other.

'To our brilliant Annie!' Tim said, raising his glass. 'Well done again, Pumpkin. I'm so proud of you.' I sighed happily, comfortable in his lemony armpit, until Claudine interrupted to say she still thought Stephen looked cheesy and self-satisfied and that his approach to hiring people sounded completely subjective and in no way professional.

'You should have married Tim,' Lizzy slurred, when he and Claudine had stumbled off home. Being Lizzy, she was waiting for an Uber taxi, and being me I was waiting with her until it arrived because I was nervous about getting on the tube so late at night and was dithering over ordering a cab of my own.

'Timmy,' Lizzy continued. 'You and him are like bloody brother and sister. I get quite jealous, you know.'

'Oh, shush.'

'I'm serious,' she said, staring at me. Suddenly – and it didn't happen often – I had Lizzy's full attention. 'Tim and you are the best people on earth and it's crazy that you're not together. I'm quite sure you love him.' She actually seemed sad for us. 'And he loves you. Kate said exactly the same thing when she was over for New Year's Eve.'

'I don't love him,' I repeated, for the millionth time. 'And he doesn't love me. I'd love to love Tim, Lizzy, but I don't and thassat. Kate should know bet-better . . . God, I'm drunk. Where's your cab?'

'It'll be here soon. Go home! I'll be fine.'

'No.'

'Moron.'

'Twatfink.'

'Love you.'

'Love you more.'

It's a heatwave, everyone's saying. Going to last two weeks! Right through to the end of summer! Maybe through autumn too!

For the girl, in this moment, there is no autumn, no September, no consciousness of anything that might be to come. There is just the shimmering heat, the smell of peaty green grass, the delicate splitting of daisy stems. She focuses all her attention on the pearly crescents of her fingernails, and the hairy little daisy stalks with their curious smell. She holds her breath every time she picks a new daisy and doesn't let it go until she has threaded it through the slit of the last.

They are making a daisy chain, the tenth of the morning, but if her mother has tired of the game she doesn't show it. She strokes her daughter's hair, running her hand down the plait she attempted earlier that morning. It was the first time her child had asked for one and the request — so clear and formal — had made her laugh and kiss her all over.

'Today I would like a plait,' she had said, absolutely confident in her mother's ability to do what the other mothers did. 'I want you to start it on the top of my head so that I look like Carrie. She says it's called a French plait.'

The plait had little blonde horns poking out of it and a kink like a broken mermaid's tail, but she was delighted with it. She had stood smiling at herself in the mirror, holding the plait in both hands as if it might fall off.

'What would you like to do with your birthday morning, sweetheart?' her mother had said. She'd given her daughter the day off

school. No child should have to spend their seventh birthday in a hot classroom with whistles and rules and shouty books. She's still not convinced she won't take both of her girls out of school and set up the home-education group she's been talking about with two other mothers in the village. It just doesn't sit right with her. They should be outdoors more at this age. Playing. They live in the middle of a National Park! Surely that's the best classroom a child could ask for.

For today, though, it's all about her seven-year-old girl with her fat plait and her white cotton dress. She'll do anything her daughter wants. She loves her today with the same ferocity that she loved her when she came out seven years ago, a squashed, messy bundle, so perfect she could barely breathe as she held her in her arms.

'I want to be outside all day,' her daughter had announced. 'Let's start with some daisy chains and maybe then we can pick me some special birthday flowers. And apples, let's look for apples.'

The woman had smiled. My little hippie, she thought proudly. 'We'll go up behind Woodford Farm,' was what she said. 'It's still covered with daisies there.'

Chapter Three

Kate

On my first morning working at Mark Waverley's yard I stumbled down the thirty-three steps to the kitchen feeling like I'd been hit round the head with a fence pole. It was six thirty a.m., still pitch black and bitingly cold, and it felt like only five minutes had elapsed since Becca had finished tutoring me late last night.

I was sick with nerves and sleeplessness. In spite of the deep exhaustion that had pinned me to my bed, I'd lain awake for hours, missing my family and wondering if there was any way I could reasonably contact them. My subsequent acceptance that I couldn't had been terrible. There was a grief that went beyond tears, I often thought, and at that moment it had settled over me, like a pillow pressed to my face.

I needed toast. I could start a day without a shower, without a newspaper and certainly without human contact. I could not start the day without toast.

Joe, the groom, was sitting by a radiator eating a piece of cheese. In spite of the freezing cold he was wearing only a stripy T-shirt and jodhpurs, and in spite of the devastating hour, he was wearing a gigantic grin. He moved his hair out of those naughty eyes and winked at me.

'Galway!' He beamed, patting a chair near to him.

'Come here to me and tell me stories of the Twelve Bens mountains. And feed me cheese.'

I dithered. Joe's eyes had lit up as soon as I'd opened my mouth when I'd arrived in the kitchen last night. 'Well, if it isn't a flame-haired little lady of Eire for me to fall in love with!' he'd shouted joyfully. 'Happy St Patrick's Day, my dear *compadre*!'

'Happy St Patrick's Day,' I'd whispered uncomfortably.

'That's a strange accent you have there, my green-eyed princess. Mayo, perchance?'

'Galway,' I'd croaked.

'The wild west.' He grinned. 'Wonderful!' Joe was a little taller than me, as lithe and muscled as a whippet. Like everyone else there, he was quite young but his face had a sandblown quality, presumably from spending all his time on the exposed hills of Exmoor.

'Tell me now, Galway.' He'd poured me a glass of wine. 'What brings you here?'

'Left my job in Dublin for a career change,' I'd trotted out. The wine was disgusting but as necessary as oxygen. 'Couldn't cope not being around horses. I've horses in my blood.'

Becca, arranging socks on the rack above the Aga, had smiled approvingly.

Joe had got me mildly drunk, told me I was gorgeous and asked me to marry him twice.

Now, at six thirty-five, he was taking calm mouthfuls of a big block of Cheddar and chatting away as if it were still last night. 'I've a mate, Sean Burke, up in Kilgevrin. Do you know Kilgevrin?'

'I don't . . . I moved to Dublin years ago.'

'It's a bit of a shitehole, Galway. Anyway, he . . .'

I zoned out, standing by the toaster while my bread had the moisture sucked out of it. Tiredness aside, I really wasn't sure if I could do this. Any of it.

Tough, I said to myself. *You have nowhere else to go, remember?*

My toast popped and I searched for a plate. I had to make it work here, and that would be a lot easier to achieve if I stopped thinking about home. And all of the Bad Shit.

'Galway?'

Joe was still eating straight from the cheese block. Little crumbs of it fell on to the large terracotta floor tiles. 'Galway, are you fantasizing about us having sex, there?'

I shook my head, forcing a smile. Last night, with the wine and the warmth of a kitchen full of people, I'd found him funny. Now I was struggling. *Come on*, I chided gently. *Crack a smile, Brady.*

Joe wrapped up his cheese and put it in the vast American-style fridge. 'Ah, Galway, you're going to drive me wild,' he said cheerfully, putting on a jumper. 'You and all that gorgeous red hair. Well, I'm going to get Kangaroo tacked up. Best give me your number so I can call if I need anything.' He pulled a hat on.

'My number?'

'It's a big farm,' he explained, digging his phone out. 'We call each other all day.' He stood in front of me, his phone in his hand.

Grudgingly, I pulled mine out and searched for my number.

'Never understand people who don't know their own number.' Joe chuckled, punching it in.

'From a man who eats Cheddar for breakfast and makes

marriage proposals at first sight,' I tried lightly. I even forced a shadow of a smile.

'Grand!' Joe tucked his phone away. 'Now I can send you dirty messages . . . Ah, Christ, Galway, don't blench like that! I'm jokin' with you!'

He pulled his gloves on, watching me. Just for a moment, the naughty twinkling stopped and a shadow of compassion passed across his face. 'You'll be fine, Galway,' he said kindly. 'We don't bite. Unless you ask us to.'

He left, and I started mechanically to eat toast, leaning against the rail of the Aga. *You'll learn*, I reassured myself. *You'll learn to relax. These are decent people, Kate Brady, you can be happy here.*

The grooms' house was a beautiful old threshing barn with a large, Mexican-tiled kitchen that had once been a grain store. The ground floor was made up of several different reception rooms, 'So it doesn't feel like a hall of residence,' Sandra had explained during my interview. There was a grown-up sitting room, a pool room, a TV room and even a reading room, but it seemed that most of the grooms at Mark Waverley's yard spent their time in the kitchen or in the laundry room where they washed and dried all the horse stuff.

Everyone other than me had lovely big rooms with views across the rolling moorland that led eventually to the Bristol Channel, although my own view of the horse yard wasn't too shabby. It was a rather lovely scene: an old stone stable block centred around a big square courtyard with a still-functional iron water pump in the centre: unusual and lucky to have so many proper old stables, Sandra had told me; none of those American-style barns with all that ugly metal. The doors and woodwork were painted a deep marine blue, which stood proudly against the yellowed stones of the stable walls. Behind the main courtyard, an ancient oak overhung a further oblong of stone stabling.

Last night I'd also met Tiggy, the Head Girl, who'd been friendly enough. In a very confident, this-is-my-empire-and-if-you-cross-me-I'll-have-you-run-over sort of a way. Like all posh women who worked with horses she had blonde hair in a messy bun and one of those attractive, capable faces that had been genetically supplied with ruddy skin and good teeth.

Tiggy. For God's sake. You couldn't make it up.

Almost all of the jobs Becca had explained to me last night involved the removal of horse poo from one place to another. 'Horses are veggies,' Becca had reassured me, 'so it don't smell too bad, pet. Although their wee's pretty bad, with all that ammonia, and they do like to take a good fart on you when you brush out their tails.'

Her final piece of advice had been about Joe. 'Don't go there,' she'd advised. 'He's had a go on everyone. He's gorgeous, if you're into that sort of thing, but it's not worth the pubic lice, my pet. Okay?'

'I may not know a horse's arse from its elbow,' I'd said, 'but I do know that I'm not looking for romance.'

'Hock.' Becca had smiled. 'Horses don't have elbows. They have knees and hocks.'

I finished my toast and pondered my next move. Neither Becca nor Tiggy had come downstairs yet and, other than stand and eat toast that I was too anxious even to taste, I hadn't the faintest idea what to do.

I wandered across the warm kitchen floor – it was

heated, I realized gratefully – and stared at a black-and-white photo of Mark Waverley on a beautiful horse. He was wearing a top hat, a tail coat and white gloves, and he was making the horse do a very boxy, poncy sort of a move. This, I remembered from the Olympics, was that mad dressage thing, where riders made horses do ballet in a long rectangular arena.

'He got twenty-six on that test,' Becca said, sliding into the kitchen. 'Fuckin' sensational. Don't think anyone's ridden a test like that in years.'

I smiled politely. 'Oh, right.'

Becca sighed. 'You don't know what I mean, do you?'

'Nope.'

'Mark's an eventer, right? That means someone who competes in horse trials. Dressage, cross-country and show-jumping all in one competition. Like a triathlon, I suppose,' she said, pulling a large box of Shreddies out of a cupboard. 'In the dressage phase you build up penalties for imperfections. Meaning that Mark got only twenty-six penalties. *Nobody* gets dressage scores like that.'

'Go away!' I said, genuinely impressed. 'So he really is good, then?'

'The best,' she said proudly. 'He may be an arsehole but he rides a beautiful dressage test. Especially on Stumpy.'

'Dressage, show-jumping, cross-country,' I repeated to myself, aware of the need to learn fast. 'Dressage, show-jumping, cross-country. That's a lot for one horse to do in a day.'

Becca smiled. 'At Mark's level, these things take place over three to five days,' she explained. 'Otherwise, aye, the horse'd die. So would Mark. So would we.'

I shook my head ruefully. 'I'm useless,' I said. 'They'll rumble me in seconds.'

'Nonsense, pet. And if you don't mind me saying, you're not going to get very far with an attitude like that.'

'Hmph.'

'We'll just stick to the story that you've had a few years off horses, so you're a bit rusty. They really don't care, sweetheart. They've got enough to worry about.'

Tiggy marched briskly into the kitchen, reeking of efficiency and good breeding. 'Come on, then, folks,' she commanded. 'Let's get this show on the road.'

But before anyone had time to get a show on the road, the door opened and suddenly the atmosphere darkened. 'Morning,' a male voice said crisply.

'Morning!' we all tinkled.

Mark Waverley. Younger than he looked in a riding hat. More handsome, too, with his dark hair and warm-toned skin, a strong, slightly Roman nose and guarded eyes. Something about him threw me straight off balance. Not in a good way.

'Who are you?' he asked. His eyes were appraising me as they might a new horse, although he didn't necessarily seem happy with what he saw. Maybe I had bad hocks.

'Kate,' I said, giving him a firm, confident handshake. 'Kate Brady, your new trainee yard assistant. Great to meet you. I'm a real fan of your work.'

I'm a real fan of your work?

'You're Irish,' he said tonelessly.

'I am. I've heard we make the finest yard assistants on earth.'

Mark just stared at me.

'I'm armed and ready for action!' I added, although my voice was trailing off.

'I forgot you were starting today.' He glanced around the room where everyone had suddenly stopped eating and talking. Instead they were zipping up coats and rolling colourful horse bandages. 'My mother hired you without passing on your CV or telling me anything about you,' Mark continued, in that cold, slightly detached tone. 'Can you come to the main house at lunch with your CV? You can tell us a little more about yourself. One p.m. sharp,' he added, and turned away.

Becca gave me a reassuring smile.

'The indoor school hasn't been raked,' Mark told Tiggy. 'I told you last night I'd be in there doing flatwork at seven fifteen.'

'We'll get straight on to it!' Tiggy said, as Mark left, without recourse to such pleasantries as 'thank you' or 'see you later'.

'You'd better take care of that,' Tiggy said to Becca. 'Teach Kate how to operate the Tank. Chop chop, team . . .'

Becca muttered about Joe being a lazy fucker, riding his own horse in there last night and not bothering to rake it afterwards. 'Come on, pet.' She sighed.

And then we were out in the freezing air, dark as night except for the old black pendant lamps, haloed by drizzle, that studded the outer walls of the stable block. Gravel crunched, ice-like, under my stupid wellies and a deadly wind made my eyes water.

This is it, I thought flatly. The first day of the rest of my life.

'I need to buy some proper clothes.' I shivered as we crunched round to the stable-block entrance. 'Today.'

A strange miasma of smells reached out as we opened the gate into the yard. Some I recognized – horse poo, straw – but many others wove together into an unfamiliar sensory blanket.

'Clothes-buying?' Becca snorted. 'You've got a better chance of going on a weekend mini-break to New York than you have of nipping off to Minehead, pet. Lunch is a twenty-minute soup break and you're spending yours with Mark. I'm going to tell you what to say this morning, and you're going to listen hard while shovelling a lot of shit and filling a lot of buckets with freezing water, okay?'

I nodded glumly.

'Only first I need to show you how to use the most dangerous machine in Somerset, known as the Tank. It rakes the indoor school, lifts up bales of straw and kills anyone who needs knocking off.'

'I really hate this job,' I muttered.

Becca roared with laughter. 'That's my girl,' she shouted. 'That's my girl!'

By lunch I was certain I was dying. I couldn't feel my fingers at all, my legs chafed where my wellies had pressed the stiff seams of my jeans into my skin, and my lip was bleeding where I'd chewed part of it off. I stank of horse wee and had hundreds of tiny pieces of horse bedding in my hair.

So far this morning I'd had zero direct contact with horses. I'd raked the indoor school, scrubbed horse poo out of the horse walking machine, picked horse poo from one of the paddocks and spent a stinking hour sculpting horse poo on a giant muck heap. I'd filled endless buckets with icy water from a heavily insulated tap and had removed yet more horse poo from the area where Joe and Mark were saddling and unsaddling an endless procession of horses for exercise.

It had been me and poo, without rest, all morning.

During the sculpting of the muck heap, Becca had tried to teach me the different names for horse colours. I had been so useless at remembering them that we'd ended up with the giggles. The serious giggles. We'd stood there on top of the muck heap, which steamed unfragrantly in the bitingly cold air, and howled for quite some time.

Mark had ridden past and glanced at us, folded over our yard forks, crying with mirth. He hadn't looked pleased, but I couldn't stop. I hadn't laughed like that in weeks.

I was so desperate for the toilet, by the time lunchtime arrived, that I almost cried when Tiggy strode into the downstairs loo ahead of me. 'Argh,' I whispered, hopping from one foot to the other outside the door.

'She's an evil one,' whispered Joe, walking past. 'I'll fight her for you, if you like.'

'Please don't be fighting anyone,' I said carefully, 'or I'll end up weeing into my sock, and that would be the end.'

Joe roared with laughter as he rolled off into the kitchen. 'I love you, Galway,' he called. 'I will love you for ever, my flame-haired Irish princess.'

I realized I was smiling, which rather took me by surprise. And then I realized I actually felt quite good. Quite happy about how the morning had gone, even though I felt I might be dead. It had been wonderful to lose myself in manual labour, to be involved in a routine and responsible for the welfare of someone beyond myself.

As the darkness had melted and our surroundings had come into view, I'd been reminded once again of how stunningly beautiful it was around there. The vivid green of the fields, sharpened brilliantly by the brown rugged hills that rose above them, speckled with yellow gorse, flint-grey rocks, white sheep.

I hadn't thought about the Bad Shit for nearly *six hours*! 'Kate Brady is on fire!' I told myself, as Tiggy flushed the loo. 'She's nailing this!'

A few seconds later I collapsed my numb, freezing thighs on to the also-freezing porcelain, and for a few moments I allowed myself to drift off on a cloud of hopeful possibility.

Then: 'PET,' Becca yelled through the toilet door. 'You've forgotten your lunch with Mark!'

I exploded out of that toilet as if it were on fire. I'd not had any direct contact with Mark during my morning's work but just glimpsing him riding round and round in that indoor school – silent as a shadow, so shut off from all the human beings buzzing around him – had left me cold.

'If he asks anything awkward, just lie,' Becca advised, as I shoved my frozen feet back into my wellies. Pain roared down my left heel, which had already blistered. 'And watch Maria. She acts like she hates Mark but she'll destroy you if she thinks you're a threat . . .'

'Ideal,' I called, running out. 'I can hardly wait.'

Who the hell *were* these people?

It didn't matter, I reminded myself. They would have to do.

I balled my hair into a bun as I sprinted across the old farmyard, which separated our barn from the main house. The sun had slid out doubtfully from behind huge sheets of grey cloud, temporarily brightening the yellow stone of the farmhouse and picking out the woody twists of wisteria that covered the south- and west-facing walls. I drew in a long, cold breath of Somerset air and prayed for clemency.

Sandra opened the door, wearing an apron saying 'SEXY GRANNY!' She was wide, wobbly and maternal, with an Alice band and glasses that magnified her kind eyes. She smelt of baking and cologne. 'Ah, Katie,' she said sweetly. 'Welcome! How are you, darling?' She made a feeble attempt to clear a path through the vast pile of wellies and riding boots that almost blocked the front door.

'Kate.' I smiled. 'And I'm grand, thanks, Sandra. How are you?'

'Love that accent of yours!' She giggled, which seemed to be her answer to my question. 'Come on through. Mark and Maria are having a little disagreement about something but they'll be thrilled to see you. Dirk?' she said to a Labrador who was eating a squeaky broccoli in a downstairs loo. 'Dirk, do you want to go to Wootton with me later? I need some stamps . . .'

Dirk squeaked the broccoli and I was waved through to an old-fashioned dining room with large windows overlooking a neglected lawn. The room contained a table and a photo in a shabby frame of Mark show-jumping, but little else, other than faded marks on the wooden walls where vast ancestral portraits might have been. There were only four chairs huddled at the far end of the table and a sense of quiet gloom hung in the air. It made a marked contrast to our bright quarters across the yard.

In one corner of the room sat a plastic Wendy house, out of which came little yells of 'WHERE'S THE STEAK? WHERE'S THE FUCKING STEAK, DAVE? I'VE GOT THREE COVERS WAITING, DAVE!'

'Ana Luisa!' bellowed a dark-haired woman sitting at the table with Mark and a mountain of papers.

'Stop swearing, sweetheart,' Mark added.

Maria sounded very exotic. Brazilian, perhaps: her beauty was wild and Amazonian and her hair fell in dramatic waves around her slim shoulders. She was wearing leather trousers with a phenomenally expensive-looking black polo-neck and a Rolex watch. I hadn't realized that people wore clothes like that outside films.

Ana Luisa, in the Wendy house, went silent. Then: 'Do you and Daddy want your fucking steak or what?'

Mark Waverley's face moved briefly in the direction of a smile. 'Oi,' he began.

'ENOUGH!' yelled the woman at the table. 'Go up to your bedroom! Our order is cancelled!'

A screaming match ensued, during which a small dark girl of around six ejected herself violently from the Wendy house, smashed it with her fist, then stormed out, swearing about her mother.

'Hello,' Mark said. His hair was squashed from being under a riding hat all morning. 'My daughter wanted to serve our lunch from the Wendy house today, but it seems that her imaginary sous-chef, Dave, has been a bit slow with the steaks.' He did that half-smile again, and even though it lasted all of a second I felt a little less nervous. 'She's been watching too much Gordon Ramsay,' Mark added.

'She is out of control,' muttered Maria. 'But that's what happen to neglected children. Maria Waverley,' she purred, standing up and placing her still hand in mine as if she were the Queen. She was both magnificent and terrifying.

'Kate Brady!' I beamed. The jolly Dubliner routine was my best and only option. 'I'm the new trainee yard assistant, great to meet you.'

Maria looked me up and down, decided I posed no threat to her marriage whatsoever, and sat down again next to Mark. 'We are having fight,' she announced. 'Because my husband he does not understand business. Kate, he has buy a horse lorry that he can only pay for if he wins Badminton and Burghley every year for the next millennium! Ha-ha!'

'Ha-ha?' I echoed.

'Maria,' Mark said tiredly. 'What part of "I have a cash sponsor for the first time in years" do you not understand?'

'Which part of "Yes, but your cash sponsor is not paying you anywhere near enough to buy that lorry" do *you* not understand, darling?'

Mark swept the papers to one side and gestured for me to sit down. 'Mum?' he called. 'Is there any lunch?'

'Of course, darling,' Sandra said, arriving with a big pan of soup and a board of bread. I suspected she'd been hiding in the kitchen doorway, waiting to be summoned. This was one of the strangest places I'd ever been.

The soup smelt like cauliflower cheese in a bowl and was served with a *boule* of oven-hot bread.

'Well, now, doesn't that bread smell like God's bakery itself?' I brayed, into the silent room. 'I could eat the lot!'

Mark stared at me, possibly wondering if I was mentally ill.

'I'm sure you could, sweetheart,' Maria said pleasantly, looking at my waist.

'Do you have your CV?' Mark asked, ignoring his wife. They seemed to spend a lot of time ignoring each other. 'And, look, I should probably tell you that I didn't ask my mother to interview anyone on my behalf. Unfortunately one of our team left while I was in Europe, trying out some youngsters, and Mum took it upon herself to solve the resultant staffing deficit.'

'Your mum and I had a lovely chat,' I tried. 'She was so nice!'

Maria snorted. 'I imagine Sandra's interview skills are even worse than yours, darling.' She gave Mark a tart, citrussy sort of a smile.

It was like a sitcom! How could they not be embarrassed, carrying on like this? I hated them both. A more miserable pair of bastards I'd never come across. I spooned some hot, cheesy soup into my mouth.

Mark turned back to me. 'So, as I was saying –'

'Please email me your CV, darling,' Maria interrupted crisply. 'For our files.'

Mark took in a slow breath. 'Please email *me* your CV,' he said. 'In the meantime you can tell me about your experience.'

'Well,' I began. 'I first sat on a pony at three years old, and since then I've –'

'You do not look like a rider!' Maria smiled, staring pointedly at my large breasts.

I blushed.

'As you were saying . . .' Mark peered at his watch.

'As I was saying, I got on a pony at three years old and went for a gallop along the beach. It was the best moment of my life. I spent my entire childhood riding, and when I moved to Dublin I kept a horse out in Bray.'

'Pony Club?' Mark asked.

'Yes!'

'Did you get your B test?'

I froze. Did I? B didn't sound good enough for Mark Waverley's yard. 'Actually, I got my A.'

'Really?'

'Yeah. I, er –'

'FUCK YOU ALL!' came a little scream from the hall-way. Ana Luisa was on her way out of the house with a little rucksack covered in diamanté. More stylish than I would ever be, she had chosen a silk headscarf and large sunglasses for her departure. She was incandescent with rage, a small bomb on two legs. 'FUCK YOU ALL! I'M LEAVING!'

'Good luck,' Maria called. Mark went to go after her but Maria grabbed his wrist with a manicured hand, bar-nacling him to the table and their argument. *Ah, go and grab her*, I thought sadly. *Give that poor sweet girl a cuddle.*

'Becca will sort her out,' Maria said, catching sight of my face. 'Ana Luisa does this regularly. It is the classic behav-iour of a child who is being abandon by workaholic father.'

Mark turned back to me. His temple was pulsing. 'Did my mother mention that you're on a trial?'

Sandra, eating her soup at the far end of the table, clapped her hands over her mouth. 'Oh, I forgot to.'

'Which is why I ask that you leave the hiring to me, Mum,' Mark cut in. Sandra, if she was hurt, did not show it.

'You're on a month's trial,' he told me. 'But that doesn't mean you're guaranteed a month, I'm afraid. I don't have millions of pounds or a state-of-the-art yard, like everyone else in the World Class squad, which means I have to be doubly fussy about who I hire.' I made a mental note to find out what this World Class thing was. 'So there's no room for error on my yard. Every little mistake can hurt us.'

He stared at me, directly, for the first time, as if challenging me to wilt and die, which I wanted to very much indeed.

Instead I smiled. 'Of course, Captain! You won't be disappointed.'

Mark's navy eyes drifted off, as if he couldn't stand the sight of me.

'So, Kate,' Maria purred, 'why you choose Mark's yard for work?'

'Well, you see, Maria, horses are my passion,' I said, verbatim. 'I left a very successful career at Google Dublin so that I could start out in the eventing world. But the deal I made with myself was that, if I was going to do it, I would only do it with the very best.' I glanced at Mark. 'So here I am, with the best event rider in the country!'

There was a brief silence, which Maria broke with an unpleasant laugh. 'Jesus.' She chuckled, in a South American way. *Hayzoos.* It seemed even more insulting than plain old 'Jesus'. 'They are all the same.' She got up and left the room. I heard her scream her daughter's name.

I waited for Mark to apologize, to make good his wife's behaviour somehow, but he didn't say a word.

'I meant it,' I tried desperately. 'It really is an honour to be working for you. The very best of the bunch, you know? Ha-ha?'

'Kate. It is Kate, isn't it?'

I nodded.

'Kate. Most eventers enjoy having smoke blown up their arses. The industry is rife with heavy-drinking, horse-doping egotistical maniacs, who cover themselves with expensive kit and make-up and get themselves photo-graphed in the champagne tent every time they go to a competition. They'll respond gladly to flattery.'

I withered. I could feel Sandra to my right, begging silently for her son to show me some mercy. 'They sound like a bunch of silly articles,' I tried lamely.

'I'm not one of them, Kate. I'm running a very tight ship here. I have no time for posing at parties, letting people tell me how great I am. If you're looking for that sort of thing, you're best off working for Caroline Lexington-Morley. What *I'm* looking for – and please be clear on this – are the most observant, meticulous, tireless grooms in the business. Because without people like that I have no hope of winning.'

'Of course, of course.' I smiled, my face bland and reassuring. I didn't like people who wanted to win.

'My staff must love my horses more than they love me, because they're the most important people here. I want them to be respected, adored, fussed over but never petted. You get out of bed at six a.m. for them, not me.'

'Understood.' I liked that he called his horses people.

Beyond that, I didn't like anything I'd just heard. 'So the horses first, you second and me last. I think I can work with that.'

Mark didn't laugh.

'So, love, tell us about your ponies,' Sandra said kindly, tucking her grey bob behind an ear. Sandra and the dogs were the only nice thing about this lunch. Dirk the Labrador sat on one side of her and an enormous grey Irish wolfhound on the other.

'I had a pony called, um, Frog?' I experimented.

Sandra's eyes lit up. 'Oh, what a name!' she cried. 'Frog! Imagine that, Mark! It's almost as good as Stumpy!'

Mark, who was shrugging on a fleece laced with horse hairs, didn't react.

'And how old were you when you got Frog?' Sandra asked.

'I was four.' I tried to remember what Becca had said about horse heights. 'He was, er, fifteen two.'

Mark's eyes had swivelled back to me. There was something going on in there that I couldn't put my finger on. 'Time to get back,' he said. 'You were late, so this conversation will have to continue later. Please make sure you're on time in future.'

Silently, sadly, I said goodbye to my soup.

'Off to shovel some more shite then!' I beamed. I was Kate Brady. I would not be beaten.

Mark stopped in the doorway. 'Email me your CV,' he said. And, just at the moment I decided he was one of the more unpleasant people I'd met, he smiled.

His daughter galloped in and threw herself at him, telling him how much she hated her mother. Mark picked her up and carried her out to the yard on his back. And, unless I was very much mistaken, he told her he completely agreed.

Sandra looked at me, and I looked at her. I felt there were many things that we both wanted to say, but none were said. She tidied up the bowls, mumbling genially about needing to pop into town, and wandered out with the dogs padding after her. 'That's Woody,' she said, pointing to the Irish wolfhound.

Then it was just me. I closed my eyes for a second, trying, through all this uncomfortable newness, to remind myself that this was par for the course. The odd employers; the strange atmosphere: it was never going to feel right straight away.

It's okay, I told myself. It really is okay. Just keep putting one foot in front of the other and before you know it it'll be dinner time. You're doing brilliantly!

I wasn't sure I believed myself, but I stood up anyway, pulling Becca's spare bobbly gloves on to my already blistering hands. 'Once more unto the breach,' I said to the empty room. 'Once more unto the bloody breach. Oh, God.'

Chapter Four

Kate

'What the hell is Mark and Maria's relationship about?' I asked Becca. We were reaching the end of my first day on the yard and dusk was stretching its long, cold fingers over the farm. Our breath, which had straggled out of our mouths like damp little clouds all day, now plumed richly like smoke. Becca was showing me how much haylage to give each horse. It was a sweet-smelling, slightly damp version of hay, the point of which Becca had explained to me and I had promptly forgotten.

'Ah, pet, don't ask me about Mark and Maria!' she muttered, loading a pile of haylage into a wheelbarrow. 'Pair of fuckin' nutters. Were they shouting at each other?'

'Mostly hissing. Although their kid did a lot of shouting. She's fierce!'

Becca grinned. 'I love that little devil,' she said, suddenly tender. 'She knows herself better than either of her horrible parents know themselves.'

I nodded thoughtfully. Ana Luisa's language might have been unusually fruity for a six-year-old but she was the only one in that room who'd actually expressed her feelings. Her mother was curdled with passive aggression and her father was a column of frost, while Sandra and I had merely cowered, like Labradors.

'Maria told her off and she tried to run away.'

A little chuckle. 'Aye. As usual.'

'Oh! Really?'

Something unreadable crossed Becca's face. 'Mmm. But we always find her.'

'Where does she go?'

'To my room, mostly.'

'How funny! Actually, Maria said you'd find her. How come?'

Becca was not enjoying all my questions. 'Dunno.'

I left it. I had enough skeletons in my own closet and, besides, we had reached the first stable door, over which hung a handsome chestnut face that looked very happy about the haylage I was carrying. 'Kangaroo', his name plate said.

I smiled, nervous but delighted to find myself face to face with a horse at last. There had been horses around me all day – being groomed, being ridden, being fed, and a bunch of mad ones galloping and bucking on the iron-hard frozen ground of the paddocks earlier, much to Tiggy's dismay – but I hadn't met a single one of them yet.

As I looked at this magnificent beast, however, I wavered. Not only was he absolutely enormous but it was now clear that I hadn't the faintest idea how to approach him. What to say to him. How even to give him some hay. 'Um, hi, Kangaroo!' I said uncertainly, sticking my spare hand out in the direction of his face. Kangaroo swung his head away, back into his stable.

'Oh,' I said, laughing to cover my disappointment. 'Kangaroo doesn't like me.'

Becca smiled. 'Come here, lad,' she murmured, and held

out her own hand. Kangaroo eventually came over, snuffling at her with his lovely soft nose. I wanted to kiss it.

'They can always tell when you're nervous,' Becca said. 'They pick up on everything. Just relax, pet, he's a lovely boy.'

I hadn't done much relaxing of late, but I tried to loosen up my body a bit and concentrate only on the beautiful horse in front of me. He was a delight. Smooth, muscled, perfectly groomed, snug in a smart red stable rug with Mark's initials in the bottom corner.

'Hi,' I said to him. 'Hi, Kangaroo.'

Kangaroo eventually took a few wisps of haylage from my hand, although he didn't seem entirely convinced by me. We moved on to the next stable, marked 'Stumpy'. He was out being lunged by Mark so I loaded his hay rack under Becca's supervision.

What lovely names, I thought, shutting his stable door behind me. Kangaroo and Stumpy. There was a Harold somewhere, and an Alfie. And a whole load of others whose names I couldn't remember, but all of them were good. None of this 'Spotty' or 'Neptune' nonsense. I wondered who'd given them such sweet names. It certainly wouldn't have been Mark.

'So are they always fighting, then?' I asked, as we moved on. 'Mark and Maria.'

Becca nodded. 'Sometimes I wonder if we're in Camp sodding Bastion, not Somerset. The problem is, she owns his best horses so he can't ever tell her to go and do one.'

I stopped wheeling the barrow. 'She owns his horses? Seriously? Why doesn't he own them?'

Becca peeled some haylage off the pile and put it into

a stable marked 'Steve'. Steve snatched a mouthful, then let half of it fall on Becca's head. She laughed, rubbing his nose. 'Thanks, Steve,' she said. 'A horse that can compete at four-star level – which is the very top – costs about two hundred grand,' she explained. 'So even the richest riders don't own all of their own horses. Zara Phillips included, pet. The real money in this game is with the owners.'

Two hundred grand!

'Mark's horses are owned by all sorts of people but his five best ones – including Stumpy, who's his World Class horse – are owned by Maria. Or, precisely, Maria's dad. But she's in charge. Daddy just signs the cheques and swanks around in the owners' tents at the events.'

'Jesus,' I said, handing Becca some more haylage. 'So it's a marriage of convenience?'

Becca glowered. 'They fell in love for a bit,' she said darkly, 'then realized they were both arseholes. But Maria doesn't want to lose out on Mark's fame and Mark can't lose out on Maria's fortune. It's a dark situation, pet, and I'll tell you that for nothing. Sharing the lorry with those two is a fate worse than death.' She straightened up a row of shovels and forks.

'They were arguing about that at lunchtime,' I said, as we moved on. 'The horsebox.'

'No surprise there. It cost him three hundred and seventy grand.'

'It cost WHAT?' I stared over at the huge silver truck with awe. 'MARK WAVERLEY, TEAM GBR', it said on the side. I could have bought a mansion with that money!

'The living quarters are like a palace,' Becca added.

'Room for eight of us to sleep. Flatscreen TV, wardrobes and underfloor heating. Even a bog and a shower!'

'Whoa,' I breathed. 'He should live in it. His house is so sad and run-down.'

'They had money, once, the Waverleys – well, you can see the size of this place – but Mark's dad died with his finances in a mess and they've had to sell nearly everything just to stay afloat. It's all a bit *Downton Abbey*, pet.'

I looked back at the vast, hulking horsebox. 'So you'll all sleep in it when you go to competitions?'

'Aye.' She indicated for me to throw her some more haylage.

'Mark and Maria too?'

Becca stopped by the wheelbarrow. 'Why are you so interested in them?' she asked.

'Er ... just morbid curiosity.' I pulled my hat down over my ears as a biting wind punched through the yard. 'My own folks are still so happy together I find it odd when I see couples who hate each other. I mean, why do they bother?'

'GALWAY!' It was Joe, approaching us on a vast, sweaty horse, which was jiggling sideways and snatching at its bit. Joe sat easily on top, grinning down at me. 'Will we be having a cuddle later?'

'We will not,' I confirmed.

'Ah, Galway! Come on!'

I loaded haylage into the next loose box. 'I'm not after the sex with you,' I told Joe, who had swung himself off the horse and was loosening its girth.

'Can you sponge him down?' he asked Becca. 'I've got to get that silly tit Harold out before it's properly dark.'

'Can you do it quickly yourself, pet?' Becca asked. 'I'm still showing Kate the ropes.'

Joe looked sulky. 'I want to show Kate the ropes. I want to show her *my* rope. I want to make sweet love to her and hold her all night. Get her some Shreddies and a nice cup of tay in the morning.'

Becca picked up a broom and waved it threateningly. 'If you and your nasty peen go anywhere near this girl, I will deck you. Now, fuck off.'

'She fancies you, Galway.' Joe winked, leading the horse off.

'So what colour is that horse Joe's got there?' I asked, as he walked away. 'Would you call it tabby?'

Becca, who'd gone bright red, roared with laughter. 'It's a roan, pet,' she said. 'Although I prefer tabby!'

We were loading another wheelbarrow with haylage just as Mark walked into the yard leading the most beautiful horse I'd ever seen. He was the one from the photo in the dining room: brilliant white, except for the dark grey mess creeping up his legs from being in the outdoor school, with lovely fat rounded ears like little satellite dishes. A very soft-looking white mane and forelock framed his sweet, open face. He stared keenly at our wheelbarrow of hay. 'Ho-ho-ho,' he whickered, and I fell in love on the spot. 'Stumpy needs more lunging,' Mark said in Becca's general direction. 'He keeps dropping his inside leg. Here,' he said to me. 'Can you sponge him down and give him his waffle?'

His what?

He held the long lead-rope to me and turned back to Becca, who was trying to engage with him while keeping an eye on me. 'I'll get Tigs to work more lunging into the schedule,' she was saying.

'Well, Tiggy says she passed the job on to *you*,' he snapped, moving away, with Becca trotting anxiously at his side. 'I want to sort this out now. Is she in the tack room?'

I fingered the lead-rope and looked up at the big, powerful animal, an extraordinary feat of natural engineering. He gazed at me, one of his comically fat ears sliding backwards. He didn't seem anywhere near as happy as he had ten seconds ago with Mark. 'Come on,' I whispered nervously, moving off towards the washing-down area that Joe was already vacating.

Stumpy, behind me, didn't move. I pulled a little bit harder, terrified Mark would turn and see us. 'Please, Stumpy,' I whispered. 'Come with me.'

Both of Stumpy's ears swung back and he refused to move. I didn't need to know much about horses to understand that this was a fairly bad situation.

Becca, seeing all of this going on, pretty much shoved Mark into the tack room.

I tugged on the rope a final time and Stumpy, if anything, leaned back. Desperate, I walked back to his shoulder. 'Please tell me what I'm doing wrong.' I gave him a stroke on the neck in case that helped. There was a curious whorl of hair just under his mane, like a little hurricane. I fingered it. Suddenly, Stumpy turned to me. A big kindly eye, fringed by long lashes, took me in while he had a good sniff of me. 'What's wrong, you weirdo?' he seemed to ask.

I remembered what Becca had said about horses tuning

into our mental states. 'Come on!' I said brightly. 'Come on, old chap!'

I tugged at the rope but he didn't move, just continued to stare at me, sniffing delicately.

Putting on a confident voice wasn't going to be enough. I wasn't calm and this horse knew it.

I took a deep breath and closed my eyes, still stroking Stumpy's warm, smooth neck. I could feel the muscle beneath my hands, and the sweet, comforting smell of horse. *Relax*, I told myself.

Nothing happened.

Relax, I repeated.

Something warm and heavy suddenly landed on my shoulder and my eyes opened. Stumpy had just calmly rested his soft, velvety muzzle there, as if that were the most natural thing in the world to do right now. I felt the warm plumes of his breath through my jacket and – just like that, without any further effort – my body slackened. It was the first time in months.

'Thank you,' I said quietly. I stroked the dark grey tip of his nose, which he wiggled under my hand like a funny hamster. Without warning I gave him a little kiss. And then we were walking calmly over to the washing-down area, with me still at his shoulder, and him ambling along beside me, a gentle giant. A feeling of deep joy and accomplishment washed through me. What a lovely thing Stumpy was. How deeply, unbelievably grateful I was to be here looking after him, rather than back in my old life, feeling frightened and out of control.

'Thank you,' I said. 'Thank you, you beautiful thing.'

It was only when we got to the washing-down area that

I realized Mark had been walking quietly on the other side of the horse.

'You forgot his head-collar,' he said briefly, slipping off the more complicated lunging head-collar that Stumpy was wearing and replacing it with a simpler version. In a two-second movement he tied Stumpy up to a piece of baling twine on a ring in the wall.

'Good boy,' he said softly, scratching between the horse's ears. 'There's my good man.' Stumpy, as if drugged, lolled his head down towards Mark's stomach. 'Silly thing.' Mark grinned, suddenly human. Smiling beautifully, he continued to scratch Stumpy's head, fondling the horse's flappy ear with his other hand.

'He's my favourite,' he said to me. I was standing, like a tool, by Stumpy's shoulder, watching this most unlikely scene with amazement. 'My weak spot. We bred him here so I sort of feel like his dad.'

'He's beautiful,' I said. 'Absolutely stunning.'

Mark was clearly pleased. 'And what a great name!' I added.

Mark was smiling at his horse as if he might actually burst with pride. It made my eyes prickle a little bit, that intense and so wholly unexpected display of love.

'His show name is Distant Thunder.'

'Like a fart.' I grinned. Mark's eyes, now gunmetal in the fading light, swivelled round to me. His smile had gone.

'Right then, silly,' he muttered, giving Stumpy one last scratch. 'Time to get sponged down.'

'They trust you if you trust them,' he said, in my direction. 'And they don't respond kindly to being towed across the yard. You have to walk alongside them.'

I nodded dumbly, appalled he'd seen it all.

'But, of course, you already know that, with your life-time spent on the back of a horse.' Suddenly he smiled again. 'Watch out. He likes you.'

I turned to find Stumpy's nose at my elbow. Without even thinking about it, I reached to scratch him between the ears, like Mark had, and once again his head lolled happily downwards, sending warm jets of air down my cold legs. 'I like him too.' I beamed. 'He's the most beauti-ful horse I've ever seen. Hello, Stumpy. Hello, you nice boy.' Stumpy pushed his head closer into my legs, eyes drooping closed.

Mark tried to stop smiling but couldn't. 'I love him,' he said. 'So much, it's hopeless.'

Then he did a double-take, as if astonished to hear the words come out of his mouth. He turned sharply and strode off towards the back stable block. 'Get him sponged down,' he called.

I watched him go, until Stumpy nudged me in the bot-tom, asking for more of that scratching.

After a long evening of tack-cleaning with Becca, during which she made me learn what every last piece of leather was called, I dragged myself up to my bedroom and Sky-ped my family. I told them a pack of lies and hated myself.

Before bed, shivering in an unseasonal vest, I did a rou-tine scan of the yard from the chink between my curtains and was surprised when my eyes found Mark Waverley standing by Stumpy's door in a big thick coat, his arms wrapped round the horse's neck. I stared at him, a solitary figure with a halo of discontent crackling around him, and felt a tug of curiosity. Stumpy poked Mark with his muzzle, as if asking for snacks. Mark reached into his pocket and fed something to the horse, which nosed him for more. Even from this distance I could tell Mark was laughing.

Ana Luisa came out and stood with her dad, who slid an arm round her shoulders and held her close. Stumpy stuck his nose into the little girl's face and even from my room I could hear her shriek with laughter. I watched them there, a strange little family, and felt tears fill my eyes as I thought about my own. I'm so sorry, I thought, hoping they might somehow be able to hear me. I'm so sorry. I love you all so much.

Mark kissed Stumpy's nose, then glanced up at my window, just as I turned to go.

Chapter Five

Annie

One month later

The day I arrived at the FlintSpark offices I decided that this was it: the first day of the rest of my life.

I was shaking with excitement and nerves as I stood in the vast atrium, swarming in all directions with people who wore trendy clothes and used words like 'programmatic' and 'synergy'.

Holy God, I texted Kate, as I waited for Stephen's PA to come down for me. *What have I done?*

Kate's WhatsApp showed that she hadn't been online since mid-March, and it was now 15 April. I made a mental note to call her tonight. It was perfectly normal for her to ignore emails – 'I spend my day on the fecking internet,' she'd say. 'Don't expect me to email in my free time.' But her absence from phone activity was plain odd.

'Annie Mulholland!'

I started. I'd been expecting Stephen's PA, Tash, but here was the man himself, wearing a beautifully fitted shirt and a glorious suntan he'd not had in March. He was smiling the million-watt smile that I hadn't quite been able to stop myself Google-imaging over the last month, only it was more dazzling than could possibly be conveyed by an internet photo. This man, I thought, pleasure steaming up my brain, is *utterly gorgeous*.

'Oh! Hi!' I squeaked.

'Come and heal this company. And the world.' Stephen beamed, gesturing towards the security gates. 'Just like Michael Jackson, only without being weird and dead.' He put his hand on the small of my back, guiding me through the crowds. People stared at him and those within his earshot stepped up their use of barmy media words. 'Platforms' and 'cut-through' and – *what*? 'Low-hanging fruits?' I was lost.

'It's really lovely to have you here,' he continued, ignoring them all.

'It's lovely to be here. Thanks so much for coming to get me. I was expecting Tash.'

'She's my PA, not my servant. And anyway, I wanted to welcome you myself. You got here okay?' He swiped me through the glass gates.

'I did, and I'm very excited about starting,' I told him. 'Although I feel like I need to ask what a "low-hanging fruit" is. And what "programmatic" means. And several other words besides. Should I have learned all the vocab before starting?'

Stephen laughed, and I felt a rush of exhilaration. 'Absolutely not. In fact, I ban you from using that or any other industry terminology. I've hired you to be a real person, not another guff-recycler.'

I grinned, thinking how extraordinary it was that a man in Stephen's position should be so personable. That he was willing to welcome me himself when I must be one of the lowliest people on his payroll.

Stephen Flint – as I'd discovered in the course of my, ahem, late-night online research sessions – was a very big cheese. The kind of man whose PA you'd be lucky to be allowed to contact, let alone the boss himself. He was one of the most written-about businessmen and innovators in the country, the head of a huge empire, the template for every young person wanting to Make It.

I couldn't understand why someone like him would want to hire a scruffy, shy, dithering hippie like me, rather than some sleek blonde who ran a Power Spa in Chelsea.

Stop it, you great big tit, I imagined Kate saying. *Have some faith in yourself, woman!*

'I'm very flattered to have the Big Cheese come to meet me,' I said, as we waited for the lift. Then I had a mild panic. 'Oh, just to clarify, I meant Big Cheese as in Big Boss, not that I think you're cheesy.'

'Oh, I'm cheesy enough.' He gestured me towards an opening lift door. 'I'm worryingly cheesy. I own some dreadful music and still make Valentine cards for my granny, and I totally believe in flowers and mix tapes and boxes of Milk Tray. I mean, who even buys Milk Tray, these days? I'm a dead loss!'

I hated lifts, but I couldn't let Stephen know. I tried not to imagine the doors jamming closed and, of course, imagined just that.

'There's nothing naff about flowers and mix tapes and Milk Tray,' I said, imagining us trapped in there and running out of oxygen. 'I used to long for someone to give me that sort of stuff!'

'But you stopped?' We zoomed upwards.

'No, I just . . .' What? *I've been single my whole life because*

I'm scared of men? I blushed. The lift came to a rapid halt and the doors slid noiselessly open. Phew.

Stephen was smiling at me. 'Well, if it's a mix tape you want, you only have to ask,' he said. 'But please keep this *grand fromagery* to yourself. I'm running a multi-billion-pound business here.' We turned to walk along a dazzling corridor, into which lights hung on invisible strings at different heights. London lazed around below us, a docile animal napping in the spring sun.

Stephen took me into the Annie Kingdom and I gasped. Everything I'd asked for was there and more besides: the special heated table with extra-soft cushioning; the top-end waxes and oils I'd hardly dared request. Flowers and plants, a state-of-the-art music system and a sleek, shiny Mac in my little office next door. Plus a MacBook Air, just in case I found myself needing two computers at once. I certainly hadn't asked for those. To top it off there was a big cake with my name on it and 'WELCOME' in slightly wobbly letters.

'I made it myself,' Stephen said. 'So it's quite bad. But it's the thought that counts, hmm?'

I stared and stared at him. The CEO of a company had *made me a cake*. Short of receiving a veg box from the prime minister, it couldn't have been more surprising. 'You – *you* made me a cake?'

'Didn't I tell you I care about my employees?' He grinned. He should have sounded naff, but he didn't. Probably because he actually meant it. 'It's wheat-, sugar- and dairy-free, and because of that it tastes disgusting, but never mind. I've called a little welcome party for you at five p.m. so I'm sure you'll persuade someone to eat it.'

'How did you know?' I felt I might cry. No man had ever been so nice to me. 'How did you know I didn't eat wheat or dairy or sugar?'

'Because you're a massage therapist and reiki practitioner and you smell of essential oils.' He looked out of the window, smiling at some private thought, and I noticed the delicate skin by his eye, little veins, like rivers on a distant map. 'And you wear tie-dye skirts. Of course you don't eat wheat or dairy or sugar, Annie Mulholland.'

Someone at FlintSpark had booked in my first two weeks of clients, and had very kindly given me the morning to 'create my space'. I put out some towels, then went off to get my security pass, my 'space' duly created. Over the years I'd come to understand that feng shui was a bonus, nothing more. What really mattered was me and the client: my ability to sense the energy and rhythm of their body, and theirs to turn off the ceaseless noise in their heads. I'd had my best massage ever in a sweltering room off a stinking alleyway in Beijing, where only the hot domes of my eyelids had prevented me seeing cockroaches scuttling across the floor underneath me.

Besides, the space was already stunning and didn't need any help from me and my 'design' ideas. (Claudine said that my house was one of the greatest recorded crimes against good taste.)

I used the rest of my morning to roam the extraordinary array of lounges, libraries, restaurants and games rooms at the FlintSpark 'offices'. How did anyone get any work done? It was like being at a festival! There were thick jungly carpets, ornate Chinese tables, beautiful industrial light fittings. The gym – or, at least, the tiny corner of it that I could see from the door – had been kitted out to look like it was in outer space. If I wanted to, I could bench-press underneath Jupiter or do some stretching on the mats beside a troop of naughty aliens.

The aliens made me smile because I somehow knew that Stephen had chosen them. I imagined those eyes twinkling mischievously as he explained his idea to a baffled designer and felt a little scrunch of pleasure in my stomach.

Of course, it was the restaurants that excited me most. Free food! Unlimited free food! I got some granola and yogurt and a crisp fresh pastry, then felt so guilty about Stephen's free-from cake that I took them back and got a smoothie with spirulina in it instead, trying not to mind too much.

'I think it's more about brand storytelling,' a man with round glasses and a beard was saying at the other side of my table. He was talking to another man with round glasses and a beard.

Beard Man II forked a piece of crayfish into his mouth and had a think. 'Agreed. But until we've run a deep dive on it, I think we should be cautious.'

Jesus Christ.

Much to my delight, when I left the restaurant I bumped into Jamilla. Jamilla had worked in the building next door to Claudine and me when we'd set up our practice. She was now FlintSpark's chief wellbeing adviser and the reason why Stephen had booked a massage in the first place. 'Hey!' I hissed. I didn't feel important enough to raise my voice in a place like this. 'Jamilla!'

'Oh, hi,' she said, wearing a glazed, distracted sort of

look. I asked her how she was but received only the vaguest indication that she was well.

I frowned. This was not how I remembered her. Did she not want me working here? Had she gone off me? 'Look, let's catch up later,' she said, noticing my face. 'Sorry, I'm just, er . . .'

I let her be. Wellness coaches were allowed bad days. I spent fifteen minutes trying to find the Annie Kingdom again, before realizing that I was on the wrong floor.

When I finally found it a workman was just finishing up after hanging a large sign above the door saying 'Inner Peace' with a big retro arrow pointing downwards. It was surrounded by Hollywood bulbs and it made me disproportionately happy, as did a huge bunch of flowers with my name on it, then some lovely welcoming emails from HR and other people whose job titles I didn't understand. The sky had rolled itself into great pillows of grey and my rooms, which seemed almost to hover in this humid cloudscape, were like a cheerful mezzanine-level entrance to heaven. I pressed my nose against the cool plate glass and wondered what the Annie Mulholland of ten years ago would have made of this.

Probably not much. But twenty-two-year-old Annie, for all her hippie leanings and rejection of Western values, had spent a lot of her time in therapy because she was unhappy about most things. Right now – here in this moment, with my breath forming hot discs of condensation on the window – I felt I might be about to get a stab at feeling normal.

My first appointment was at one thirty, and I'd been promised that a list of names would be left in my little office by midday. Thus far, nothing had appeared and it was one twenty-five.

'We left it on the desk,' said the girl whose number I'd been given as a contact. 'Next to your computer?'

'Oh, God. I'm so sorry. I threw away one of the computer manuals because there were two identical ones . . . I must have binned the client list too. Goodness, what a bad start . . .'

I scrabbled around in my bin for the schedule but found nothing. One of those efficient ninja cleaners had been in already.

I was crouching over the empty bin when Stephen Flint walked in.

'Oh. Do you normally wait for clients under your desk?'

I stuck my head out. My hair had already started to come out of its plait and was falling all over my face. 'Actually, I do. It's an ancient shamanic ritual.' Instantly, I blushed. I'd just made a joke! At a man!

Stephen laughed. 'Everything OK?'

'Yes, fine. I threw out my client list for the afternoon. But the cleaner's taken it already. I'm sorry, Stephen, I'm not normally such a shambles.'

Barefaced lie. I had to get better at this stuff. I *had* to.

Stephen was unfazed. He offered a warm hand to help me out from under the desk. 'Well, you needn't worry too much. Your first client is me. I called shotgun.'

'Oh!'

Suddenly – shockingly – the thought of running my hands along Stephen's back had become thrilling.

Boundaries, I told myself sharply. 'Good for you,' I

said, jogging off to the treatment room so he wouldn't notice the red in my cheeks. 'I'm sure Jamilla'll be very happy with you.'

Stephen grinned. 'She's never happy with me.'

There was a blanket of tiny freckles all along Stephen's shoulders and, as he breathed in and out, I imagined them filling my hands, like warm little pebbles. He was more knotted than before, and had a large spasm in his lumbar region. I thought about what he'd said, about having had a really shitty year, and wished I could give him a hug. I knew all about that sort of year.

I pressed my entire weight down into my interlaced palms, feeling his muscles release, stretch out, relax. I loved every minute of his hour: me, him, the gentle rhythm of breath and the clouds trundling slowly past.

Massage had been my only constant since I'd crashed out of school, wrecked and hopeless, with only four GCSEs to my name. Without massage, and the respite it brought me from a head that felt like it would never heal, I was quite sure I wouldn't have survived.

Up, along, round. Up, along, round. I started on his bunched trapezius and found myself staring fondly at the soft hairs on the back of his neck.

Careful, I warned myself.

I'd learned massage in places where the focus was on *chakra*s and biorhythms, rather than things like ethics, but that didn't mean I wasn't clear where the line was.

Although what was I worried might happen? Stephen was almost certainly married. And, if not, he'd be in a relationship with a dynamic woman. And, if not, he'd never be interested in –

STOP IT, YOU TIT, I imagined Kate snapping. *Stop wallowing around in the Bad Shit!*

A tiny slice of pale blue eye opened as I tiptoed out to leave Stephen to dress. 'You've ruined me,' he moaned. 'Help . . .'

I sat at my desk, waiting for him to change, and grinned like a teenager. I loved having this effect on my clients, but I particularly loved having it on Stephen Flint.

He texted me at eleven thirty-seven p.m.

I was in the bath, poking a finger into my belly button and thinking again about Kate, whose phone had been switched off when I tried her. A tiny part of me was worried, even though Kate was made of tougher stuff than I and was, no doubt, fine. Knowing her, she'd have taken a sabbatical and gone to build a school in Venezuela or somewhere. It was just slightly odd that she'd not told me: during the course of our close eight-year friendship we'd never gone longer than a week without talking.

I was thinking also about the stupendous evening I'd had. During my welcome drinks, Stephen's PA, Tash, had told me that I was invited to a secret gig taking place in the music venue in the basement. Expecting some beardy bloke singing rubbish folk music, I'd been fairly astounded to see Elton John wander in. He'd done six songs, then left the room in a state of pandemonium.

'This is UNREAL!' I shouted in Stephen's ear, when he appeared halfway through Elton's performance. 'I CAN'T BELIEVE THIS IS HAPPENING!'

Stephen was clearly very pleased. 'This is how we roll.' He touched my shoulder briefly. 'Wonderful to see you smiling,' he said, then turned to talk to Jamilla, who seemed perkier now. She'd told me earlier she'd not been in touch with Claudine for a while, and I thought, privately, that I didn't blame her. Claudine was teetering on the brink of downright offensive at the moment. Last week she had told me that if I was entertaining notions of a crush on my boss I was being a deluded child. 'Don't be stupid, just for once,' she had said. 'Men like him are bad news. And they never go for women like you.'

Thanks, I'd thought. *Thanks a lot*. I wondered if Claudine would be so bloody rude if she actually met Stephen and saw for herself that he was just a really nice bloke.

Beside me in the crowd, Jamilla was listening to Stephen with a slight smile on her face. In spite of her improved mood she still seemed shattered. Stephen patted her back kindly before wandering off. I loved that he made an effort to talk to everyone, no matter what rank they held.

I'd floated home on my bike, boggled and delighted. My world, I saw, had become very small over the last few years. My time had been divided between the tube, silent treatment rooms and exhausted, dreamless sleep. I'd lost the energy and courage that had once flung me across Asia with a rucksack on my back, and I'd kind of lost the ability to interact with other humans, which wasn't good. But suddenly, gloriously, I could see the sky again.

When my phone beeped from my bedroom, even though there was no reason on earth why he would be texting me – especially at this time of night – I somehow knew it was Stephen.

I lasted sixty seconds before I heaved myself out of the bath to go and look.

I'm so pleased you're working for us. You are a dream! Everyone's raving about you already! X

Do I reply? I wondered. Certainly, said my furiously texting thumb.

You're welcome!! Thanks for taking me on board!!

Too many exclamation marks.

As his reply arrived in my inbox my excitement turned to something I wasn't so familiar with.

After my massage today I realized I really wanted to get well. Learn how to relax, eat healthily. All the things Jamilla keeps telling me to do. But it was you and your wonderful work that convinced me it's time for a change. Thanks again, Annie. x

I took the phone to bed and popped it on a Japanese silk cushion, as if it were a sacred object.

'PULL YOURSELF TOGETHER,' I whispered fiercely into the empty room. 'HE'S YOUR BOSS.'

But I couldn't. I had never been able to let my guard down with strangers, especially men. Yet with Stephen Flint my guard had vanished into thin air. It was April; it was spring. Maybe today really *had* been the first day of the rest of my life.

Chapter Six

Kate

Six thirty a.m., a Tuesday in April. A lone girl walks through an empty landscape at daybreak. Around her is a web of fine white lace, a million tiny pearls of water scooped up from the English Channel and carried high over Exmoor before settling in the fields. Her footsteps follow the line of the hedge, which is stuffed with black-thorn flowers and early-morning bumblebees already hard at work. Every few paces she turns and looks at the little footsteps she's left, as if to check she is still alone. She listens, straining to hear something, but all that's audible is a steady drip, drip, drip from the little coppice of beech trees behind her. Up ahead a tired light appears in the window of the old stone farmhouse and she walks on towards it, both relieved and disappointed that her solitude is to be broken.

Sometimes I did that. Pictured myself as if I were in a film script: a lone woman picking her way through an empty landscape, checking every few steps for preda-tors. It was the sort of thing that only the maddest article would do, probably, but it kept me on my toes. 'Never forget the man in your shadow,' I muttered to myself, sliding into the yard without setting off the squeaky gate that Sandra kept forgetting to oil. 'Never forget that some aul' bastard could pop out and grab you any time, Kate Brady . . .'

I giggled. I sounded like an old man in a shebeen somewhere in the wilds of Connemara, not an ex-Google employee from Dublin who'd run off to hide with the horses. Which was a good thing, because Joe said I was already beginning to sound English. 'The shame of it, Galway,' he'd tutted.

I inhaled deeply as the smells of the yard snaked in. Thank God for this place. Here all I had to think about was whether the water buckets were full; whether I'd cleaned the right tack for Mark tomorrow; whether we were running low on haylage or chaff. Becca had been right: I had learned quickly, and that was because here in this remote corner of Somerset there was peace and simplicity, absolute freedom from the incessant noise of my old life.

An early starling was watching me from the dovecote, but apart from that, the yard seemed empty; most of the horses would still be lying down in their stables. I felt a great swell of affection for my beautiful new friends, stretched out on their beds, trusting that soon people would appear to feed, exercise and love them just as they did every day, come hell or high water. They were so trusting, those creatures, so gentle. One in particular.

In the far corner of the courtyard, a handsome white head was already hanging over the stable door. Stumpy made a quiet whickering sound as I approached him, his satellite-dish ears strained far forwards and his eyes focused excitedly on me.

'Hello, silly,' I said quietly, reaching into my pocket for the pieces of carrot he knew I was carrying.

'Hoo-hoo-ho-hoo,' he whispered, and – just as I did every morning – I smiled like a little girl. I was completely in love. Hooked. Done for.

'Oh, you are just so *lovely*,' I said, and kissed his nose. He butted me gently, impatient for the carrot. Food before love, he was saying. Come on, Kate Brady, you know my priorities.

I gave him some carrot, then scratched underneath his forelock, smiling as his big head drooped and his eyelids closed. 'I love you, Stumpy,' I said. 'I think you're the nicest person I've ever met. I wish you were a man. Actually I don't. Men are horrible! But you, my boy, are perfect.'

I kissed one of his now-floppy ears, running my nose up the fine, soft hair, brushing my eyelashes with the tip of his ear. Everything about working on this remote farm was helping me heal, but if there was one thing, one person, responsible for bringing me back to life, it was Stumpy. (He was definitely a person. Far more a person than many humans I could think of.)

I'd discovered quickly that Stumpy was like a mirror to my often-turbulent mental state. If I was upset, Stumpy knew. He would stand quietly while I leaned, exhausted, on his shoulder the morning after one of my still-frequent nightmares, or he'd blow on my neck when I got upset about lying to my family all the time. If I flinched when my phone went off, or stared fearfully at cars coming down the driveway, he would stiffen or turn away, signalling clearly that he found my anxiety unpleasant. Whatever was going on with me, the horse knew and, however bad it was, got me back on track.

He was a miracle. I still had a long journey ahead of me

but with Stumpy at my side I felt certain that I'd be my best self again one day.

'Look what you've done to me!' I said, and kissed his nose again. 'Look! It's pathetic! I'm the lovelorn moron over here!'

'He has the same effect on me,' said a man's voice. Mark gave Stumpy a Polo and patted his neck, then caved in and kissed his nose too, even though I was watching. He blushed as he did it, but couldn't stop himself. 'You've really fallen for him, haven't you?' he said, not quite looking me in the eye.

'How could I not? He's the most adorable horse in the world.'

Stumpy reached up and rested his muzzle on Mark's head, even though it was six feet off the ground and made the horse visibly uncomfortable. 'Get off, idiot.' Mark grinned.

He turned and looked straight at me, with the lopsided expression I was coming to recognize as a smile. 'You come out here every morning,' he said. 'Stumpy's always waiting for you. Sometimes you go for a walk first but you always come and see him. Every day, before the rest of us are up. You always seem so happy.'

How had he seen me? (And why was he watching?)

'My room looks over the yard,' he explained, almost kindly, as if to spare me discomfort.

'Oh, I see.' I concentrated on getting fine pieces of bedding out of Stumpy's mane. 'He makes for a good start to the day, don't you think, boss?'

Everything I felt about Mark was confused. In many ways, he was exactly as Becca had said – cold, monosyllabic, completely disengaged from the lives of his team. And yet I'd catch him, sometimes – he caught me too: we seemed to have an odd habit of coming across each other during a soppy moment with Stumpy – betraying a softness that I found incredibly touching.

'So,' Mark said, 'how do you think it's all going? Your month's trial is up today.'

'Oh.' Shit, I'd forgotten. What if he thought I wasn't up to scratch? What would I do then?

'I've had the best four weeks of my life,' I said simply. I couldn't stand the thought of leaving; trying to sound detached and professional would be a waste of time. 'I love the work, I love the craic, I love the horses and I love watching you ride. Watching how you are with the horses – I didn't know competition riders were so sweet with them, I . . .'

I trailed off and chanced a look at him. To my amazement, just as my eyes met his, he smiled properly. A big, beautiful smile that creased the skin around his eyes like tracing paper. 'Er, thanks. Although I thought we'd agreed. No blowing smoke up my arse.'

I tried to ignore the strange lightness in my stomach. 'Sorry. No flattery. I think you're a terrible rider.'

Mark actually chuckled. 'You're doing a great job,' he said. 'I'd be delighted to keep you. In fact, even though it'd be peanuts, I'd like to offer you a tiny salary. You're not keeping a horse here, after all.'

He rubbed Stumpy's velvet muzzle. 'Unless you want to bring your horse,' he said casually. 'We could do that instead, if you wanted?'

'No, no!' I said quickly. 'And there's no need to pay me

either. I'm happy. Your mum feeds us beautifully and I enjoy the work.'

'Well, that's nice to hear, Kate, but I still want to pay you.'

'No!' It came out far too loudly. 'Sorry, I mean, no, thanks, you're all right. Keep your money for the eventing season, boss. You're bound to need it.'

'Are you turning down money?'

'I am. Money's not an issue for me. I had a great job in Dublin.'

'Could we pay you in another way? Do you want some lessons, maybe? I never see you exercising the horses . . .'

'No, really! I'm fine! I enjoy my shit-shovelling more than you'd know!'

Mark was looking more and more suspicious. 'Some time off? I could get you a ticket back to Dublin to see your family.'

'Ah, no, I can speak to them on Skype.'

'Kate,' Mark said carefully, 'you're being quite weird. I want to pay you. Please tell me how.'

I racked my brains. What could I ask for to keep him quiet? How could I explain to him that just by having me here he was saving my skin?

'A competition!' I cried. 'Let me come to a competition some time. I'd love that! Badminton, maybe – that'd be a dream come true!' Badminton was not far off, and I knew there was no way on earth I'd be allowed to go under normal circumstances. On the rare occasions that Mark needed anyone other than Tiggy he took Becca. 'I don't want to put you on the spot,' I added hastily. 'I know you need your best people at Badminton. So Belton Park would be fine if that's better.'

'Badminton it is,' Mark said, without turning a hair. 'You've got to learn somewhere. And it's a cracking place to start. Absolutely bonkers, about as old-school as it gets. Bowler hats, shooting sticks, mad old women in pearls. I'm only taking two horses so it's not like Tigs'll be overwhelmed.'

'Are you sure?'

He shrugged. 'Why not?'

'But what about Becca?'

'Like I said, I'm taking two horses,' he repeated patiently, 'And Becca comes to events when I'm running four or more.' He scowled. 'Although if Maria has her way I'll be competing all five of her dad's bloody horses.'

I shifted from one foot to the other, unsure whether to join in. 'You don't want to compete them all?'

'No! Apart from the fact that it's against the rules, it'd be impossible. I'd die.' He did a hand gesture that meant 'enough of that'. 'So, do you want to come?'

'Um, yes!' I said, delighted. 'Thank you so much, Mark. How exciting!' I turned to Stumpy, who was nibbling a piece of hay stuck to my shoulder. 'I'm going to come and see you at Badminton!' I told him. 'I'm going to see you jump the biggest and scariest jumps in the whole *world*, little Stumpman!'

I heard Mark chuckle again, and before I knew it I'd joined in. 'Your man thinks we're total eejits.' I gestured at Stumpy.

'Rubbish. He thinks we're great.'

We. My head was getting noisy. I needed to end this conversation. 'Well, thanks again,' I said. 'I'd better let you get on with your day.'

'Okay,' Mark said. He, too, began to withdraw, to dismantle the flimsy bond that had sprung up between us. 'So that's sorted. You're staying on. Excellent news. I'll get Mum to put you up on the website as a permanent member of staff.'

'NO!' Stumpy jumped, his ears swinging back. 'Please don't do that! I'm like you. Not in it for the fame . . .'

'Oh,' Mark said, after a bemused pause. 'You really are odd,' he added, with another of those big smiles. 'Refusing to let us pay you, telling me my horse's show name sounds like a big fart, roaming around my fields at six in the morning. Are you on drugs?'

Mark had never made a joke with me before. It was so nice to see him smile.

'All of the drugs.'

'Great.' He chuckled. 'We'll have some drinks later to welcome you formally to the team, and you can share your drugs then.'

'That'd be lovely.' I beamed. 'They're great.'

'I'm glad you like them all. Joe's not been too much, has he?'

Last night Joe had burst into my room at eleven o'clock, shouting, 'GALWAY! ME LOINS ARE ON FIRE! I CAN'T TAKE ANY MORE! WILL YOU PLEASE SHOW THIS MAN SOME MERCY AND GIVE HIM A RIDE?'

Becca had thrown a satsuma at him from her doorway and roared that she'd kill him. He'd roared back that she was a jealous old lesbian and I'd sat in bed, crying with laughter, amazed at how well I was fitting in.

'No, Joe's okay,' I said, smiling fondly.

Mark was watching my face. 'Oh,' he said. 'Oh, I see.'

'Oh, Jesus, no, I'm not after Joe!'

There was a long pause, during which we both self-consciously reached out to stroke Stumpy, who was getting bored of us talking outside his door. Then Mark turned on the heel of his riding boot and marched off. 'You should probably get them fed,' he called.

I watched him go, and thought, *I don't want you to think I fancy Joe.*

And then: *This is worrying.*

I didn't get a chance to tell Becca I'd passed my trial until much later on, when we were washing down Jolene and tacking up Harold respectively. Harold was in a very bad mood and kept trying to bite Becca's bottom.

'Bugger off,' she told him, swiping at his snapping teeth. Harold responded with redoubled attempts, and Becca had to move away. 'What's wrong with you, pet?' she asked him, hands on hips. 'Have you been possessed?'

'Mark said he's going to get the chiropractor out,' I told her. 'He's worried Harold's got something wrong with his back.'

Becca stroked the horse until he stopped biting.

'I have news!' I whispered.

'What's that, pet?'

'I passed my trial! I'm staying!'

Becca swung away from Harold. 'Kate!' she cried, jumping over and hugging me. Becca didn't do much physical contact. I was touched. 'That's fantastic news, pet!' I smiled happily, thanking myself once again for running away to Somerset. 'So you'll be staying? Indefinitely?'

'Yes!' I scraped the water off Jolene's quarters, keen to

have her rugged up before she got cold. 'Your man said he thought I was doing a grand job and even offered to pay me! He's going to take me to Badminton and we're to have some drinks tonight to celebrate.'

'Really?' Becca paused.

'Yeah!'

'He's taking you to Badminton? And throwing you a *drinks* party?'

'I know! Madness!'

Becca went back to Harold's saddle. 'I see,' she said. Something about her tone made me turn. There was a lovely ease and fluidity in Becca's movement normally, but suddenly she was hunched and pinchy. Harold turned to bite her again, and this time she slapped him hard on the shoulder. 'STOP IT.'

Harold turned away sulkily and Becca called over to Joe, who was approaching. 'I've put Harold's road studs in,' she said to him. 'He's all yours.' And before Joe had a chance to thank her, or I had a chance to get a proper look at her face, she'd gone.

One of the many things I'd had to look up recently was the World Class squad that kept being mentioned. I'd learned it was a programme to support the horse/rider combinations that made up Team GBR – 'Lots of coaching and horse medicine and support,' Becca had explained, 'that'd cost them a fuckin' packet otherwise.' Mark had been in the programme for five years with a succession of fantastic horses (all owned by Maria's father) and was now in it with Stumpy: he was planning to take him to the World Equestrian Games later this year.

From time to time the coach, a man called Pierre, would visit the yard to train Mark, and Caroline Lexington-Morley would come over to join in.

Today they were show-jumping in the outdoor school.

It had turned into a warm spring day and the sheep in the field next door were standing in the sun, comically stupefied, as Mark and Caroline cantered around. Clouds scudded lightly overhead and pigeons called lazily to each other from the beech copse. It should have been a perfect afternoon, really, except Becca had sunk into a dark mood and had barely spoken at lunchtime.

Caroline was flirting openly with Mark. I found myself taking more notice of this than I'd have liked.

'It's none of my business,' I said to Joe, who was leaning on the post-and-rail fence, watching the session with great interest, 'but isn't Caroline married?'

Joe smiled. 'Of course, darlin',' he said. 'But that seldom stops anyone in this business.' He turned back to watch Mark, who was sailing down a hefty line of jumps with perfect timing and balance. I knew now that the rows were called combinations and that it was bloody tricky to do them well. Mark and Stumpy, though, calm as clouds, made it look easy.

'Beautiful,' Joe said. 'Absolutely beautiful.'

Caroline – noisily confident with her pink lipstick and expensive leather-palmed gloves – shouted, 'God, Waverley! Can't you be shit for even a *minute*, sweetheart?'

Mark set off and did the combination again. 'Gorgeous,' Caroline yelled.

Leave him alone, I heard myself think.

That sort of thought has to be banned immediately, I

told myself, staring determinedly at Stumpy and ignoring Mark. Twists of alarm were beginning to spiral up my abdomen.

Stumpy was making a strange noise as he trotted, a sort of deep, hollow squeaking. 'What's that sound?' I asked Joe, just as Mark pulled up next to the fence we were leaning on.

But Joe had already gone.

'What sound?' Mark asked.

'Oh. Um . . . The noise your man makes when he's trotting.'

'Air in his sheath,' Mark said, turning to watch Caroline take her turn.

'Sheath?'

Mark turned back to me, a definite smile in his eyes. 'The thing that hangs down between his back legs, protecting his penis.'

I stared at Stumpy's neck. I daren't look at his sheath. Or Mark's sheath. Crotch. Face. Anything.

Help.

'Oh,' I said flatly. 'Air. Right.'

'Yup.'

I tried not to laugh, I really did, but it was futile. Stumpy had a shouty crotch! You couldn't make it up! A loud peal of laughter rolled out of me, in spite of my best efforts to stop it, followed immediately by a similar one from Mark. Stumpy gazed at me like I was really strange, which just made me laugh even harder. We laughed until I was actually crying, and didn't stop until Ana Luisa marched up and shoved a posy of weeds through the fence towards her dad, who stopped laughing long enough to thank her profusely and instruct me to put them in a special vase.

'Why are you laughing?' she asked impatiently, and I had to leave because I couldn't answer.

I took the posy and put it into an old jam jar on top of one of the many rickety chests of drawers that lined the walls of the tack room. And even when Maria stormed in, looking for Mark, and snapped that I wasn't there to sit around doing nothing, the smile didn't leave my face.

The woman watches her daughter press one of the daisy chains up to her nose. Her face is scrunched with comic puzzlement.

'Why are daisies so stinky, Mum,' she asks eventually, 'when they look so pretty?'

'That's just how Nature made them.' Her mother smiles. 'The daisies probably think we smell weird, too.'

Her daughter giggles. She's so beautiful, the mother thinks. So milky pale and pretty, with those huge blue eyes and little pixie ears, the softness in her features that is born entirely of her rare trust in all people. She makes friends wherever she goes, this girl, marches up to strangers on those slim little legs and tells them her name without any of the haughty self-consciousness that cripples her elder sister. Sometimes she'll shake their hands or even say, 'You can kiss my cheek, if you like.' She is a delight. A free spirit, just like her mother, *they say in the village.*

'Here,' the woman says. 'Put some more sun cream on. The sun's baking us like potatoes.'

The girl continues with her daisy chains. 'You do it,' she demands. 'It's my birthday.' She flashes a quick smile at her mother to check it's been received in the spirit it was meant, and is pleased to see that her mum is chuckling.

'Cheeky,' Mum says. She starts with the child's slender little arms, moving the straps of her white cotton dress so she can cover her shoulders.

Without warning her daughter twists round and kisses her mother's nose. 'I love you, Mummy,' she says, and the woman thinks, If I died today, I would die so perfectly happy.

She decides she'll talk to Bert later about this Africa trip. Maybe it's too soon. Maybe she should just let their beautiful little family breathe for a while. Does she not have everything she could possibly want, right here? Does she not know happiness that transcends every mountain daybreak, every remote beach, every huge sky she saw travelling the world? She knows Bert will do anything she asks, but she knows, too, that his heart isn't fully in the plan. She feels an almost indecent swell of love for the quiet, generous man she married, with his open face and his hopeless love for her, his long, spidery fingers and his gentle voice. He's starting his novel today. She was so proud this morning that she had to leave his little study so that he wouldn't see the tears in her eyes.

'Right,' her daughter says, hanging the final daisy chain carefully around her neck. 'Let's play hide and seek.'

Her mother assents, rubbing the last splodge of sun cream into the back of her little girl's neck.

It's the last thing she will ever do for her.

'You hide first,' she says, and her child goes sprinting off across the field, shouting, 'CLOSE YOUR EYES AND COUNT TO TEN! NO, TWENTY! NO, THIRTY! COUNT TO ONE ZILLION BILLION THOUSAND MILLION!'

For the rest of her life she will wish that she had turned round to shout those things directly at her mother, rather than into the rippling shelves of hot air that hover over the field. She will wish that she had seen what she knew to be behind her: her mother sitting in that carpet of daisies at Woodford Farm, her hands over her eyes and laughter spilling out of her.

She will wish more than anything else that this was the last memory she had of her mother, rather than the one that, after nearly three decades, she still can't erase.

Chapter Seven

Annie

It was Saturday and Tim and I were at the Counter in Hackney Wick, eating *huevos rancheros* with great big blobs of spicy chorizo and thick sourdough bread. A warm May sun was climbing rapidly into the sky and we were sitting out on the café's higgledy-piggledy wooden jetty, watching the light sparkle and wobble on the surface of the River Lea. Lizzy had blown us out because she was hungover and Claudine had said she would rather eat swords than hang around in Hackney.

'Wow.' Tim smiled. A narrow boat was chugging past bearing a girl in a leopard-print leotard and bright red lipstick. Nothing else. Behind her the Olympic Stadium squatted fatly in the sun.

Hackney was not the place it had been fourteen years ago when I'd rented my little house off Murder Mile. Luckily, my ancient landlord had not seemed to notice that it had become an extremely fashionable and expensive place to live, so I was still paying less rent than other friends now paid for one-bedroom flats. I really must tell him what his house is worth, I thought guiltily. The problem was that, even though he was probably perfectly nice, I could never quite bring myself to phone him in case he wanted to come to the house and talk to me there alone.

Tim had been telling me about Mel, who apparently slept with her face down in the pillow and was allergic to pork.

'Poor thing,' I'd said. 'I know how she feels, with me not being able to eat wheat or dairy.' I spread a piece of sourdough toast thickly with butter.

Tim seemed to be quite keen on Mel, and I was pleased to find that I was truly happy for him. 'Maybe we're getting there,' I said. 'Me finding a decent job and you finding a decent girl. It only took us sixteen years, Tim.'

'Is that how long we've known each other? Seriously?'

It was. When I'd first met Tim on my first day at the support group, he was wearing a hoodie and those big trainers that always smell of wet dogs. He'd been going to the group for three weeks already and had befriended me with a fierce desperation as soon as I'd walked through the door. 'If we're really as mad as these people, we should consider killing ourselves now,' he'd said, all curtains haircut and bum-fluff chin. He'd gestured bleakly at the collection of depressed teenagers sitting in a circle at the far end of the church hall.

'I'm afraid I'm definitely mad,' I'd apologized. 'I have a psychologist's file to prove it.'

Tim nodded glumly. 'Me too. Is it not bad enough to be a teenager? Why do we have to be fucked up too?'

Now look at him. All tall and preppy, happy and successful, a clever psychiatrist with a big flat in Bethnal Green and now a girlfriend! 'We just need to find you a decent man,' he said. 'Then everything will be complete and we'll never have another difficult day.'

I thought about saying something but stopped short.

What exactly could I say? *Oh, I've got a crush on my boss, so hopefully I'll be all loved up soon myself?*

'What?' Tim was watching me in the annoying way he had, which said, *I can see what you're thinking.* 'What's going on in there?'

'Meh.'

'Don't you dare.'

'Honestly. Nothing.'

'Annie! You're lying!'

I busied myself with my eggs, swirling in the spicy red oil of the chorizo until my plate was orange, concentrating on the clink of cutlery and the low hum of conversation around us.

'Is it your boss?'

'Meh.'

'It's your boss!'

Eventually I agreed. 'Nothing to say, though, Tim, so don't even bother. He's just a bit fit and funny, that's all. I shall get over it, like I always do.'

Tim finished his eggs. 'So he's unavailable. That's a surprise.'

It wasn't yet confirmed but I had, rather sadly, begun to fear it was inevitable. For a while I'd allowed myself to hope that Stephen's recent dark time had been to do with a break-up, but yesterday his PA, Tash, had said 'they' when she was talking about Stephen's house, and there was a picture of a child in his wallet. Plus he had said during his massage yesterday that he was off to Paris for the weekend, and men only went to Paris if they had a woman in tow.

'It's under control,' I said. 'A passing crush. It means nothing.'

Tim put his fingertips together and watched me.

'Stop it, Tim.'

'Okay . . .'

'Worry about your girlfriend instead. She can't eat bacon sandwiches.'

Tim laughed and the little thread of tension was cut. I would get over my crush. Although it would help if Stephen stopped coming for massages. He'd had three this week alone – 'I'm completely addicted,' he said cheerfully – and the better I got to know his body the harder it was to feel nothing about it. There was a little dink at the top of his neck where he'd once been cut with a barber's razor, and a mole on his left ankle with a curious ellipsis round it, like a planet. I enjoyed his body far too much.

It also hadn't helped that, after my first month, he'd sent me a massive hamper of beautiful food to say thank you for 'turning my senior management team into relaxed little puppies'. It was full of expensive superfood supplements and lovely farmers' market things. And a pair of Reebok shorts! He'd remembered what I'd said about never having time to exercise or cook!

I was very confused about my relationship with my boss.

No, I wasn't.

Yes, I was.

Oh dear.

Tim and I left the café and mooched around the paintings in the Stour Space. After less than a minute we admitted we hated them and moved on into the midday sun, drifting over Regent's Canal and picking up the bank of the Lea Navigation, talking about Lizzy, who had added a third boyfriend to her portfolio and was some-what manic.

'Don't you long for a time when everyone in Le Cloob is just normal?' I sighed. 'There's always at least one of us in some form of the Bad Shit.'

Tim picked up a stone and tried to skim it across the river towards the Olympic Park. It plopped and sank straight away. 'I don't wish we were all normal,' he said thoughtfully. 'Although I know what you mean. Life is a rich tapestry, Pumpkin, highs and lows, happies and sads. It's all in the natural order of things.'

'Life is a rich tapestry, eh?' I grinned.

'Unfortunately I did say that, yes. But you know what I mean.'

'Yeah.'

'By the way, talking of the Bad Shit, what's the latest on Kate? Have you heard from her?'

'No, but I think she's okay. I called her landline and some girl answered, saying she's renting Kate's room for a while because Kate's gone away. I guess she just forgot to tell me. She'll be in touch.'

'Oh, phew,' Tim said.

'Yeah. Although she'd better not have gone off to Asia without me.'

'Well, if she has, you're not allowed to go running off after her. You've got a proper job now, Pumpkin, time to lay down some London roots for a bit.'

Tim was often on at me about my tendency to fly to the other side of the world. Like my therapist, he thought it was unhealthy; he claimed it only happened when my anx-iety got out of hand and that it was all about disappearing.

Disappearing emotionally: running away, skirting off sideways, rather than continuing the uphill battle to stay sane.

He was quite right, of course, but I felt that was my prerogative. For all Tim's training, and for all the many conversations we'd had about my mental state over the years, I still didn't think he quite understood how exhausting it was for me to stay afloat. If the work required just to feel neutral was a constant struggle, did I not have the right to skive off from time to time? I mean, at least I disappeared to fascinating places for six months, rather than to my bed.

Also, as I'd tried to explain to him many, many times, it wasn't just about disappearing. I *loved* travelling. I loved the landscapes, the big skies, the freedom. Most of all I loved the surprising feeling of safety it gave me. I'd hand over my rucksack at the check-in desk, pass through security and . . . *there*. It was as if my very soul breathed out. Suddenly I was just another girl, a nameless face in a sea of travellers. I'd collect my bag at the other end, dive into a humid scrum of waiting rickshaw drivers and nobody would know – or really care – who I was.

I looked up at the sky, a thin sheet of vivid blue. 'I won't be going travelling any time soon, so you needn't worry. Um, Tim?'

'Yes?'

'Are you in love with Mel?'

Tim frowned, picking up another stone. He did another terrible skim. 'Love?'

'Yes. That. Are you in that with her?'

'When you fall in love, it's like being hooked up to a drip,' Tim said thoughtfully. His eyes had taken on an intensity that surprised me. 'A drip that delivers the very breath of life. I don't feel like that with Mel – not yet . . . But she's great. I certainly think I could fall in love with her.'

A naughty beagle galloped past us. 'Wow,' I said, surprised. I glanced sideways at my friend, who was in a world of his own. 'I've never had that. The intravenous-drug thing.'

Tim shrugged. 'It just means you've not found your One. Or, at least, you've not allowed yourself to.'

'Oi. No psychologizing.'

'I'm a psychiatrist.'

'No psychiatrizing, then.'

He laughed despairingly, muttering something about me being a mad badger and testing the diagnostic capabilities of even his cleverest colleagues.

I ignored him. Something wasn't quite right. 'Er, Tim, forget for a second that I'm a maddo. Can we instead talk about who *you've* been in intravenous-drip love with, please?'

Tim looked away. 'Sorry?'

'You just said a really hair-raising thing about what love feels like. And I'm asking who, exactly, has made you feel like that?'

Tim looked very uncomfortable. 'I . . .' he began. I waited.

'That's just what they say,' he said eventually. 'In books and films. And even psychological literature. I wasn't talking from personal experience.'

That was not how it had sounded to me. But I left it. Tim and I were good at knowing where to stop. Maybe he had fallen head over heels in love with Mel already and didn't want to admit it.

We walked on.

A man up ahead was taking photos of the water, balanced precariously on the scrubby grass of the bank with a very expensive piece of kit dangling close to the rippling surface. 'I'd laugh if he fell in,' I said, even though I probably wouldn't. And then, as I saw the set of the man's head, the slope of his nose, I realized it was Stephen.

I stopped. I turned to walk in the other direction, then turned back. Then turned again to walk away. Then I stopped completely, paralysed by indecision.

'Annie?' Tim said.

'Come here,' I hissed, walking away again. Tim came, obviously perplexed. 'That's him! That's my BOSS!'

Tim looked round. 'DON'T LOOK AT HIM!' I whisper-yelled.

It was too late. Stephen must have sensed that we were stalled on the towpath and turned sideways, straightening slightly. The lens of the camera caught the sun and flashed off my bright red face.

'OH!' I bellowed. 'HI!'

Stephen hung the camera round his neck. 'Are you stalking me?' he called, loping over to us with one of those dazzling smiles. 'Hello,' he added pleasantly to Tim.

'Um, Stephen, Tim, Tim, Stephen,' I said. I felt the same wash of pleasure that swept over me whenever I saw Stephen. Although what on earth was a man like Stephen Flint doing out here in the wilds of Hackney?

'Hi, mate,' Stephen said, shaking Tim's hand. To my

great surprise he was wearing trainers, although they did appear to have cost five thousand pounds.

Tim scuffed the earth with his thirty-five-pound Converses and Stephen asked what had brought us there.

'I live here,' I told him. 'Well, in Lower Clapton. We were just having breakfast at the Counter Café. Do you know it?'

Stephen beamed. 'I do! And how funny – we're almost neighbours.'

Tim and I stared at him. 'You live in Hackney?'

Stephen whipped up his camera and took a quick photo of our stunned faces. 'Shock-horror.' He checked his screen. 'Corporate twat lives in EAST LONDON! I have a house in Clapton Square.' He picked up a stone and did a perfect skim.

'Ha,' Tim said. 'You sound like you have a property portfolio!' He was grinning as if that were impossible. He didn't know quite how rich Stephen was.

'Actually I have,' Stephen admitted. 'Awful.' He grimaced apologetically and we all laughed. It was impossible to dislike Stephen. Even the slightly radioactive-looking duck straggling past us looked as if it would mate with him if he tipped it the wink.

'I thought you were in Paris this weekend,' I said.

'I cancelled the trip about fifteen minutes after my massage with you. Decided to have a lie-in, go for a walk, take some pictures . . . You were right,' he added. 'I needed some rest.'

I beamed.

'Annie's brilliant,' Stephen told Tim. 'Really helping me out. An asset to FlintSpark, and a very good influence on us nasty old corporate capitalists.'

They started talking about Stephen's camera and I stared at the water, excited and a little distracted.

I liked the way Stephen took the piss out of himself. And lived in east London, rather than Surrey, and shuffled off on a Saturday to take pictures of the water just like I did when I was travelling. I particularly liked that he was not carrying a child or holding the hand of some beautiful woman.

I was full of chorizo and May sun and a big heart-pounding crush.

' . . . with chorizo? Holy moly! Unparalleled!' Stephen was looking at me.

'Eh?'

'I said, have you ever tried the *huevos rancheros* with chorizo? Holy moly! Unparalleled!'

Tim and I looked at each other. 'That's exactly what we just had!'

In my head I started singing the tune of 'Can't Take My Eyes Off You'.

'We order it every time,' Tim said. 'But it's quite a challenge – Annie basically eats all of mine if I don't watch my plate.'

Stephen cocked his head to one side. 'You two are a fantastic double-act. You even laugh at the same time. Have you been together long?'

I went bright red. 'Oh, no! Just very old friends!'

'Oh, come on. You're like peas in a pod!'

We shook our heads hopelessly, and Stephen began to look guilty.

'Oh, crap,' he said, realizing he'd blown it. 'In spite of running a global company I'm actually outstanding at saying the wrong thing. Sorry. I'll go now. Carry on taking pictures of stupid things. I spent half an hour photographing a floating Pepsi can earlier. You truly belong in Hackney when you find yourself doing things like that.'

I smiled. 'I still can't believe you live here.'

'Ha. Well, there you have it. I'm not what you might think, Annie. Lovely to see you, and Tim, nice to meet you.'

'Likewise,' Tim said, shaking Stephen's hand again.

'Wow,' he said, as we walked away. 'Even *I* have a crush on him. What a charming man.'

'Stop it,' I said. Then: 'Argh, Tim. Isn't he *gorgeous*?'

Tim nodded. 'He is.'

I smiled hopelessly. 'I wish he was single. And not so nice. Because if I stood a chance with him, I think I'd just go for it. Try my hand at the old dating thing.'

Tim watched me. 'Really?'

'Yeah. I want to blow a big mating horn and make a charge for him!'

'I'd advise against that.'

We both laughed, although I could tell Tim was holding something back. 'Just take it easy,' was all he said.

Later that night I read my tarot cards. Just out of curiosity, of course. I wasn't really into tarot, but I'd inherited a pack during my travels and found them useful when I entered into my latest obsession.

I got the Knight of Cups and the Ace of Cups. Which meant new love, new beginnings, excitement and happiness, with a bit of knight-in-shining-armour thrown in for good measure.

I forbade myself to connect this with Stephen, then caved in after less than a minute. I thought about the sun on those eyes of his, about those nice hands cradling his camera as if it were his child, and the easy way he talked to my dear friend Tim Furniss. Was he my Knight of Cups? My Ace of Cups? The intravenous drug that Tim had talked of?

'No,' shouted the tiny part of me that was still mostly sane. Stephen was my boss, the CEO of a vast company. The fact that I'd had this level of contact with him was a mere fluke and his ownership of a house on Clapton Square was not a Sign.

I was doing quite well with this line of thought until twenty past ten when my phone buzzed with a message from him.

Was great to see you today. At the risk of being done for harassment, I just wanted to say that I thought you looked lovely. Those mad ethnic things you wear really suit you (and I never thought I'd hear myself say something like that). Stephen X

Chapter Eight

Kate

My official welcome drinks were held in the paddock by the outdoor school at seven. Drinking commenced immediately and was fast and furious.

By nine o'clock, when we all lurched off to do our final check on the horses, there was still no sign of Mark. I tried and failed to stop myself asking Sandra if he was coming.

'Oh, he's having a nice dinner with Maria and Ana Luisa,' Sandra said. 'I got them some lovely pork chops from Normington's this aftenoon, only four pounds for the lot!'

She dropped yet another burger through the grill of the barbecue into the hot coals, sighed and took a glug of her Campari and orange. It had been Sandra's idea to have a barbecue – a very nice idea it was too – but she was doing a fantastic job of destroying all the meat she'd bought.

I said that the pork sounded like a fantastic bargain, took a charred burger so that she'd feel better about her grill skills, then wandered off, feeling sad and stupid. Why had I imagined that Mark would join us? All he'd said was that he wanted to organize some team drinks. '"Team" meaning us grooms, you eejit,' I muttered to myself. 'His slaves. Since when was he part of the team?'

I decided to get very drunk.

Becca, whose mood change I still hadn't managed to unravel, had obviously had the same idea. She was sitting on the fence, slightly away from the rest of us, smoking roll-up after roll-up and steadily chugging her way through a box of Shiraz. When I took her a burger she shook her head. 'I'm fine,' she said curtly, when I asked her if she was okay, and fiddled with her wine box until I went away.

Half an hour later Sandra wobbled off to bed, then returned after less than five minutes. She admitted that Mark and Maria were having another terrible argument and that she'd given Ana Luisa earplugs. 'I couldn't take a moment more in the house,' she said. Her hands trembled as she accepted another Campari and orange from Joe, who was actually being very sweet with her. 'Maria really is a devil. Trying to make him run all sorts of horses that aren't ready, just so that she and her dad can spend every weekend in a different champagne tent. The devil! The little devil! My poor Mark! She's just screaming at him, even though the little one's in bed!'

She sank into a chair and burst into tears. 'It's too much,' she sobbed, into Joe's arm. 'Too much, Joseph. It's like the past repeating itself.'

I thought it would be inappropriate for someone as new as me to pile in, plus Joe seemed to have it under control, but my heart ached as I watched Sandra cry. She was Mark's manager, his PA, his press secretary and his accountant, and beyond him she seemed to have nobody. How sad that a family so successful and glamorous from the outside was little more than an empty vessel in reality.

In the grooms' barn there was kindness, warmth, respect and laughter; in the main house, shouting or silence.

I thought about my own family and a pain swelled in my chest that almost knocked the breath out of me. I had let them down so ruinously. And my friends. What sort of a monster was I? I wondered if they would ever forgive me, when they found out the truth. I'm so sorry for what I did, I thought. Mum, Dad, everyone, I'm more sorry than you'll ever know.

I topped up my glass.

Caroline's grooms turned up in a taxi, having heard there was free booze down the road, and things quickly went feral. Even Dirk and Woody the dogs, were drunk, thanks to Joe, who'd been slipping them cider. When Tiggy found out she whacked him on the arse with a lead-rope. 'Stop spanking me, you bully,' Joe grumbled, rubbing his bottom. 'Galway, Tiggy's after attacking me again. Will you come and make my poor little bottom better, darlin'?'

'I will not.'

'Ah, Galway, I BEG you.'

'No!'

'YES!'

'Oh, for God's sake.'

More drunk than I had been in weeks, I waddled over to Joe with a horse blanket wrapped round me. He was standing by the barbecue looking sad, wiggling slightly to Haddaway's 'What is Love', which was coming out of Sandra's portable radio.

'Right there,' he whispered, pointing to his buttocks. 'Help me, my darlin' beautiful Galway. I'm a victim of terrible abuse.' Shaking with laughter, I rubbed Joe's bottom, and Caroline's head groom said I was done for now. I told him he might just be right: Joe's bottom was the best I'd ever handled.

'A bit more, Galway,' Joe said, smiling like a naughty little angel. 'Maybe a bit more round towards the front, too . . .'

'Joseph!' Sandra cried. 'Behave!' But she was laughing now, too. Everyone was laughing, except Becca, who was still sitting on the fence, slightly away from the group.

'Becca!' I giggled. 'Help!'

She looked at Joe and me, Joe with his arms around my waist, pretending to kiss my neck while moaning a folk song about roses, and shook her head. 'Actually, I'm off to bed,' she said. 'Night, all.'

I karate-chopped my way out of Joe's arms and went after her but before I had a chance to draw level she turned. 'Don't, pet,' she said. In the light from the lanterns her face seemed taut as a drumskin. 'I'm tired, I'm pissed off and I need to go to bed. I'll be right as rain in the morning.'

She looked at me directly for the first time since that morning. There was a question in her eyes that I didn't understand. 'Whatever I've done, I'm sorry,' I said uselessly. 'I thought you'd be pleased I'm staying. I don't understand what's happened.'

'You haven't done anything,' she said, after a long exhalation of breath. 'You haven't done anything at all, Kate. And I should at least be grateful for that.'

She turned to go again but I grabbed her arm. 'Becca, please tell me what's up.'

'Pet,' Becca said, staring fixedly at the ground, 'let me go, please, and get back to your party.'

And then she went, and I let her, because I was too confused to do anything else.

By midnight, everyone was in a terrible state. We'd moved to the grooms' barn, and Sandra had gone to bed. There was no sign of Becca but the dogs had somehow found their way in and were stretched out in front of the Aga, dead drunk. 'Look what I did.' Joe giggled, curling up next to Woody, wrapping one of the dog's limp paws around his middle. 'Look what I did! God will kill me for my sins.'

Tiggy was dancing with Caroline's head groom, who was the campest thing I'd ever seen, and the others were playing strip-poker at the table, which I was keen to avoid. Too drunk either to stand up or dance, I lay down on the floor with Joe and the dogs. Dirk opened a sleepy eye, thumped his tail a couple of times, then went back to sleep.

Joe rolled over so he was lying next to me. He sang along to the Cure about how we'd kissed as the sky fell in. Joe never stopped smiling. He never stopped being nice to people, or finding a joke when things were dark. I would go for you, I thought, smiling into those lovely hazel eyes, I really would go for you, if it wasn't for the fact that I have this great big crush on our boss.

I rolled away from Joe, appalled. STOP THAT, I told my head. Do you not think you're in enough bloody trouble?

Joe rolled over and spooned me. 'Kate, he said, nuzzling into my hair. 'Katie, darling, please can we do a bit of the french kissing? All casual, like? I can't bear it any longer.'

As if I were watching from a corner, I watched myself roll back over to face him. I felt frightened. And not because I was inches away from Joe's face. I was frightened because my heart had just admitted that I had a big crush on Mark Waverley.

'Hi, sex pest,' I said weakly. 'It seems we're lying on the floor.'

'I don't care where we lie.' He smiled. 'I just have to snog you, Katie. A man can only take so much teasing.'

I can't have a crush on Mark, my head shouted. Mark of *all people*. I CAN'T.

And so, without really caring that I was in a room full of drunk people, and that gossip in this world spread with the speed and intensity of a forest fire, and that Joe was the biggest whore in the West, I let him lean in and kiss me. A long, soft kiss on the lips, laden with cider fumes and barbecue relish. I felt Joe's lips smile and I allowed mine to do the same.

Then someone at the table spotted us and started shouting that Kate and Joe were having full sex by the Aga, and the kitchen door opened and Mark Waverley walked in, and the first thing he saw was Joe and me lying on the floor between his dogs, kissing each other. The colour drained from his cheeks. Time stood still as he looked down at me, and I looked up at him.

'Oh, hello, boss,' Joe said, waving. 'How're ye?'

When I stumbled upstairs a few minutes later, my mind a drunken tangle of embarrassment and self-loathing, I saw that a light was still on in Becca's room. I paused. Becca was disappointed in me, in that sad, sorry way that my folks used to be when I was naughty, and I didn't have the faintest idea why. All I knew was that I hated it. I wanted things to be as they were. Becca was the only good friend I had access to, these days. I needed her. And, more to the point, I adored her.

I'd heard the front door slam as I'd come up the stairs – Mark leaving – and then the low murmur of scandalized conversation downstairs turning into a roar. 'I got a snog with Galway!' I could hear Joe yelling. 'I bloody knew I'd wear her down in the end! Oh, we'll be rumping in the feed room before you know it.'

I wanted to cry.

Cursing myself for my stupidity, my selfishness and my disgusting weakness as a human being, I knocked on Becca's door and pretty much fell in.

'Hello,' I said. I knew I looked like a withered old drunk. I didn't care. I just wanted to apologize for whatever I'd done so we could sort out the mess together.

'So you got off with Joe,' Becca said, drawing her duvet up to her chin. It had a summer-flowers print growing delicately over it and was the most un-Becca-like duvet in the universe. 'I heard the yelling.'

I winced. 'I hate myself. I really do, Becca, so please don't feel like you need to hate me too. Really, I've got it all covered.'

Becca stared at me, then smiled. It was a sad sort of a smile, but it was a start. 'I don't hate you.' She sighed. 'It's impossible to hate you. Besides, you're my friend.' She blushed slightly, pulling the duvet up even further. 'It's me I hate, pet.'

I sat down on the floor because the room was going a

bit lopsided. I intensely disliked being so drunk. Why did it always seem like a good idea?

'If you hate you and I hate me, maybe that cancels us out,' I suggested.

'Interesting logic.' She pulled herself up in bed. 'Want to get in?' She lifted up the duvet. I crept into Becca's bed, like a naughty dog. She must have showered after walking out of the barbecue: she smelt of synthetic raspberries and clean hair.

'Please talk to me,' I said. Tears sprang into my eyes. 'Please tell me what's up, Becca. I can't stand us not talking.'

'Me neither.' She picked at some bobbles on her duvet cover, perhaps composing herself. Then: 'Mark,' she said simply. 'I love him.'

I turned to stare at her.

'No, I don't love him. It's limped on long enough now for me to know that it's just an obsession. But love or obsession regardless, I can't shake it off.'

'So you're not gay?' I blurted out. Wow. I really hadn't thought it possible to hate myself any more than I had ten seconds ago. 'Ah, Jesus,' I said. 'What a stupid and rude question. Please don't feel you need to answer. I'm so sorry, Becca.'

Becca was chuckling. 'I'm not gay, pet. Although my mam says I do a pretty good impression. She's a shrink. Reckons that by making myself look like a stereotypical lesbian I'll successfully defend myself against the possibility of intimacy with a man, or something like that.'

I nodded stupidly. Too cerebral for this time of night.

'Maria had a bigger-than-usual affair four years ago,'

she said flatly. 'She left Mark, for a while, left Ana Luisa here, too, which was nice of her. It was someone from the Fédération Équestre Internationale she'd met at Gatcombe. She decided that he was even more useful to her than Mark. Mark caught them in the lorry at Burghley the very next week. He finally had a long-overdue go at her and she left him, just like that, because she won't have anyone criticize her. Sandra went to pieces and Mark even stopped riding for a few days. I was the only other woman on the yard back then so they moved me into the house to help look after Ana Luisa.'

She paused. 'I loved that child. She was so fucking sad, Kate. So lost and frightened and confused. Once Mark regained the power of speech he went the other way, wouldn't stop talking. He was on at me day and night about his *feelings*, their relationship, even his relationship with his dad. I mean, for fuck's sake.'

I listened, deeply moved.

'He was so shocked that Maria had actually gone, and so scared about the effect it would have on the little one. And he wouldn't admit it but he was sick with fear that she'd take away her horses. He cried, Kate, he cried every day.'

A tear dropped out of Becca's eye. She rubbed her chapped hands fiercely across her face, but the tears kept welling up and sliding out. 'And stupid old me, who'd never really been close to a man before, got all confused, and thought it meant something. And my stupid old heart decided that I loved him. And that maybe he felt the same way.'

I threaded my arm round her tattooed shoulders.

'But obviously, pet, he didn't. After two weeks of gabbling at me he stopped, because Maria had decided to come home and he was back in his miserable, shit, trapped life again. He hates it, pet, but it keeps him so busy he doesn't have to think about it. He's got the horses, the trophy wife, the batty kid and his mam warbling around, pretending everything's fine.'

Becca was sobbing now. 'He just took her back as soon as she decided he was too useful for her to lose. As if his happiness didn't matter.' Her shoulders shook. 'I still can't believe what a fuckin' idiot I've been, pet. I'm so sorry I got the hump this morning. I was just jealous that he wanted to take you to Badminton, and throw you a drinks party when he's never even made me a cup of tea. I was jealous that he actually managed to say more than one sentence to you. I convinced myself that he liked you. And that you liked him back.'

And with that she curled her head into my shoulder and howled.

I hugged her, rocking backwards and forwards. I hummed a song that my mum used to sing when I'd fallen over and hurt myself until, eventually, she stopped crying.

'Becca,' I said, when it was all over. 'Becca, listen to me. I don't fancy Mark. And he doesn't fancy me. I just kissed Joe, remember? There's nothing between Mark and me. No spark, no nothing. There never has been, and there never will be. Do you believe me?'

Becca's eyes were all red and blurry. She wanted to believe me. She wanted to believe what I'd said almost as much as I did.

And I knew in that moment that what I'd just said

would have to be true. There never had been a thing, and there never would be. And that was that. I relaxed a little. I was a bloody expert at blocking out the Bad Shit, these days. I'd simply add my messy feelings about Mark to the ever-growing Access Denied Department of my head and get on with my job.

'Thanks, pet,' Becca said eventually. Her voice was trembling but I could feel that stoic strength building slowly back in her. 'I do believe you. Thank you, Kate.'

Chapter Nine

Annie

In the week following my unexpected Hackney encounter with Stephen, I noticed that I was somehow sneaking on lipstick when my back was turned, and managing more than once to go and get my hair blowdried into something tumbly and voluminous. It was duplicitous behaviour of which I did not approve. One day Claudine met me for lunch at work. As soon as she saw me, she scowled. 'I knew it!' she hissed. 'You fancy your boss! Annie, you are deluded. Men like Stephen are *bad*.'

The next day I waited for Stephen to turn up for his massage, ready to compile a list of reasons why she was wrong.

But Stephen did not come that week, or the next. In fact, it was nearly three weeks before I saw him again. Tash told me he was in Hong Kong. 'Having far too much fun,' she said, rolling her eyes. I rolled mine too and felt desperate.

I checked my phone constantly in case he sent one of those lovely text messages again, which he did not. I spent an evening eating stinky Comté cheese from the deli on Chatsworth Road, stalking him furtively through newspaper articles and Facebook. I began to curse myself. Could I not – just for one week, one day even – form an appropriate crush on an appropriate man?

When I found an interview with him in the *Spectator*, in which the interviewer himself had quite clearly fallen in love with Stephen, I ate even more cheese and finally admitted to my (sadly indifferent) sitting room that I was smitten with Stephen Flint.

On the seventh evening of Stephen's absence my phone rang at just gone ten o'clock from a withheld number. I threw myself at the phone like it was the last on earth.

Then I waited. 'Er, hi?' I'd never sounded so casual.

'Annie, you old tinker,' shouted Kate Brady. 'How're ye, darling?'

'Kate . . .' I closed my eyes, full of warmth at the sound of her voice. 'Kate, I thought I'd never hear from you again. Where've you *been*?'

Kate sniggered. 'I know, darling, sorry. I was after running off to the countryside.'

'What? Running off? With who?'

'With myself, Annie. Myself and a load of horses. I'm having a blast, although I look like a fecking muck heap most of the time.' And with that she was off, explaining – as if this was the kind of thing people did all the time – that she'd got fed up with Dublin and decided to take a countryside sabbatical.

'I love it,' she said. 'It's a bloody dream, Annie. The mornings are so beautiful and the weather's been lovely . . . I could do this for ever.'

We spoke for a while about her life on the farm. It sounded like a wonderful way to live but – although I couldn't quite put my finger on why – I couldn't help thinking there was something she wasn't telling me. I let her be. A lifetime of being mentally prodded and poked by psychologists and doctors had taught me to back off when people didn't want to share information.

'So what're you up to?' Kate asked. 'How's things?'

'I'm standing naked in front of the mirror in my bedroom,' I admitted.

'Oh, right. Grand.'

When she'd called I'd been staring at myself, wondering what Stephen would think if he were ever to see me naked. A man with film-star good looks and a wardrobe to suit, removing the worn Indian cottons of a deathly white, slightly baggy girl with what I believed to be a fairly average appearance, aside from her lovely long blonde hair. I'd look like an old white plastic bag next to Stephen and that toned brown skin. And what was I even doing, wondering what he'd think of me naked? He'd been surprisingly welcoming, which was probably standard practice for him, and he'd sent me a couple of late texts – probably from his desk, knowing his schedule – and now he was away, not thinking about me. There couldn't have been less of a story.

I'd been feeling quite lonely with my crush. Claudine had made clear that she didn't like the sound of Stephen, so talking to her wasn't an option, and Lizzy, for all her initial excitement, had cautioned me against getting involved with my boss when I admitted to my little crush. Even Tim had been a bit off when I'd tried to talk to him.

So I told Kate. I told her about every last text message, the hand on the small of my back, and the strange sensation I had that I was coming alive after years in hibernation, and how I was positive that this had everything to do with Stephen.

'Oh, sure, give him a ride,' Kate said, when I finished.

'If he's not flirting with you, Annie, I'll eat my hat. Remember, you're twenty times prettier than you think you are. You know all my boys in Dublin are mad about you.'

I smiled shyly. One of them had asked me out for a drink when he'd come to London recently. I'd made myself say yes but had cancelled three hours before when I'd realized I was having mild palpitations and couldn't eat. 'Claudine doesn't like him.'

'Oh, Annie, she doesn't like *anyone*. Anyone other than that big farty husband of hers. Sweetheart, just go for it. If he asks you out, say yes. What's the worst that can happen?'

Then, one morning, he was there.

It was eleven o'clock and I was preparing to massage Jamilla. Instead, in wandered Stephen, grey and exhausted. 'Annie!' he croaked. 'Thank God! I've just spent fourteen hours on a plane. I'm dying. Only you can heal me.' He slumped into the armchair in the corner, looking far more like a lovely tired boy in a rumpled suit than a multimillionaire.

'Hiya,' I said casually. 'Good trip? Did you oust Jamilla from her massage slot? I'm meant to be seeing her next.' I pretended to do something with my massage oils because my hands were shaking.

'No.' Stephen slipped behind the silk screen to change, leaving me slightly wrong-footed. Normally I waited next door while my clients got changed, but the thought of him there, separated from me only by a length of silk . . . 'No. Jamilla's left, actually.' *Whump*. His clothes started to hit the floor.

'Really? Why?'

'Oh, we had to let her go.'

'*What?*'

'She was trying to do us over. Well, she was helping a competitor try to do us over.'

Whump.

I stared at the silk screen. 'No! No way!'

Stephen's head poked over the top. 'I'm afraid so. She'd been a little erratic for a few weeks, but I just thought she had some stuff going on at home. Then I had some auditing done on a department that has absolutely nothing to do with her . . . Only it turns out it does. She – Actually, Annie, I shouldn't be talking about this. Not until the facts are established.'

I couldn't believe it. 'Okay . . . But *what*? How? I just don't get it.'

'Mike and I have a lovely afternoon ahead with the auditors and probably the Fraud Squad working it all out,' Stephen sighed. 'Which is not what I need.'

He emerged in a dressing gown. 'I thought she was great,' he told me. 'I'm desperately upset about this. All that wellbeing advice she gave me, as if she cared.'

'But how? How could she have commited fraud? She was a *wellness coach*!'

Stephen smiled thinly. 'A wellness coach with access to everyone and everything. We have you guys on a fairly loose rein, security-wise, but I'm afraid that might have to change.'

I was dumbstruck. Jamilla had always seemed so lovely.

Mildly panicked by this news, I wondered what would happen if they knew I'd been looking Stephen up on the internet. Would *that* count as snooping? Would I be sacked? Would they be allowed to search my phone and my computer at home? My heart began to race. I had to be careful. Stop being so mad.

'So now I have no wellbeing coach, until we've replaced her,' Stephen was saying. 'You, Annie Mulholland, must fix the Leader of the People. Bad luck.' He chuckled. 'Very bad luck. I've been really naughty and my body's all messed up.'

'Naughty? In what way?' I wasn't sure I wanted to know.

'As in working too hard and not sleeping enough,' Stephen replied, sitting on the edge of the massage table. He looked wrecked, the poor thing.

Thank God.

And: *Get a bloody grip, Annie.*

'God, you're good.' He yawned as I finished. 'I got off the plane this morning dying of tiredness, then found out about Jamilla and felt really depressed. But now I feel as strong as a . . . a LION!' He gave a sleepy little roar.

'I'm glad you're getting so much from these massages,' I said. 'That makes me happy.'

'It's one of the lovely things about you,' said Stephen the Lion. His mane was all messed up and I didn't remember having fancied anyone so much in my life. 'You really *want* to make other people happy. You're very nice, you know.'

I forced myself next door into my office so he could change. It wasn't the first time he'd told me I was a nice person. Was he actually right?

Then there was a snort of laughter. 'Um, Annie.'

'Yes?'

138

'Come here, please.'

I went through to the massage room. Stephen was holding his phone. 'I just picked this up from the side because I thought it was mine. Only it must be yours because a picture of me popped up when I pressed the home button.'

Oh, God. Oh, no. I prayed it wouldn't be the picture I'd Googled that morning before he'd arrived.

It was the picture of Stephen I'd Googled that morning before he'd arrived.

'Care to explain? Do I have a little stalker on my hands?'

And there was nothing – *nothing* – I could say.

'My friend wanted to know who you were,' I said hopelessly. 'She works in media, thought she might have come across you . . .'

I had never been so utterly mortified. Not once in my whole life. How could I have left the phone there? And what was I *doing*, Google-imaging my boss?

Oh, for sudden death.

'It's fine.' He grinned. Then he peered at me. 'Seriously, Annie, it's fine. I don't really think you're stalking me. Please don't be embarrassed!' A pause. 'Please.'

Outside the sun had just punched through some clouds and someone had started playing a piano in the music lounge next door. Stephen sang along under his breath as he read something on his phone. He's already forgotten about it, I told myself. You're okay. Just stop stalking him.

'Right,' Stephen said, putting his phone away. 'I've just decided I'm going to take myself out for a coffee before going back to the coalface. Would you care to accompany me?'

'Um, I've got clients until midday,' I began, but Stephen interrupted. 'I'll have Tash sort it. I have a proposition I'd like to discuss with you, Annie Mulholland.'

'Okay!' I heard myself say. 'Sounds lovely.'

Stephen took me to a cool little coffee place round the corner, a little cubbyhole with old wooden benches and workmen's lights. Heads turned as we came through the door and I glowed, like a stupid great Belisha beacon. Stephen must surely be the best-looking man in London, and I was here in this café with him. Although the fact that I was in a café with any man was quite impressive.

'Oh dear,' he said, as we approached the counter. 'I bet you don't do caffeine . . .'

'I need a coffee after that.'

The police had arrived just as we'd left the building. 'Fraud Squad,' Stephen had said grimly. He'd wavered, knowing he would probably be needed, then shrugged. 'Bugger it,' he said. 'Mike's the best corporate lawyer in the world. If he can't deal with it I'm sacking him.

'Annie, I'm joking,' he'd said, catching sight of my face.

So off we'd gone, me wondering what on earth must have gone so badly wrong in Jamilla's life that she'd felt the need to do whatever it was she'd done. I'd felt sick at the thought of her held in a room with policemen and lawyers. It was almost inconceivable.

We sat and waited on a bench inside a big open window, watching sunny Clerkenwell flitting around us. 'You're quite right,' I told him. 'I don't drink coffee, except I totally do. I did some reiki training in Melbourne once, about ten years ago, and had my first ever proper flat white there.'

Stephen smiled. 'I bet it was a revelation.'

'I couldn't believe coffee tasted that good! When Antipodean coffee finally made it to London I almost wept. Don't tell my nutritional therapist, though. I don't drink caffeine. Or alcohol. And I don't eat sugar. Or wheat. Or dairy.'

'Ha-ha! You are such a funny little thing, Annabel Mulholland.'

I tried not to let my face split in two. People like Kate Brady were funny. Not me!

'I had my first proper coffee in Sydney,' Stephen was recalling. 'Artisan flat white is all I'll drink now.' He grinned. 'What a pair of twats.'

The coffee arrived and we drifted off, somehow, into tales of childhood holidays. It turned out that we'd gone to the same little beach in Wales and had even stayed at the same caravan site. 'I used to love those waffles they sold at the little post office,' Stephen was recalling. 'Do you remember the ones? Those round things? Oh, God . . .'

'*Yes!* I used to bully Dad into buying them for us!' I was probably a bit red-faced and shouty, but I was astonished. I'd never met anyone who'd heard of Tresaith before, let alone run around naked on its beach as a child! And the waffles! The waffles!

'Oh, the waffles, Annie Mulholland.' Stephen sipped his coffee, watching me. 'I couldn't help noticing that you've mentioned your father a few times, but not your mother. Is she evil?'

My smile faded. 'No . . .' I felt my heart skip a beat, as it always did when someone asked me about Mum. 'She died when I was little.'

Stephen's face fell. 'Oh, I'm so sorry,' he said. 'I shouldn't have asked. I . . . Oh dear, I'm so very sorry.'

'It's okay.' I clasped my hands together for strength. 'It was my seventh birthday, the day she died. Very occasionally I can still picture her face. Her real face, I mean, rather than photos. So at least I have that.'

Stephen looked anguished. 'Oh, God, you poor girl.' Without warning, he put his hand on mine. Warmth fireballed up my arm and I felt confused, then ashamed. I shouldn't be feeling like that while I was talking about Mum. Although wouldn't Mum have liked him? Once she'd got over the whole corporate thing?

I looked timidly at Stephen's face, over which a long shadow seemed to have fallen.

'I lost my own mum just after Christmas,' he said, to my surprise. 'She had Hodgkin's lymphoma. And I know that however "fine" it is, it isn't. Not really.'

'Oh, no,' I said, appalled.

'Oh, yes, sadly.' Stephen's face didn't change but I knew his pain: still blade-sharp and unhealed.

'I'm so sorry,' I whispered. Imagine going through all that agony and having to be a big brave leader to thousands of people. I'd just crawl into a little hole.

His phone went off – for perhaps the fourth time since we'd been there – and he snapped. 'Fuck *off*,' he hissed. 'Fucking fuck off.'

I flinched. It didn't matter how justified anger was, I never felt comfortable near it.

'Sorry,' he said, turning his phone off.

'It's, er, fine. Goodness, I had no idea. No wonder you've been feeling so rotten.'

Prince's 'Raspberry Beret' came on the radio, and I thought about Dad and his funny stories of dancing with Mum. She was mad about dancing, he said, danced in the kitchen, the garden, the fields . . . 'She even insisted on dragging me to the little disco in Bakewell when she was pregnant with you,' he'd smile. He liked to act like he'd thought she was mad, but his face always betrayed him. He'd thought she was the most wonderful woman on earth. 'When that "Raspberry Beret" song came on, she twirled around like a teenager,' he had once said. 'Whirling and swirling with you tucked away inside her. The locals always loved it. Thought she was absolutely batty.'

On a whim, I shared the memory with Stephen.

'She sounds brilliant.' He paused. 'Was it cancer that got her too?'

I checked his face. Did he know? Sometimes people would work out who I was but they'd pretend not to know. I hated that.

Stephen, as far as I could see, hadn't the faintest idea.

But I couldn't tell him. I opened my mouth to speak and nothing came out.

'It's okay,' he said, seeing my distress. 'It's really okay – I shouldn't have asked you.' He sighed. 'Bereavement gives you a slight edge, doesn't it? A slight sense that the world is altered, and that your place in it has changed. Like you're part of a different race that you never knew about or wanted to join.'

That was exactly how it felt, although for me there was also the awful sense of hyper-visibility that I'd fought so hard. The knowledge that, as soon as I said my name, people's faces would scrunch up as they tried to remember where they knew it from. And then the awkwardness – the *awfulness* – when they remembered.

'Well, Tim seemed like a good bloke,' Stephen said softly. 'I'm sure he looks after you. I certainly hope so.' He fiddled with his coffee glass, rolling it around the table in front of him.

'Tim? Yes, he's a good friend to me.'

'Are you sure that's all? You two seemed so . . . so in tune!'

'Quite sure.'

'Oh.' Stephen looked pleased.

'Me and Tim . . . We're just very good friends. We go back a long way.'

He actually smiled. 'Well, that's nice. There's something awful about being single, then bumping into happy couples on a Saturday morning. You think you're happy pootling around on your own and then . . . Oh. Right. *There's* what happy looks like.'

I felt a bit crazy. 'But you're not single,' I said desperately. 'You've got a kid!'

Stephen seemed confused. 'Not the last time I checked. What do you mean?'

My heart was in my mouth. The talk of Mum, and now this. Too much. I felt my shutters trying to close but they seemed jammed: I was still there, still exposed.

'Oh, the picture on your office wall,' I muttered. 'Of the child. And, er, there's one in your wallet I just noticed at the till . . .'

Stephen laughed. 'You *are* stalking me! You're a proper stalker!'

'Oh, no, no, I just thought . . . you know, the pictures, the Paris trip . . .'

'I don't have a wife, or even a girlfriend, and I was actually going to Paris on my own that weekend, to take photos. No child either, I'm afraid. But I do have a damnably handsome little nephew, Barnaby.'

'I really wasn't stalking you, Stephen. I –'

'Sure about that?' His eyes were twinkling.

'Positive.' My face was boiling.

'Oh, Annie, I'm joking! Please, you look terrified! I'm sure you have far better things to do than stalk me.'

I couldn't say anything. I just hated myself. Hated being this mad and complicated.

'Look, I wanted to ask you,' Stephen continued – perhaps trying to rescue me, 'if you might be able to join my senior management team in the South of France next month. We're having an Out of Office at a château near St Émilion and the gang are all clamouring for you to come and do massages. We need something lovely in our midst, Annie. Otherwise it'll just be wine and cigars and chat about penis-extension cars. Please come!'

I was dumbstruck.

He leaned back to appraise me, smiling at me with those extraordinary eyes. 'I'd love you to come,' he said simply. 'Never mind what my team want. *I* want you there. I like you. You're a breath of fresh air around here.'

'I . . . What about my other clients?' I managed to say.

Stephen merely laughed. 'Oh, come *on*. Are you really going to argue with me?' He locked his eyes on mine. 'Well, Annie?'

'I have my two best friends' birthdays,' I mumbled. Tim

and Claudine had been born on the same day. Le Cloob had a tacit agreement that nobody went away during this double celebration. But my heart was hammering and I knew I was going to say yes. Not because I loved France with a passion and the thought of walking through soft green vineyards on a summer evening filled me with joy. Not even because I'd be able to eat all of the cheese east of the English Channel. But because, even though it was beyond ridiculous, patently absurd, completely inexplicable, I saw in his eyes that Stephen Flint was planning to seduce me. And I knew that, for whatever reason, I was finally – *finally* – ready to be seduced.

Chapter Ten

Kate

The first thing I noticed, when Mark's truck growled into the lorry park at Badminton, was that everyone looked like members of a secret army. There was a sizeable regiment of attractive women driving enormous horseboxes with absolute confidence, their hair in messy buns, all slim arms and sleeveless shirts. Theirs was matched by a regiment of tall, slim, ruddy men, with names like Harry, Horatio and Hugo. And bringing up the rear was a great sea of middle-aged women in felt fedoras, upturned collars and pearl earrings, striding around with cups of coffee and surprisingly obedient dogs.

It wasn't the poshness I found strange, I decided, as Mark flashed his parking permit at the security stewards. These had to be some of the hardest-working people on earth; they could be as wealthy or well schooled as they damned well liked. No, it was just the sense of having entered a parallel universe.

We'd passed three parked police cars on the A46 and I was still feeling jumpy. The sight of them had made my heart stop and my hands were shaking even now. The police are really not here for you, you fool, I reminded myself, as Mark and Tiggy jumped out of the cab. Stop being so silly! I stayed for a few minutes, determined to get my head straight and my body calm. I breathed slowly, finding comfort in the equine smells drifting through the open window: horsefeed, hoof oil, fly repellent.

In . . . and out.

In . . . and out.

Stumpy whinnied in the lorry behind me.

I could do this. I'd get out and help, and over the next few days I'd do everything with a smile on my face.

Since he'd caught me kissing Joe on the kitchen floor, Mark had gone back to talking to me only when he had to, moving through each day with his face set, detached once again from the world around him. I couldn't pretend I wasn't disappointed but I knew that in the long run his coldness would make things easier for me. He'd go back to being Mark Waverley, the closed door, and I'd go back to being Kate Brady, the cheeky little fecker from Dublin.

I got out in time to see Stumpy towing Mark down the ramp. The horse was excited. His head was at least eight feet off the ground, and he pranced around like a colt. 'Hoohohohohooo!' he shouted, skittering sideways into Tiggy.

'Stop it,' she said, slapping his quarters, then marched up the ramp to calm Harold, who was stamping and whinnying.

'Is everything all right?' I asked Mark. I'd never seen either horse like that.

Mark looked vaguely in my direction. 'You know what they're like when they arrive at a competition,' he said.

'Oh, yes.' I blushed. 'Yeah. Mad little bastards, horses!'

As Mark tied up Stumpy I caught him smiling, which lifted my spirits.

Mark went off with Sandra, who'd driven behind us in her falling-apart Clio, to register at the horse-trials office. Tiggy and I walked the two horses down Badminton village's little high street and into the stabling complex, where Stumpy started jogging again.

'You,' I told him, as he towed me through a vast old arch into the stableyard, 'are being very silly.'

The yard was full of people and horses, tousle-haired young men with walkie-talkies, signs and noticeboards everywhere. Yellow-stoned, huge and beautifully historic, the stabling ran off down the side of the enormous bulk of Badminton House with a rather lovely duck pond thrown in, lest any of the horses failed to notice that they were living now with the aristocracy. Mark's two were to be stabled in the 'under the clock' section, which was so lovely it made me feel quite emotional. I'd been expecting huge temporary stable blocks, not something that looked like the set of *Black Beauty*.

'Noisy in this section, but lovely to be in the thick of it,' Tiggy told me.

'It's beautiful,' I breathed, shutting Stumpy into his ancient stable with its smart red walls and cast-iron rails. His name was already on the door. 'I can't believe I'm here!'

I took Stumpy's bandages off, checking his hind leg for warmth or swelling. Three weeks ago he had had a swollen fetlock and all hell had broken loose: Mark had decided immediately to withdraw him from Badminton and Maria had screamed that if he did, without giving the horse a chance to recover, she would take Stumpy and all of her father's horses away to another rider. Stumpy, Harold, Madge, Alfie and Kangaroo, Mark's very finest horses, all probably capable of winning Badminton.

Had I been allowing myself to think about Mark at all, I'd have been heartbroken for him. Every time I had dealings with Maria I was struck by the concrete hardness of the woman, her casual cruelty, her extraordinary lack of respect for the man she'd married. If, as Becca had intimated, Mark felt stuck with her because he would otherwise be horseless, his life must seem impossibly bleak.

Stumpy's leg was fine. Phew.

Later on, after a thunderstorm had hammered across the site like a gun battle, Stumpy and Mark went off to the trot-up in front of Badminton House. Tiggy explained that it was a rather old-fashioned demonstration of each horse's soundness and rather entertaining. 'Go and watch,' she said. 'I really don't need you here. Oh, and look out for Jochim Furst – he's one of Mark's biggest rivals. German. He's shagging Maria.'

I stopped. 'He's *what?*'

Tiggy shrugged. 'He's shagging Maria,' she repeated, applying a quartermarker to Stumpy's bottom. 'Everyone knows.'

'Including Mark?'

She frowned. 'Not sure,' she said. 'It's not the easiest thing to say to someone, is it? "Your wife is shagging your rival and everyone knows."'

The crowd went wild when Mark and Stumpy appeared through the stable arch. I watched them trot along the gravel, dumbfounded by what I'd just heard. Didn't anyone *care*? Mark's wife was cheating on him! The mother of his child was at it with one of his closest professional rivals!

I noticed the tightness in Mark's jaw as he ran alongside his horse in front of the bowler-hatted officials and knew how much he would be hating the attention. Caroline Lexington-Morley, who'd gone before him, had worn a short skirt and heels and had been devoured by the cameras. She and Mark could not have been more different.

I suddenly felt an overwhelming sympathy for my quiet, introverted boss. He worked so bloody hard at this, gave it every atom of energy he had, and there was his wife making a mockery of him while everyone gossiped behind his back. I wanted to help him, but how? What could I possibly do for a man who wouldn't let me anywhere near him?

Just be cheerful, I reminded myself.

'Nice work!' I said, as we led Stumpy back to the stables.

Mark shot a grateful look in my direction. 'Really?'

'Really, boss. I was impressed. A fantastic arse you've got there in those trousers.'

It was a risk, but Mark, to my intense relief, was quite amused. 'Oh. Thank you.'

'You're welcome, Captain!'

Stumpy's hoofs clicked and clattered over the uneven cobblestones.

'I hate all that shit,' Mark admitted. 'I wish I didn't have to do it.'

'I know,' I said sympathetically. 'I totally don't blame you.'

'Really?'

'Really. Whatever you might think, Mark, I don't enjoy noise and attention either. In fact, I hate it. That's why I love working on your farm so much.' I paused. 'It's the nicest job I've ever had.'

To my amazement, Mark smiled right at me. It was the first smile he'd sent my way in quite a long time. 'Thank you,' he said quietly, and I glowed because I knew he meant it.

There's no one really on your team, I thought, as Mark handed Stumpy to Tiggy. Your mum loves you, but she's useless. Your daughter loves you but she's six, and your wife is shagging someone behind your back. Your grooms are all far too scared of you to be your mates and you don't have time for proper friends.

No wonder he was so close to Stumpy. He was lonely. We actually had quite a lot in common, Mark and I.

Mark turned to find me watching him. 'Want to walk the cross-country course with me?' he offered. As soon as he asked, his cheeks coloured. 'Tiggy doesn't need you at the moment,' he explained quickly. 'I think she wants you off her hands.'

Three hours later, as the sun set over the uneven roof of an old barn at the edge of the lorry field, I was sitting in the cab of our box having a secret brandy from Sandra's supply.

There were two reasons why I was drinking alone while everyone else was at dinner. The first was fear. Mark and Stumpy couldn't possibly make it round that course alive! It was *monstrous*! Mark had caught me lying down in a big ditch over which was suspended an enormous tree trunk – a trakehner jump, apparently. I had lain down first to see how many of me could fit lengthways across it and had stayed there because I was so shocked and frightened at the thought of Stumpy trying to clear this abyss that I couldn't get up.

The second reason I was drinking was that in the last three hours I had become very seriously confused. Mark had really come alive as we'd walked round in the bright post-thunder sun, chatting quite animatedly about the history of the course. 'But of course you know all of this,' he'd said, as we stood by a giant lake into and out of which he had to jump. 'I'm sure you don't need me to tell you.'

'You're right,' I'd muttered, dodging a posh bloke in wraparound sunglasses who was driving a golf buggy at high speed. 'But it's, er, much more helpful to hear it from an expert.'

Mark had laughed. A lovely, gravelly, sweet laugh that had split his face in two and made the polo-shirted girls following us round the course take unashamed pictures of him. 'Oh, Kate,' he'd said, at my beetroot-red cheeks. 'How much longer are we going to keep this up?'

Oh, shite.

'Kate Brady,' Mark said, still smiling – a gorgeous, bashful smile that completely eclipsed the dazzling beauty of the Duke of Beaufort's estate, 'I *know* you're not a horse person! There was no pony called Frog. There was no childhood spent galloping around on ponies. I seriously doubt that you'd so much as patted a horse before you arrived on my yard.'

I'd just stared dumbly at a huge Mitsubishi advert next to where Mark was supposed to jump out of the lake. 'Um, what was that?' I'd said eventually.

Mark had thrown back his head and laughed. 'Kate,' he'd said, walking towards me. My stomach lurched. *STOP IT*, I hissed at it. *THINK OF BECCA. THINK OF THE BAD SHIT. AND THEN THINK OF EVERYTHING THAT'S GOOD ABOUT YOUR NEW LIFE, STOM- ACH, AND STOP LURCHING.*

'Kate, the first thing you told me was that you sat on a fifteen-two horse and went for a gallop when you were three. That was, er, pretty surprising.'

I sighed. A couple of weeks after that awkward lunch I'd thought back to what I'd said and felt a bit sick. Already I knew it had been laughable. I'd just hoped they'd thought they'd misheard me.

I looked helplessly at Mark, because I didn't know what to say, and then I looked away because he was absolutely gorgeous, grinning straight at me with his hair doing that wavy windblown thing and his face all burnished by the late sun.

'And Frog,' he said, sniggering. 'Outstanding.'

I found my lips beginning to smile. How had I ever thought I'd get away with it? I was a joke!

'You told me you'd got your A test at Pony Club. Even though only about ten people in the country take it each year. And really, Kate, every time you opened your mouth for the first two weeks, you gave yourself away. Pretty much everything you said was bollocks.' He sat on the grass because he was laughing so much. 'And yet you just carried right on!'

'Oh, God.' I sat down beside him. I dipped my head away as a photographer pointed a camera at us. I was going to have to be careful of that.

Mark was laughing so hard I couldn't help but join in. The harder he laughed, the harder I laughed. It went on for what seemed like for ever.

'So why did you keep me on?' I'd asked eventually. 'Why did you let me have the job? You told me you needed the best grooms on the planet.'

'I gave you the job because I liked you,' he said simply. He turned to me and, against my better judgement, I turned to him. 'Your Irish charm won me over. I was having a horrible fight with Maria and you just bowled in telling loads of lies. With a nice smile and lots of steamrollerish good cheer. You were very funny.'

'Funny doesn't make a good groom.'

'No.' Mark turned to the lake now. 'It doesn't. But desperation does, and you had that in spades.'

I swallowed. 'What do you mean?'

'Kate.' Mark's voice was kind. Dangerously so. 'I know what it's like to feel trapped and desperate, and I wanted to help.'

I thought about Maria, the awful things I'd heard her say last week when she was on at him not to withdraw Stumpy. She had called him a coward and a small man; she'd said he was a disappointment to her father, who'd invested so much money in him; and she'd rounded off by telling him he was the laughing stock of the eventing scene, which was completely untrue.

Yes, he probably knew a thing or two about trapped and desperate.

'Well, thank you,' I said eventually. 'You're right, I was desperate. Really very desperate indeed.'

'Poor you. I heard it was a burnout, over in Dublin.'

'Oh. Who told you?'

'Tiggy.'

I'd supposed it would only be a matter of time before Mark found out. I knew Becca would have kept it to herself but then Joe had started asking questions so I'd blurted it out before he'd started reaching conclusions of his own. And, of course, once Joe knew something, it was open season.

'Sorry I lied,' I muttered.

Mark shook his head. It didn't matter.

'And thanks again for giving me the chance,' I added. 'I hope you think your risk paid off.'

'You're shaping up to be a fantastic groom,' he said. 'You've given it your everything, like I knew you would, and because of that you've learned fast.' His cheeks coloured faintly, and of course mine followed suit. 'You're great, Kate. I know I'm not very good at communicating these things – at communicating anything, really – but I do value you very highly indeed. You're the best thing that's happened to my yard in a very long time.'

I couldn't stop looking at him. At those mysterious eyes, which were beginning to give away their secrets.

'Well, your yard is great already,' I said weakly. 'You don't need me to improve it! It's the dog's bollocks, Mark!'

'It scrapes by,' he said, unconvinced.

'It more than scrapes by! It's a bloody king among yards!'

'Oh, Kate! It's nothing of the sort. It's shabby, it's chaotic, it's poorly laid out and everything's falling apart. If you saw a proper eventing yard you'd know what I meant.' He shielded his eyes from the low sun. 'But as you've probably heard my father drank all of the family's money away before, er, drinking himself to death when I was twelve. So there just isn't any. We do the best we can and we let the world laugh at us for running such a ramshackle place. And until such time as I get twenty extremely rich owners and sponsors lining up to throw cash at me, that's just how it's got to be.'

I stared at him. 'I didn't know,' I whispered, horrified. 'Jesus, Mark, I'm so sorry. I thought he'd died of cancer or something. That's absolutely terrible.'

'By the end it was better for Mum that he died,' Mark said. 'He was in a dreadful state, had been for years. It's appalling, watching someone destroy themselves against their own will.'

No wonder it's so hard to get near you, I thought sadly. You poor thing. I imagined a frightened little Mark watching his father fall apart. It made my chest hurt.

He must have spent every penny he had in making the grooms' barn nice while living all the time in a house with shonky electrics and holes in the roof.

'I can't tell you how sorry I am, Mark,' I said quietly. 'But this just proves that your yard – no, your *career* – is a huge triumph, and you'll not convince me otherwise.'

Mark looked pleased, in a tired sort of a way. 'Thank

you. And sorry, I don't know why I suddenly told you about Dad.'

'Because you wanted to talk about it?'

Mark coloured.

'Stranger things have happened,' I said, 'than human beings wanting to talk to each other about things that make them sad.' I held my breath. Was that too much? Too far?

Not quite. Mark smiled. 'Talk about my feelings? Me? You're fired.'

We shared an easy silence.

'Well, if there's anything I can do for your yard, tell me,' I said. 'You've helped me more than you'd know.'

'Work your corporate Google magic and get us a couple of million pounds, maybe? That'd be helpful.'

'Ha-ha-ha,' I said, hoping he didn't mean it. 'What I will do is work until my back breaks. I'll work on my days off, if you need me. Just say the word. I want to help.'

'You have an interesting approach to recovering from burnout,' Mark said. He was watching me like I was a nutter.

'Ah, well, it was more mental than physical. I'm happy here. Happiness gives you energy.'

'Interesting,' he said thoughtfully. 'Well, you don't need to break your back. You're doing fine just as you are. You do us so much good, Kate, all those bad jokes and that cheeky talk.'

A fly landed on his nose and I wanted to reach forward and brush it off so that I could touch his face. I sat still.

'Well,' Mark said, 'we'd better get on with this course. Thanks,' he said. 'For, er, you know. Conversational things.'

We stood up. 'All I'll say,' Mark added, and I could hear both nervousness and determination in his voice, 'all I'll say is that I really hope you stay at the farm, because I want you on my team, Kate Brady. I really do.'

In the lorry I poured myself another brandy. I needed to sort myself out, urgently.

The girl's hiding place is good, she knows that, but Mummy should surely have found her by now, shouldn't she? The stream is loud here, where a clump of smooth rocks, like the tops of mushrooms, have made a little barrier against the cold water. She didn't hear Mummy shout, 'Coming to get you!' Nor could she see her because of the boulders and bushes everywhere.

It's been ages now.

Slowly, carefully, she stands up and tries to survey the field where they were sitting. No sign of Mummy. Perhaps she shouldn't have run so far.

She scratches her clavicle where the daisy chains lie against her skin. Tiny beads of sweat have appeared on her chest and she swipes at them as she crosses back over the stream. In her face there is still laughter; the expectation that, in a few minutes, she and her mother will spot each other, scream at the moment of discovery. Scream and laugh and probably chase each other around the daisy meadow.

On the other side of the stream, she has a better view. Still no Mummy.

She looks over her shoulder towards the woods. She has a strong feeling that Mummy is there, although she cannot imagine why.

She starts walking up towards the wood.

She and Lizzy have a little den a bit further in, made by fallen branches. They've swept it out so it's all tidy. It's cool and muted green at the moment, but until recently there were a thousand million bluebells spread out in a squashy carpet of purple. Mummy had allowed them to pick enough bluebells to fill one small vase but no more than that. 'We're friends of Nature,' she'd said.

'I SEE YOU!'

There she is! Mummy! She's quite a long way off, visible only because she's standing on a path. She's — oh! She's talking to someone! The little girl squints and recognizes the man they sometimes see in the village, with the skinny legs. He's holding Mummy's arm and she seems to be both moving towards him and away at the same time. Are they dancing? She crinkles her nose. 'Mummy?' she calls. She doesn't feel so happy now. She wanted this morning to be just her and her mother, not the man from the village with the skinny legs.

Her mother doesn't hear her because she's shouting. The girl doesn't like it when her mother shouts. It happens very rarely so when she does shout it means someone has done something really bad.

Uh-oh, she thinks. The man must be being really bad. Odd that he's not shouting back, though. Maybe he knows he's in trouble.

He and Mummy are moving even further away now, Mummy wriggling and shouting and doing strange, jerky, dance-like moves. The little girl realizes that Mummy isn't going to join in again with the game any time soon: she's doing some boring grown-up thing, didn't even look round when she shouted. She marches back to the daisy meadow to wait.

She is angry with the man with skinny legs, and angry with Mummy. It's her birthday.

She decides to start another daisy chain, only for some reason she can't. She feels upset and restless and she wants a drink. 'Mummy,' she calls, but she knows her mother can't hear her.

Without understanding why, she starts crawling fast towards the longer grass by the old stone wall. She feels as if people are watching her out here in the daisy meadow and she wants to be invisible.

She sits in the shadow of the wall with long fronds of prairie grass tickling her chin. She watches the woods, ears straining for any sound of her mother.

Mummy has told Lizzy off for laughing at the man from the village with skinny legs. She's said to Lizzy that he is ill and that he deserves kindness and respect. Maybe she'll change her mind now, the girl thinks. The man didn't look very kind just now.

Suddenly she reaches for her throat and rips off her daisy chains.

She continues to hide, to wait, until a sound from the wood snaps her head up. It's screaming. Loud, frightened screaming, which is suddenly cut off.

She huddles closer to the wall and starts to cry.

Chapter Eleven

Annie

I arrived at the château just as a large Chinese-lantern sun bled its final pools of orange on to the terrace where Stephen and his team were drinking champagne. The air was heavy with the scent of jasmine, and the clink of glasses muffled by lazy birdsong. Tash was waving from the doorway, reassuring and orderly in a crisp linen vest. Above her rose the wisteria and jasmine-covered house, grooved and pockmarked like an old hand.

I paused before getting out of the airport car. Suddenly, in this gentle bowl of a valley, at the end of a long drive over which *platane* trees arched like a leafy roof, it began. Stephen was drinking wine just there and it was not impossible that he liked me. Enough, even, to do something.

Claudine had been disgusted to hear that he'd invited me. 'You 'ave been there two *months*!' she'd hissed. ''E cannot just invite you on a work jolly after that time! It is something that you are offered if your service is consistent in a long-term fashion! 'E is a slimeball! 'E just wants to seduce you!'

I'd smiled because, being Claudine, she'd actually said 'consistent in a long-term fashion'. She was such a funny thing. But my smile had incensed her further, and in the end I'd just changed the subject. Kate Brady, who had no

known weirdnesses when it came to men, had fully con-
doned the plan, and I was going with her judgement.

'*Et voilà,*' said the driver, for the second time.

'Sorry. *Pardonnez-moi.*' I got out and dragged my new
trolley suitcase across the gravel towards Tash. What stupid things they were, trolley suitcases! I should have
brought my rucksack.

'Hey!'

'Hey, Tash! This is amazing!'

She grinned, taking my bag. 'Isn't it? They're all very
happy. I don't think they'll cause us any trouble this weekend.'

'Well, now, Miss Mulholland.' My stomach jolted pleas-
urably. There he was, striding over from the terrace, a long
evening shadow trailing elegantly at his heels.

He kissed me on both cheeks and I was spellbound.
His face was on mine, just for a second. Warm, slightly
abrasive, lightly scented.

'I'll get her sorted,' Stephen said to Tash. 'You should
put your feet up – you've been working far too hard today.'

'I haven't!' Tash protested. 'I only set up the conference
call and made sure the –'

'Oi,' Stephen said. 'Don't you answer me back. Go and
have a nice swim and some of that beautiful stinky
Époisses and I'll take Annie into the house.'

Tash gave in gratefully.

Outside it was still very hot but the interior of the
château was as cool as a monastery. A smiling woman in
the long, stylish kitchen took my bag away and handed me
a glass of champagne, and Stephen and I wandered round
the ground floor. His arm brushed against mine as we

stood in the doorway of a *bibliothèque* and I felt every atom in me buzz.

'The owner of the château is a diehard fan of the surrealists,' he was saying, 'which is extremely convenient because I am too. There's some beautiful first-edition biographies in here, everyone from Le Corbusier to Éluard to Picasso.'

He turned to look at me. 'Hmm. Pretentious?'

'No!' I said. 'I love them too! I think Penrose is my favourite, though. I went to see his house in Sussex recently. It was wonderful.'

Stephen grinned. 'Penrose, eh? Right. Well, please step this way, madam.' He took me along an uneven corridor and on into a smaller room with long, low sofas and a slightly bizarre collection of paintings from every era. Late sun bobbed and swayed through the leaves of the trees outside.

Stephen waved at the fireplace, above which hung a wildly fantastic collage that could only have been made by Roland Penrose. I gasped. 'No way. No effing *way*!'

Stephen exploded with laughter. 'Did you just say "effing", Annie?'

I was too awed by the painting to be embarrassed. 'Yes. Look! Look at it! Is that Notre-Dame poking out behind the . . . Oh, my God. It is. I can't believe I'm seeing this!'

Stephen put an arm round my shoulders for a beautiful moment. 'You're even cooler than I thought,' he said, then wandered off to take a closer look at the painting. 'None of the guys got excited about it.' Dizzy with it all, I followed him, walking in the warm slipstream of his body. A bell rang somewhere deep inside the house. It was all so swimmingly perfect that it bordered on the absurd.

We stood and stared at the collage, and I wondered how I would bear it if I'd got it all wrong and Stephen just liked me in the same way he liked Tash. I imagined me jumping on him – in some moment of total madness, clearly – and him gently but firmly pushing me away, and me getting sacked and having to start over again and –

Then I turned and saw him looking at me and my anxious thoughts abruptly stopped. It was not the same as with Tash. I had no experience with men and chemistry and signals but I knew, nonetheless, that this look Meant Something. *Holy Mother of God*, I thought, weak with shock. *I might actually kiss a man.*

After a long pause, Stephen opened his mouth to say something, just as one of the staff walked in and told us that cocktails were being served on the terrace.

Stephen sighed, breaking eye contact.

'Come on, then, my surrealism-loving masseuse,' he said. 'Let's go and have some cocktails.' He didn't move. Then, very slowly, very deliberately, he reached over and took my plait, which had swished over my shoulder, and laid it back on my spine, running his hand down it to straighten it. 'This plait is such a lovely thing,' he said. 'It's my favourite.'

I clenched my fists, as if that would help me focus. 'Are you sure you want me out there?' I asked weakly. 'Shouldn't I be . . . er, hanging out with the rest of the support staff?'

For a moment Stephen looked confused. Then he chuckled. 'You're here as a guest,' he told me. '*My* guest. Of course I want you to come and have cocktails. And there's only Tash. We can all survive without our PAs, you know. I cook for myself and clean my own toilet. No, I don't. That's a lie. But I totally could if I wanted to.'

'Flint?' called a voice from the corridor. 'Flint? Where are you?' Rory Adamson's large belly arrived through the door, followed by Rory himself. He was sunburned, very merry and, for some reason, rather adorable out of his suit.

'Oh, hello, Anna,' he said pleasantly. 'Pleased you've come to indulge us! Flint, we need to talk to Chicago about this acquisition before we get too drunk. And then we need to get too drunk.' Rory was Stephen's right-hand man. They'd been to a posh school together: they hadn't got on famously, Stephen had admitted, but they'd liked each other well enough for Stephen to be able to poach Rory from his job nine months ago.

'Rory Adamson, you fat twat,' Stephen said. 'Her name is Annie.'

'Of course!' Rory was genuinely contrite. 'Sorry, Annie. They keep giving us this wonderful *grand cru* from St Émilion and we're all wasted. As if *any*one could forget the name of our massage queen.'

I grinned. 'Forgiven. I'm coming to join you for a drink, if that's okay.'

Just for a second, a tiny hairline crack of a second, Rory glanced sharply at Stephen. *Really?* Stephen, unflinching, held Rory's gaze.

He guided me out of the room and I shivered, remembering that, however human, however funny and self-deprecating he was, Stephen Flint was a monumentally powerful man. And however much I liked him it would take real guts to let go and trust him completely. But I was ready to try.

Dinner was served when the last violet smudges of light were swept clean from the sky. We ate under a beautiful canopy of fairy lights strung between fruit trees; a perfect dinner table with starched tablecloths, gleaming cutlery and wild flowers in vases. And, of course, serious quantities of wine that probably cost per bottle more than my monthly rent.

All around me, Stephen's team were throwing big chunks of juicy steak into their mouths like club-wielding cavemen. And I could barely eat a mouthful. The trees rustled lazily above us, cutlery clinked on china and the conversation buzzed around me, but all I could hear was Stephen's voice.

This was the intravenous drip Tim had told me about. Its power astonished me. Patrick, the chief finance officer, was on my right, slurring on about how he loved the way I used so much of my own weight to press and squash his tight muscles. Everyone was talking to me about massage. Presumably they didn't imagine I had anything else to talk about. It didn't matter. I wasn't listening.

Stephen was talking to Janique, the senior counsel, and all I could hear was his voice.

My phone buzzed in the pocket of my long skirt.

I COMMAND YOU TO COME HOME, Claudine wrote. *We need to talk. You are making a big mistake, trying to sleep with your boss. It will come to no good, I am sure of it.*

I deleted the message and slipped my phone back into my pocket. Enough. I'd tried to be understanding, to appreciate that this was just Claudine's way of protecting me against potential trouble – but it was *my* potential trouble, not hers. I was tired of feeling patronized. Of being the small person. Hadn't I spent enough time being small? Hiding?

She had even arranged to take me for an emergency afternoon tea last weekend, so she could try for a final time to talk me out of going to France or having any involvement with Stephen. "E is not right for you at all,' she had told me, in a most uncompromising tone, never actually having met or talked to him. 'I counsel against sexual intercourse, Annie. In fact, I forbid it.'

For the first time ever – largely because I seemed to have no choice over my feelings for Stephen – I had directly disobeyed her. 'I hear what you're saying, Claudie, and you may well be right . . . But I'm afraid you can't stop me. Not even *I* can stop me.'

'Women do not sleep with their bosses in this day and age!'

'Oh, for God's sake, Claudie! Of course they do! And why not? We're both humans. Who cares if he pays my wages? Don't try to turn this into a feminist concern when it's not. It's about two human beings, who appear to like each other. And that's that, you cynical old git!'

Claudine had gasped. For a moment she stared murderously at me and then, quite deliberately, she had stabbed her knife into my scone. 'I forbid it,' she said. 'You need to approach potential relationships in a balanced and cautious fashion. Nothing about the situation with that slimeball man is balanced or cautious. I forbid it – you understand? I forbid it!'

I stared right back at her. Enough of her mad talk about relationships. Enough of her thinking she could somehow save me from my past with careful management. And enough of her talking about Stephen as if he were just some stereotypical corporate arsehole with a penchant for the ladies when, in fact, he was turning out to be the absolute opposite. 'Tough, Claudie. I'm going to France. And if sex is on offer, I'll be taking it.'

And I'd reached out and stolen her scone.

Stephen was watching me. He carried on talking to Janique, and I resumed my conversation with Patrick, but all the while he held my eye.

I didn't know what I was doing. I drank too much Bordeaux and took off my shoes so I could feel the grass between my toes. Stay connected to the earth, I reminded myself. Feel the earth.

It calmed me down a bit. But not much.

I woke early, hungover but full of restless energy. Dawn was poking needles of light through the ancient shutters on my bedroom window and the luxury quilt I'd pulled over myself last night was now stifling. I got out of bed, grateful for the coolness of the stone floor under my feet, and opened my shutters. Below my bedroom there was a clear blue oblong of water through which a man was swimming. He cut across it like a knife through butter: straight, precise and unimpeded. The water barely rippled around him. Nearby a cock crowed half-heartedly, perhaps stupefied by the coming heat.

The man reached the end of the pool and tumble-turned perfectly.

Stephen. Swimming at daybreak, even though he had been up until at least three a.m. I watched the ripple and surge of his back muscles, those lean, powerful arms. I wasn't being crazy in the slightest. The man in the pool below me was, hands down, the best-looking man on earth and he was making all the signs of being interested in me. I had every right to be feeling like a woman who should be in a secure facility.

I am being very reasonable and sane, I replied to Claudine. And then I marched downstairs in my new silk pyjamas with an old wrap from the north of Argentina that I hadn't quite been able to resist packing. I could hear pans and chatter and tinny music from the kitchen but otherwise the place was deserted. It couldn't be much later than six.

Padding along the uneven stone flags, past the room with the Roland Penrose collage, I grinned. Stephen and I had hundreds of things in common. Who cared if he was a multi-millionaire and my boss?

I slid through an old terrace door and strode along a little avenue of gently moving limes round to the back terrace where the pool was. He was still there, cutting through the water. A pair of sweet old slippers sat by the side of the pool with his watch, which curled round as if trying to remember the shape of his wrist. I wanted to put it on. Slide my feet into the old slippers. Instead I sat on a marble bench and waited for him to turn and swim towards me.

'*BONJOUR!*' he shouted, doing just that. '*Comment ça va, ma jolie?*'

I grinned. I hadn't even bothered to look in the mirror,

just marched outside in my old wrap, yet he was calling me his *jolie*. Of course he was. Weren't all women beautiful when they were in love?

Steady on, I cautioned myself. *No need for the L word.*

'I'm well,' I called. 'What a stunning morning!'

'It's a peach, isn't it?' He pulled himself out of the pool, water sliding off the strong brown body I was beginning to know so well. I looked away. It wasn't right. It wasn't decent. *Forgive me, Father, for I have a serious desire to sin . . .*

'Wait for me a second and I'll show you some more brilliant things. This is my favourite château in the whole of France!'

I laughed. 'Oh, to be so familiar with all the châteaux in France.'

'Ah, yes. Twat.' He looked bashful. 'Let me at least take you inside for a naughty breakfast.'

'Naughty?'

'Come with me.' He threw on a stripy cotton shirt and old cargo shorts, which had been hanging on a tree. I'd never seen him in shorts. Naturally, he looked perfect.

We walked, talking easily. Before long Stephen steered me sideways through a door and I found myself in the main kitchen. It was vast. Many areas were taken over by gleaming metal counter-tops and uninspiring racks of pans, but the end we'd arrived in was as it might have been a hundred years ago, with a foot-pump tap and old grooved wooden worktops dotted with bits of china, half-drunk cups of coffee and trays of croissants ready for the oven. The kitchen staff smiled but carried on making *chocolatines* and juicing plump golden oranges.

'Good morning, Mr Flint,' said the woman who seemed

to be in charge. 'I hope you slept well. Can I get you the usual?'

'Please, Sylvie!' Stephen said. 'This is my favourite bit!' he whispered conspiratorially. He looked like a boy.

'Shoo,' Sylvie said, pushing us off to an ancient counter by the window. I took a seat next to some boxes of lemons and fresh mint leaves drying on a tea-towel. Before I knew it Sylvie had put two mismatched mugs of hot chocolate in front of us, proper thick, creamy French hot chocolate, with brioche for dipping. She added some bread and dishes of half-used jam and butter, and left us to it. '*Bon appétit*,' she murmured, sliding quietly away.

'Aah.' I sighed, sipping the velvety chocolate.

'Try this,' Stephen whispered reverently, passing me the jam. 'It's fig, from the orchard. Incredible.'

It was. Everything was. Especially the fact that this was Stephen's naughty secret. 'There's only so much formality I can take,' he told me, stuffing chocolaty brioche into his mouth.

Eventually we sat back, full and happy, and watched the kitchen staff at work. 'It must make you proud,' I mused, 'seeing all these people, beavering away for your massive important company that everyone wants to please.'

Stephen frowned. 'I guess so. I just hope they don't think I'm a rich idiot.'

'You keep saying that,' I replied. 'But I don't think that about you, and I really doubt these guys do either. To be honest, I find it quite hard to reconcile you with your job. You seem so . . .' I trailed off, embarrassed.

'So what?'

'Real,' I muttered, blushing. 'And normal.' You're a

jam-with-blobs-of-butter-in-it kind of a person, I thought, but didn't say. And I like that very much.

There was a long pause, during which Stephen looked at me and I looked at my bread. I ate some of it. 'I'm glad you think that,' he said. 'I'd be really sad if you thought I was in some stuffy Old Boys' league.'

I continued eating.

'You're not what you seem either.' He smiled. 'You wander round in those clothes being all earthy and ethical and stuff yet you eat like a bastard and you aren't afraid of a good drink. You're a disgrace to your nutritional therapist.'

'I'm not!'

Stephen laughed. 'Oh, Annie, come *on*!'

I looked at the space where my bread and butter, my jam, hot chocolate and mountain of brioche had sat, and considered all the cheese I planned to eat later on. 'I used to be good,' I grumbled. 'But I'm lapsed. It's terrible.'

Stephen couldn't stop laughing. 'But what's the point in life without cheese and wine? And cake? And bread? Not to mention flat whites?'

'I can't officially agree with you. Unofficially, however, I totally agree.'

The kitchen staff were picking up pace. 'We'd better get on,' Stephen said. 'But I'm glad we had that breakfast.'

'How come you invited me?' I asked boldly.

'Because I want you to see who I really am.'

'I'd better go and shower,' I mumbled. 'I've got my first massage at eight.'

'Have a good morning,' Stephen said. 'I'll see you later. I'm booked in with you this evening.'

*

That morning, I did three massages, and in the afternoon I went for a walk along the Dordogne. Stephen and his gang had gone off to some vineyard by St Émilion, Tash with them to facilitate cars, so it was just me, Sylvie and her team. She gave me a beautiful little picnic of *saucisson*, bread, garden lettuce and thick, oozy *chèvre*, wrapped in a proper checked cloth, like something from a children's fairytale.

It was a perfect afternoon. I wandered into a second-hand bookshop in a long barn by the water and bought an old issue of *Vogue* with Lee Miller on the front.

I watched a couple ahead of me stop again and again to kiss each other and sat down on a bench by the water, almost overwhelmed by the rushing excitement inside me.

My hands shook as I prepped the treatment room I'd been given, ready for Stephen's massage. I'd heard them arrive back, patently drunk and in high spirits, and had felt so nervous that I'd not even come out to say hello.

I never talked to Mum. I'd never believed she was following me round like a gentle, omnipresent shadow. That was part of the problem: I'd always believed her to be trapped in some terrible violent Purgatory. But occasionally I had a fleeting sense of her. A waft of something here, a warm cushion there, and now, just for a minute, I could smell her. *The lavender*, I thought. Mum had used lavender oil for almost everything.

I closed my eyes, breathing her in. The room became more peaceful, somehow, and my breathing slowed down. I could do this.

'Hello!' Stephen said, bursting in without warning, radiantly happy and healthy. '*Bonsoir*, Annie! *BON-BLOODY-SOIR!* What a stunning evening! I don't want a massage, I want to get back out into that beautiful country-side. Will you come with me?'

'Of course.'

We left the house through the back door, out of sight of the others. We both avoided the subject of why. After a short walk along a stone path that gave way to chalk, we entered a rustling section of woodland and picked our way uphill through the evening chorus, talking about our families. To my amazement, Stephen had remembered from one of our earliest conversations that I had a sister called Lizzy who worked in programming and that she was two years older than me. He was extraordinary! 'Is she like you?' he asked.

'No! She's about as similar to me as a Buddhist monk. Although there's not much Buddhism about Lizzy. And even less monk.'

'There must be some similarities. I bet I could see you in her face.'

The wood was petering out into acre after glorious acre of vineyard, carving soft green lines out of the undulating earth.

'You'd probably recognize bits of me,' I said doubt-fully. 'She's a knockout, though, in a proper film-star kind of a way. I'm not saying I'm a minger but Lizzy's the red-carpet one for sure.'

'Film stars are not real women,' he said. 'Specially that Jolie creature. I must be the only man on earth who doesn't fancy her. She scares me. It's not just those enormous lips,

176

it's everything. *And* she stole Brad off Jen and I'll never forgive her that.'

I stopped walking and looked at him. 'Did you actually just say all of that? Are you in fact a woman?'

Stephen tried not to laugh but couldn't help himself. 'I'm completely nuts about you,' he said suddenly. The laughter stopped but his smile didn't. 'I can't eat, I can't sleep. I can't do anything except think about you, and the way you move around a room, the way your hands feel on me, the way you get little blonde horns escaping from your plait. I can't stop watching that tiny little snub nose of yours and the way your freckles speckle across it like little tiddlywinks, and the smell of soap on your skin, and the way the bells jingle on your skirt when you're working on me, and the fact that you couldn't give a shit that I'm a rich businessman. I can't stop thinking about the night I met you, and how you blatantly didn't want me there because you were tired, and how peaceful and sweet you looked when I found you asleep in Reception, all curled up on the sofa like a little mouse. I can't stop thinking about the way you bite your lip when you're thinking, and that delightful little laugh you have. All those funny earth-mamma clothes you wear, and how graceful and calm you always are. I'm worried that you and that bloke Tim are in love with each other, and I'm worried that I'm your boss, and this is all completely inappropriate, and I don't know what to do. I'm consumed by it, like a woeful character from Shakespeare wandering around the forest, pounding his chest. I'm done for, Annabel Mulholland, totally done for. I can't –'

I never remembered how it had happened, who moved

first. I just knew that suddenly he stopped speaking because we were kissing each other. I wasn't shaking with fear like I'd thought I might be, I was firing with chemical excitement, up on a rolling high. Stephen smelt faintly of cologne and his body was as firm as metal against mine. He kissed hungrily, deeply, pulling me even closer to him.

Once again I wasn't sure how it happened but suddenly my vest top was off, flung somewhere among the vines next to Stephen's T-shirt, and his bare torso was against mine. Fragmentary blasts of excitement erupted and flamed. I was no longer in control of my own body.

'Annie . . .' he muttered, kissing my neck. There was a frantic struggle as we both tried to remove the rest of our clothes, then I was on bare soil and Stephen was on top of me and before I even knew what was happening, had time to think about things like contraception or the stones digging into my back or the bee buzzing loudly near my ear, it was happening. Intense, heady sex that hurt me only fleetingly before the chemicals took over again and I flew high into the universe.

Stephen held me so tightly afterwards that I could hardly breathe. I didn't want to breathe anyway. Crushed into his side I felt a tear of relief, of pride, of all sorts of things, slide out of my eye.

I wasn't broken. Underneath everything, all the ache and the fear, there was a woman: a normal, functional woman, ready, at last, to rejoin the human race.

Stephen kissed the side of my head and pulled me even tighter, and told me it had been amazing. Then it started again. At *my* instigation.

I'm all over this sex stuff, I thought proudly.

Shut up, I thought, embarrassed.

By the time we got back to the château it was dark and dinner had started. I couldn't speak and my lady parts were in shock. I held on to Stephen's arm, as if it were a life raft.

'Er, right then,' Stephen began, as we hit the stone path again. 'So, do you come here often?'

I breathed hard, suddenly returning to the scents of the evening. Seafood, garlic, jasmine. Stephen's body. The ancient wooden floor creaked as we stopped in the hallway.

'I don't want to have dinner with them,' Stephen murmured. He moved away from the stripe of light under the dining-room door. 'Can we go to my room? I don't want to let go of you.'

The high. The transcendent high. The chemicals, the whizzing neurons, the firing synapses. The pulsating, pumping high. Why had I spent my adult life running from this? I wondered, as Stephen slid his hand down my trembling belly.

Hours later, when the sun has gone and the fields are still and grey, a policeman finds her curled up in a tight ball in the shadow of the wall. He takes her home, where there is a row of white cars with blue lights.

A policewoman leads her to the couch where she sits her down and explains to her that her mother is not alive any more, but Annie already knows. From a room upstairs come terrible noises; noises that sound like jungle animals more than they do Daddy. But Annie knows it's Daddy because from time to time she can hear him cry, 'Georgie, Georgie, my girl, my Georgie, no.'

Lizzy has cried herself to sleep. She is a defeated ball in the corner of the armchair.

The policewoman seems to wait for Annie to cry, but she is silent as a mouse. When the policewoman asks if she understands what she's told her, Annie just nods.

She stares at the fireplace where there's a misshapen wicker basket that Mummy once bought in an Abroad Country. It's surrounded by a collection of shoes from last night, when they all played 'throw the shoe into the lumpy basket'. Over there on the wooden table is a mug that still holds the remains of the cinnamon tea Mummy was drinking last night. And over the chair a big silk scarf that they bought in that thing called a flea market that was full of smelly clothes.

Annie sits perfectly still with her hands folded in her lap and just shakes her head when Mrs Wilson from the village arrives and asks her if she wants a sandwich.

'Or maybe a tissue, sweetheart?' The policewoman tries again. 'Some lemonade? A nice glass of milk?'

I didn't reply because, already, I'd gone. I'd disappeared from my own life, just like Mum had from hers — only I wasn't put in a box and buried. I had to stay.

Chapter Twelve

Kate

Three days into Badminton Horse Trials I stood in the crowd overlooking a cross-country jump called the Vicarage Vee, which Mark had told me was one of the most famous on the course. The air was hot and humid and the vast crowds that had been pouring in over the last two days had swelled yet again. Fear pulsed in my temples as I imagined Mark and Stumpy galloping around that impossible course. Please, I prayed feverishly to my occasional God, please, God, I beg you, keep them safe. I'll do anything – I'll even go out for sherry with Maria, if you want me to. I could become a proper Catholic, or work at a shelter or donate a kidney. Just don't let any harm come to them.

Away from my daily routine in Somerset, I was finding it far harder to maintain the growing sense of calm I'd felt over the last few weeks. Intrusive flashbacks from my past – the whole bloody mess of it – had kept me awake the last two nights as I'd tried to sleep on my narrow bunk with Mark only metres away. And, try as I might, I couldn't control the strong physical sensations I felt when I was around him. When he'd done his dressage test yesterday, then removed his top hat at the end to bow at the judges, his hair had blown loose in the crisp morning air. I felt like

I'd been hit in the face. 'You're beautiful,' I'd whispered, and then felt sick in case anyone – including me – had heard.

I'd tried to run off and have a drink with Tiggy last night but Mark had cornered me and said, all nice and relaxed, 'Why don't we take our favourite horse for a walk along the lanes?' And I'd found myself in a beautiful sunset once again with a horse I adored and a man I –

A man I nothing.

'Let's let Stumpy graze for a bit,' Mark had said, when we reached a large field with the double gates left open. 'I don't like him being in a stable all the time.'

Stumpy had been very happy to oblige. We'd sat on an old stone wall while he had mown down the corner of some unsuspecting farmer's land. I laughed every time I looked at my big grey friend; Tiggy had taken his plaits out after the dressage and his mane looked as if it had been given a tight perm.

'There's a lot of indignity in being a horse,' I observed, watching him. 'Perms, people doing baby talk at you – not to mention all that ridiculous dressage stuff.'

'What do you mean, "all that ridiculous dressage stuff"? Stumpy loves it!'

I laughed. 'He can't! It's ridiculous! No horse would enjoy that!'

'Stumpy would disagree. You don't do dressage that well if you hate it.'

I loved the ease with which Mark chatted when he was away from home. He was like a different man here in this honey-stoned village; a man unafraid to smile and laugh and show the world who he was.

'You seem so different out of the yard,' I said.

Mark looked at me, and I felt little prickling sensations all the way down my back.

'So much happier,' I added, rather wishing I hadn't piped up in the first place. 'You really love these competitions, don't you?'

'Yeah, I do.' He sighed.

Silence.

'I live for the competitions, although they're exhausting. But, really, I –' He broke off, and I looked away. Strange things happened when I spent too long looking at him.

'Really you what?'

'Doesn't matter.'

'Sure?'

'Ah, fuck it,' he said. 'Fuck it, Kate. The truth is, I just love being away from Maria.' He breathed out in a big whoosh. 'And it's such a relief to say so, even though it's an awful thing to admit.'

I hadn't expected that.

'As soon as I drive that lorry out of the yard I feel . . .' He searched around for the right word. 'Free.'

'Oh.'

'And for the record . . .' he sighed '. . . I dislike myself enormously for saying that. Quite apart from the fact that it's so disrespectful to talk about Maria behind her back, I couldn't bear it if Ana Luisa thought I liked being away from *her*. I don't. I love her. I love her so much it hurts at times.' His eyes welled suddenly.

'But you're right. I do love being away at competitions. It's like stepping into a different world where I . . . hold some value as a human being.' Mark concentrated hard on his hand, which was clutching Stumpy's lead-rope with a white-knuckled ferocity.

'You do hold value as a human being,' I said, because I couldn't not.

Mark didn't react. He just stared at his hands. 'That's not what it feels like in my house,' he said eventually. 'In my house I'm a low-value human.'

Leave her, I thought sadly. You're too special for this. Mark deserved someone who loved him. Respected him. I wanted to shout, 'Look what you've achieved, for crying out loud! And after having your childhood ripped away from you by your dad. You're a miracle, Mark, you deserve better!'

But then I looked at dear, lovely, sweet Stumpy, chomping away so happily at the grass, his tail flicking lazily at flies, and I thought of Ana Luisa, sitting up on the saddle in front of her daddy last week, shrieking excitedly, her father's arm tightly round her middle, and I knew it wasn't that simple. Mark had everything to lose if he threw Maria out.

So I just said, 'I understand.'

'I'm sure we'll work it out,' Mark said tiredly. 'Relationships are hard, right?'

'Don't look at me,' I told him. 'I'm the last person you'd want to ask about relationships.'

'I see. Well, I'm sure Maria and I'll sort it out,' he said, and neither of us believed him.

We had talked until the golden fields around us began to turn grey, and by the time we got up to leave I felt crazy. When Mark smiled at me, and said, 'Thanks, Kate. That was really nice,' I swear my legs wobbled like something from a historical romance.

'Daddy!' shouted a small voice, in the mêlée of grooms and riders in the stable block.

Before we even saw her, I felt Mark stiffen. 'Ana Luisa?'

Maria and Ana Luisa were meant to be in Portugal for ten days, at the luxury villa of one of Maria's relatives. It was unusual for Maria to be away during such a major event, Becca had said, but evidently the offer had been too good. 'She never turns down the finer things, pet,' Becca had said disparagingly. 'Nasty old skank.'

'Daddy!' Ana Luisa shouted. There she was, all done up in a posh little blouse and ruby-coloured trousers. 'Mummy's made me wear stupid clothes,' she grumbled, throwing her arms around Mark's legs. 'I think we need to get one of those stylists,' she added, and Mark laughed loudly.

'How do you know what a stylist is?' He reached down to scoop up his daughter.

'Anyone who's *anyone* knows what a stylist is,' Ana Luisa said, and Mark hugged her hard.

'You're mad,' he said. 'I'm so happy to see you!'

'It's Mummy who's mad,' Ana Luisa said. 'I hate these clothes! Can I wear Stumpy's instead?'

'He'd be delighted to lend you a rug, I'm sure.' Mark kissed her head. 'How come you're back early? Is everything okay?'

'Everything's fine,' Ana Luisa said. 'Mummy just said we had to come back to take care of business. You know what she's like.'

'But where is she? Who are you here with?'

'Monica,' Ana Luisa said airily.

'Monica?'

'She works for that German man with the weird name.'

'Jochim?'

'Yes. Daddy, I need some different clothes.'

'Why did she leave you with Jochim Furst's groom?'

He has no idea, I thought.

I put Stumpy into his stable and rugged him up for the evening, smiling as Mark and his daughter discussed the merits of horse blankets as human clothes, but fuming as I thought about Maria. Leaving her daughter with Jochim's groom while she went off for a shag? What kind of mother behaved like that? I tried to imagine how I'd have felt if my own mother had pulled such a stunt but gave up because it was so inconceivable that she'd have been so bloody selfish in the first place. Ana Luisa was *six*! Six years old! And it was nearly dark!

Where the hell was she?

'I came to make sure you ran Stumpy on the cross-country tomorrow,' Maria purred, arriving just at that moment. With the click of her leather-heeled boots came a swampy fug of expensive perfume.

'Oh, hello,' Mark said. He made to kiss her cheek but she moved away. 'You cancelled your holiday?'

'I cut it short,' she replied. 'My father asked me to. He did not want to leave matters to chance.'

'Leave what matters to chance?'

'Matters such as you doing the wimp out and not letting Stumpy run the cross-country,' Maria said, as if talking to a challenging child. 'I know what you are like, obsessing about problems that do not exist.'

Mark took a deep breath. How he stayed calm around her I had no idea. 'Stumpy's warm fetlock *definitely* existed,' he said. 'And it was only three weeks ago. So forgive me for exercising caution.'

'The horse is fine,' Maria snapped. 'He just hit his fetlock on something. The swelling went down within the day! We will not have you threatening your place in the World Equestrian Games team because of minor thing that happen months ago.'

'Three weeks ago,' Mark repeated, but I could tell he'd given up. 'Look, I'm planning to run him. He's passed his vetting, he's passed the trot-up, he's been perfectly sound and he did a beautiful dressage test. Of course I'm planning to run him. But obviously I'd pull him straight away if I didn't think he was up to it.'

'For fuck's sake,' Maria snapped. 'Why you *always* look for the negative? Why you always look for excuses not to run my horses?'

'Can you not swear in front of our daughter?' Mark asked. 'Just for five minutes? Have you heard her language recently?'

'Oh! *Now* you worry about your daughter! *Now* you step in to be good father!'

I stroked Stumpy's neck. I was going to have to get out of there at some point, and I strongly suspected that Ana Luisa would want to escape this. But I was scared of Maria, too.

Then: Sod her, I thought. I'm Kate Brady and I won't stand for this.

'Hi, Maria,' I said, emerging from the stable. 'How are you?'

Maria barely glanced at me. 'Fine.'

'Mark's taking great care of your horse,' I said. 'Which is why he should be fine to run tomorrow.'

She turned to look at me. Too far?

'I'm *sorry*?'

Definitely too far.

'I said, Mark's taking great care of your horse.'

Maria's nostrils flared. 'I'm sure you have things to do,' she said softly. 'We are busy here.'

'Fancy a hot dog?' I asked Ana Luisa.

'Yes,' she said. 'And an ice cream, and a burger, and maybe some sweets.'

'Deal.'

As I walked off with his daughter, I felt Mark smile, even if the gesture hadn't quite made it to his face. You're welcome, I thought. I'd do anything for you.

And that, I knew, as I took Ana Luisa's hand, was very frightening. What about Becca? And Maria? And this confident little girl powering along beside me?

If you don't get this under control you'll have to resign, I told myself shakily.

But where would I go?

The smooth, moneyed voice on the Tannoy told me that Mark Waverley and Distant Thunder were clear of the Outlander Bank and heading towards the Gatehouse New Pond. Only one jump until they were in my line of vision, tackling that most hideous of obstacles. My heart was thumping loudly in my ears. Stewards were blowing warning whistles and the public crossing was closed to clear the way for my boss and his horse.

And there they were. My beautiful, beautiful Stumpy, nostrils flared pink, sweat foaming over his breastbone, yet so strong, so fast, so confident as he galloped up the green slope. Mark sat light as a feather in his saddle, face set on the jumps ahead, already reining in Stumpy to make sure he was on the right stride. Adrenalin lifted me high above the crowd and I hovered there, tremulous and sick, as everyone turned to follow Mark over the first part of the jump.

Stumpy leaped as if the jump were nothing, Mark crouched over him. I began to smile as they flew through the air. Thank God!

Then Stumpy stumbled on landing. He stumbled and, in slow motion, began to somersault.

For a split second I didn't believe it. Didn't believe that, of all the horses and riders in this competition, of all the jumps on this course, *my* horse and rider should have an accident. Right there, in front of my eyes.

No.

But Stumpy was flying right over in a dreadful somersault and Mark was rocketing off him.

No.

Mark was thrown forward, but not far enough. Half a tonne of horse landed on him with a sickening cracking sound, then everything went quiet. My vision tunnelled; my breathing stopped.

Stumpy did not move. And, underneath him, neither did Mark.

I was running. A steward tried to stop me but I threw her off as if she were made of paper. As I arrived by his side Stumpy made a terrible noise and managed to roll off

Mark, who lay still on the ground, bent at all the wrong angles. Next to his beloved horse, he was like a child's broken doll, forgotten in the grass. 'HELP!' I heard myself screaming. 'HELP THEM! SOMEONE HELP THEM!'

Finally, as the stewards and the vet's Land Rover arrived at the fence, I was dragged away. Terror sawed right through me. This couldn't be happening. Not here, not in front of me.

An ambulance 4x4 came tearing over the hill. Two of the stewards held me at a distance, sobbing and pleading, as a white tent was erected over Stumpy and the paramedics surrounded Mark.

Chapter Thirteen

Annie

The day after I returned to London I dragged my weary body up to a damp Derbyshire to see Dad. I felt like a shameful old tramp, arriving on his doorstep after five steamy days in France, but I'd promised to spend the weekend with him and was already a day late, having lost my passport and then having to spend a day at the British consulate in Bordeaux getting an emergency permit to travel.

I hugged myself all the way up to Chesterfield, still barely able to believe the last few days. But the closer I got to home, the sadder I felt. *I want Daddy to have this*, I thought. *I want him to fall in love again. Let go. Be happy.*

'Some people get many loves,' Dad often told us, 'but not me. Georgie was my one and only. My girl.' There was a picture of them on honeymoon by his bed. He was all shy and handsome in shorts and a linen shirt, Mum beautiful in a cotton tunic covered with a swirling Indian print. Apparently she'd made him try some mushrooms and they'd had a wild night running around a tiny Greek village chasing giant imaginary squirrels. From what I could tell, Dad would have done almost anything Mum asked of him.

'Hello, Flannie.' He held out his arms at the front door.

When Lizzy was little she'd called me Flannabel or Flannie and Dad had loved it so much he'd never given it up.

'Hello, Dad.' I grinned into his shoulder. I felt his tickly beard on the side of my face and forgot everything for a moment. I loved my daddy so much. 'It's so nice to see you.'

'Likewise, my love,' he said cheerfully. A spot of rain landed on my nose and he shook a fist at the sky. 'Come in, come in. Let me give you some money for the taxi.'

I took it, because I knew it made him feel better about not being able to collect me from the station any more, but I felt a great tug of regret as I did so.

'How are you, Dad?'

'Very well, very well. Getting the window boxes ready for autumn.' I smiled right through the sadness this news brought me. In his time Dad had been a wonderful gardener; Lizzy and I had loved digging up potatoes with him and reaching for runner beans that spiralled up tall canes into the sky. But his grief and trauma seemed to have grown over the years, rather than diminished, and these days Dad was pretty much trapped in his own house. Even venturing into the garden was too much.

'And work?' I asked brightly. 'How's it going?'

'I'm on a pig of a project, darling. An absolute honker!'

Dad translated literary Spanish novels into English. He and Mum had met in Barcelona at a party thrown by one of his authors, which Mum, passing by on a pedal bike, had wandered into. That was typical of Mum, he said.

Luckily for Dad, Mum had been backpacking for the last three years and was a little tired of living out of a rucksack. She gave in quickly to his repeated pleas for her to marry him, and within three months Georgie Whelan had become Georgie Mulholland. She had moved into his house in a village called Great Longstone near Bakewell and painted beautiful murals and patterns on the walls.

She had borne Lizzy and me, managed to persuade Dad that we should all go travelling round Africa for a year, then been raped and murdered on my seventh birthday.

Just like that. The record stopped, the future cancelled.

Dad said Lizzy and me had given him a reason to carry on but we both knew that a large part of him had died with Mum, a part that could never come back. He'd been a wonderful father, rolling up his sleeves and suffering princess role-play and fairy-cake baking sessions; he'd taught himself to cook so he could feed us properly and, in later years, would insist on picking Lizzy up from nightclubs at two or even three in the morning, rather than have her come home with a dodgy cab driver. When, at the age of sixteen, I ended up in a psychiatric ward he was by my side all day, every day, and if he was frightened by what had happened to his little girl he never showed it.

He was our rock, our friend, our daddy. But there was a hole in him that nothing and nobody could fill, or would fill, ever again. And that was just how it was. We accommodated his increasing list of neuroses and fears, we allowed him to abandon hope of ever writing his own novels, and we never shamed him.

Privately, of course, it broke our hearts. His life became smaller every time we visited.

We sat in the kitchen, which seemed a lot tidier than it had been in recent months. Dad served homemade lemon cake on an old willow-pattern plate with chips in the glaze that was probably only in circulation still because it had been one of Mum's favourites. We chatted while the house-martins scrabbled around in the low eaves and the clouds disgorged thick sheets of rain on to the Peaks.

Dad told me about the book he was translating, a 'somewhat wanky but rather beautiful' novel about a man who bought an abandoned church in the Andean foothills in Chile, and I told him about the new lease of life I'd taken on with work. 'I'm thinking of going to Tibet soon,' I told him, 'to do some more training. I had incredible massages there. And I'm going to talk to them about having one afternoon per week reserved for reiki. I love it, Dad!'

'Wonderful,' Dad said. 'I can't tell you how happy that makes me, pet. Another piece of cake?'

Dad passed the plate to me, then rested his chin in his hands, watching me with a twinkle in his eye.

I watched him back. I noticed that his eyebrows, which had begun to go a bit sprouty in recent years, had been tamed. And he was wearing a new shirt, a lovely navy thing with orange stitching that wouldn't have looked out of place on a cool young man. Or indeed – my stomach flipped ecstatically – on Stephen.

The mutual watching continued.

'Where did you get that shirt?' I asked him.

'The internet, of course.' Dad grinned. 'Enough about my shirt. Anything you want to tell me?'

'Eh?'

He laughed, leaning back in his chair. 'About the man?'

'What man?'

'The man who's making your face go bright red, Flannie.'

I didn't want to tell him about Stephen. Not yet. But –

'GAH! Oh, *Daddy*! You're a pain!'

Dad nodded. 'And I'm your dad. You didn't think I wouldn't notice, did you?'

'Evil,' I muttered.

'I'm just your old dad, Flannie,' he repeated. 'And I can see you've met someone. Are you going to tell me, sweetheart? Or am I going to have to work it out for myself?'

So I told him.

I told him almost everything, save for the bit when Stephen and I had had sex three times in a darkening vineyard, or the bit where we were spotted kissing passionately in a corridor at two a.m. by a big gay chef, who had bellowed, '*Quel scandale!*' and had to be given a bottle of wine worth five hundred euros to keep his silence. Neither did I tell Dad that Stephen had told me he was in love with me. Even I – high as a kite, and declaring the very same right back – knew that that was a bit fast.

It didn't make it any less real, though. I was hooked right up to that drip. 'And that's about it,' I said. 'Still early days, Dad. No need to write a wedding speech yet.'

Dad frowned. 'I'm not so sure,' he replied. 'You're like a live wire. I've never seen you like this about anyone, Flannabel.'

I tried not to do the mad smile of the smitten but it was impossible. 'Argh,' I whimpered.

Dad chortled. 'Oh dear,' he said. 'It's worse than I thought!' He sat back again, cradling his coffee cup against his chest. 'Sweetheart,' he began hesitantly. 'He's a good man, isn't he? A decent man?'

I thought about the expensive flowers Stephen had sent me when I got back from Heathrow, even though he'd had to spend six hours with me in the British consulate at Bordeaux while I'd waited for the emergency travel permit. And the texts he'd sent me this morning, wishing me a lovely day with my dad and just being generally sweet and completely like nothing I'd ever imagined a CEO to be. 'Yes, he's decent. He's lovely. The genuine article, Dad, I don't think even you could find fault with him.'

Dad looked slightly embarrassed. 'I'm sorry,' he said. 'I hate the idea of you seeing me as an interfering old granny . . .' His beard wobbled slightly.

'I don't think that, Dad,' I said. 'Not at all. I know how much you worry about me and Lizzy, and I completely understand why.'

'I just want to be sure that he's a nice man. Who'll keep you safe. Never harm you.' A tear fell from his eye and my heart twisted savagely. Even more than I wanted happiness and freedom for myself, I wanted it for my dad.

I smiled. 'He's great, Dad. You don't need to worry about him at all.'

'Do you have friends in common? Do you know all about his past? No children, ex-wives, nothing like that?'

I sighed. 'Dad, come on. Of course I don't know everything about him. As I said, it's early days. But if he has an ex-wife and child he's lied to my face, and Stephen's a very heart-on-sleeve sort of a guy. I think his problem is more that he's incapable of being *dis*honest!'

'Some men are good at lying,' Dad insisted. I could tell he hated himself for this.

'Stop it. You don't need to worry about me, Daddy. I've met a really, really lovely man. He makes me laugh, he's humble, he's generous and he has this really strong moral code. I've found a good 'un.'

Dad stared at his hands, and I went over to crouch next to him. 'Nobody on earth is more obsessive about my safety than me,' I said. 'If there was a whiff – so much as a *particle* – of trouble with Stephen, my radar would have gone off weeks ago. Come on, Dad, you know that.'

He sighed, and into me swung the great weight of his grief and fear. 'Okay,' he said eventually. 'I'm sorry, darling. I love you so much, I just want you to be all right.'

Later on, as we sat listening to records in the sitting room with all of Dad's cosy lamps on I noticed – rather to my amazement – that he had Facebook up on his laptop. 'Really?' I said, as he went off to wash up. 'Facebook?'

Dad stuck his head out of the kitchen. 'I know! Who'd have thought? I've decided to enter the world of social media.'

'Don't be ridiculous!'

'Straight up,' he called. 'I'm rather enjoying it, you know, Flannabel. All sorts of funny stuff out there!'

Maybe, after nearly thirty years, things were on the move.

'You should use your new-found internet skills to try a bit of dating yourself,' I said gingerly, as Dad came back.

'Is it time for your train yet?' Dad asked. He looked distinctly shifty and shot back to the kitchen.

Holy God, I thought. Is he dating *already*?

'I'll order a taxi in a few minutes,' I called. 'Stop pretending you didn't hear what I just said.'

Dad cleared his throat in the kitchen. 'My love life is none of your business,' he said, and I could hear the smile in his voice. 'But for the record, you nosy beggar, yes. I'm dabbling.'

I gaped at the kitchen doorway. The old fox!

I whipped my phone out, quick as a flash, to tell Lizzy, then put it away again. God knows, it must be hard for him, I thought. The last thing he needs is us gossiping behind his back. Still, my heart soared as I heard him crashing around in the kitchen.

'Don't call a taxi,' Dad said, popping his head round the door again. 'I'll take you.'

I opened my mouth and shut it again. 'Sure?' I said casually. Dad hadn't been able to drive me to the station for six years.

'Sure,' he said, and I had to fight very hard with myself not to cry.

Just as we were preparing to leave for Chesterfield, the phone rang in the hall. Dad was poking around upstairs, trying to find me a book he wanted to lend me, so I picked it up. 'Hello?'

There was a short silence at the other end – not a computer silence, but a person silence – then the line went dead.

Puzzled, I looked up the stairs in Dad's direction. My definitely smarter-than-normal daddy, with his nicely trimmed beard, under-control eyebrows and new shirt. Daddy, who had somehow found the confidence to leave the house and drive me to Chesterfield.

And then everything fell into place. Dad had already tried internet dating. He was past that stage now.

Dad had a *ladyfriend*!

I smiled all the way back to London. Maybe things were changing for my family. Maybe we were starting to heal.

Shagged someone else last night, Lizzy texted me at Birmingham. *Oops!*

Or maybe it'd take a little more time, I conceded. But progress was being made, I was sure of it.

I went to bed and tried – as I did every night – to picture Mum's face. I couldn't imagine ever giving up.

Chapter Fourteen

Kate

A girl sits in the pale gold light of a summer morning, shards of sunlit dust dancing lazily around her. Apart from the slow rise and fall of breath, the morning is silent.

It isn't peaceful. It's the silence of loss, of absence; the kind of silence that is noisy because of its very existence. She closes her eyes and recalls the sounds that she wants to hear: the clatter of hoofs, the gentle sounds of eating, the swishing tails and comical snorts that once filled the many cracks of her life. She adds human sounds: laughter, banter, water-bucket filling. She feels an old smile inside her, although it doesn't get as far as her face.

A single dog bark in the yard – in the real yard, the quiet rectangle of waiting, empty stables – brings her back to today. To this otherwise silent morning, and to the two tonnes of white-grey miracle with whom she is sitting on a straw bed.

That bit really *was* like a film. He'd made it! My beautiful Stumpy had done the near-impossible. Not only had he survived a fractured pastern bone but he'd done so with courage that would have brought a tear to Mark's eye, had he been there. 'I'm so proud of you,' I told him, as I did every morning.

Slowly, careful not to frighten him, I stood up to go and

make his morning feed. 'You stay there, my man,' I told him.

Stumpy looked at me as if to say, 'Seriously, will you please stop talking to me? It's six forty-five in the bloody morning.'

I once used to enjoy making feeds: all those smells of sweet chaff and nutty competition mix, the buckets of thick gloopy sugar beet when it was cold, but these days I couldn't stand it. Whatever jolly spin I put on things there was no denying the sadness of making just two feeds each morning, rather than thirty. A farmer's pony had been drafted in to live in the stable next to Stumpy's, so he didn't get lonely, and that was it. Two horses; two buckets.

Stumpy made some jolly noises as I returned with his breakfast, although he looked a bit baleful. 'You miss your dad, don't you?' I said, giving him his feed.

He was already too busy eating to reply.

'I miss him too,' I said, staring sadly at the huge white bandage on the horse's leg. 'I miss him far too much.'

For a moment I allowed myself to close my eyes and let Mark inhabit my mind. Those dark, secretive eyes that I had been slowly learning to read; his quiet voice talking to his horses. And, indeed, the peace I had begun to feel around him; the heart-warming realization that he found me funny and refreshing, not a thorn in his side at all.

You lost your chance, Kate Brady, I thought miserably. He liked you. He just didn't know how to say it.

I glanced around furtively in case someone might be able to see the contents of my head. The man had been married, for crying out loud!

'Galway, you old whore,' Joe shouted, waving at me as

he strode across the yard. It was going to be a hot day and he looked like something from a gay disco in jodhpurs, boots and a navy vest. A moustache and whip would have been ideal but I supposed you couldn't have everything.

'How're ye, my princess?'

'I'm grand,' I told him, kissing the spot on his cheek he was pointing to. Nowadays Joe and I were like an old couple: we occasionally cuddled for comfort, kissed each other on the cheek every morning and drank lots of strong Irish tea on the sofa while watching shit TV. We even had our own child in the form of Sandra, who had completely fallen apart and needed watching (not to mention cooking for) every day.

'Yourself?' I ducked back into Stumpy's stable to fetch his water bucket.

'Ah, you know,' Joe said. 'Tolerable.'

If Joe hadn't stayed on at the yard – insisted on staying on, even though there were no horses for him to ride or pounds with which to pay him – things would have been considerably more grim. Within a week of the accident everyone had been given their notice by Tiggy, who had thankfully entered a shell-shocked operations mode, brokering the sale of Mark's own horses and co-ordinating the return to their owners of the rest.

Maria had taken hers away first, in Jochim Furst's lorry. 'They are moving to Oxfordshire,' she emailed us. 'Please don't try to visit.'

One by one the rest of Mark's owners had driven their lorries sheepishly down the driveway until, one hot, empty day at the beginning of June, the yard was quite empty. Tiggy had taken a job at Sarah Hutton's yard in Berkshire and Becca had been offered one at Caroline's down the road.

'I can't leave,' she'd said, when the offer had come through. Tears had trembled in her eyes. 'I can't leave, pet, this is my home.' She knew I was staying to look after Stumpy; understood without asking awkward questions that there was nowhere else for me to go.

'You have to,' I'd said. 'If you stay here we'll both be really depressed. It sounds fun at Caroline's yard, Becca. You'll probably have a far better time there.' I felt a big lump swell in my own throat. 'And, besides,' I said, 'if you turn Caroline's job down the next offer could be five hours up the motorway, not five minutes down the road.'

She'd known she had to take it. We'd cleared out her room together, and I'd cried as I'd pushed her totally un-Becca-like flowery duvet into a black bag.

'Time for a new start,' she said, when the car was loaded. Joe, who at that point was staying 'just for a week, to look after Sandra', waited patiently in the driver's seat while we cried and hugged each other.

'I needed this,' she mumbled into my shoulder. 'I feel awful, pet, fuckin' awful right now, but I needed something like this to happen. Time to move on, you know?'

And then she, too, was gone. There were no pupils arriving for lessons with Mark any more. No Team GBR coaches, no vets, no reps from the horse-feed companies, no saddlers, chiropractors or press. No Ana Luisa running round throwing comical insults at us all, playing in her tree-house or bossing her friends around when they came to play.

Maria had left for ever, taking her daughter, and had

finally shacked herself up with Jochim Furst, who'd won Badminton while Mark had been airlifted to the Major Trauma Centre at Southmead with bleeding to his brain and a body crushed like a compacted car.

Some fairly damning articles had been written about Maria in the eventing press but she really wasn't the sort of person to give a shit.

What the press didn't know, however – had I been braver, I might have told them – was that Maria had ordered that Stumpy be put down, even though he had every chance of surviving. After lying winded for a few minutes he had managed to haul himself up, holding one of his forelegs off the ground. The equine hospital had found an incomplete stress fracture in his pastern bone: nothing to do with his lameness the month before, just a nasty wearing of his pastern that could have gone at any moment. They told us his chances of survival would be much higher if they put steel pins into the bone immediately.

'I am not willing to pay for surgery,' Maria had said on the phone, when I called to explain Stumpy's options. 'And a horse needing four months' box rest is no use to me. Tell them to put him to sleep.'

I had begun to get hysterical, which only seemed to strengthen her resolve. Indeed if it hadn't been for Tiggy, who had confiscated the phone and reminded Maria that it would cost more to have Stumpy put down than it would just to sign the horse over to Mark, she would probably have got her way.

Tiggy had handed me back my phone. 'I'll stay with Stumpy,' she said. 'You go to the hospital. I don't see how

Mark is going to survive this.' Her voice rose in a desperate sob. 'But if he does, he'll need a friendly face when he comes round. I'll send Becca there too, to help look after Ana Luisa. And Joe to look after Sandra. I'll get there as soon as I can . . . Oh, God, Kate.'

Joe leaned over Stumpy's door. 'You're a handsome bastard, aren't you?' he said, patting the horse's still-muscled neck. 'I'm glad you didn't croak it. Poor thing, cooking that little bastard of a fracture all that time and none of us any the wiser.'

'What's happening today?' I asked, trying not to giggle at his outfit. Joe, knowing full well what I was thinking, flexed his muscles and did a few squats. 'Well, Galway,' he said, 'I've thirty more companies to call and then a meeting with Terri James.' He smirked. 'I reckon by the time I've finished with her, she'll promise us that three-year-old mare.'

'You are the worst of all whores,' I said to him. 'You put our country to shame.'

Joe shrugged. 'Mark Waverley didn't die,' he said simply. 'He made it, Galway. Feck knows how but he did. One day he's going to be ready to get on a horse again and when that happens, Galway, I swear I'll have the best feckin' horses in the land, all up and running so he can just hop on and go.' His eyes filled suddenly and he turned away from me. 'And if I've to make tender love to Terri feckin' James, Galway, then that's a duty I'm ready to take on.'

'I love you, Joe,' I said tenderly. 'You might be a whore but you're a very, very good one.'

His determination to keep Mark's career alive was, I'd come to understand, simply Joe's way of dealing with what had happened. He'd been there through those agonizing hours outside the operating theatre, holding Sandra firmly in his arms as if she might leak in all directions, like sand out of a broken egg-timer. He had looked after us – the whole team of us – when one of the surgeons finally emerged after fifteen hours to tell us that Mark had survived and we all broke down. And that night Joe had made Sandra her dinner, then put her to bed and sat on a chair in her room all night so that she wouldn't be alone.

Stepping into a head-of-the-family role was not what I'd ever have expected of Joe Keenan but, then, surviving a devastating trauma was not what I'd expected of Mark, and nursing a horse back to health was not what I'd expected of myself.

We were limping on.

'Right, Galway,' Joe said, wiping his face on the back of his hand. 'Feck off up to Bristol and see your man, now.'

'He's not my man!'

Joe looked puzzled. 'As in, Mark, Galway. Your man. Like we say in Ireland?'

I blushed, swiping at my still-watery eyes. 'Sorry. I just wouldn't want you to think I thought he was *my* man. Because he's not, never has been and never will be. I'm really not interested in him. At all. Never have been, Joe.'

Joe stared at me. 'Okay, Galway,' he said. 'Thanks for gettin' me up to speed, princess.'

'How's he doing?' I asked one of the nurses on Mark's ward. His bed was rumpled and empty, which meant he must be at physiotherapy, although my heart still stopped every time I found his bed without him in it. I wouldn't admit it to anyone but I lay awake most nights, blind with panic that he could be dying right now. That his heart might have stopped beating, or that the chest infection had come back. When I wasn't lying awake panicking about Mark, I would be asleep having nightmares about my past. Nightmares in which the police knocked on Sandra's door, asking if I was there. Nightmares in which my family found out what I'd done and told me they would never talk to me again.

Sometimes I'd have to go out in the middle of the night to sit with Stumpy, and only then would I calm down.

'Mark's doing well,' the nurse said carefully, 'but it's a tough journey that he's on.'

He's still immobile and extremely depressed, was what she meant. 'Do you think he's at least where you'd expect him to be, given the scope of his injuries?'

She frowned. 'To be honest, I've never seen trauma injuries as bad as his,' she admitted. 'So I've no informed idea of where he should be at. But that's because I've spent a lot of my career in oncology,' she added, as my face crumpled. 'I'm still new to this unit, love. I think that, given the number of fractures he sustained, he's probably doing brilliantly. Chat to the consultant, okay?'

'Thank you,' I said. 'I will.'

Up the corridor a trolley emerged from the lift. Was it him? Was it Mark? My stomach fluttered nervously. 'Thank you for all you're doing for him,' I added. 'You guys have been quite wonderful. I'm sure he's not an easy patient.'

The nurse smiled. 'It's a pleasure and an honour,' she said. 'And you should be thanking yourself too. He lives for your visits!'

I looked up the corridor. It was Mark. In a panic, I slipped sideways into the toilet. He was at his lowest and most vulnerable when he was being wheeled around the place, furious and trapped in a body that no longer worked. The last time I'd witnessed him being brought back after a scan he'd gone white and not spoken to me at all. He'd just lain there, staring at the ceiling, battling angrily with the tears he would never allow to fall.

I had cried those tears for him later, my face buried in Stumpy's soft white mane.

Mark did not live for my visits, I thought, listening to the trolley as it trundled past the toilet door. I didn't really know what Mark was living for any more. He was desperately low. He barely ate. I knew his lawyer had been in a few times to talk about custody of Ana Luisa but Mark never mentioned it to me. He didn't talk about his little girl at all, or his soon-to-be ex-wife, or any of the horses he'd lost. He didn't talk about Sandra, or the financial peril that hung over the farm, or the pain he must be in. He just answered my questions. If it weren't for his interest in Stumpy's recovery, we would have sat in silence every day.

Not that that would have stopped me coming.

I left it for a few minutes, then slipped through his curtains, pretending just to have arrived. Mark shared a ward with two other beds and, in typical Mark style, always kept his curtains firmly closed.

'Top of the morning to you,' I said, in my very worst leprechaun accent. 'It's nice to see you, so.'

Mark looked briefly at me. 'Hi.'

'How are you on this glorious day?'

'Shit.'

That was fair enough. The man was recovering from a head injury, a pelvic fracture, a broken hip socket and a broken arm and leg. He'd also suffered something called a flail chest, which – like the head injury – should really have killed him but, miraculously, it hadn't. That injury, in turn, had bruised his lungs and caused a major chest infection; the damage to his pelvis and hip joint meant that he still couldn't really move his legs, and the fact that he'd broken his right arm and left leg meant that he wouldn't be considered safe enough to go home for at least another three weeks. Oh, and he'd had plastic surgery to his leg where the tibia had broken through and his skin was still laced with the eerie shadows of faded bruising.

'Shit' was fair enough.

I hovered by the end of his bed. 'I could go and get some lunch and come back later?'

He stared at the ceiling.

'Or I could just come back tomorrow . . .'

Mark shrugged. 'Up to you,' he said. 'I don't want to take up your time.'

I smiled, even though he was refusing to look at me. 'I'm not all that busy with just the one horse and his friend.'

Mark, as I'd predicted, couldn't resist. 'How is he doing?' he asked, turning his head carefully towards me. A little light had appeared in his dark, watery eyes.

'Wonderful,' I said, unable to hide my excitement. 'The vet came to change his bandage yesterday – it's so huge –

and although it's far too early to tell, she said it was all looking good. He's so patient, Mark. So brave!'

Mark nodded, and I knew he wasn't speaking now because he couldn't.

'We're all very proud of him,' I said softly. 'He's fighting.'

Mark resumed his silence. I sat there for a few minutes, humming a non-existent tune and digging out some dirt from my fingernails.

'So, Joe's been working hard with the sponsorship calls,' I tried.

Nothing.

'Oh, and your mum actually got a haircut yesterday, so that's good. She was beginning to look a bit wild there.'

Mark's eyes closed.

'The nurse said she thought you were doing really well,' I said desperately. 'She said she'd never seen someone with injuries as bad as yours. But look at you, eh? Making all this progress?'

'He told you then,' said Tony, the physio, marching in with his white trousers and squeaky trainers.

'Told me what?'

Mark looked cross.

'We got him into a wheelchair today! Wheeled him out of the front door and into the outside world!'

I stared at him, then turned to Mark. 'Are you SERIOUS?'

Tony tutted. 'Oh, *Mark*,' he said. 'Come on, mate! This is a big day! I've also said he can start taking showers, so things are on the up.'

Still Mark said nothing.

Tony rolled his eyes at me. 'I just popped by with your wallet,' he told Mark, putting it on the bedside table. 'You left it in physio.'

Mark failed to thank him and Tony left.

'This is incredible news!' I cried. 'You must be thrilled!'

There was a pause. Then Mark turned his head to me.

'I'm not fucking thrilled, Kate. Sorry if that doesn't fit in with your vision of my life, but that's just how it is. I'm far from thrilled. I've got pressure sores and my muscles are wasting and I'm sharing my room with a complete *mental* whose wife keeps sneaking vodka in for him, which just reminds me of Dad, and the whole world is talking about my wife fucking off with Jochim, which apparently everyone knew about other than me. I'm terrified she'll try to take Ana Luisa away for ever, and I haven't even the money to hire a lawyer good enough to stop her. And, if all of that wasn't bad enough, I have to put up with you just marching in here, day in, day out, being all chirpy and – and *Irish*. I wish you'd all just fuck off, with your good news this and progress that and exciting whatever, because from where I'm standing – except, no, I'm not bloody well standing, I'm lying – there is no good news here.'

I stared at him, my cheeks burning red.

'Just go,' he said. 'Leave me alone.'

To think he'd dreaded my visits, every day. To think I'd fooled myself into believing he enjoyed my company, when he actually just thought I was an idiot.

I tried to collect myself so that I could make a controlled exit, but I just found myself staring furiously at the wallet Tony had left on the bedside table, trying to stop tears falling.

Mark took that wallet to all of his appointments, tucked into his hand under the blanket; I'd thought it was an odd financial thing. Perhaps an unconscious need to keep his money close in case Maria took that too.

But as my eyes finally focused I realized that Mark was doing nothing of the sort.

There was no money. The only thing left in his sad, baggy, empty wallet were two photographs in the clear plastic sleeves. One of Ana Luisa at the school fête, dressed as a bowl of sherry trifle, and one of Stumpy, stretching his nose towards the camera as if he wanted to eat it.

I looked at his two little mementoes and knew that it was time for Mark to start fighting. He couldn't carry on lying there like a miserable old broken corpse, because he wasn't. He was a father and a son, not to mention a medical miracle. He'd survived the unsurvivable, just like his horse, and he had everything to live for.

'You left the hospital for the first time in six weeks,' I said. 'I know things are dreadful. But, Mark, can't you see that you're on the up? Can't you see that you're getting there?'

Mark rolled his eyes angrily.

'You won't acknowledge how brilliantly you've done, Mark? You won't admit that this is a triumph the size of the Republic of sodding Ireland?'

'Just shut up,' he said. 'You're boring me. I thought you were interesting, Kate, but you're just like the rest of them.'

'I'm trying to help.'

'No, you're trying to make yourself feel better,' Mark said.

Was I?

'I sat there, completely helpless, while they wheeled me out,' he muttered. 'They could have wheeled me into the path of an oncoming lorry and I wouldn't have been able to do anything to stop them. The accident was nearly six weeks ago, Kate. This is not a giant leap for mankind. Tony was just being over the top. He's an idiot.'

I broke. The rage, the despair, the fear, the loneliness, the regret, every crushing feeling I'd had to bite back over the last few weeks, it all exploded.

'An idiot?' I shouted. 'A fucking *idiot*? Are you for real, Mark fucking Waverley? He's a physio at one of the best fucking spinal units in the country! How dare you?'

Mark stared at me.

'And what the fuck do you mean, it wasn't a giant leap for mankind? You should be dead!' I cried, my voice breaking already. 'You had blood pouring into your brain, Mark, three of your ribs detached themselves from your ribcage and crushed your lungs, and your thigh bones smashed your hip socket to pieces. Yet you're mobile again! They're talking about letting you go home in the next few weeks! What will it take to make you realize what you've got? You lived, Mark! You lived! And Stumpy lived!'

Mark was white-faced with shock and rage. Well, fuck him.

'Fuck you,' I shouted. 'Fuck you, Mark! Where's your gratitude? I'll stop coming up if you don't like my company but you can at least show some fucking dignity, and some respect, and speak nicely about the people who are busting their fucking arses to get you home!'

I stood up, shaking with fury. 'I've not seen Stumpy lying there muttering under his breath. I've not seen him shoot down every tiny bit of progress he's made. He's fighting really hard and he's doing it like a gentleman. Are you going to be beaten by your horse? Are you really?'

And without waiting for an answer, I swept back the curtain and left it open, shouting that he was not a fucking hermit, and I left.

'Have a nice afternoon, love,' called the nurse, as I steamed past.

Chapter Fifteen

Kate

The next day I drove up the M5 for the final time. I needed to apologize, several million times over, and then I needed to offer to walk out of Mark's life.

'You are a stinker,' I shouted at myself as I drove. 'A rotten, stinking, putrid old boil, Kate Brady. You're a bastard and a tinker and a feck. You screamed at a man suffering major trauma! You suck! I hate you!'

It was amazing how quickly I'd stopped shouting at Mark and started shouting at myself. I'd been at it for eighteen hours now.

I didn't know the hard facts of Mark's mental health at the moment because, obviously, it was not something he was keen to discuss with me. But I didn't need to steal his medical notes to know he'd be suffering post-traumatic stress disorder. To have survived being crushed by a half-tonne horse going at thirty miles per hour, being airlifted to hospital, then spending a combined total of thirty-five hours in surgery with*out* suffering major psychological trauma, Mark would have had to be a non-human life form. Especially since his wife had chosen that moment to leave him, taking his child, his horses and his sole source of income.

'The man has nightmares and flashbacks and he's in

pain all the time. He can hardly move and he has to shit into a pot with a nurse there. And look what you went and said to him,' I continued, as I came off the motorway at Filton. 'Gah!'

'Hiya, love,' said the nurse at the station, when I slunk in fifteen minutes later.

'Hi, Jean,' I said. Until now, I'd not even had the manners to check her name badge. God, I was loathsome.

'He's in there,' she told me, as if to say, 'Batten down the hatches!'

'I hate myself,' I told her. Jean just smiled.

'Hi,' I said, sliding into Mark's cubicle. My voice was barely audible.

Mark's eyes slid over me, then away again.

'Um, how are you?' I tried.

'Okay.'

'God, Mark,' I whispered. Tears welled in my eyes before I had a chance to stop them. 'I can't believe I said what I said. I don't think I'll ever be able to forgive myself. I am so incredibly sorry.'

Mark's eyes came back to me.

'I don't think you're undignified or ungrateful. I think you have the kind of courage that people write about in novels, and the kind of patience that only saints should be allowed.'

Mark closed his eyes.

'I'm sorry, Mark. I was suffering from the delusion that you needed to hear that stuff, but I was wrong. You have every right to be sad and angry and frustrated. I think you're one of the bravest and nicest people I've ever met, and you have no idea how much you've done for me, letting me stay at your yard. You are my hero. You've saved my life. And to think that that's how I repaid you.'

I started to cry.

'I'm so bloody ashamed. I won't come here again. I'll stay at the yard and look after Stumpy, and when you're ready to come home I'll have gone. I'm sorry, Mark Waverley. I'm so sorry. You're one of the best men I've ever met.'

I turned to leave. 'Oh, and Maria is an absolute twat,' I said over my shoulder. 'She needs a brain transplant, leaving a man like you.'

I opened the curtain and slipped out.

'Kate.'

I froze.

'Come back.'

I didn't.

'I said, come back, you irritating fool.'

Slowly, barely able to believe it, I turned. He was smiling. Mark was actually smiling.

'Come back in here, please.'

I came.

'Shut the curtain.'

I shut.

'Maria is an absolute twat,' he repeated slowly. 'She needs a brain transplant.' And then he laughed. He laughed! It was the best sound I'd ever heard.

'Thank you, Kate,' he said, trying not to laugh too hard. His ribs were doing okay but laughing probably wasn't great. He laughed until his lip started trembling and suddenly tears were falling out of his eyes and into the pillow.

I went over to mop them up and ended up dropping my own all over his face.

After an undignified scramble with a box of tissues, I sat down and Mark turned to look at me. Dear Mother of God, he was lovely.

'I think your methods could do with some tinkering,' he began, 'and perhaps the volume could have been turned down a bit but, contrary to what you might think, you said exactly what I needed to hear.'

'But I insulted you. And I said fuck twenty times over. I hate that word.'

'I needed some fuck.'

'Really?'

'Really.' He was smiling again. 'It's not been the best time,' he said. 'And I'm still very wobbly. And I've never used the word "wobbly" before in my life, and I wish I hadn't because it makes me feel stupid as well as vulnerable. But you're right, Kate. I need to be grateful, and dignified, and positive. Because otherwise I'm going to end up with a fixed body and a broken head, and what kind of a life would that be?'

'A shite one?'

Mark laughed again. 'A shite one.'

'I don't want a shite life,' he went on quietly. 'It's been bad enough, with Dad dying and Mum being a liability and us never having any money, then talking myself into marrying a complete monster, suffering the indignity of her constant affairs and the never-ending fear that she'd take my baby away from me. But, for whatever reason, I've been given a second chance and you made me see that I have to grab that chance by the balls.'

'The balls,' I echoed.

'My arm and leg have healed, and I'm able to put a little bit more load through them every day. And the whole pelvis catastrophe is fixing itself, which is why I'm in a wheelchair at last. My ribs are stuck back in place and all of my brain scans have been fine. Basically, I'm going to make it.'

'Because you're a miracle,' I reminded him.

Mark smiled. 'Maybe.'

'Definitely.'

'Okay, definitely.' He sighed. 'I think part of the problem is just being so immobile. Maria told me that I'm a workaholic. That I stay busy from dawn to dusk to stop myself actually dealing with anything. Much as it pains me to admit it, I think she's right.'

'Oh . . .'

'It's very easy to do a runner from your own life, you know?'

'It is.' I smiled sadly. 'It really is.'

'It's especially easy to do a runner from your life in my line of work. I just get on a horse at seven a.m. and that's it until I'm so shattered I go to bed. Busy, busy, busy. Life? What? Problems? Eh? *Feelings?* Don't be ridiculous!'

He paused, thinking. 'I guess that's part of why I've been so particularly miserable. Being stuck with myself. It's not much fun.'

'I see what you mean there, boss . . .'

'I have everything to play for,' Mark admitted. 'I had a really good psychotherapy session today because for the first time I actually wanted to feel better, and I managed to write a few sentences in my journal with my right arm, which I wouldn't have been able to do if the nerve had suffered permanent damage. Plus Kelly's on nights at the moment,' he added, 'and she's brilliant. So things are pretty good.'

I smiled, as if to say, 'How wonderful!' Rather than 'Who the hell is Kelly?'

'Kelly's married to Tony,' Mark said. 'Isn't that funny?'

'HILARIOUS!' I roared with relief.

'So, thank you,' Mark repeated. 'There's a long way to go with this head of mine, and a very long way to go with this body, but you've reminded me that I'm not going to get there sitting in here like a furious hermit.' He grinned, and I tried not to stare adoringly at him. 'I might even get you to open the curtains when you leave.'

'Steady on,' I said. 'Let's not get ahead of ourselves there.'

'So how are *you*, Kate?' Mark asked.

'I'm . . . I'm fantastic,' I said. 'More fantastic than you could possibly imagine, hearing what you've just said.'

There was a long silence through which we both smiled, and it was not in the faintest bit awkward. 'Oh, and I took a photo of Stumpy this morning with food all over his nose, look.'

'Oh, Stumpy,' Mark said, smiling at the photo. 'Oh, my Stumpy.'

'He said to say, "Please come home soon, Dad."'

'I want to see my fields again,' Mark said simply. 'I want to get back up on my feet and feel fresh air on my face. I want to see Stumpy run round the paddock with my own eyes and I want to get out there and fight for joint custody of my daughter.' Carefully, I sat down on the side of his bed, even though there was a big sign by it, saying, 'PLEASE DO NOT SIT ON THIS PATIENT'S BED.'

'Please keep coming, Kate.' I felt his good hand slide hesitantly towards me. I saw it touch mine, shaking slightly, and I heard Mark's breathing peak with the effort of making that tiny gesture.

That enormous gesture.

I looked at him, even though it felt dangerous to do so.

'Joe is doing a wonderful job, by the sound of things,' Mark said. 'And Mum is doing her very best. But you, Kate Brady . . .' he moved his hand fully over mine '. . . you're giving me a reason to live every day.'

His eyes bulged with tears again, and before I knew what I was doing, I lifted up his good hand and pressed it against my face. We stayed like that for several minutes.

'Oh, not you, too,' I said eventually. 'Not you at the crying as well. Joe was after crying yesterday morning. Great bunch of girls, you are.'

I held his hand against my cheek for a final, precious moment.

'It's Stumpy I'm doing it for, anyway.' I grinned. 'Not you.'

Chapter Sixteen

Annie

'Aha!' Lizzy shouted, as I arrived in the restaurant. 'She's alive!' I stopped, confused. I was in Shane's, a tiny little place round the corner from my house, and I was meant to be meeting Tim for a quick dinner. But with him were Lizzy and Claudine.

'Er – is this Le Cloob?'

'Damn right it's Le Cloob!' Lizzy said. 'You've gone and got yourself a boyfriend, Annie, and you've already disappeared off the face of the earth. Did you really think we were going to let you and Tim just have a cosy catch-up on your own?'

I stared at them stupidly. 'But we're only allowed to meet in Clapham.'

Tim and Lizzy turned to Claudine. 'Well, we were wondering . . .' Tim said.

Claudine stared defiantly back at us all. And then, to everyone's surprise, she let out a naughty snigger. 'Oh, my little espadrilles.' She sighed. 'You are all very entertaining. Do you really think I refuse to eat anywhere other than French restaurants?'

'Um, yes?' Lizzy said doubtfully.

At this Claudine laughed. 'Ha-ha! I could have kept it up for years!' She took a slug of wine. 'You must all think

I am some very strange sort of nationalist French peasant. I am a cosmopolitan woman. I like all food and all restaurants. I just fancied playing wiz you all.' She was delighted with herself. 'Ha-ha!'

'You,' Tim said, frowning at Claudine, 'are a little shit.'

Tim never told Claudine off. Neither did he ever call anyone a little shit. 'You are!' he protested. 'All those times we've travelled down to Clapham to keep you happy!'

'I know! You losers!' She pronounced it 'losairs'. I loved Claudine.

I sat down and took a long, lovely sip of the crisp Greek wine – served, of course, in those trendy little beakers – and smiled. Life felt very good at the moment. It was summer and I was abuzz with wild, zinging feelings that had barely allowed me to sleep since Stephen and I had first kissed nearly three weeks ago. I was crazy with it, glued to my phone like a lovesick teenager when I wasn't with him, and glued to his side when I was.

'Well, now,' Claudine said, once we'd all ordered. She sounded more severe. 'Well, now, my small cheese block. You are obviously going to have to tell everything. And perhaps you can start by explaining why you 'ave not answered your phone in three weeks.'

Then her face changed. 'Sorry,' she said. 'Sorry. I am cross with you, but I should at least pretend otherwise.'

Lizzy laughed but I was suddenly silenced. Was Claudine right? Had I really gone to ground?

'I think you should start at the beginning,' Lizzy said, fanning herself with the menu. The windows and door were wide open but it was still boiling. 'And tell us everything. Except for sex, I could do without that.'

'So could I,' Tim said firmly, and Lizzy shot him one of her you-are-totally-in-love-with-my-little-sister-and-it-drives-me-mad faces that I always did my best to ignore.

I told them everything I could think of, apart from the bit about Stephen and I having sex literally all the time. Even I was taking a while to get used to that. 'I wake up every morning feeling like I'm on speed,' I finished dazedly. My food had arrived and I'd barely even noticed. 'I'm smiling, I'm zinging, I say yes to everything and I don't even get tired. I hardly recognize myself!'

'We hardly recognize you either,' Claudine remarked helpfully. She stabbed a piece of purple broccoli in a fairly violent manner.

I told them about Stephen's fantasy house in Clapton Square, how it looked like God himself had become an interior designer and put together a showroom in Hackney. 'Literally everything in that house is stunning. And among all the beautiful design he's still got loads of old books and pictures and stuff. Even his downstairs toilet is a work of art!'

I didn't mention the loo picture of a six-year-old Stephen dissecting a frog in his back garden: as yet I'd failed to make him take it down. (He thought it was hilarious and sweet; I thought it was depraved.) But I did say that I'd always thought a person's house to be a reflection of who they really were. And that this house boded very well for Stephen.

'Isn't it just wonderful that he lives there, and not in a ten-million-pound house in Kensington? Doesn't that just show you what a great bloke he is? He is just amazing! Amazing, I tell you!'

Rein it in, I told myself. This is nauseating! But I couldn't. I felt like I'd won the lottery. Years and years of loneliness, nothingness, a painful inability to engage with men on almost any level and now *this*? Even I barely believed it.

'I'm smitten,' I admitted. 'Completely in love. It's hopeless.'

'*Love?*' Claudine barked. She put down her cutlery. 'Did you just say love?'

I nodded guiltily. 'I know what you're thinking, but you're wrong. We're not being mad and impetuous, we *are* in love. Madly in love. It happens all the time, so stop looking at me like that! It happened to you, Claudie, you were married within five weeks of meeting Sylvester!'

Claudine, who could not argue with this, was silenced, although not for long. 'You are totally out of control,' she said. 'My darling, you have been together two and a half weeks! Look at you! You 'ave moved *far* too fast!'

'Claudie . . .'

'No! You do not know this man! You are being ridiculous!'

'Oh, Claudie!' Lizzy began. 'Don't be mean. What about love at first sight?'

She would defend me to the hilt, Lizzy, but she looked rather worried, too. They demanded that Tim expound some wisdom on the possibility of love at first sight and I zoned out, suddenly anxious.

What if Claudine was right? What if I was just caught up in some mad blaze of hormones? What if the pure, racing joy of the last seventeen days had had more to do with madness than it had with love?

I'd let no man near me for years. I'd agreed to go on the odd date, often under extreme duress, but the tiny handful of men I hadn't panic-cancelled at the last minute had – in spite of being mostly very nice – touched deep icy memories that I wanted nothing to do with. Gradually, in the same way that Lizzy and I had stopped trying to do something about Dad's agoraphobia, Le Cloob had stopped trying to set me up with men.

My unexpected willingness to place my trust in Stephen – to let myself fall for him – had felt to me like a landmark victory. A miracle! I couldn't bear it if it wasn't real. If it was just me being crazy.

'Hey.' Tim had reached across to tap me on the arm. 'Are you OK, Pumpkin?'

I shrugged miserably.

'Right, will you two please be quiet?' Tim said, and Lizzy and Claudine stopped. They turned to him, then to me. 'Annie's doing her best here,' he said. 'It would probably help her if you weren't arguing over whether or not she's sane. Right under her nose.'

'Oh, darling, sorry,' Lizzy said. 'I was defending you! But of course Timmy's right. Sorry.'

Claudine poured us all some more wine. 'I am sorry too,' she said. 'But please understand that my intentions are always good.'

'I know.' Of course I knew. 'But I wish you'd trust me more, Claudie. I wish you'd allow me the possibility of being genuinely happy, of having made a really good, brave decision, rather than just assuming I've gone mad again.' I knocked back some wine. 'Trust me, Claudie. Trust me, *all* of you. I'm constantly on the lookout for

227

cracks in my mental health. Yes, it concerns me that I feel this strongly after such a short time. And, yes, I know it all seems too good to be true. But could you please give me a chance? Look for the best possible explanation, rather than the worst?'

Claudine paused before answering. I knew what she was thinking. I knew she still held in her memory the fragile nineteen-year-old I'd been when we'd first met at a nutrition seminar in London. I knew how protective she was of that girl; how she'd fight for her with her bare hands, if need be.

'Okay,' she said. 'Okay, Annie, my small apple. I am sorry. If you tell me that you think it is good between you and Stephen then I am 'appy.' She reached over and touched my hand. 'Really, I am sorry.'

I squeezed her hand. 'Well, I'm sorry too. I didn't know I'd gone all crap at answering the phone. I'll get a grip, I promise, and I won't let Le Cloob suffer.'

'Group hug,' Lizzy said thickly, prompting a very awkward clasping of shoulders around the table. 'End of group hug,' she announced. 'Far too bloody hot. Plus I've got BO.' She flapped at her armpits and Tim chuckled, appalled but amused.

'Talking of relationships,' I said, keen to deflect the attention from my own, 'how's Mel, Tim?'

A shadow crossed Tim's face as he filled his wineglass to the brim. 'Erm,' he began, then petered out.

'Everything okay, Timmy?' Lizzy asked. She was very sweet with Tim sometimes. Like he was her puppy.

Tim cracked his knuckles, as he always did when he was nervous. 'Er, Mel and I split up.'

We all gaped at him.

'What?'

'Eh?'

'*Quoi?*'

He wriggled uncomfortably. 'Yeah. We split up. I'd probably rather not talk about it, if you don't mind. I'm a bit raw. Still processing it.'

'But —'

'Of course,' I interrupted Lizzy. 'We're here when you need us.'

Claudine showed less respect. 'Who dumped whom?' she demanded.

Tim flinched. 'It was my decision.'

'*Vraiment?*' Claudine asked. 'But why?'

'Let's leave him alone,' I said sharply, and Tim gave my knee a grateful bump. God, poor Tim. It had been just two and a half weeks but I knew already that I wouldn't be able to function if things between Stephen and me went wrong. Even if we went for two hours without at least a text message I felt a terrible hole opening in my heart. I'd die without him. I would literally die.

'Let's talk about something else,' Tim said. 'I mean it,' he added, as Claudine opened her mouth to fire another question his way.

Lizzy started telling us about one of her boyfriends who was up for an innovation award, whatever that might mean, and I drifted off, dreaming of maybe living in Stephen's house with him one day. Imagining having a kitchen that size, and beautiful great big folding doors into the garden.

And then I frowned.

Stephen. Stephen was at a table a few metres away with a girl. A little wispy Hackneyite wearing what looked like a vintage nightdress and bright orange lipstick, her hair in a topknot. She looked like an art student, perhaps, couldn't have been any older than eighteen. I hadn't noticed him because he'd had his back to me but now he was turning sideways to talk to the waiter. And it was him. Stephen. It was my man.

In spite of everything that had passed between us in the last two and a half weeks my heart ground to a halt. Who the hell was the girl?

Tim, seeing my face, glanced at the table. 'Oh,' he said, as Stephen cut off a bit of his steak and put it on the girl's plate, chatting away comfortably as if they'd known each other all their lives.

My head tried to rationalize. She was too young, for starters. A child. He couldn't surely . . . Not in my little local restaurant either. We were within ten metres of my front door!

And our beautiful shiny new relationship, the whole explosive energy of the last few weeks! There was no *way* that wasn't real! There must be an explanation.

Perhaps sensing our gaze, Stephen looked over his shoulder and suddenly saw me. And, to my heartfelt relief, I saw not so much as an atom of panic in his face. He just looked delighted. He beckoned me over, explaining to the girl who I was.

'Er, hang on a sec,' I said vaguely to Le Cloob. I floated over to their table, holding on to an unsuspecting diner's chair for support.

'What a lovely surprise!' Stephen said, standing up and

kissing me softly on the cheek. The feeling of his face against mine sent me reeling. 'Annie, this is my niece Petra,' he said. 'Petra, this is Annie.'

Petra smiled limply. 'Hiya,' she said.

Thank God. Thank God.

I shook my head, as if to dislodge the awful thoughts I'd been having, and smiled at Petra. I could tell straight away that she was a brat. She was sullen and resentful and didn't say a word in the conversation that followed.

'I finished work before eight for once,' Stephen beamed, 'and here we are in the same restaurant! Mad! Splendid! Petra's just moved to Clapton before starting art school,' he continued. 'And her dad, my big brother, has asked me to keep an eye on her. So here I am, reporting for duty.'

Petra rolled her eyes but I was weak with relief. 'Of course,' I gasped. I sounded insane. 'So are you Barnaby's big sister, Petra? Stephen carries a picture of him in his wallet. He's gorgeous!'

'Yeah,' she muttered, evidently disgusted at having to talk to me. 'Yeah, he's my brother.'

'Well, it's nice to see you,' I said, slipping my hand into Stephen's, out of sight of his niece. He kissed my cheek again, a lingering kiss that smelt of clean skin and verbena, and said he'd come over to say hi to Le Cloob when they'd finished eating. 'Hello!' he called in their direction.

'Flannie . . .' Lizzy handed me some water as I sat down. 'Are you okay?'

I took a sip of water. 'Um, sorry?'

'Darling, are you okay? Your hands are shaking. You look like you're going to faint.'

A pretty waitress refilled our glasses and the sudden smell of wine made me feel sick.

'That's Stephen!' I said. 'And that's his niece. For a moment I thought . . .' My voice wobbled off into nothing. 'I'm such a freak!'

Claudine was scowling at Stephen and Petra. 'How do you know he is her niece?'

'Oi,' Tim said sternly. He poured me some water out of a carafe. 'Claudie, he introduced the girl as his niece. We all heard him. I think, if she was his secret lover, she might possibly have objected.'

Claudine began to argue but he and Lizzy told her to shut up. I tried to breathe myself back down to some sort of equilibrium.

'Sorry about that,' I said, when they'd finished arguing. 'I wish someone had warned me that love turns you into a paranoid lunatic, ha-ha!'

Tim and Lizzy exchanged glances, which annoyed me. 'Pumpkin,' Tim began. There was a delicate expression on his face. 'Pumpkin, you looked . . . er, very anxious back there.'

'As if your life were 'anging in the balance,' Claudine added unhelpfully.

'Well, if he'd been cheating my life would have been hanging in the balance. Oh, come *on*, guys. We've just been there! I'm okay! I'm just in love!'

Tim did the face I knew he must use on his patients. Polite, respectful but ever-so-slightly concerned. 'I accept that,' he said gently. 'But just take it easy, okay? Relax into it, Annie. If you're right for each other there needn't be anything to worry about.'

'I agree, darling,' Lizzy said. 'Maybe you should do some of those meditations you like, keep yourself nice and balanced. I mean, it's normal to worry a little bit, of course, but you did seem, er, like you were about to die.'

I pushed my salad round my plate, hoping nobody would notice that I'd hardly eaten. I was fed up with having to defend myself and my relationship, and even more fed up that they were probably right. I mean, Stephen had spent the past seventeen days telling me how madly he was falling in love with me and yet I'd gone into freefall when I'd spotted him having dinner with a teenager. That was not sane behaviour.

Tim had been hassling me about the fact that I'd stopped seeing my therapist when I'd run out of money. His view was that now I was earning again I could afford it. My view was that I couldn't stop smiling: why would I want to go back to the gloom of my therapist's armchair?

Now I wondered if maybe I should. Tim was seldom wrong about these things: not only did he know me inside out but he had the added benefit of having sorted out his own shit quite spectacularly.

Tim and I had met at that support group as sixteen-year-olds when we had begun to implode. He had lost his big sister to a brain tumour around six months before and had been harming himself. I had decided on my sixteenth birthday that I was done with being alive. All of my birthdays had been bad since Neil Derrick had been urged by voices in his head to 'punish' my mother while we played hide and seek on Woodford Farm, but that one, nine months after I'd started having panic attacks, had been impossible. I'd woken up unable to remember Mum's face and had had an attack. By lunchtime I'd had four more, and as my fifth had moved in on me, like a rotating saw, I'd agreed with myself that that would be that.

The on-duty psychiatrist at A&E had prescribed anti-depressants and referred me for psychodynamic therapy. At some point a psychologist had taken charge of me and suggested several other things I should try. The guilt at what I'd done to Dad and Lizzy was so crushing that I'd tried everything on her list, which meant – among other things I didn't want to do – attending a weekly support group.

I'd found the group to be pointless and had kept on going only because of my family, and because I liked Tim so much. Perhaps it was because he was so fragile himself, or simply because he was such a beautiful, kind person, even back then, but in Tim Furniss I'd found a man with whom I'd felt safe.

As the months had passed, however, I'd watched him grow and change; watched him discard the ragged mantle of his past and step into a vital and focused existence of which I could only dream.

He'd done it. He'd recovered. And I . . . Well, I'd limped on as best I could.

Fine, I thought wearily. I'll go back to therapy if I need to. I'll read books. I'll do anything I have to do to keep this relationship going.

'Just give me a chance, guys,' I said, picking up my fork again. 'I totally hear what you're saying, and I accept that I need to calm down. So let me just get on with that in my own time, okay?'

Tim smiled. 'Good on you, Pumpkin. And remember, we love you.'

Stephen and Petra got up to go while we were all arguing over desserts. He shepherded her to our table before leaving, telling Le Cloob he'd come back for a glass of wine once he'd walked Petra home. 'If that's okay,' he added. 'I don't want to be That Boyfriend who just gatecrashes everything.'

Lizzy giggled. 'I had one of those. But I can tell you're not the same. We categorically demand that you return, Stephen. It's not optional.'

'Nice to meet you, Petra!' I said. It was a relief to be calm again. 'We'll have to go for coffee some time – we must be neighbours!'

'We are,' she said.

'Oh! He told you where I live, then? Just there on Blurton Road?'

'Uncle Stephen has told me *all* about you.' She gave me a sickly sort of a grimace. What a charmer!

Well, I'd work on her, just like I'd work on myself. Maybe if I played my cards right she'd even come to see me as a sort of cool (or most probably not cool) aunt.

Uncle Stephen, so impossibly handsome in his rolled-up shirtsleeves, caught my eye and winked.

Two hours later, we were engaging in some casual nudity on the big Inca rug in my front room. It was his first time at my house and, after a brief tour, most of which he'd spent removing my clothes, we'd had a bit of a marathon in front of the fireplace, which I'd filled with candles. We were both sleepy and a bit drunk but every now and then one of us roused ourselves out of our stupor long enough to kiss part of the other. An elbow here, a rib there. The candlelight made long shadows across Stephen's lovely tanned skin and I thought once again that he looked like a mythological god.

'This is like a film,' I said timidly. 'Midsummer sex in candlelight. Feeling this good.'

Stephen rolled sideways so that he could see my face. 'But, Annie, you have three large locks on your front door, and you keep your keys in a secret cubbyhole, which makes me feel like we're in a thriller. And let's not forget that you did run off to vomit while I was bestowing tender kisses on your neck.'

The morning-after pill had caught up with me; the second in a fortnight. I hated taking it; hated what it meant; hated what it did to me. But that was the problem with love. It stripped you of sense.

'We have to stop having unprotected sex,' I said. It worried me that I wasn't looking after myself properly.

'I agree.' Stephen yawned. 'How do I know you aren't infecting me with rotten diseases?'

I smiled thinly. 'Hmm.'

'Hey . . . Annie? What's wrong?'

'Nothing. Well, just the morning-after-pill thing. I shouldn't let it happen.'

Stephen kissed my forehead. 'And I shouldn't either. Stop worrying. We made a bad mistake and then we made it again. But that's that.'

I relaxed. 'Thank you. And sorry for ruining this little film scene we're having here. Look!'

I scampered over to my little house-key cubbyhole. 'Look, I'm going to be all casual with my house keys, see?' I tossed them into the air and they landed on the sofa. 'Look! There they are, just sitting on the sofa. In full view of the street. That's how relaxed I am . . .'

Stephen started laughing. 'They'd be in full view of the street if you didn't have your curtains closed.'

I looked forlornly at my big pile of keys. How shiny they were, I thought, my jailer's hoard. Of course I couldn't just leave them in view of the street. Far too shiny. Far too obvious. 'I may need a bit more time on the keys front,' I admitted, putting them back in their cubbyhole. 'So if you could cope with feeling like you're in a thriller a little longer, that would be great.'

Stephen just chuckled. 'Come back here.'

I came. 'Stephen, thank you for being amazing tonight. You charmed the hell out of everyone.'

'I did not! Claudine was looking at me like I was some sub-species of crustacean!'

He wasn't wrong. When he'd returned to the table Claudine had grilled him for a good five minutes before Tim had stepped in and told her basically to be quiet. Stephen, being the good-humoured man that he was, had taken it in his stride, but I'd felt like I might die of embarrassment.

Luckily, Lizzy and Tim didn't seem to have any problem appreciating Stephen. Lizzy had been reduced to tears of laughter when Stephen told us about his elder brother, Petra's dad, who apparently used to throw bananas and oranges at Stephen's head while he slept and spent his summers sitting in a pear tree reciting the lyrics from *The King and I*.

By the end of the night Lizzy was declaring quite openly that she thought Stephen was the best man she'd met in years. 'And to top it off you're appallingly good-looking!' She giggled. 'Well done! I think you've even won Claudie over.'

Claudine declared he had done nothing of the sort, but did at least manage to kiss Stephen's cheek when we left the restaurant. Tim and Stephen had even had a manly hug, much to my delight.

'He's so handsome,' Tim whispered, as Stephen ordered Lizzy and Claudine cabs on the FlintSpark account. 'And just great. He's basically the perfect man.'

'Isn't he?' I'd blushed.

Tim looked at me. 'Yeah,' he said sadly. 'I wish I had some of his charm.' He had gone home looking depressed.

Poor old Tim. The Mel thing must have hit him hard.

'Claudine will take time, but they basically all think you're amazing,' I told Stephen. One of the candles sputtered and his face swayed in and out of the shadows. 'And they're right,' I told him. 'You are amazing.'

Stephen pulled me close and kissed me. 'I'm glad they liked me. I liked them. I have hopes of one day becoming a member of Le Cloob. Or at least a sort of recognized guest.'

'And that's another thing! You remembered that we're called Le Cloob! I was so proud!'

'Of course I remembered, silly.' Stephen ran his fingers along my arm. 'You talk about those guys all the time.'

'I'm sure I do . . . I can barely remember anything of the last two weeks. It's just been like a perfect blurry blur.'

Stephen kissed me again. 'Your memory is really quite

extraordinary,' he told me. 'In a very bad way. I honestly don't know how you ran your own business before we met.'

'Neither do I. Trust me, I made many, many mistakes.'

Stephen sat up suddenly. 'Which reminds me! I have something for you.'

He got up, walked over to the hallway where his work satchel was hanging and returned with a little maroon booklet. 'Look what arrived on Tash's desk this afternoon. You massive goon.'

'WHAT?' I sat up. 'No! Where? How?'

Stephen grinned, handing me my passport. 'You are hopeless,' he said, snuggling back around me. 'Sylvie at the château found it and the courier dropped it off today.'

'God,' I said, mortified. 'How could I have been so stupid? I looked everywhere! I spent a fortune getting that emergency travel thing!'

Stephen kissed my ear. 'It's all part of your mad charm,' he said, nuzzling my neck. We lay there for a long time, the candlelight flickering over our bodies and the dark room behind us. The heat of the day had finally passed and the warmth of my man wrapped around me was blissful.

Being here now, so completely calm and happy, I couldn't quite believe I'd felt so hysterical when I'd spotted Stephen and Petra earlier. It seemed like something from a different world.

'Penny for your thoughts,' Stephen asked.

I smiled sheepishly. 'You may not want to hear them . . .'

'*Au contraire.*'

'I panicked when I saw you with your niece earlier,' I admitted. 'I was terrified she was . . . you know. Silly me.

I was just thinking how pathetic it is that I got into a panic. How sad and stupid.'

'Oh, Annie.'

'I know.' I paused. 'It frightens me that I can just fly off the handle like that. I don't want to be one of those paranoid women.'

'Have you been like that in the past?'

I went quiet. Stephen knew that I was not exactly flush on the ex-boyfriend front but I had yet to tell him that there had been basically no one. 'I've never had the chance to find out,' I mumbled. 'There's, um, never been anyone as amazing as you.'

'Well, keep talking to me,' he said gently. 'Don't suffer all those nasty thoughts on your own. They're destructive and horrid and they only grow in size if you keep them to yourself.'

'I know.'

Stephen pulled me closer to him. 'Annie,' he whispered. 'You're safe with me. If you're struggling, I want to help you.'

I stroked Stephen's hair. 'Thank you. I'm just a bit . . . a bit odd when it comes to men.'

Stephen watched my face but he didn't probe further. I had yet to tell him about Mum.

He smiled suddenly. 'If it helps, I felt the same about Tim. He fancies you, I'm absolutely certain of it.'

Dear God, love made you vulnerable! I almost laughed. 'He most definitely does not,' I told him. 'If I'm sure of anything, it's that Tim isn't interested in me.'

There was just the thin edge of a frown on the outskirts of Stephen's brilliant blue-eyed smile. 'I'm telling you, he fancies you! I'm a bloke. I know what we do.'

'He doesn't!' I insisted, less certainly.

'Well, I can only say what I see,' Stephen said. 'He's a good-looking chap and a nice bloke by all accounts, but there's something a bit . . . I don't know . . . *predatory* about him. At least around you. You probably think I'm being a dick now.'

'Tim! PREDATORY?' I laughed like a drain. And then stopped laughing like a drain because even though it wasn't true it was still a horrible thought.

'I'm not sure I'd win if he turned on the charm,' Stephen smiled, seeming slightly embarrassed. 'And I'm rather poor at losing.'

'Oh, Stephen Flint,' I said. 'There's no battle going on between you and Tim. But if there was, you've won it already. I'm yours! I'm the spoils of your victory! Annie Mulholland, a paranoid, sniffling mentalist, with cheap candles and stinky joss sticks all over her house!'

Stephen, satisfied, chucked me over his shoulder and took me up to bed. 'I like mentalists,' he said.

Chapter Seventeen

Kate

A little while after he had returned home, Mark drove his wheelchair all the way along the drive to the beech coppice where I was sitting under a tree, writing a letter to my family that I wouldn't be able to send.

'Well, would you look at you?' I said. 'Whizzing yourself all the way out here!'

It was a scorched, dry afternoon in August and Mark glowed in front of me like a fine Renaissance painting: olive-skinned, wavy-haired, humble and yet glorious.

'If you will keep on skulking in the woods like a hobo,' he grumbled.

I blushed at his tone: so familiar, *so unlike Mark*. It had been easier with him in the hospital bed. His immobility had made things safer. I'd been able to get close to him without feeling I needed to worry about what it meant. But here on his farm, the fields ungrazed and empty, the heather blowing up on the moor and nothing else for miles – no nurses, no machines, no fluorescent lighting – the thing between us, whatever it was, made me anxious.

'Sorry, I just don't like the film crew. They make me feel . . .' I trailed off, waving my arms.

'Exposed?'

I nodded gratefully. 'That's the one.'

Mark smiled. 'Kate, they're making a documentary about me. How do you think I feel?'

'Super-exposed?'

He sighed. 'And then some. I have no idea why I agreed to the bloody thing.' A documentary crew had been following Mark for the last couple of weeks as he prepared to take his first steps since the accident. 'We'll just blend into the background,' they'd promised, and, of course, had done nothing of the sort. I seemed to spend half my life dodging them: wearing baseball caps and sunglasses or hiding behind the livery horses Joe had managed to get in for some extra cash. I'd told them straight away that I didn't want to appear in the thing and would not sign one of their consent forms, and they were all, like, 'Of course! No *problem*! We're totally comfortable with that!'

I didn't entirely trust them, though, so I was spending quite a lot of time in hiding.

'Well, I'm sorry if it's made you uncomfortable,' Mark said. He was watching me curiously. 'I had a feeling you were just being helpful when you said you were okay with it. I should have probed further.'

'Ah, no problem. I did some special ops training a few years back so I'm decent enough at staying hidden.'

Mark chuckled. He did that quite often, these days. 'Are you being mysterious and odd, Kate Brady?'

'Mysterious and odd,' I confirmed. 'It's our family motto. *Nescio et mirum.*'

'You are very *nescio*, and monumentally *mirum*,' Mark agreed. 'Although I'm impressed you know Latin.'

'I'm not just a pretty face, boss.'

Mark smiled. 'How are your morning walks, talking

of odd? I don't catch sight of you, these days, what with having to sleep downstairs.'

'Oh, grand, you know. I love stomping around at that time of day.' I crossed my fingers behind my back.

He was pleased. 'I bet it's lovely before the heat settles in. Sometimes I imagine you out there at the crack of dawn, and think, That's the first thing I'll do when I'm walking properly.'

'Well, if you play your cards right I'll invite you along some time,' I said, before I had a chance to stop myself.

Thanks to the combination of a broken left leg and a shattered right hip socket Mark was still a few weeks off walking, which was lucky because I wasn't actually taking my walks at the moment. Since a police car had arrived last Thursday I'd been having nightmares: long, traumatic dreams followed by hours of broken sleep in my hot little bedroom. It was only when the day arrived in golden streaks under my curtains that I was finally managing to fall into an exhausted slumber.

I yawned. I was shagged.

'So I've decided to teach you to ride,' Mark announced.

'You have?'

'I have.'

'And can I ask why?' I was stalling.

'Don't you want to ride?' he asked, puzzled.

'I don't know.'

'Are you being mysterious and odd again?'

I nodded apologetically. Of course I wanted to learn to ride. But the idea of learning with Mark felt alarmingly intimate.

'You do want to learn, don't you?' he persisted.

I nodded again. I really did.

'But for reasons you're obviously not going to share, you also *don't* want to ride.'

'That's about the size of it, boss.'

Mark shook his head despairingly. 'Kate,' he said, 'I'm stuck in a wheelchair and I won't be on a horse's back for months. Perhaps ever. You can't even imagine how much I want to jump on and ride through Allercombe Woods, just me and the clump of hoofs on earth. If you won't learn to ride for you, is there any chance of you learning to ride for me?'

'You're a total fecker,' I gasped. 'That's blackmail!'

Mark sniggered.

'SHOULDERS BACK!' he roared, two hours later. 'IT'S ME WHO'S FULL OF BROKEN BONES, NOT YOU.'

'I'm comfortable like this,' I shouted back. I could see from the big mirrors on the wall of the indoor school that I was all hunched over like Quasimodo but for some reason this position felt safer.

'PUT YOUR HEELS DOWN, FOR CRYING OUT LOUD!' Mark yelled. 'Are you listening to *anything* I'm saying?'

I jogged down to where he was sitting and pulled up Marmalade, one of our livery horses, in front of him. 'Mark,' I said, 'aren't teachers meant to be nice when it's someone's first lesson? Aren't they meant to be encouraging and jolly and that?'

He was sitting in a shard of sunlight that fell through a hole in the roof. 'That was never my style.'

'Well, if teaching is going to be your sole source of

income until you can ride again, I suggest you think about revising it.'

He laughed. 'Fair. How about "You're doing okay"?'

'No, that sucks too.'

'"You're on track"?'

'Jesus, Mark. You blackmail me into learning to ride and then you abuse me for two *hours* when my arse feels like someone's been at it with the cheese grater, and the nicest thing you can say to me is that I'm on track?'

He was chuckling. 'But you look like a hunchback and your reins are too long, your toes are pointing down and you're riding about as badly as it's possible to ride. Plus you're doing it with a face of fury, which makes you look even worse. What am I meant to say?'

'The fury is concentration.'

'Whatever it is, you're terrifying. But I tell you what, I can go one better than "You're on track." Kate, I still think there's hope for you.'

I tried and failed to stop myself laughing. 'You're a massive shitebag, Mark Waverley. A massive, stinking, fly-infested shitebag.'

'Oh, Galway,' said Joe – I hadn't spotted him leaning against a metal beam. 'You're quite the charming little article, aren't you?' He was smiling but I could hear his mind at work.

'Why are you just sitting there?' Mark asked. 'Walk on, please. We're going to try trotting again.'

I groaned.

'I'm sorry, Kate, what's that? Are you suffering executive stress again?'

'What?'

'Executive stress. The thing you came here with.'

'Oh, that!'

'Yes, that. You look ever so stressed by this riding business. I'd hate to bring on a relapse.'

I coloured. 'No relapse, boss. But my *arse* . . .'

'Behave yourself,' said Mark, with a lightness to his voice that made me want to sing. And made me also want to turn the horse in the direction of the gate and gallop far, far away from there.

Twelve hours later, I woke with my heart pounding and sweat drenching my sheets.

It was that police car. That bloody police car. They'd only come to hand out a leaflet about outbuildings security, Sandra said. The Gillinghams had been burgled last week. But as I'd seen it cruising slowly down the drive that day last week I'd felt a sense of pure, unfiltered dread that had pinched at me ever since.

I sat up and drank some water, wondering if I had the energy to change my sheets.

I would Skype my family in the morning.

Chapter Eighteen

Annie

I stared at the man standing in front of me.

Yes, it really was him.

It was Stephen Flint! Right here, at St Pancras! And he had our train tickets in his hand!

'Argh,' I cried.

'Hello to you, too.'

I shook myself. 'Are you really here?'

Stephen looked round. 'I think so. I was about to get into the shower when I saw these tickets on top of the loo. I had a feeling you'd need them.'

'Argh,' I repeated. 'Hang on.'

I phoned Lizzy, who had gone off to buy us some new ones when it had become clear that I – not for the first time – had lost our pre-booked tickets. 'I left them on the loo and Stephen's brought them so don't buy new ones,' I shouted.

'Okay,' she shouted back. 'You big freak.'

I ended the call and smiled. One of those huge, all-consuming smiles I couldn't stop doing at the moment. 'I think we may need to look into hiring you a personal assistant,' Stephen suggested. 'I mean, the loo? Seriously?'

I snuggled in and kissed him. 'Thank you,' I told him. 'You're my knight in shining armour. I must have left them there so that I wouldn't forget them.'

'Well, that went badly,' he observed.

I had been even more scatterbrained of late: I'd left my phone in the fridge, I'd lost my security pass twice, and I'd managed to leave my Annie Kingdom unlocked several times. I doubted anyone at FlintSpark would come in and steal towels but it was poor practice and I'd have died if Stephen found out, especially after what he'd gone through with Jamilla earlier in the year.

Was there something you could do about poor memory? I wondered, as Stephen kissed my forehead. My head was so unreliable at the moment.

'Stephen, you're our saviour,' Lizzy said, arriving back. 'Thank you a thousand times over.'

'You're welcome. She's quite a worry, this one. But very endearing.' He slid his arm round my waist.

'Tell me about it. Well, we'd better go. See you soon, Stephen.' She kissed his cheek.

'Thank you again,' I said, throwing my arms around my man as Lizzy wobbled off in her Peak District-unfriendly sundress and heels. 'I promise to stop being so useless.'

Stephen tucked my hair behind my ear. 'I'm keeping an eye on you,' he said. 'If it gets really bad we'll ask Tim for a consultation. Anyway, I'm glad to be seeing you again. I wanted to give you a special Mum's-birthday cuddle.'

He held me tight and I felt great swells of both happiness and grief. 'Thank you,' I whispered into his chest. 'Thank you.' As our relationship and the summer had progressed, I'd found myself still unable to tell Stephen about Mum. He knew she was dead, of course – we'd talked often about how it felt to be in the world without a mother, but I hadn't found the right moment to tell him how she'd died, or how it had eventually led to my teenage crisis. Then one day a couple of weeks ago he'd arrived in my Annie Kingdom just as I was about to break for lunch, his face white with shock.

'Tell me,' he'd said. 'Annabel Mulholland, the Peak District, 1987. Tell me Georgie Mulholland wasn't your mum. Oh, God, please tell me I've somehow got it wrong.'

I had sighed, closing the door behind him so that we had some privacy. I loathed it when this happened. I had yet to find a way of coping with the horror that crossed people's faces when they realized I was *that* Annabel Mulholland. The poor girl whose mother was raped and murdered in the woods during a birthday game of hide and seek. The girl whose face had been in every newspaper for weeks, whose name was branded on a generation of minds. When I'd finally got myself sufficiently together to try a day at a sixth-form college in Chesterfield some awful man from a tabloid had sprung out of nowhere and taken a picture of me. 'Daughter of Murder Victim Starts College' the headline had read.

I had never gone back.

'Tash just sent me a link to an old article,' Stephen had said quietly. 'She said she'd always thought she recognized your name and . . . Oh, God. I don't even know what to say. My poor, poor sweet little girl.'

Now in the station he held me tightly. 'I'm sure your mum knows you go up and celebrate her birthday every year. I bet it means the world to her to know you're both still looking after your dad.'

Announcements were made, tickets were bought, trains were missed. I was in a little sub-dimension of my own. Everything felt good when Stephen was nearby, even on days like today. He helped me on to the train, then insisted on putting my overnight bag on the luggage rack.

We stood in the vestibule by the door so he wouldn't get trapped, kissing and giggling like teenagers. Stephen kept squeezing my plait. Lizzy came out and told us to get a room.

Eventually the train manager got on the Tannoy and asked anyone not travelling to disembark, and Stephen gave me one last lingering kiss.

Just as the doors locked.

'Shit. I'll climb out of the window.'

'No!' I cried. 'That's mad and dangerous. What if the train pulls away?' I grabbed his pocket, as if that was going to stop him.

'I have to get off! I have back-to-back meetings this morning!' He pawed at the window as the train began to move.

'You'll die! Which is at odds with my plans for you! You'll have to get off at Leicester.'

'*Leicester?*' Stephen pulled the window down, his handsome face creased with laughter. 'I DON'T WANT TO SPEND THE DAY IN BLOODY LEICESTER! LET ME OFF!'

It was too late. The train was gathering pace. Stephen and I stared at each other, then burst out laughing. 'Leicester it is,' he said resignedly. 'I'd better call Tash and have her reschedule everything. Unbelievable!'

When we found Lizzy, she was unsurprised. 'Twat-finks,' she said. 'You'll have to come to see Dad, Stephen. He'll be very excited.'

Stephen smiled. 'I doubt that,' he said. 'I'll get off at the next stop.'

I was thinking hard. Maybe he should come. I'd wanted to wait until . . . until what? Until I knew he was someone Dad could trust? I knew that already!

'I actually think she's right,' I said. 'Dad would be thrilled to meet you. I told him about you the other week-end and he was really pleased.'

That was a slight lie. But Dad would have been suspicious of anyone I got involved with.

Stephen looked worried. 'It'd be a bit rude to just barge in without having been invited,' he said. 'Your dad's probably really looking forward to seeing his girls. And from the sound of it, this is quite a big deal, him going for a walk with his daughters after being trapped for so long in his house. It should be just the three of you.'

Lizzy brushed him aside. 'Tosh. He'd rather meet you.'

'Are you sure?'

'Yes!'

'Okay! But I'd have brought something for him if I'd known. I've got a lovely book about Borges that he'd enjoy. And some lovely Rioja. Damn.'

I slid my arms around him. 'How did you know he likes Rioja? And Borges?'

I could feel Stephen shaking his head above me in Lizzy's direction. 'This girl forgets literally everything,' he told her. 'Every conversation we've had just disappears out of her mind. And she seems to be getting worse, not better.'

Lizzy agreed. 'She's forgotten my birthday five times in the last ten years. Once she called me Andrew. *Andrew?*'

Having failed to persuade us to upgrade to first, Stephen went off up the long, snaking train to buy us pastries, and Lizzy and I settled in for a good gossip.

We'd hardly dared talk about the changes that Dad seemed to be making in his life lest we jinx the whole thing. But as the weeks passed it had got harder to deny that things were on the move. He was doing his own grocery shopping, he was posting letters and he'd even started gardening.

'Dad's really gone to war with agoraphobia,' Lizzy said proudly. 'And all without our interference. Isn't he wonderful?'

'Beyond wonderful,' I agreed. 'Today is huge.'

Dad had emailed last week asking if we were planning to come up for Mum's birthday, as usual. We'd both said yes and then – to our absolute astonishment – he'd replied saying that he wanted to go for a *walk* along Froggatt Edge, Mum's favourite in the Peaks, and afterwards he wanted to go for a cream tea at a pub Mum used to take us to when we were tiny.

Lizzy and I had called each other and cried.

'. . . and I didn't want to say anything,' I told her now, 'but I have a feeling he might have a girlfriend.'

Lizzy was gob-smacked. 'WHAT? Tell me everything you know!' she hissed.

I told her everything I knew and she looked slightly disappointed. 'Oh. Is that it?'

'What do you mean, is that it? There's more than enough evidence here! He's admitted he's dating, he's cleaned the house and he's buying new clothes. No jogging bottoms in sight! The dropped call was the clincher, though.' I giggled. 'The sly old fox.'

'But how do you know it wasn't a marketing call?' Lizzy still wasn't convinced.

'I just knew. Remember when we were teenagers? Calling boys? We'd always put the phone down if one of their parents picked up!'

'I didn't.' Lizzy snorted.

'Oh. Well, I did.'

'Of course you did, Flannie. God, I'll be so happy if Dad's met someone.'

'Me too. I love him so much.'

'Well, he loves you too,' Lizzy reminded me. 'He loves you very much.'

'Who's that?' Stephen asked. He bore a bag of pastries and a smile. 'Tim?'

'Eh?'

'Tim loves you very much?'

Lizzy looked confused. 'No, we were talking about Dad.'

'Oh! Silly me. Sorry.'

'Although I'm convinced Tim does too,' Lizzy muttered.

'Oh, Lizzy, don't . . .'

'Me too!' Stephen jumped in. 'I'm certain of it! Didn't I tell you, Annie?'

'You did. And I'm telling you. Both of you. There's about as much chance of Tim fancying me as there is of Lizzy seducing Boris Johnson.'

Lizzy frowned. 'I've always had a bit of a thing about Bozza, as it goes . . .' She looked preoccupied. 'Stephen, this is really interesting. Do you really think Tim's pining after Annie? Because I've thought that for bloody years.'

Stephen looked at me, to check I didn't mind this conversation happening. I did mind. 'Stop it,' I said. 'Both of you.'

'He turned up at her house the night before last,' Stephen stage-whispered to Lizzy. 'Late.'

'*Eh?*' Lizzy and I said, at the same time.

'You went to bed before me, remember? I was downstairs catching up on emails and he knocked. I saw him through the peephole. He was visibly drunk so I crept away. Does he do that often? Because it seemed a bit weird to me.'

I was thrown. Why on earth had Tim turned up at my house? Could Stephen actually be on to something?

Lizzy was pretty grossed out, too. 'That's just weird,' she said. 'Doesn't sound like Tim. God, Annie, maybe you've made him lose his mind.'

'I'm not having this conversation. This is Tim we're talking about, not some freak. He often works late at Homerton Hospital – he was probably just walking past.'

'Walking past your house on his way to Bethnal Green? Really?'

After a long pause, during which I had to admit to myself that it was indeed quite strange, Stephen said, 'Just keep an eye on him. We men are pretty determined when we want something!'

Lizzy shoved a pastry into her mouth. She didn't like it either.

Dad and Stephen got on like a house on fire. Dad had lent Stephen a summer waterproof and some walking boots from his own sizeable collection – which had sat unused for more than a decade – and thought Stephen looked 'very fine' in them. I agreed readily. Every now and then I weakened and tried to kiss him unobtrusively, and every time Dad clocked us and I felt like a teenager caught groping her spotty boyfriend.

Dad and Stephen walked together for a good hour while Lizzy and I trailed behind. Froggatt Edge was beautiful today: rugged and scrubby, the heathery wildness of White Edge looming off to our left and the Derwent snaking through the valley far below. Only tiny shreds of cloud broke up the vast blue sheet of sky overhead.

'This is the happiest day,' I said to Lizzy. 'Look. Look at Dad, just *walking*.'

Lizzy nodded. 'I can't believe it,' she said softly. 'Daddy.'

'And he even seems to like Stephen. Would you believe it, Dad agreeing to trust him, just like that?' Dad laughed at something Stephen was saying.

'There is literally nothing not to like about your boyfriend, though.'

'It makes it very easy, being with a man who gets on so well with everyone. I have no idea how he does it – he just seems to fit in wherever he goes. He's so bloody charming! And yet it's all real, too.'

Lizzy made a vomiting noise.

'Sorry.'

'No, I'm just jealous. And you're right – having someone you know everyone'll like makes all the difference. When's he going to meet Kate?'

A hawk was circling overhead, uninterested in the monumental events that were unfolding below. 'Soon, hopefully. She's been quite shit at keeping in touch since she went off to this farm, but Stephen's up for taking a trip to meet her, maybe in September. I just need to get her to be a bit less vague and flaky so we can actually make a plan. I mean, I don't even know if the farm's in Ireland! All I know is that it's really remote because her phone doesn't work any more. She's being very mysterious, you know.'

'Sounds like a scandal to me!'

'Probably, knowing Kate. Well, next time she calls I'm going to demand full disclosure and a farm invite. I need her to meet Stephen – she's very excited about him.'

'Ah, young love.' Lizzy beamed. 'You're so proud of him, and it's very sweet.'

'Your turn next, Lizzy Lou.'

'Maybe.' She gazed out at the view, a little shadow falling over her pretty face. 'I really must stop this stupid dating nonsense and try to meet a proper person I want to be with *all* the time.' She tucked a windblown strand of hair behind her ear. 'Although that's pretty scary.'

I wanted to hug my beautiful sister. I wanted to tell her that what we'd been through was not a life sentence, that it could be overcome and the patterns broken.

But I trusted her to find this out for herself. She was a formidable woman, Lizzy Mulholland, and the fact that we were even having this conversation meant that she was on her way.

Later, we went to a pub tucked away by the river outside Hathersage. We sat outside, even though it was still windy, and ate scones, cream and jam, and drank three large pots of tea between us, which left us a bit wired and maybe a little more open than we would normally have been.

'I want to propose a toast to this fine young man,' Dad said, raising his mug. 'I think he's superb.' Over the years Dad had picked up a faint Derbyshire accent. Lizzy and I both smiled at the way he said 'superb'. I couldn't have been happier than I was at that moment, surrounded by the people who mattered to me most, Dad making his way back into the world.

'I was so embarrassed to crash your day, but I'm glad I did,' Stephen said. 'And I'd love to have met Georgie so that I could thank her for bringing this beautiful little hippie into the world . . . But I'm delighted to be meeting you, at least, Bert.'

Dad's eyes filled with tears and he raised his cup again. A blackbird landed in the tree behind him and broke into song. 'To my Georgie,' he whispered, 'who would have been so happy today.' He smiled at Stephen, as if to say thank you, and a tear slid quietly down his face.

'To Georgie,' Stephen repeated. Then, softly: 'And to my own lovely mum. Miss you.'

The vivid green of the peaty grass blurred as my own eyes filled with tears. The blackbird warbled again, a beautiful ripple of music against the chatter of the river.

'I might go and ask if they've got any cakes,' Lizzy said eventually. 'Is that a good plan, everyone?'

'Yes,' said everyone, and the mood was restored.

Hello, Mum, I said in my head. *Isn't this a lovely day?*

Chapter Nineteen

Kate

'Bye, guys,' I said, waving one last time before shutting down the Skype window.

I rested my head in my hands for a few moments, fighting, as I did every time I saw my family, to steady myself before the guilt took me over. They still hadn't the faintest idea. 'Please come home soon,' they'd said just now. 'We miss you so much.'

It wasn't just the guilt that killed me, though. There was something else that was beginning to happen when I spoke to them. A jumpiness, a frustratingly unspecific sense of trouble ahead. *Tick tock, tick tock, tick tock*, it whispered, refusing to elaborate. The summer had ambled into autumn and the trees had begun to speckle gold. Soon winter would be here, with its freezing mornings and endless rug changes.

Tick tock, tick tock.

It wasn't just the changing seasons, though. It was something else. Something bigger.

You've stayed here too long, whispered the Bad Shit, as I pulled on some riding gloves. *You're going to get found out* . . .

'I want you to start riding Stumpy,' Mark said that evening. I'd just padded into his dining room in my socks and jodhpurs, as I'd been doing every day since he'd had his accident and Joe and I had agreed to keep Sandra company in the evenings. When Mark had come home we'd somehow just carried on eating there: we were no substitute for Ana Luisa but we made sure things were lively and upbeat.

'What?'

'I want you to start riding Stumpy.'

'But you've retired him!'

Mark sat down, moving a pile of paperwork to one side so I could have a space opposite him. 'Retiring him doesn't mean he needs to sit in his stable with a pipe and dressing gown, Kate. He's young and strong and he'll get really depressed if he never goes out.'

I gaped at him. Nobody was allowed to ride Stumpy! Mark had broken him in when he was four and had been Stumpy's sole rider ever since. But last week, after months in the stable with his enormous bandage, Stumpy's X-ray had indicated that his pastern had healed and he was to be allowed some controlled exercise on the lead-rope, followed by gentle riding.

'Are you *serious?*'

'Yes. I know how much you love him. I heard that you threatened to – what was it? – to deck Maria if she had him put down.'

I blushed. 'Oh, that.'

'So that's settled. You'll ride Stumpy. And don't you dare get emotional.'

'Roger,' I muttered, fighting tears with an iron fist. 'Um, where's your mum, anyway?' The kitchen was dark and Dirk and Woody were sitting in the doorway looking suicidal, which meant they hadn't been fed.

Mark glanced around. 'Oh! Of course. She's gone on a date with George.'

'REALLY?'

Mark grinned. 'Yes. She was wearing a skirt when she left. I nearly fainted.'

'Well well well.' I giggled. 'I've a mind to put a curfew on that one if she gets frisky. Oh, good old Sandra. And good old George!' George was one of the owners of the livery horses. He was a delightful man who wore a tweed jacket and a tie every single day, and he'd been asking Sandra out for ages.

'Ana Luisa said, "Gran, be careful. George might get ideas if you show him too much leg."' He shook his head, laughing at the memory. Ana Luisa was staying for the half-term holidays and Mark couldn't have been happier. 'She's an outrage, my daughter.'

'She'll need feeding,' I said.

'She will. Ana Luisa?'

Nothing.

'Ana Luisa!'

'Dad, I'm busy,' came the shout from upstairs. 'Will you leave my dinner outside my bedroom door, please? And soon. I'm starving.'

Mark and I looked at each other. Joe was out seducing the new receptionist at the vet's and he was normally the back-up cook when Sandra wasn't around. It was dawning on us both that we were going to have to cook a meal. Together. And eat it together, without even the ferocious company of Ana Luisa.

Get a grip, Brady, I told myself. You are more than capable of having some food with your boss.

Forty minutes later we had something that was reasonably similar to sausage and mash. I'd shoved the sausages head first into the mash so they stood up out of the potato and Mark had put together some quite bad gravy and overcooked peas.

Ana Luisa, unable to wait any longer, had come down to harry us along.

'Dad!' she shouted, when he put the dish on the table.

'Yes?'

'DAD!'

'What?' Mark had his hands on his hips.

'*Everything,*' she replied derisively. 'Just everything. This is the worst meal I've ever seen!'

'It's an unpleasant-looking thing,' Mark admitted. 'But it tastes good. Look!' He pulled a sausage out of its mash mooring and dipped it into his thin gravy. 'Mmmm!' He ruffled her hair and she slapped him off, smoothing down her shiny mane.

'You are a tragedy,' she told him. 'This is a terrible dinner! What if Granny goes off and marries George? What are you going to eat then, Daddy? You could die of bad food!'

Mark was shaking with laughter. 'You may well be right,' he said.

'I'm going to get a packet of crisps and I want you to think about what you've done,' she told him. 'I love you, Daddy, but this is just not good enough.'

Mark and I cried with laughter as his daughter marched into the kitchen and then back out with a packet of McCoy's hanging disdainfully from her fingers. 'Shocking,' she said. 'Absolutely shocking, the pair of you.'

She paused to kiss her dad on the way, then stomped out, her hair all flicky and stylish, a proper little lady.

Mark mopped his eyes. 'Right. Well, it's just you and me, then.'

'Indeed. A date!'

What had I just said? I had never hated myself as much as I did at this moment.

'Er, yes . . .' Mark said. Then: 'Um, no. Ha-ha. Ha-ha-ha.'

'Obviously I was joking . . .'

At least Mark had the decency to look as embarrassed as I felt. I sat down and pulled one of my legs up on the chair next to me. Just to show how casual I was. Just to show this was not, and never would be, a date, Mark pulled out a sausage with his thumb and forefinger and started eating it like that. *Casual*.

Ana Luisa reappeared in the doorway. She leaned against the door frame, one leg crossed over the other, appraising us coolly. 'You're on a date, did you say?' She ate a crisp. 'I was just outside, listening in.'

Mark started to tell her that eavesdropping was not a great quality in any human being but she interrupted him. 'You *are* on a date, aren't you?' she said. 'You're both looking very strange in the face, and Kate is wearing make-up and she never wears make-up.' She looked at me. 'Do you fancy my dad?' she asked.

I had a forkful of mash halfway up to my mouth. 'Huh?'

'Do you fancy my dad?' she repeated. 'Everyone else does, apart from Mum. All the mothers at school and all the women he teaches riding to. And everyone else. Everyone fancies my dad. Do you?'

'Of course not!'

Ana Luisa wasn't pleased. 'Why not?'

Oh, holy God.

'Ana Luisa . . .' Mark began. I could see he was torn between terrible fear and terrible amusement. 'Look here –'

But she cut across him: 'She fancies you, Dad. Why don't you grow a pair and ask her out?'

Chapter Twenty

Annie

Autumn. London grew colder and brighter; the days shorter and the nights sharp. I was still as high as a kite, dizzy with looping, spiralling love.

Le Cloob were meeting tonight, having had quite a poor summer.

Stephen was in West Sussex with his father. I was rather relieved he was there because if he'd been at home I'd probably have cancelled Le Cloob. He would never have tried to stop me seeing my friends, of course, but I couldn't stand the guilt of leaving him in that great big house, all stressed and lonely.

Poor Stephen was having a horrible time. Something – everything, it seemed – was going wrong at his New York office and he was having to spend half his life either working late in London or, frequently, flying to New York to deal with it in person. Meanwhile his father, whose grief was rolling on with the grim determination of a five-tonne lorry, had become suddenly needy and Stephen had been summoned down there several times, often late at night.

He was exhausted. Eating badly, drinking too much, often very scratchy and tense. I watched him running around, trying to make things better for his grieving father and I loved him. The man was at his physical and mental limits, yet still he took his dad's calls, still he drove down to West Sussex, even though the round trip took more than four hours, and even though he was on his knees with tiredness.

I had no idea what I could do for him, so I'd decided just to be the best girlfriend I could be.

Tim and Claudine were at a table next to the bar, talking over a candle. My heart swelled.

'Hello!' I cried.

Claudine had a scowl as long as a baguette. And Tim looked like someone had stuck a baguette up his bottom.

'I am surprised you came,' Claudine said, by way of a greeting. 'And where is your sister? She is always late. I am sick of it.'

'I'm sure she's on her way,' I said. 'What do you mean, you're surprised I came?'

Claudine just shook her head.

'Um, hello,' I said, bending down to kiss Tim.

He took my hand and squeezed it very tightly. 'I've missed you,' he said. He looked tired and unusually scruffy.

As summer had turned into autumn Tim had seemed to become sadder, not happier. Stephen thought it was because he was pining for me; I thought he just wasn't over Mel.

Claudine poured some Merlot then fixed her beady eyes on me. 'So, Stephen has kidnapped you and you are not allowed to spend time with us,' she said.

'Sorry?' Not this again.

She merely raised an eyebrow.

'Well, he's having a pretty bad time at the moment,' I

began. I glanced at Tim – *help me out here* – but he was just watching me with glassy detachment. 'But, um, I've only missed one Le Cloob, haven't I?'

'You 'ave missed three,' Claudine said coolly. 'And you do not reply to my messages, and Tim said you've ignored several voicemails that he 'as left you. Tell me, Annabel, is this the behaviour of an old friend?'

I stared stupidly at them. 'What do you mean I've missed three? What? Voicemails? Messages?'

Claudine looked impatient. 'Oh, please,' she muttered.

I began to panic. I surely couldn't have been that bad? Could I?

Shit, I thought miserably. I probably could. There had definitely been voicemails I hadn't listened to and it wouldn't surprise me in the slightest if I'd managed to completely overlook text messages. I'd been doing it for years. But never to the extent that I'd offended Le Cloob. *I have to sort myself out*, I thought anxiously. *These people would move mountains for me, yet I can't even reply to their text messages?*

'I'm really sorry,' I said, slumping into my chair. 'I . . . It's been really busy. We went on a few little holidays in the summer . . . And now, well, there's just lots of shit going on for Stephen. I've been trying to help him. Dry cleaning, looking after his house, cooking for him, that sort of stuff.'

Claudine was disgusted. 'You 'ave been acting as 'is 'ousekeeper?'

'No! Of course not! And he's forever trying to stop me! I'm just helping out when I can.' I tried to look stronger than I felt. 'That's what you do in a relationship,' I added.

'Good to have some variation, though, don't you think?'

Tim said mildly. 'You do seem to be with him most nights, Pumpkin. And doing his laundry the rest of the time. Do you not think it might be a good idea to have some other things going on?'

I stared at him in disbelief. Tim? Tim was jumping on the bandwagon, too? 'I am *not* with him all the time!' I said. 'And the laundry was just an example! Stop acting like I'm That Girl!'

Claudine fixed me with her deadliest stare. 'Well, then, stop *being* That Girl.'

Lizzy arrived. 'Hi, darlings,' she said, without kissing any of us. She fell into her seat and reached over to grab my wine, which she downed in one. 'Urgh,' she said.

Well, I'm glad I came tonight, I thought. *Cheers, everyone! Good health!* I went to the loo and asked myself to please be nice and consider that not everyone was as lucky as I was right now. I had a little text-off with Stephen and as usual I felt better. He was the best drug. He should have been available on the NHS.

When I got back to the table, Lizzy asked me what was going on. 'You've disappeared off the face of the earth, darling,' she said.

I sighed. After Le Cloob had bollocked me *en masse* in the summer I'd tried really hard to improve matters, but Stephen was having such a particularly difficult time at the moment, and on the rare occasions he was free he had a rather lovely habit of whisking me away for nights at beautiful hotels. What was I meant to do? Tell him, 'No, thanks'? 'You all just think I've gone mad, don't you?' I said. 'You just think I'm in this mad whirlwind of obsession and I'm letting my life slip by the wayside.'

Nobody argued, and I felt tears spring to my eyes.

'It's fine, sweetheart,' Lizzy said flatly. 'Just make a bit more you time. And reply to your bloody messages!'

'I do!'

Le Cloob rolled a collective eye.

The evening limped on in a crappy fashion. Lizzy told us that both of the men she was dating had found out about each other and dumped her. She was 'a bit upset'. 'But more just disappointed in myself,' she said, in a moment of uncharacteristic self-reflection. 'What am I doing?'

Tim, who probably knew exactly what she was doing, merely stared at her in an unfocused sort of a way.

I went to the toilet again.

Everything there was a lot more jolly: I'd had another text message from Stephen, who was making dinner for his dad. *How is Le Cloob? Have you told them our news? I cannot wait, my little Pumpkin. Literally cannot wait. Love you xxxx*

Funny. Tim had always called me Pumpkin. Maybe I looked like one.

I called him.

'Everything all right?' he said. The TV in the background faded as he moved off to talk to me.

I sighed. 'Not really. Stephen, have I just been with you for the last few months? Have I really just shut myself off from the world? They said I'm either with you or running around doing your errands.'

There was a silence. Then: 'Well, my little Pumpkin, I guess, thinking about it, you have been a bit too kind to me recently. Perhaps they're right. Perhaps you should be spending more time with them.'

I bit my lip.

'I mean, you love spending time with them, don't you?' he continued. 'They're your best friends.'

'They don't feel very friendly, these days,' I admitted. As soon as I'd said it, I hated myself. But it's true, I thought. They've given me nothing but shit since I started going out with Stephen. Which would be reasonable if he was bad news, but he's the nicest man in London!

'Pumpkin?'

'Tim calls me . . .'

'Tim calls you what?' Stephen sounded faintly suspicious.

'Nothing.' I didn't want to tell him Tim called me Pumpkin too. Something told me he wouldn't like that.

'Look, Pumpkin,' Stephen said. 'The most important people to spend time with are the ones who make you feel fantastic about yourself. Who you enjoy seeing every time, even when the chips are down. If Le Cloob make you feel like that then of course see them more. I'm certainly not expecting you to run around doing my chores, even though it's been unbelievably sweet of you to do so.'

But they don't make me feel fantastic about myself, I thought. In fact, these days, they make me feel rubbish.

'Go and tell them our news,' Stephen urged. 'I think their reaction will tell you all you need to know! I'm sure they'll be thrilled.'

He was right. It'd be a good test.

'I love you,' I told him, and marched back out to the restaurant.

'I have news!' I said, sitting back down. 'I'm moving in with Stephen!'

Le Cloob stared.

'I finally told Mr Pegler what his house was worth, and he tried to let me stay on at the same rent but his son had other ideas. It's going to cost me a fortune now so I've handed in my notice. And Stephen asked me to move in. So – ta-da! We're going to cohabit from Christmas onwards!'

'*What?*' said Claudine, eventually.

'Jesus!' said Lizzy, looking really upset.

And: 'Oh,' said Tim.

I took a good look at them. All three of them. *None* of them was happy for me. Not even Lizzy. In fact Lizzy, to my horror, burst into tears.

'My lovely Annie,' she said, wiping her eyes with her sleeve and trying to hug me sideways. 'I'm so, so sorry. Ignore me. I'm truly excited for you, darling, I really am, but I just . . . Oh, God, I'm sorry.'

I pulled back, staring at her in bewilderment. 'But what? What's going on?'

Lizzy grabbed a napkin from the bread basket and shoved it in her face, crumbs flying everywhere and sticking to her tears. This was not like my beautifully presented sister at all. I repeated my question.

'Love,' she replied sadly. 'Or lack of it. I'm so sorry, I don't want to ruin your moment, darling, but you've kind of pulled the rug from under my feet. We'd been doing so well at avoiding love, you and me, and then you went and got all brave and let Stephen love you and I just . . .' She sobbed into the napkin until Tim, as if roused from the dead, passed her the packet of tissues he always carried around.

Lizzy eventually cleared up her face. Claudine, I noticed, had not said anything.

'Apols,' Lizzy said weakly. 'This is awful behaviour. I'm just feeling rather sad and left behind. Scared I'll never be able to do it. Bollocks, maybe *I* need therapy.'

'You'll be fine, Lizzy Lou,' I said gently. 'If you're ready for love then love will sure as hell be ready for you. You're every man's dream, darling, you have it all.'

'You do,' Tim chimed in, although he sounded fairly unconvincing. 'You're lovely, Lizzy. And gorgeous. Not to mention super-clever.'

Lizzy made her best and bravest attempt at a smile. 'Kate,' she said. 'We need Kate Brady. I'm sure she'll be thrilled for you, Annie, my love. None of the awful reactions you're getting from us bunch of old goats.'

Privately, I couldn't have agreed more. I hoped Kate would ring me soon. I needed a friend who was always happy for me, whatever I did, whatever I said. A friend who didn't always have my past in mind, who didn't think they knew what was best for me.

'She will be happy,' I agreed. 'And, Lizzy, I mean it. Your time will come soon.'

Claudine said, 'I am going to order the plum clafoutis for dessert.'

'*Really?*' I said. 'That's all you have to say?'

Claudine's eyes flashed and my heart sank. I had roused the tiger. We all went out of our way to avoid rousing the tiger.

'Actually, I am not 'aving the plum clafoutis,' she said stiffly. 'If I 'ave to listen to this bullshit a moment longer I will have to poison your desserts. So I am leaving. I am sick of having friends who disappear up the arsehole of their own love-lives. Call me when you 'ave something better to talk about.'

Ʌnd with that, she left.

'That went well,' I said.

Tim gave me a funny look. 'Well, it's all pretty sudden, Annie. You've really not known him very long.'

How's it going? Stephen texted. *Have you told them yet? I'm sure they'll be thrilled for you. X*

I walked to the tube with Tim at the end of the night. He'd apologized, earlier, for taking a crap all over my news, but we both knew it was too late. My friends were clearly convinced that I was insane, and I was terrified that they might be right. It reminded me painfully of being seventeen, of watching myself constantly for signs of another downward turn, waiting for the tightening sensations that would herald the return of the panic attacks.

I was sick of it. Sick of never being able to fully trust myself.

As we drifted down into the tube station, behind a crowd of drunk young people singing some song I was clearly too old to know, Tim suddenly stopped. 'You really are in love with him, aren't you?'

'I am.' I felt it fill my chest and lungs. 'It was just as you said, Tim. A drug. The breath of life. Everything.'

I saw intense pain in his eyes. 'Oh, Tim,' I said softly. 'Timmy, what's going on? Is it Mel? Are you still heartbroken? Please talk to me.'

But please don't say anything I don't want to hear.

Tim carried on staring at me, as if sizing up whether or

not to share. Then part of him withdrew. 'I'm all right,' he said. 'Just thinking about love, and feeling sad – same as Lizzy, I suppose. It's harder to pretend you're okay about not having it when you can see it happening to someone else.'

I put my hand on his shoulder, wishing so desperately that I could help. 'But you'll find it! Tim, of all the men I know . . . you're wonderful. How could you not find love?'

He was staring blankly at the advertising screens sliding past us as we descended the escalator. 'I did find love,' he said when we got to the bottom. 'I found love unlike any-thing I could've imagined. I've loved this girl for years.'

A train whined in beside us on the southbound platform, letting out a cloud of drunken shouting. Its passengers streamed past us and up into Clapham Common station. I stood rooted to the spot while things in my head moved slowly and unevenly.

Tim's eyes gaped with sudden tears. 'But unfortunately the girl I loved didn't love me back. She still doesn't. I'm sorry, I need to go.' He followed the noisy crowd on to the ascending escalator. I stood at the bottom, watching his slumped, sad back struggling up into Clapham Common station and tried with all my strength to squash my thoughts before they gained traction and became real.

I felt a bit sick. I needed to get back to Stephen.

After what I thought to be a decent interval I walked back out of the tube station and hailed a cab I couldn't afford.

I didn't care. The Underground was making me feel panicky and I needed to hear his voice.

Stephen's phone nearly rang out, but at the last minute it was answered.

'Hello?' said a girl's voice.

I checked my phone. I'd definitely called Stephen.

'Hello? Who is this?' she asked.

As if winded I fell backwards into the taxi seat.

No. No no no.

We crawled past the dismal bars on Clapham High Street, overflowing with mini-skirted girls and overweight men, and the driver turned on his radio.

My chest felt like someone was sitting on it.

I went to call Lizzy, but couldn't. None of Le Cloob wanted to talk to me.

Kate, I thought desperately. I'll call Kate Brady. But as I scrolled frantically for her number I remembered that she was still on her farm in the middle of nowhere.

'Mum,' I whispered, as the first tear appeared. 'Mum, I need you.'

Chapter Twenty-one

Annie

I let myself into Stephen's house and got into his bed, my knees pulled up against my chest. If I went to my own house it would be like admitting there was a problem.

From time to time I managed to be rational. I mean, when would Stephen have an affair? Every moment he wasn't at work, he was with me. And he really *was* at work when I thought he was: he answered if I called his direct line; he'd send me selfies of him and the team pulling self-pitying faces by the conference phone, or he'd have Tash call me and tell me how late he was running.

And on top of there not being enough hours in the day for him to have an affair, there was the fact that he loved me. And told me so frequently. You could fake many things in life, but not love.

Which meant that I was being insane and irrational. Again.

Some time later I heard a key in the front door. 'Annie? Pumpkin?'

Stephen stood in the bedroom doorway, ragged with exhaustion. 'You keep cancelling my calls. Sweetheart, what's going on?'

'A girl answered your phone.'

Stephen frowned. 'What – Tara?'

'Who's Tara?'

Stephen leaned against the door frame. 'Oh, my God. Tell me this isn't what I think it is.'

I said nothing and Stephen began to look angry. He wasn't meant to look angry. He was meant to look contrite and reassuring.

'Tara is Dad's sister, my aunt,' he said flatly. 'Whose house I spent half my childhood playing at. Who is more like my mother than ever, now that Mum's dead. Tara is my aunt,' he repeated. 'And if she picked up the phone it's probably because she thought it was Dad's.'

He ran his hand over his face. 'God,' he said, to no one in particular.

'You've never mentioned her,' I whispered.

Stephen put his head back against the wall. As if to say, 'Give me strength.'

'I have,' he said eventually. His voice was kinder than his face suggested. 'I promise you, Annie, I have. I think I even mentioned her when I met Le Cloob back in June. In fact, I know I did. We talked about my aunt Tara and Claudine's aunt Juliette. Why don't you call one of them?'

'Because they'll think I'm mad.'

Stephen watched me. Then he came over and sat on the side of the bed. I could smell the faint shadow of his man perfume, expensive, sophisticated, alluring. Christ. What was a man like this doing with someone like me? 'Let me show you a picture of Tara,' he said, scrolling through his photos. 'There you go. That's who answered the phone just now. If you want we can ring her.'

'Then she'll think I'm mad, too.'

The woman, who looked tall and slightly vague, was

most definitely not like Stephen's lover. I gazed at my man, who was stooped and exhausted after another long day at work and an evening with a grief-stricken father. And I knew he was telling the truth. 'I'm sorry,' I muttered. 'I did it again, didn't I?'

Stephen shrugged. 'I won't pretend I'm not upset, and a little insulted, because I am. I've never given you any reason not to trust me, yet you seem not to.' I cringed. 'But I get it, Annie,' he said softly. 'I get it.'

'You get what? That I'm mad? Stephen, I don't *want* to be mad. I want to be happy and normal and trusting! I hate that I see the worst in everyone. It's awful!'

Stephen took my hand. 'Stop that. You've just gone through a hell of a lot in your life, and you've ended up a lot more . . . anxious than most. "Mad" is a very unkind word.' I ran a finger over his stubble. 'But you have seemed more paranoid in recent months. More forgetful. More kind of, like, I dunno. Like you're slightly in a world of your own.'

I started to cry. Shit. *Shit.*

'Oh, Annie, don't cry. That doesn't mean I think you're mad,' he said. 'But maybe we just need to get you a bit of help. A bit of coaching? Or some counselling maybe.' He looked doubtful. 'I don't know much about that stuff. Do you think you should talk to Tim? He knows the most about your past, doesn't he?'

'Yeah.' I was horrified. Was it really coming to this? Was someone other than me suggesting I needed help? 'I don't want to talk to Tim.'

Stephen was taking off his shoes. 'Why?'

'He was weird tonight.'

Stephen shoved his shoes under the bed and slid in next to me in his suit. 'Well, I won't say I Told You So. What happened?'

I told him everything, about how hostile Le Cloob had been, how attacked I'd felt but how worried I was that they were right. How worried I was that my head wasn't functioning very well. And, finally, how worried I was that Tim might have been talking about me when he announced his long-term broken heart. 'That's the worst bit,' I whispered. 'The thought of Tim thinking about me in . . .' I swallowed '. . . in *that way*.'

Stephen lay on his back, staring at the ceiling.

I watched him. 'What are you thinking?'

'Nothing.'

'Stephen . . .'

He rolled over to face me. 'I'm thinking your friends seem neither to like nor trust me. And *you* don't seem to trust me either. And now your best male friend, who I've been telling you is in love with you from day *one*, has now pretty much admitted to just that. And I'm thinking I just don't like any of this but I don't feel like there's anything I can say. They're your best friends. Your family, even. They've helped you get through a difficult life and have been there for you, always. What can I possibly say against them?'

To my intense surprise, Stephen's eyes had become dangerously shiny. 'You and me are like . . .' he paused '. . . this beautiful thing. This simple, lovely thing that's not like anything I've had before. And yet it just seems like around us there are all these obstacles. Sometimes I wish we could shut everyone else out and just be you and me on our own.'

He rolled on to his back again. 'But I know that's not reasonable,' he added.

I shuffled into his side, smelling his tired skin and faded man perfume. 'I know what you mean.'

'You do?'

'I do. I'm not enjoying seeing Le Cloob at the moment. I don't agree that they don't like you but they . . . I dunno. They just aren't supportive.'

Stephen grimaced. 'I'm sure Tim'd support you.'

'Stephen, don't. We don't even know it was me he was talking about.'

'Oh, come on!'

I sighed. I had never received even the faintest signal that Tim was in love with me. That three-week fling we'd had when we were nineteen had been driven not by intense feelings but by intense confusion: how could we be so close and *not* feel that way towards each other?

Since then: nothing. Not a whiff. From either of us. But when he'd gone all intense and started talking about his unrequited love earlier, my body had gone into emergency lockdown. The panic had come before my head had even had time to process what was going on. And while I wasn't all that willing to trust my head, these days, I knew I could always trust my body.

Something was there. And I didn't want it.

'I can understand why you'd rather think he wasn't talking about you,' Stephen said. 'But I'm afraid I have to disagree. For the third and final time, I'm a man. I know how we work. And Tim has more than a passing crush on you, sweetheart. I mean, quite apart from the way he looks at you there's the fact that he turned up at your house at, like, midnight or something, all mad and drunk. Then he dumps his girlfriend, ooh, surprise surprise, not long after you and I start going out. He realizes he can't carry on with her. And now he's just telling you that he's been in love with "someone" for ever and she doesn't feel the same!' Stephen was almost laughing, although he didn't sound very jolly. 'Come *on*, Annie!'

Little worms of fear began to move in my stomach.

'I don't think he's in love with Claudine or your sister,' Stephen said mildly.

'No.'

'And is there anyone else in his life it could be? Any other girl he's known for years?'

I thought about it, even though I already knew the answer. 'No. Just me.'

Stephen was watching me. 'Annie,' he said, 'I don't want you getting all worked up about this. I mean, I know you don't trust men very much, for understandable reasons, but him having thoughts about you doesn't mean he's suddenly dangerous or anything.'

He stroked my face. 'Pumpkin? Are you in there? I said, I don't want you worrying.'

I shuddered. I didn't want Tim or anyone else having thoughts about me. Not those sort of thoughts.

My phone broke the silence. Stephen's face said, *I bet that's Tim.*

It was.

I looked at my watch. Ten past midnight. What should I do? The idea of having to go the whole night without knowing what he wanted was even worse than the idea of having to talk to him.

Stephen shrugged. 'Answer it.'

My finger shook as I swiped to answer the call.

'Tim?'

'Hiya. I just had a call from Gastro.'

'Sorry?'

'The restaurant. You left your bank card there. The booking was in my name so they called me. Just thought I'd let you know.'

'Oh, thanks,' I said, profoundly relieved. 'I'll, er, I'll text you tomorrow about maybe picking it up from the hospital on my way home from work.'

'Left your bank card?' Stephen whispered, smiling. I nodded.

'I can drop it round after work, if you want?' Tim was saying. 'Or we could go for a drink?'

'Oh, right, um, maybe.'

Tim paused. 'I feel like I said things tonight that were confusing and unclear and I . . . I want to say them properly. You mean too much to me to let them go half said.'

'It's fine!' I said. 'No need!'

'No, I really do need to talk to you. Can I call you when I finish work?'

No, you can't. 'Um, okay.'

'Night then, Pumpkin,' he said. 'Sleep well.'

Stephen pulled me close to him. 'Stop it,' he said. 'Stop worrying. Tim is not dangerous, Annie, he's your friend. But I can't imagine you're very keen on this "chat".'

I'd never been less keen on anything in my life.

I watched a tiny bug make its way across Stephen's dove-grey wall. It was six thirty and still dark. How quickly the autumn had come, I thought, after what felt like the summer of my life.

I'd barely slept. At one stage I'd had a lucid dream when I'd thought Tim was in the room, watching me, only I couldn't move, couldn't talk, couldn't do a thing. I was paralysed.

When I woke up properly, I told myself not to be so silly. Reminded myself of what a lovely, sweet, respectful man Tim Furniss was, and what a precious friendship we had. But the spirals of panic multiplied and my heart continued to thump at a rate that was never going to allow sleep.

At four o'clock I had decided I was going to call my therapist today. Stephen was right: I was not in a great place, and if this thing with Tim was what I feared it to be, I was going to need help.

'He's always staring at you, Mum,' Lizzy used to say, when Mum told her off for being mean about Neil Derrick. 'I think he's weird. Why does he have to have such skinny legs?'

'Neil's a sweetheart,' Mum would say. 'He's just a bit different from you or me, Lizzy. Please be nice to him, darling.'

But Lizzy had been right. He was always staring at Mum. Always crossing the road to say hello in that funny voice of his.

Stephen was still asleep, an arm flung across his face, his chest rising and falling slowly. His phone vibrated continually with messages and emails but he slept on.

Just as he began to stir, my own phone vibrated.

Tim.

Can we meet at 6.30 tonight? At the Elderfield? Could really do with a chat. Let me know. Tx

I put the phone down to find Stephen's ice-blue eyes watching me. 'Hello,' he said, stretching cat-like across the bed. 'What's going on?'

'Tim. Wanting to see me tonight.'

Stephen yawned, curling himself around me. 'And what do you want?'

'Not to see him.'

Stephen buried his nose in my hair. 'Pumpkin, I'm worried that I've made you unduly paranoid.'

'You haven't. I do a good line in paranoia without any need of help.'

I felt Stephen smile into my hair. 'Do you want me to put him off for you? Buy you a bit of time?'

I pulled back to see his face. 'Would you mind?'

'Of course not.'

'Then yes, please. Stephen, I –' I took a deep breath. 'I'm going to call my therapist. Get an appointment.'

Stephen hugged me. 'Good girl. We'll get through this. I'm taking the liberty of giving you the day off, so you can get your head straight. And I'm giving myself the liberty of a morning off to look after you.'

I filled Stephen's beautiful cast-iron bath while he called Tim and told him I had food poisoning and wasn't going anywhere today. I jumped when I heard my own phone ring, and panicked when I saw it was from a withheld number. I let it ring out, and felt sick when a message came through.

But it was Kate. Rambling on happily about her life on the farm, telling me I was a funny old fool and that she missed me, she'd be sure to visit London soon. I smiled. Good. If anything was going to help glue Le Cloob together, it would be our Irish friend.

Stephen let me laze around in the bath for a while before he climbed in, too, ignoring his phone, which buzzed imperiously and without pause. 'How did he take it?' I asked.

'He'll survive.' He tugged at one of my soapy toes. Hot steam gave him wet, starfish eyelashes, which I wanted to kiss. 'Unless he's a complete psycho, in which case he'll come and find us and kill us.'

I let Stephen massage my feet. I felt strangely detached from the world, as if there were a fog around me. The only things I could see clearly were Stephen and me.

'At least you and I are fine,' I said. 'Everything else feels a bit sub-standard but you and I feel good. Oh, and Dad. He's doing brilliantly. And Kate, when she bothers to call. So I guess everything is okay, really, apart from Le Cloob. And, er, the state of my head.'

Stephen rubbed his thumb right into the ball of my foot. 'You do seem to feel crappy when you've seen Le Cloob, these days.'

'I know.'

'It's difficult,' he acknowledged. 'When you have this wonderful friendship and suddenly it's causing you loads of pain and shit. And you're thinking, Hang on. This is meant to be my safe place. My good place.'

'Yes! That's exactly how it feels!'

'I had a friendship like that,' Stephen said. 'Philip. Me and him went back years. But he just got ... I dunno, messy. There was always a *thing* or an *issue*.

Every time I came away from the pub when we met up, I just thought, That was shit. Really difficult. And it shouldn't be.'

'So what did you do? I don't think I've heard you talk about him. Although with the state of my brain at the moment anything's possible . . .'

Stephen smiled, too polite to agree with me but knowing full well it was true. 'Walked away. It was harsh, but it was right. I don't get much free time and what I do have needs to be spent with people who leave me feeling really good. Quite a simple rule, but it works.'

I closed my eyes, taking in long draughts of fragrant steam. I wasn't going to be walking away from Le Cloob any time soon. But something needed to change. Quite urgently, really, if we were to move on.

And then, as I pondered my dilemma, I did something really, really terrible.

I did an enormous, noisy, underwater fart.

I froze. No. No? Yes? Had that happened?

I opened a crack of an eye, to see Stephen staring at me in absolute amazement. I closed my crack of eye. 'No,' I whispered.

'Er, *yes*,' Stephen bellowed. 'Yes, you just did that. IN MY BATH!'

'No.'

Stephen started to shake. 'Yes.' He was laughing. 'Yes, you did. And I FELT it. Oh, God! URGH!'

'No no no . . .' But I'd gone already. I laughed and laughed and laughed, and Stephen did too, and we laughed until we couldn't breathe. Tears ran down my face and my chest ached. 'No,' I cried, from time to time.

When we finally recovered, I took Stephen's foot and started a massage by way of apology. 'No farting,' he grumbled. 'This bath has had as much as it can take.'

'I'm always happy when I'm with you,' I said. 'I love every minute we have together. And these days I find every minute I spend with Le Cloob difficult. I'm going to have to take some time off. Tim, I don't want to see Tim for a while. Claudine, ditto. And Lizzy needs a good talking-to, because I'm not going to stop seeing her.'

Stephen was watching me. 'Well, if that's what you want,' he said. 'I'm certainly not going to tell you to stop seeing your friends.'

'You don't need to,' I said sadly. 'They've made their own bed.' Already I felt calmer. Less shit. Less strife. Had I not had enough in my life?

My phone, sitting on the chair next to Stephen's, came to life. Stephen hauled himself out of the bath to take a look. 'It's Tim,' he said.

'Oh.' I didn't like that. 'Leave it.'

Stephen got back into the bath with me and I concentrated on soothing the sudden jumpiness in my stomach. 'It's all cool,' Stephen said. 'Stop worrying!'

My phone started ringing again.

'Tim again,' Stephen said. I swallowed.

The third time Tim called, I was feeling sick. 'Can you get rid of him?' I asked. 'I don't like it. I mean, you told him I have food poisoning.'

I watched Stephen's long, strong body pad across the floor, bubbles and water sliding off him.

'Hi, mate,' Stephen said politely, hitching a towel round

his waist. 'Yeah, she's still in a bad way, I'm afraid, poor thing . . .'

He wandered off down the hallway and I realized I was holding on to the side of the bath, my knuckles white like china. *It's fine*, I told myself. *It's all totally fine. Tim's probably just worried about me.*

'Hmm,' Stephen said, when he reappeared a few minutes later. 'He said he was calling because he was really early for work and could pop over to check up on you, if you wanted.'

I stared at Stephen, who smiled reassuringly. 'He thinks you've got food poisoning, remember?'

'I know! But you told him you were looking after me! Why is he trying to come over anyway?'

Stephen held out a big towel for me. 'I told him very specifically not to come, Pumpkin,' he said. 'So you can relax.'

Stephen took me to the bakery on the corner of the square, where he bought me some banana cake and a strong flat white. I'd expected him to hold forth on what an obsessive weirdo Tim was but, to my surprise, he did a great job at calming me down. 'Maybe we were both wrong,' he reasoned, running his tongue along his upper lip to catch the tiny bubbles of *crema*. 'Maybe we've both read too much into it.'

'Maybe,' I said doubtfully. 'Perhaps we've both been too hasty.'

I didn't believe myself, though. So it seemed the least surprising thing imaginable when I glanced out of the window, down which rain poured thickly, like syrup, and saw Tim coming towards us from Mare Street.

'Shit!' I whispered. 'Stephen, he's here . . .' The words stuck in my throat.

Stephen peered out. 'Oh, come *on*,' he said irritably. 'Leave her alone, you idiot.' He touched my arm. 'It's fine. I'll go and tell him to bugger off.'

For a split second, I thought about stopping him – I didn't want to cause a scene, after all – but it suddenly mattered to me more than anything else in the world that Tim Furniss did not come into this shop. So I nodded. Stephen got up and slid out of the bakery, just as Tim turned off into Clapton Square.

I crouched, my chest a tin hollow, waiting for something to happen. For Tim to go back towards Mare Street, or for Stephen to reappear. But nothing happened.

I counted ten breaths.

Still nothing happened. The rain continued to smudge down the windows and a toddler came and stared at my banana cake.

Nothing happened.

When I couldn't bear it any longer, I went outside.

They were standing in front of Stephen's house, arguing. Before I had time to decide what to do, Tim was storming down the street towards me. He saw me straight away. 'Annie,' he shouted. 'Annie, listen . . .'

In dreams where I was being chased by a man I could never run: my feet just pedalled uselessly in the air and sound secreted itself in a corner of my throat. In reality, I was able to run faster than I'd ever run in my life. I sprinted off past the library and the crummy estate agent, Tim's voice lost in the acceleration of a 38 bus. I ran round the corner of Lower Clapton Road, past the bric-a-brac shop and into a greasy spoon full of construction workers.

By the time Stephen found me I was stalled outside the pawn shop on the corner, staring blankly at the forlorn rows of gold-plated '18' and '21' pendants; discarded celebrations of birthdays passed. The rain had stopped but the pavement was still drenched. Buses rumbled past. I felt hopeless.

'Oh, Pumpkin,' he said, putting his arms round me.

I leaned into him. I was tired. I wanted to take a sleeping pill.

'Annie, what happened?'

I hugged him hard, hoping he'd stop asking questions.

'Annie?'

'Overreaction,' I said into his coat. 'A big one. Sorry. I'll call my therapist when we get home. Maybe my doctor. I won't let this get the better of me, Stephen. I promise.'

Stephen kissed my forehead. 'Come on,' he said, taking my hand and leading me away.

'What did Tim say?'

Stephen sighed. 'He just kept saying he had to see you, it couldn't wait. I said, "Mate, she doesn't want to see you. Or anyone else." So he called me all sorts of things. He was a bit unhinged. But, Annie, I don't think he'd come to kill you. I shouldn't have joked about that – I feel guilty now.'

'Did he chase me?' I asked, as Stephen led me back down towards the square.

'No. He just watched you run off. He looked sad and then left, although not before he'd called me a wanker.'

A few minutes later he tucked me into an armchair and gave me a brandy. 'Perhaps you need some anti-anxiety medication or something,' he said tentatively. I'd started crying again. 'You seem very tense, Pumpkin . . .'

'Maybe.' I put my hands over my face. 'Maybe I do. Stephen, please don't leave me. Promise me, you won't leave me?'

Chapter Twenty-two

Kate

'So you're shagging the boss, Galway?' Joe asked, as we cleaned the tack one evening.

A cheek-piece fell out of my hand and into the water bucket.

'Oh dear.' Joe sniggered. 'Galway's flustered. How could you do it to me, princess? How could you?'

I fished out the cheek-piece. 'I'm not shagging the boss. Nor do I plan to ...' I trailed off. 'Dammit, Joe, stop embarrassing me!'

'Galway,' he said, 'I happen to think you and the boss'd make a lovely couple. You pretend to be a Dublin ball-breaker but you don't fool me, darlin'.'

'What?'

'You're as soft as he is.'

'Feck off,' I growled. 'And, for the record, I'm not blushing.'

'Ah, Galway, but you are so.'

'Am *not*.'

'Oh, Galway.'

'What's he on about, pet?' Becca was standing in the doorway. I almost gasped.

'Bloody hell,' I said, staring at her. 'You look lovely, Becca!'

Becca had been growing her hair for the last few months, although whenever she visited us it was pulled back in an unforgiving ponytail. But tonight it lay against her shoulders, dyed a new chestnut brown and all styled like she'd just left the salon. She was in jeans, not jodhpurs, and – I gaped – a tight-fitting jumper! Whatever next? She'd be wearing make-up and perfume at this rate! I sort of hoped she wouldn't. 'Stop looking at me like that,' she grumbled. 'Caroline's grooms have signed me up for some dating thing and they bought me a blow-dry this afternoon. It's my first one ever and I feel like a huge old twat.'

I got up to hug her but couldn't quite bring myself to do so. 'You look too nice and clean,' I explained, squeezing her hand. 'I'm so pleased you're dating! Any good ones yet?'

'Jesus, no. All madder than a box of frogs. But it's been quite fun.'

We smiled at each other, acknowledging silently how far she'd come.

'You do look nice, Becca,' Joe said, standing up. 'In fact, you look so nice I might ask if you fancy a few jars later.'

Becca looked at him in utter horror. 'Joe, pet,' she said clearly. 'I'm dating because I'd like to meet a nice man. Not an Irish whore.'

Joe just sniggered.

'Go and get the wine from the fridge,' I told her. 'I'll make sure he doesn't follow you.'

Joe whistled as Becca went off, all shiny, bouncy hair, in the twilight. 'You're pathetic,' I told him. 'She gets a Hollywood blow-dry and suddenly you're sniffing around her ankles like a randy dog.'

Joe batted his eyelashes at me. 'What's that, Galway? A Hollywood blowjob?'

He ducked as I threw a bar of saddle soap at his head. 'Galway, behave! This is the answer! You can seduce the boss – because, dear Christ, girl, he's cryin' out for you to seize the day, there – and I'll have some cosy nights in with Becca, and then we can all open our presents together round the tree at Christmas and have some babies and great craic. Wouldn't that be the best, Galway?'

Becca arrived back with the wine. 'Becca, I'm afraid Joe's talking about having babies with you,' I reported. 'And he said that Mark's crying out for me to seduce him,' I wanted to add. Was he? Was he really? Had he said something to Joe? Little flutters of excitement and panic broke out inside me.

'You can fuck right off, pet,' Becca was telling Joe. 'I'd sooner mate with a goat. Right, let's get this thing open . . .'

Mark's documentary was on at nine o'clock and in her excitement Sandra had invited almost everyone she had ever met. She'd been preparing food for days, even though we barely had enough to feed the four of us. 'Pork pies,' she'd been muttering this morning. 'Pork pies – I want everyone to have a pork pie . . .'

Becca found a perch on a chest with clean stable rugs piled on it. 'How's Mark?' she asked.

'Walking without his stick now!' I beamed. 'Not for long, but it's big progress. He's been so brave, Becca, you can see how much it hurts him.'

Becca was delighted.

'Galway fancies the living daylights out of him,' Joe said. 'And he fancies her right back. Holy Mother of God, you should've seen them over the last few weeks, Becca – it's been enough to break a man's heart.'

He guffawed into the profound silence that followed. 'Right, I'm off to get showered so I can seduce you later, Becca. Galway's got one more bridle to do – make sure she doesn't skive.'

'Go away, Joe,' Becca said. She was giving me some serious raised eyebrow.

'Joe's talking nonsense,' I told her, when he'd sloped off. 'Mark does not fancy me. And I don't fancy him. So you can stop looking at me like that.'

'I see,' she said, her eyes twinkling.

'Stop it! There's nothing! Nothing at all! Ever!'

Becca poured me some wine. I heard jingling – she was actually wearing bangles. 'Kate, pet, you needn't worry about me. I got over it as soon as I left, like I knew I would. I was just stuck, my love. Stuck in a rut here, convincing myself that Mark was the answer to all my problems.'

I concentrated on cleaning Stumpy's bit.

'Oh, pet, look at me.'

Grudgingly, I put it down and met her eye. 'Kate,' she said softly, 'when I arrived here, I'd just had to terminate a pregnancy because I found out that my fiancé was shagging someone else. I was broken, my love, crushed like a rabbit in the road.'

'Oh, no, Becca . . .'

'I was very happy to get caught up with Mark and his

problems. I thought he'd fix me. But he didn't, pet. *I* fixed me. Time fixed me, just like it's fixed you. I'm not interested in Mark Waverley, my little love, but I think you are, and I think you have been since you arrived here.'

I let my eyes drift up to the row of faded rosettes that Mark had won as a boy, pinned to the wall by his proud mother all those years ago. I thought of his face, so precious, so kind and brave, the way he pushed me every day to improve, the trust he'd invested in me by handing me his beloved Stumpy. And I thought about the way I still looked out of my bedroom window and saw him cuddling the horse over his stable door, giving him Polos and talking to him. Hopelessly in love with his furry friend.

Becca was right. I was mad about him.

'I don't fancy him,' I insisted. 'I don't fancy him at all.'

Becca stared at me long and hard. 'Okay. I guess it'll just be me and Joe at Christmas then. Me, Joe and some hot loving.'

Then: 'Eew,' she muttered.

The documentary started well enough. Lots of stuff about Mark's glittering career, the way he'd come out of nowhere with no money and a tragic past. They had photos and a couple of old video clips of ten-year-old Mark that did funny twisty things to my stomach.

But they didn't waste much time with that. The accident came soon after, documented with terrible precision by the cameraman on his tower above the jump. Mark and Stumpy flying through the air, like discarded toys, then all of the officials and paramedics sprinting towards the awful pile of misshapen horse and rider.

And me, running at full tilt towards them, my screams a thin line of panic drawn high and jagged above the stunned silence of the crowd.

They showed my run in slow motion. My face, screwed up in sheer agony, right there in the centre of the screen.

The world went silent as I stared at myself.

Oh, God, I thought. *Oh, God, no . . .*

I felt Becca's hand touch my shoulder. 'Pet?' she whispered. 'Pet, are you Okay?'

I got up to leave but realized I'd draw more attention to myself, so I sank back into my chair. Blood pounded in my ears. I had to go. I had to leave *right now.* Tonight. As soon as the documentary had finished. I had to put as much distance as I possibly could between me and the farm.

In the ad break, Becca marched me out to the kitchen. 'Right,' she said. 'Enough. Tell me everything, Kate, and do not give me any more shit about a burnout.'

So I did. I'd be gone by the time anyone came for me, anyway.

She tried to make me stay. Tried to reassure me that there was no reason why anyone would connect me to Mark. 'You were just a horrified onlooker, pet,' she said gently. 'Listen to me. Did you not notice the shots of other people doing exactly the same thing? Screaming? Running? Crying? Why would anyone know you work for Mark?'

She held my shoulders firmly, as if I might otherwise evaporate. I was shaking like a whippet.

'Pet, you have to calm down. I can see the problem, but running off into the night isn't going to solve anything.'

I whimpered.

'Come and watch the rest,' she said. 'And afterwards we'll decide what to do. You can come and bunk at mine for the night if you want.'

She peered at me. 'Breathe, pet,' she said quietly. 'Breathe in and out, please.'

Mark was watching me as we came back for the next section. He raised a tiny fraction of an eyebrow. *Are you okay?*

I ducked my head. It was too painful to look at him, knowing that by the morning I'd be gone.

The film rumbled on and I barely saw a thing. Towards the end they showed him standing up for the first time, his legs wobbling and his face white with exertion. Everyone in the sitting room had tears in their eyes, but I was frozen.

Suddenly the screen had my attention again. 'Mark has been teaching his one remaining groom, Kate, to ride,' said the voice-over. The camera was all on Mark's face with me an unfocused blur in the background. 'It's okay,' Becca whispered, squeezing my hand. 'You're not even a tiny bit recognizable, pet.'

I looked up wildly at the window, as if expecting there to be faces staring in at me.

Back on screen Mark was breaking into a big, proud smile as I executed my first ever flying change. 'Good girl,' he shouted. 'I owe Kate a lot,' he told the camera, in an unexpected moment of candour. 'She visited me every day when I was in hospital.'

'Why do you think she visited you every day?' the director asked off-camera. They didn't miss a trick, those guys.

'I have no idea,' Mark said. 'I wouldn't have done if I were her. But she did. Her visits were the high point of my day. She brought me videos of Stumpy and cracked lots of bad jokes. She pulled me up when I was wallowing in self-pity.'

The director left a pregnant pause. 'It sounds like she's gone above and beyond the call of duty,' he commented.

Mark's eyes followed me round the school. 'She did. If she hadn't, I'm not sure I'd be walking today. She gave me hope and made me fight . . . She was a force to be reckoned with.'

The director left a loaded pause – and, to my amazement, Mark took the bait. 'She shouted at me more than once. Told me to stop wallowing and be grateful I was still alive. It was quite full on but it was exactly what I needed.' In the background, I swore loudly as I bungled my second flying change. 'But it wasn't just that. There's something about Kate. A determination to find good in the bad. She always has a joke, or a ridiculous comment to hand. She's always smiling. She's unlike anyone I've ever met.'

'She's very special to you, then,' the director asked. His excitement was almost palpable.

Mark turned away. 'More inside leg,' he shouted at me. He ignored the question.

Back in the sitting room Mark was staring fixedly at the screen. I felt as if I might throw up.

When it was over, everyone clapped and then went silent so that Mark could make a speech. Being Mark, he didn't make a speech. 'Stop it,' he told them. He grabbed a handful of peanuts and stared at the floor, his cheeks singeing red.

I slipped out of Sandra's sitting room and left the house, closing the door quietly behind me. Dirk and Woody were asleep in the porch; they thumped their tails lazily on the floor as I stepped over them and escaped to the stable block, checking all around me for trouble. 'It would be at least four hours until anyone could arrive,' I reminded myself. 'Minimum. Probably even longer.' But there was a trail now. A trail to Kate Brady of Hythe Farm in Somerset.

It was windy and snippy outside; little spots of rain buried themselves in my hair as I ran over to Stumpy's stable.

He was still up, pulling away at his haynet.

'Hello,' I said. My eyes filled with tears as soon as I touched his nose. 'I've come to say goodbye.'

Stumpy dropped a load of hay on my arm. 'Do you have treats of any sort?' he wanted to know. 'Polos? Carrots? Anything at all that I can eat?'

And with that I started sobbing.

Stumpy paused in his crunching for a second, staring at me.

'I love you, you silly thing,' I whispered. 'You saved my life. You and your dad.' I slid my arms round his neck, pressing my cheek against his warm, sweet-smelling hair. 'I owe you so much,' I told him. Stumpy stayed still for a few moments but in the end his stomach won and he moved away to take another mouthful.

But he was back straight away, watching me with those big kind eyes. 'I'll miss you for the rest of my life,'

I whispered, tears streaming down my face. 'You big brave bugger. You lovely person. You funny boy.'

And before I had time to argue with myself, I made myself turn and walk away. No looking back, Brady. Move in a straight line, leave no trace.

'What are you doing out here?'

I screamed. My voice was snatched up by the wind and hurled across the paddock, where the big oak swayed and swirled chaotically across the surface of the half-moon.

'*Kate?* What's wrong? It's me!'

Mark, in a hopelessly unfashionable jumper with his sponsor's name emblazoned across the front. His attempt at 'dressing up' for his guests, which had made me feel all smiley and warm when I'd seen it earlier. Before my life was blown wide open again.

'Sorry, boss,' I muttered. 'You took me by surprise, there.'

Mark cocked his head to one side. He smelt of woodsmoke from the sitting-room fire. 'I brought pork pies,' he told me. 'Mum was getting very anxious that you hadn't eaten one. Plus everyone was staring at me and using words like "bravery" and "hope".'

I laughed, in spite of my pounding heart. 'I love your mum.'

'Same,' he said. 'But the pork-pie thing is pushing me over the edge. Look, let's just get this over with. Shall we?' He gestured at the paddock gate.

I glanced at the drive, picked out by lamps. Nothing yet.

I went over and leaned on the gate next to Mark and his crutches.

'Er, cheers,' he said, bumping his pork pie against mine. He took a large bite of his and I wondered how I would force myself to eat.

You have to go! shouted my head. *Now! Get the merry hell out of here!*

The problem was, I couldn't. Almost equal to the fear was this intense, visceral feeling I had standing there with my boss, watching the eyes I'd come to know so well, both of us aware of what he'd said about me on camera. I managed to take a bite.

We stood there in the windy night, eating Sandra's pork pies.

'So what's going on?' Mark asked, when we'd finished.

'Oh, er, you know,' I said, dusting myself down with shaking hands. 'Things.'

'I see.' He smiled. 'Kate, you're shivering. Do you want my jumper?'

'No.'

'Really? You're shaking like a leaf.'

I checked the drive. 'If I take your jumper then you're cold too,' I said lamely. 'I don't want that.'

He took his crutches and walked off to the tack room. 'Stay there,' he instructed.

I stayed. I watched the drive.

Mark came back with a stable rug, which he wrapped around us both. Closer than we had ever been, we stood stock-still and gazed out at the fields. The wind was brutal against my face and the rain still spiky and cold. I felt none of it.

'So here's where I am right now,' Mark said, emboldened now that he wasn't looking directly at me. 'I'm going through a divorce, I'm fighting an evil woman for joint custody of my beautiful little girl and I've got a skeleton that's only just beginning to stop feeling like a beanbag. My physio is exhausting and I'm shitting myself that I won't be able to compete again. And shitting myself that maybe I don't even *want* to compete again. And you know what the funny thing is about all of this, Kate? In spite of the above, I actually spend most of my time thinking about something else entirely.'

My hands were still trembling, even though my body felt oddly calm. 'I can relate to that.'

'You can?'

'The last few years are like this big war zone in my head,' I said carefully. 'All these unexploded mines everywhere and yet all of that's sort of gone into soft focus. There's this other thing. This other . . . person.' My voice wobbled and bowled off in the wind.

I could feel Mark's warmth through my jumper now. God, the miracle of life. This man could have been dead by now. Could have died at Badminton, or in the helicopter. Instead he was here: vital, alive, the loveliest man on earth at this moment.

'Good to hear it's not just me,' he said slowly. 'You know. Feeling preoccupied.'

'Yes.'

There was a long pause. Fallen leaves skittered across the yard behind us and I smelt the wet earth and the woodsmoke. My home.

(For how much longer? An hour?)

'I think someone should say something,' Mark said. 'I think we should both say something brave.'

'I don't,' I said quickly. 'I think we should both be great big stinking cowards.'

'But I don't want to. I want to be brave, Kate.'

'You've been brave! You were brave as, I don't know, a *bear* in that hospital! A big bear, you know, that can pull down trees and fight lions and stuff . . .'

The delightful rumble of Mark's laughter filtered through his jumper into mine. 'I don't think bears and lions live in the same place,' he said. 'But I like being a bear.'

He took a deep breath. 'Kate . . .' His voice was ragged with nerves but I heard the determination. Don't let him say it, I thought, starting to panic. You've ruined enough lives as it is. Don't ruin his too! *Get out!*

I felt a warm tear drop down my cheek. 'I can't have this conversation,' I said. 'I'm so sorry, Mark, but this isn't the time. I have to go.'

'What – to an empty barn? With all your team next door? And me trying to say –'

'I've a stomach ache,' I said hopelessly.

Mark turned to me. 'I don't know what's going on here,' he said softly. 'But I have proper words to say. Words that should never go unsaid. And I want to say them. Will you let me?'

I shook my head as tears filled my eyes yet again. 'I have words too, Mark. But we can't have this conversation. You'll have to trust me.'

Mark watched my face. To think I'd once imagined that there was coldness in these eyes. To think I'd been so blinkered that I saw meanness and cruelty where there was warmth and generosity, masked only by shyness.

'Kate,' he said quietly. 'Look, Kate, I thought you'd had a burnout. I don't understand why that means you're not allowed to . . . to like someone.'

'I know,' I said, trying pointlessly to wipe my face with my hand. 'But I really can't. Especially the someone we're talking about here. Even though that someone is in my mind all of the time, and even though that someone makes me feel all strong and happy.' A huge sob burst out of me. I couldn't stand it.

'But what if the person likes you back, Kate? What if they lie awake listening to the mice in the roof and wonder what it would be like to hold you while you slept?'

Strands of Mark's hair blew against the side of my face. 'I care about them far too much to let them do that,' I whispered. 'If I thought that was the case I'd leave. Because it couldn't work out well for that lovely person listening to the mice.'

'But that person has suffered just about every harm going,' Mark persisted. 'And he's survived. Part of the reason he's survived is that you've given him hope. He's full of you, all day and all night. What could you have up your sleeve that could possibly hurt him?'

'A lot,' I cried. 'An awful lot. Mark, please don't do this. I'm in trouble. A lot of trouble.'

Mark went silent for a while. Then his eyes, dark as the sky, swivelled back to mine. 'I just checked with the man who's mad about you,' he said, and I saw the corners of his mouth turn up in a beautiful smile. 'And he said he's fine with whatever you've got.'

Mark's arm had somehow slid around my waist. 'Your broken rib,' I said.

'Shut up.'

'I smell of pork pies,' I added, and once again felt the soft rumble of laughter through his jumper.

'Me too.'

I could feel his breath on my forehead. I was blind with confusion and desire and panic. I was meant to be Kate Brady, the chirpy little whatsit from Dublin, yet I barely knew my own name at that moment, let alone what I should do.

'You could go,' he said, and our faces somehow angled round towards each other. 'Or you could just try it for five minutes. Saying some words. Or even not saying some words.'

Our noses were brushing now. I'm falling in love with you, I thought. This is a nightmare. The most perfect, beautiful nightmare.

Another tear fell down my cheek. 'I don't dare,' I whispered.

'I do,' he said.

And then he kissed me, and everything slowed down. Mark slid his hands gently into my hair, and for the first time in my life I caught a glimpse of love. Not love from films or poems, or the illusion of love created by a lonely and desperate mind, but real love, bigger than all of its many problems.

I had to leave tonight.

Yet I couldn't, and I wouldn't.

Chapter Twenty-three

Annie

Lizzy and I sat cross-legged in front of a new fire in our pyjamas, opening the sprinkling of Christmas presents that Dad had got us. He never went mad but each gift was always perfect. This year he'd bought me an antique silver watch, because mine had broken, and a waterproof cover for my rucksack so that my stuff wouldn't get ruined if I did go to Tibet for the massage training.

'What did Stephen get you?' Lizzy was asking. She had been given an antique necklace and a pair of very cool sunglasses that Dad had been recommended 'by Janet off Facebook'. His burgeoning presence on social media was insane. Every time I saw him pop up on Facebook he'd made another friend, or joined another group, and (to my great embarrassment) had made a photo album of me and Lizzy as chubby little girls.

'He's giving me my presents in Paris,' I said. 'I'm so excited – I can't believe I've never been!'

Stephen hadn't called me yet, which I was completely fine about. No, really, *completely* fine. It was his family's first Christmas without their mum and it would be monstrously selfish of me to get upset about his radio silence. He was taking me to Paris for a week on the day after Boxing Day – was that not enough?

New Year's Eve was always the province of Le Cloob but this year we'd not made any arrangements, so I didn't feel particularly guilty about the trip. Since our disastrous meeting in October we hadn't met as a group. I was still very upset with Claudine, and although I suspected Lizzy agreed with quite a lot of what Claudine said, her loyalty would always be to me. And then, of course, there was Tim.

Tim.

Howling it out in therapy had helped, a little, and the longer we went without contact, the calmer I felt. On good days I wondered if perhaps I'd made it up, or at the very least overreacted. But the fact that Tim had not been in contact for two months spoke volumes.

Sometimes the guilt at just abandoning him was unbearable, but the fear was bigger. I could not have a man in my life, even one I'd known and trusted for years, who was *thinking* about me.

Trying to prevent Lizzy from realizing that Tim and I weren't talking had been rather difficult, as had going back into therapy while I was dealing with a man who was at the end of his tether through work stress. I was far from fixed and Stephen had had to have serious words with me when I asked him if he'd put an extra lock on his front door.

It had been a slog. But it felt like change was in the air. Stephen and I were off to Paris for the New Year and when we got back I was moving in with him officially.

'I definitely think we should get Dad drunk and cross-question him about this possible girlfriend,' Lizzy said, leaning forward to blow at the fire with Dad's ancient leather bellows.

'Agreed. He's a sly dog, our daddy.'

'Oh, really? How so?' Dad walked in with Mum's wonky old tray, laden with stunning canapés. 'A little something to tide us over until lunch,' he said, smiling at our astonished faces.

'DAD! How the hell did you do these?'

'I saw them on Pinterest,' he explained earnestly. Lizzy and I bellowed with laughter. 'And then I cooked them last week. I did get a bit of help,' he added, blushing slightly. 'I froze them. Didn't want to spend all of Christmas Day in the kitchen.'

We fell on them like savages.

'These are bloody delicious!' Lizzy shouted, through a mouthful of spiced lamb cutlet. 'You clever thing!'

Dad, nibbling something wrapped in delicate pastry, positively glowed.

'Right.' Lizzy poured him a glass of sherry. 'Daddy, we've had enough. You're going to have to tell us about your ladyfriend immediately. Who is she? What's the deal? Is she off the internet? Is she fit?'

Dad stared at Lizzy and then, to our absolute horror, his eyes filled with tears.

'Daddy, no,' Lizzy whispered, appalled. She ran off to get some tissues and I abandoned my crostini to comfort him. Dad batted at the tears, which were leaking silently out of his eyes.

'Here,' Lizzy said, shoving a big pile of balled-up toilet roll into his face.

Dad mopped at his cheeks and, slowly, pulled himself together. 'Sorry about that,' he said. 'Just got a bit sad. A bit guilty. I know Georgie would've wanted me to meet someone, but seeing you two here I felt like I'd betrayed her. You know.'

We nodded understandingly, privately thinking that Mum was probably furious with him for having waited nearly thirty years.

'I have met someone,' he said bravely. 'Linda, although I call her Linnie. She lives in Bakewell. Has a teenage boy called Rob who hates my guts. She's a physics teacher, would you believe?' He did a little swoony smile and I felt my stomach lurch happily. A physics teacher! Perfect! Bakewell! Perfect!

'DADDY!' Lizzy jumped on him, somehow landing neatly and curling up on his lap, like she used to when he made up stories for us.

'She's lovely,' Dad said, from underneath Lizzy. 'An absolute treasure. She runs the Bakewell women's choir and she's been wonderful about my, er, cautiousness.'

We all giggled. 'It only took you the best part of three decades,' I said. 'You definitely don't want to rush that one.'

Dad told us about 'Linnie', and how great she'd been at helping him get over his guilt and sadness at having finally met someone. 'She didn't bat an eyelid the first time I cried about Georgie,' Dad added. 'Not a whiff of jealousy, or insecurity, or any of that nonsense. In fact, she encouraged me to write a diary about all the happy things that have happened since Georgie died. Seeing my little girls grow up, transforming the garden, working with all of those fantastic authors ... It wasn't all sad, was it, my darlings?'

'Absolutely not,' Lizzy said.

'No, it wasn't. I thought it was very clever of Linnie to help me see that.'

I felt like my heart would burst.

'I decided to do an online diary instead of a handwritten one,' Dad continued, 'one of those blog things, so that if I got to a point where I was ready to stop writing it, it'd always be there.'

'Lovely,' I said.

Dad looked proud. 'I designed an extremely cool page, you know.'

Lizzy and I roared with laughter again.

'But I think I've done with it now,' he said. 'I'm going to use my blog-writing time to get going on my novel. I've been sitting on it for more than a quarter of a century now, I think it might be time . . .'

After quite a lot of persuasion and a couple of glasses of brandy, Dad showed us his blog. Lizzy and I divided our time between reading his posts and making Christmas lunch. Because Mum had been vegan we'd always had hippie food at Christmas, but this year Dad had gone completely mad and bought a turkey. Nobody had any idea what to do with it. We flicked between Delia's website and Dad's blog, laughing and sometimes crying as we viewed all those lovely photos of us as children – frightened, sad, bereaved little babies – but, as Dad wrote, 'Strong, stubborn little beasts.'

'I really, really love it, Dad,' I said, wrestling with a big bag of sprouts. The kitchen was full of steam and chaos, which Lizzy was making worse by playing a badly recorded CD of a *mariachi* band who'd been busking at St Pancras. It had been a long, long time since I'd seen the kitchen so full of life.

Dad was shyly pleased. 'The local newspaper rather likes it too,' he admitted. 'They put it up for some award! Loads of people have read it and got in touch! Whatever next?'

'It's beautiful,' I told him. 'Our whole lives are there – everything!'

'How's Tim?' Dad asked, looking at a very old picture of the two of us together.

'Fine,' Lizzy said. I exhaled, relieved. She still didn't know. 'Le Cloob is slightly on strike because Claudine was horrible to Annie about Stephen, but I'm sure we'll all meet up soon.'

Dad looked sharply at me. 'She decided he wasn't right for me,' I told him. 'But it was based on nothing. Everything's fine, Dad. Stephen's still fantastic and I'm still happy.'

'Sure?'

I could feel Lizzy watching me too.

'I've never been so sure,' I said. 'The only thing that's wrong with my relationship is that everyone seems to question it. It's depressing.'

And then, as we all stood there in awkward silence, my phone rang, and it was Stephen. At last.

'Hi, Pumpkin,' he said. 'Happy Christmas!'

Lizzy went back to her gravy.

Stephen was not having quite as nice a day as we were. 'I've had to go for a walk,' he said, wind crackling down the line. 'Else I'll end up punching my dad. He's being a nightmare. I should have come to Bakewell with you.' I could hear the strain in his voice.

'Can't your brother look after him for a bit? Or Petra? You can't look after him all the time . . .'

'Oh, they're all at my sister-in-law's parents. It's just me and Dad.'

'Well, he'd be on his own otherwise. You're doing a good thing.'

'I suppose so. But seriously! He's playing *computer games*!'

'Your dad? Really?'

Stephen laughed drily. 'My dad is not who you might imagine him to be.'

'Tell me about your day,' I said. I didn't like it when Stephen sounded terse: it was so unlike the twinkly-eyed man I loved so much. 'Tell me about your walk. What can you see?'

'Nothing special,' Stephen said. 'Presently, a family of fat people letting their bull terrier shit on the pavement. Ho-ho-bloody-ho.'

'That's not how I imagined the village to be!'

Stephen's dad lived in a village called Wisborough Green, which I'd done a Google image on at the beginning of our relationship just because . . . Well, there was no good reason for that, beyond nosiness. It was a chocolate-box place with village greens and duck ponds and beautiful old pubs, nice-looking men walking spaniels amid flowers and carefully pruned trees. Not the kind of place where bull terriers did poos on the pavement in front of their indifferent families.

Stephen humphed. 'Okay, okay. It's not a fat family and it's not a bull terrier. Just an old lady and a poodle. I'm being moody, trying to paint a dark picture, you know. We men aren't good at sulking.'

I couldn't help but laugh. I could almost hear him sticking out his lower lip.

'Want Annie,' he said sulkily. 'Oh, are you near your rucksack?'

'It's upstairs.'

I could hear him smile. 'Well, then go up and check the top pocket. The tiny one.'

I ran upstairs. Stephen was so lovely with his little surprises.

A jewellery box had been stuffed into it. A blue velvety one, the sort of box I'd never held in my hand before. My jewellery tended to be of the wooden bead variety.

For a second, my heart slowed down. Surely not . . . I sat down suddenly on my bed, staring at the jungle mural on the wall that Mum had painted when I was small.

My life flashed before me, my hopes, my fears, those years of agony tucked away in the past.

'Are you alive?' Stephen asked.

'Yes.'

'Well?'

'Hang on.'

I took a deep breath and opened the box. It was not a ring. Inside was a little silver pendant on a chain, with the letter P.

'Er . . .'

I pulled it out, just to check that my eyes weren't playing tricks. 'Er, it's a P.'

My mind tried to work out what was going on here, but came up with nothing.

'For Pumpkin!' Stephen said. He sounded delighted. 'Oh, shit, would you have preferred an A?'

'No!' I felt suddenly weak. What the hell was going on with me? Would I *ever* be able to trust a man? 'No, a P is perfect. I'm your Pumpkin, after all. And it's beautiful.' It was. It wasn't something I'd ever have chosen myself – and Stephen was normally very good at fitting in with my off-piste tastes – but it was, actually, stunning. So small and simple and pretty. I stared at it, sitting quietly in my hand, shining tiny spokes of light on to my fingers.

Stephen laughed. 'You *are* my Pumpkin. My sandalwood-scented girl. I love you, Annie.' I heard a door close behind him as he walked back into his dad's house.

'I love you too,' I whispered.

'Stephen,' called a man's voice in the background. 'Lunch!'

'Who was that?'

'Dad.'

'Oh! I thought he was on the Xbox?'

Stephen sighed. 'He is, but luckily for him he has a son who can cook. I just asked him to stir the gravy while I spoke to you. Now he's wearing an apron as if he's spent the last four hours slaving away at the Aga.' He chuckled. 'He's a bugger, my old man. I reckon we can introduce you now. He seems to have got his head round the idea of you and, actually, he's not been too depressed today.'

I was happy to hear it. 'Good! Maybe we can pop over to see him when we're back from Paris.'

Stephen agreed. 'I'd better go,' he said. 'I don't trust Dad alone in the kitchen for long. Love you, little one, speak later.'

I went to put on the P, but stopped. I didn't know why,

but I felt a bit disappointed. Pumpkin was our private name but it also reminded me of Tim.

I left the necklace on my bed, sitting prettily in the jade green swirls of my Sri Lankan bedspread, and promised myself I'd not be such an ungrateful girl in future.

Chapter Twenty-four

Kate

Dearest Kate,

I'm not sure about leaving you a letter on Stumpy's door. What if Joe gets at it first? He'll never shut up. Literally, we'll have to tolerate his sniggers and double-entendres for the rest of time.

On careful reflection, though, I've decided to go ahead anyway. I know this is how you start each morning and I love that. I know you'll find this letter, and you'll read it right here by the door and Stumpy will try to eat it and you'll turn round and kiss him. I hope you'll smile. I hope you'll be feeling as mad with excitement as I do at this moment.

We kissed last night. Six and a half long hours ago, if you're interested in fine detail.

I can't believe it! Me and Kate Brady, with all her wild red hair and her cheeky chat and that glowing, lovely smile. We kissed over pork pies in a windy wintery field and it felt so good I carried on doing it for an hour without needing my crutches.

Kate, I'm going to lay my cards out. This probably isn't very smooth but – as you've noticed by now – I'm about as smooth as a field of sheep. I entertain dreams of one day being a normal member of society – of being able to pick out an outfit, for example, that doesn't make me look like a mannequin from the farm shop. Or of one day being able to just walk into a room and chat with people, all casual and engaging.

Small steps, though. For now I'm still learning — and I'm learning a lot of these things from you — and because I'm still learning, I'm going to say it straight:

I think you're wonderful, Kate Brady, and I'm mad about you. You saved me from self-imposed death-by-self-pity when I was in hospital, and you saved me from my marriage by barging into this farm and showing me that women can actually be lovely. Respectful, thoughtful, kind; all the things my wife, bless her soul, was (is) not. You even saved my horse's life when Maria tried to end it. You saved my mum's life when she was at her wit's end. You saved us all, you mad Irishwoman. Even Ana Luisa likes you, although she would no doubt try to take that terrible secret to her grave.

I'm feeling very impatient about when I might be able to kiss you again. (I'm not hiding in Stumpy's stable watching you read this, by the way. I've gone back to bed.) But I want so badly to smell your hair and feel you here in my arms. All alive and funny and obstinate and sweet.

I can't wait to start our future together. I think about you literally all of the time.

Please will you be my girlfriend?

Thanks. Love Mark x x x x x

I can't leave, I thought, as Stumpy started trying to eat the letter, just as Mark had predicted, and I laughed and kissed him, just as Mark had predicted.

I can't leave this place.

I was going to have to tell Mark everything, every single thing, and then I was probably going to have to call the police myself.

Panic expanded in my stomach. I don't want to! I don't want to talk to them! I don't want to talk to anyone!

Stumpy rested his muzzle on my shoulder.

'Maybe I'll give it a couple of days,' I told him. 'See what happens.'

He let off a big, bored sigh.

The sudden sound of an engine on the drive made me jump, but it was only the feed merchant's van.

I steadied myself against Stumpy's door with a shaking hand. Yes, I had to stay. Every part of me knew that. But it could prove one of the most stupid and dangerous decisions of my life.

Chapter Twenty-five

Annie

'This is the wrong check-in desk,' I said, scanning the row of BA signs above us. 'This one's for New York.'

'It is, my Pumpkin. We're going to New York!'

I gaped at Stephen. 'Eh? But I was there when we booked the tickets! We're definitely going to Paris!'

Stephen grinned. 'The problem is, you have an embarrassingly wealthy boyfriend, who sometimes can't control himself. He wanted to treat you to something super-special, and take you somewhere you'd never been, so he kind of cancelled the Paris tickets and booked some New York ones instead.'

I stared at him. 'We're going to New York? Seriously? But what about that visa thingy?'

'Um, I kind of applied on your behalf using your passport,' he confessed. 'I hope that wasn't too naughty of me . . .'

'Oh, my God!'

'And I'm afraid I've been really naughty and I've not booked us in somewhere mad and bohemian. I've booked us in somewhere extremely cool and expensive, and we're going to be really vulgar and eat in all the most expensive places and buy absolutely anything we want. Okay?'

I laughed, a slightly mad cackling sound. 'OKAY!' I shouted. 'THAT IS SERIOUSLY OKAY!'

I had been to New York, in fact, about ten years ago during a layover from New Zealand, but had only been there ten hours and had made the mistake of going to Times Square. After several weeks' hiking in the glacial calm of the South Island mountains, I had felt over-whelmed and lost. Some mentalist had grabbed my arm and shouted at me about THE WHITE BIRDS while I'd been queuing up to buy a crappy fruit salad in CVS Pharmacy and I'd completely freaked out and run five blocks with my giant rucksack on my back. Then I'd sat on a pavement and cried, until an unsmiling cop had told me to move on, presumably thinking I was a hobo.

'I know you're upset about how things have been with Le Cloob,' Stephen said, 'and that's part of why I wanted to treat you. Remind you that some people, aka me, think you're amazing.'

I grabbed him and kissed him, right there in the first-class queue. Which was not a queue, so really we were just kissing in front of the nice lady.

After staggering around in a jetlagged fug I finally started to fall in love with the city. Stephen had booked us into the very poshest suite at the Nomad, complete with private roof terrace and expansive views of the city. We were served fantastic breakfasts that seemed to appear as soon as we woke up, and Stephen even talked me into a shopping trip.

The slight problem – although really it was quite a big problem – was that Stephen's New York office, which had been causing all of the trouble lately, had got wind of his arrival in town. At least once a day, Stephen received a call he couldn't ignore and – swearing, apologizing and promising he wouldn't be long – he would have to get into a big, posh American-style car heading for the FlintSpark offices. Every time I told him I didn't mind.

And I sort of didn't, but sort of did. I was learning to love New York, learning to fall into step with its energy and speed, but only with Stephen next to me. He was completely at ease in the city: he could hail a cab in seconds and knew where everything was, whereas I just sort of skulked around, feeling bewildered.

What could I say, though? The trip must have been costing him an appalling amount of money. And when he was with me, he was lovely. He even braved the suite's big bath with me, in spite of my recent (and not insignificant) fart-transgression.

So I said nothing. 'I'm fine,' I told him, then stayed in the hotel until he was free again.

On New Year's Eve, Stephen had to go and firefight for several hours. He'd taken the work summonses reasonably well so far, but I could tell that this call had made him angry. He marched away from me, swearing into his phone, and came back sparking with anger like a loose cable.

I didn't like it. Although neither, I reminded myself, did he.

As an apology, he sent me to the Bliss spa for an outrageously decadent afternoon, although I'd rather have stayed at the hotel. It felt odd, having nice women working away at my horrible feet and witch-like talons. I worried about Stephen and concentrated so hard on trying to relax and enjoy myself that, of course, I didn't enjoy myself in the slightest.

By seven p.m., when we were meant to be leaving for a restaurant, there was still no sign of him. At seven forty-five a bell-boy came up with a box containing a lovely cashmere shawl. 'Wrap yourself up and snuggle,' said the typewritten note. 'It's chaos here. Will get away as soon as I can. Am so sorry.'

I watched *Law and Order: SVU* and ate a big kale salad. They were wild about kale in this city.

Nine thirty-five p.m.

Stephen sent me a string of furious-sounding messages, apologizing, raging, swearing.

Nine minutes past eleven: *I am sacking everyone*, he wrote. *They have let me down in just about every way.*

Finally, at eleven fifty-five, Stephen arrived back. He was the angriest I'd ever seen him. I could feel it straight away, a nasty, crackling energy that filled the room. Pre-emptive fireworks were already spiralling up into the sky across Manhattan and a banner was running across the bottom of the TV channel, telling me – in case I hadn't noticed – that it was five minutes to NEW YEAR!

'What happened?' I called. He had marched straight through to the bathroom, saying he needed the loo. He clearly did not. He went in, locked the door – which he never did – and then there had been a horrible angry silence.

'Stephen? Are you okay, darling?'

Nothing. New Year struck and a great eruption of fireworks lit the sky; tiny *whumps* of sound through our triple-glazed windows.

I turned off the TV and stared at the darkening screen as I worked out what to do. I didn't like anger. I especially didn't like angry men. Red flags were unfurling.

I slid a foot out of bed, then slid it in again.

Stephen came out five minutes later, his face set in a smile that didn't quite make the grade. 'Sorry,' he said quietly. 'A very bad day at the office. Not that I should have had to be in the fucking office on New Year's Eve when I'm on fucking holiday. I'm fucked off. I'm really fucking fucked off.'

I was frightened by the snarling energy coming off him but I held out my arms anyway. It wasn't reasonable to expect him never to get angry, just because of my Stuff. He paused, then turned away.

'Let me have a shower,' he called. 'I'll have a shower and I'll turn my phone off. Even if the entire New York office goes up in flames, which it looks like it fucking might do, we'll enjoy what's left of the night.'

'Okay,' I said to the bathroom door, which had once again closed in my face.

Poor Stephen. I wondered if he'd ever imagined it being like this, when he'd started FlintSpark all those years ago. That he'd be pulled and stretched in all directions by people in suits all over the world, needing him in meetings, needing him to make decisions, needing him to authorize unimaginable sums of money.

He emerged once more, and once more I held my arms out.

'Jesus! Can you stop . . . Can you please stop being so *nice*?'

I stared at him, my heart pounding. 'Sorry?'

He looked at me for a very long time.

'Sorry,' he said. 'Sorry, darling Pumpkin. I think I should just go to sleep. We can start again in the morning, yes?'

'Okay,' I whispered. 'That's fine.'

At two a.m. I was still awake, lying on my back as Stephen slept soundly beside me. His chest rose and fell rhythmically, the anger drained and spent.

Pull yourself together, I told myself. It wasn't as if he had threatened me.

Twenty minutes later, I heaved myself out of bed and padded over to my phone, which had been buzzing with *Happy New Year!* messages since seven o'clock when midnight had struck in London. I thumbed through them, smiling absently.

Nothing from Tim.

I checked my email. Claudine had sent me a message in the last hour. I frowned. What on earth was she doing awake at this time? It must be seven in the morning in the UK. She was not the type to party all night.

'Urgent,' said her email.

I opened it. And even though my life had changed the moment Stephen Flint had walked into my office, I only realized it now.

Annie, I have bad news. Forgive me for the brevity of this message. I have to tell you. Stephen is dating online. I have a profile myself which is how I know. It's a long story but I can tell you that he is active right now. In fact, he has been trying to persuade me to go on a date with him in the last twenty-four hours. I am dating with a blurry picture, because I am married, and he must not have realized that it is me. I am ashamed of this, and a lot of things I've done lately, but this is not the time to talk about me.

I am so sorry. This is awful. I will try to explain better when I see you. Please do not tell anyone I have an online dating profile, and please come home. I am attaching a screengrab of his profile so that you know it is not just me being a nasty old skunk. He is cheating. And I think he has been since you met.

When you told us about Stephen I was already aware of him and I'm afraid I already had reason to believe that he was bad news. I suspected then and I know now that he is everything people hope CEOs are not, Annie – ruthless, dishonest, manipulative . . . It would not surprise me if he was a psychopath. Many men in his position are; I read a book about them recently. I have watched you grow more and more dependent on him; I have watched you push everyone else away and sink gradually back into your old fears and paranoias. And I cannot help but think that this is his fault, not yours. I am quite sure you have convinced yourself that you're just mentally unstable, but my feeling is that he has made you feel that way.

I do not want you to worry that he is unsafe, because I am sure he is not, although I do think it is better not to confront him while you are out there alone without any support. My advice is to slip away, come home, let me explain everything and then we can decide together how you should proceed. I am here for you.

Again I am so sorry. I have battled with myself for weeks about how much of this I should tell you, but I needed evidence, Annie. Now I have it.

Come home. Love, Claudine

I put my phone down and found myself holding one of my toes. I stared at it, as if it belonged to someone else.

I picked up my phone and read Claudine's message

again, opening the screenshot of Stephen's supposed dating profile. There he was, an arm around me. All but my plait had been cropped out.

It was impossible that this could be true. Claudine must be trying to ruin my trip, the little cow. What was *wrong* with her?

I read her message a third time, and felt a deep, lurching movement in my stomach, as if a door marked 'horror' had opened just a crack.

There was a helicopter flying near our hotel. A hum from the temperature control. A little drip from the shower that Stephen hadn't fully turned off.

And the sound of his breathing. Big, handsome, lovely Stephen. Asleep in bed, metres from me.

Chapter Twenty-six

Annie

I sat on the wide, flat toilet seat. I thought distractedly about American toilets. How low and flat they were. How much more comfortable.

I didn't think much about Stephen. Something happened when I tried to. A sort of ripping, a fierce tearing that felt like death.

Another text message arrived in my hand, with a little self-important buzz. *Have you read my email?* It was Claudine.

Stephen is a total bastard and you need to come home, she texted two seconds later. *Please read my email. I do not say this often enough, but I love you, my little friend.*

I wondered who I should call. I couldn't call Claudine. I couldn't hear her voice, heavy and laden with facts that would destroy me.

Lizzy. Lizzy would know what to do.

I stared at Stephen's washbag as my phone tried to connect us. 'Flannie?' she mumbled. Her voice sounded like pillows.

'Has Claudie called you?'

More pillow. 'No. What's wrong? Is she okay?'

I took a long, shaky breath. 'She's fine. She emailed me and told me Stephen is cheating on me. He's internet dating. She forwarded me an email of him asking her out, and a screenshot of his profile. He asked her out this afternoon, while I was having my nails done. In orange.'

I stared hard at that washbag.

'What?' Lizzy asked. 'I . . . *What?*'

I had a feeling that tears were coming; and with them would come the end. I pressed my eyes hard on my forearm and took a long, shuddering breath.

'Stephen wouldn't do that, would he? And what do you mean Claudie found him on a dating site?'

'I don't know what she's up to. But there's a screengrab of his profile. He's called himself "LeaderOfPeople". That was his joke. He used to say to me, "I am the Leader of the People." Sometimes he'd call himself God. Lizzy, I really can't do this. I'll die.'

I heard Lizzy pull herself up in bed. 'Darling,' she said softly. 'Darling baby girl, I am so sorry. Come home. Get on the first available plane.'

I pressed my wrist harder into my eyes. 'No. I think Claudie's just stirring.'

A pause.

'Really?'

'Really. Look how weird she's been! She's been terrible, Lizzy! She's disliked him from square one! From the *moment* I mentioned him!'

I could imagine my big sister: eye mask pushed up on to her forehead like Carrie Bradshaw; soft cotton pyjamas from the White Company. My beautiful, perfect, damaged sister.

'Annie,' she said eventually. 'I think you should probably come home anyway. Just while you figure it out. Maybe

Claudie is stirring, but it's probably best if you find out when you're –'

'Pumpkin?'

Stephen was in the bathroom. All six foot two of him, naked, blinking, confused.

'Pumpkin? What's going on? Are you okay?'

'Airport,' I could hear a voice in my ear saying. I ended the call.

'What's going on?' Stephen yawned.

I looked up at him. The air between us seemed thick, heavy with my confusion and fear. 'Claudine emailed me saying that you were internet dating,' I said.

Not so much as a muscle moved in Stephen's face. There was no flash of guilt, no tiny shred of worry. He just looked at me. And then he smiled. 'Oh dear,' he said. 'Has she gone mad?'

I smiled back, a tired little glow of hope in my stomach. 'Possibly.'

'I mean, for starters, Claudine is *internet dating*? I thought she was married! To . . . What was his name . . . Sylvester?'

'Yes. She is. I think she just doesn't like you. Which says a lot more about her than it does about you. What a horrible, horrible thing to make up. I don't know what her agenda is.' My eyes bulged suddenly with tears. 'It's not true, is it? Stephen?'

Stephen slid his hands around my face. 'No. It is not true. It could never be true and it will never be true. Annie, I love you. You're my One.' He pulled me into his chest. His heart was beating faster than usual.

'She sent me a screengrab of the profile. And of the messages between this person and her. It was you.'

Stephen stroked my hair. 'It wasn't me, Pumpkin,' he said sadly. 'Of course it wasn't me. It might be some psycho using my photo . . . Or it might just be Claudine. But it certainly wasn't me. Show me.'

I slid my hand into my pocket to get my phone. My hand was shaking. It was shaking very hard. Stephen half carried me back into the suite, turned a lamp on and sat me gently on a large cream sofa. Below us Broadway hummed and growled.

Stephen's arm clamped me firmly in place so that I couldn't leave his side and for a split second – a tiny, tiny slice of time – I felt another, deeper, fear that went way beyond the possibility of losing my beautiful relationship. It was the fear of a little girl crouched in a field with prairie grass tickling her chin; a little girl waiting for something very bad to happen.

I loaded Claudine's email photos, looking blankly at the suite full of our things; small deposits of us all over the polished wood floor and the elegant furniture. The hotel suddenly seemed a disgusting extravagance.

'Here.' I passed the phone to Stephen. His expression was first astonished, then amused, then astonished again. And then angry. Viscerally angry. The arm around my shoulder became a vice.

'I need to call them,' Stephen said quietly. 'I need to call this website and find out who the fuck is doing this to me, and how they let it happen. And then we need to call your . . .' he paused, and I felt the anger radiate crazily out of him '. . . your *friend* to ask her what the fuck *she's* doing. How dare she just email you like this, without any facts?'

I sat still as a mouse, my heart pounding. I thought, I want to believe you more than I have ever wanted anything.

Stephen read the whole thing again. 'Fuck's sake. I do not need this. Not on top of everything else. How dare they? How dare she?'

'But, Stephen, she said –'

'I couldn't give a *fuck* what she said,' he yelled, grabbing my phone. He threw it across the room and I yelped, terrified. 'How dare she? And how dare you, Annie? After all the shit and paranoia you've thrown at me, how dare you do it again, here, now? After all I've done for you?'

I cowered. I had to get out. *I had to get out.*

'I'm sorry,' I whispered.

'I've been good about your fucking friends,' Stephen shouted. His eyes were ice-cold, furious. 'I've never once told you what I really think, which is that you should tell them to fucking fuck off, because they make you feel shit and anxious, but, my God, Annie, I wish I had. Look what she's done! That bitch! And look how easily you've believed her!'

He stared at me and I felt fissures crack open all around me, like an ice sculpture finally beginning to melt. My chest was ballooning with panic.

'I can't be in a relationship with someone who doesn't trust me,' Stephen said. His voice was quiet now, as still as glass.

'Don't,' I began. 'Don't say that. I do trust you, I just don't know how to explain what Claudie –'

'FUCK CLAUDIE!' Stephen yelled. 'FUCK HER!'

He stood up, towering over me, and I heard myself crying hysterically, begging, pleading.

And then something was switched off.

'Oh, God,' he said suddenly, crouching in front of me. 'Oh, God, I'm doing exactly what she wants. Oh, God, Annie, I'm so sorry. Forgive me, my beautiful girl. I've played right into her hands.' He leaned forward and held me to him.

I couldn't feel the warmth of his body. I couldn't feel anything other than my screaming nervous system. Stephen pulled back to look at me, and it was only then that it really hit me.

I don't know you, I thought. *I've never known you.*

'Come to bed,' he whispered into my hair. 'Come to bed, sweetheart. We'll sort it in the morning. Please, Annie, come to bed. I will never shout at you again. I promise.'

And so we climbed into the gigantic bed and I held him until he fell asleep and I fell into a terrible, sick trance.

When I woke up, Stephen was in the walk-in shower, singing a song I didn't know. Behind the luxurious blackout curtains bled razor-thin strips of daylight. 06:00, said the clock by the bed.

New York, new year.

I lay still for a few moments, feeling each different part of my body, as if it might have disappeared.

And then I reached over and picked up Stephen's phone and opened his emails. I ignored his BlackBerry messages: it was the personal mails I was after. I scanned through his inbox; nothing. I scanned down the list of his email folders; nothing. Stephen was still singing.

I clicked on his sent items.

'Here we go,' I said to myself in a strange voice. 'Here they are.' Because there they were. Responses to messages from the dating site, saying, 'Sarah_Smiles has sent you a message'; 'BrixtonGirl30'; 'HaleyTheSailorGirl'. Messages to girls called Roisin, Becky, Kerri.

I clicked on a recent reply he'd sent to Arty_Girly. What a curious moniker for a girl in her thirties. Only she wasn't. Arty_Girly looked like she couldn't be much older than twenty. Her picture appeared automatically in every email response, a pouty, silly, self-conscious girl, barely out of her teens, all vintage and net and samey hairstyle. All *Hackney*.

I looked at Arty_Girly with a dreadful coldness and heard the shower stop. I thought, This girl is very familiar. And then I thought, Oh, it's Petra. Petra is not Stephen's brother's daughter. Petra is a girl from the internet whom he's fucking.

Stephen's replies to Arty_Girly via the dating website became personal emails with a girl called Petra Navarro in mid-June. Around the time we were newly 'in love'. I picked one from mid-July.

My psycho ex Annie is still stalking me. For your safety I think we should carry on meeting away from Hackney, just for now, although if you bump into her I think it'd be best that you continue to pretend you're my niece. You saw what she was like at that restaurant! I think about you all the time. I came again and again last night, thinking about what we did in Berlin. You are so fucking hot, Petra, I'm crazy about you. Let's meet up on Thursday night. Your humble sex slave, Stephen xxxxxxxx

'Good morning, Pumpkin,' Stephen said, walking into the room. He was naked, apart from a fluffy white towel round his neck. His phone was warm beside my thigh. 'Did you sleep okay?' He came over and kissed me long and lovingly on the mouth.

I made a little sound.

Stephen sat in front of me on the bed. 'Sure?'

I nodded. I needed to think, fast, yet I couldn't think at all.

That was, until his phone, nestling close to my thigh, started ringing. Stephen looked round, then down, and then at me. 'Is that my phone?' he asked softly.

I nodded, and saw something tiny change in his eyes.

Stephen reached under the duvet and took it, staring at me with a dangerous curiosity. 'You were snooping on me? Checking Claudine's bullshit story out?'

I shook my head. My vision had tunnelled.

'I emailed the dating website,' he said coldly. 'And they've written back to me already saying that I *do* appear to have had my identity stolen. The card linked to this account apparently belongs to someone else, but they can't tell me who. They're looking into it. In fact, they've passed it on to the police.'

He didn't break eye contact with me. 'If you pass me my BlackBerry I'll show you the email they sent me half an hour ago.'

Help. Help me. I have to get out.

'This has been the worst twenty-four hours of my life,' Stephen said. 'But finding out that you don't trust me is the worst part of it.'

I was frozen.

'Don't do this to me,' Stephen said. 'Please don't let some bitch do this to us, Annie. I love you.'

A vein bulged above his eye.

'But Claudine showed me your profile. It was –'

'Will you fucking *shut up* about Claudine?' he yelled, right into my face.

I gasped and flattened myself against the pillow.

'Sorry,' he muttered. 'Sorry, sweetheart. I'm incredibly stressed. I can't believe this is happening. You know I'm not like that.'

I cowered, terrified.

Before I knew how to respond Stephen had my wrist in a vice-like grip and had yanked me out of bed. 'Listen to me!' he hissed. 'Stop acting like I'm some kind of murderer, Annie! Some kind of psycho! I am not the man who killed your mother! I'm your boyfriend! Your lover! Your best friend! STOP FUCKING WELL DOUBTING ME!'

I tried to back away but he followed me, until my back was against the wall. His face had changed yet again. There was a deadly calm in his eyes.

'Listen to me, Annie, and listen carefully.'

A tiny snatch of air made it into my lungs.

'I came and plucked you out of a shit life that had you trapped,' he murmured, his face right next to mine. I could smell his toothpaste and his clean, cold skin. 'I gave you a job and I gave it to you at a fantastic salary. I gave you everything you wanted. I took you to France. I took you on holidays and breaks. I've brought you to New York. I have picked you up and dusted you down *every single time* you've fucked up, Annie – I've helped you find the things you've lost, I've replaced your phone every time you've managed to abandon it somewhere, I've protected you from your psycho friend Tim, who lies awake at night dreaming about fucking you.'

I began to cry.

'And I've tolerated all of that panic and crying you're so fond of because . . .' he took a long, slow breath '. . . because I love you. You owe me, Annie. You need me. You cannot function without me.'

Small ragged snatches of air. I concentrated on each tiny breath as it gasped into my lungs. Just another. And another. And another.

'Your life doesn't work without me, and you know it.'

He ran his lip along my jawline. 'So stop fucking around,' he whispered. 'Stop listening to the people who have been making your life a misery. Your sister, who's too busy with her boyfriends to be there for you. Claudine, who seems actually to hate you and want you to be alone. And Tim, who's so obsessed with you he took to stalking you in your own home and you didn't even *notice*. Stop fucking around listening to them, and listen to me. Because I make you happy, and they don't.'

He pulled back so I could see his eyes. They were deadly.

My wrist throbbed where Stephen had it jammed into the wall.

'I'm so sorry,' I said, tears running down my cheeks. 'I'm so sorry. It's Claudie, she did this to me. Of course I trust you. I love you so much.'

Stephen let go of my wrist and took me into his arms. 'Thank God,' he said. He pulled me even tighter, stroking my hair. 'I thought I'd lost you to the dark side then.'

'It's okay,' I whispered. Stephen held me so tightly I

could hardly breathe. 'I just let Claudine mess with my head.'

Stephen held me there, while I fought for my breath, murmuring into my ear about how much he loved me. Then breakfast arrived, and we ate a perfect plate of eggs and chicory and truffled bacon, and Stephen went for his morning number two, like he did every day after breakfast, and I pulled on my jeans, took my passport, my coat and my scruffy handbag – so out of place in a hotel like this – and left the room. I took the lift down to the lobby and then I ran faster than I'd ever run in my life, out into the freezing, steaming street, exploding into a taxi and telling it to take me to Newark, because I knew Stephen would look for me at JFK, and if there was one thing I was utterly, fantastically certain of, it was that I did not want him to find me.

As we turned left to start picking our way across east Manhattan I saw Stephen running out of the hotel, looking left and right. Even from there, I could see the fury in his face. It was the kind of fury I had seen in my dreams since I was seven.

Chapter Twenty-seven

Annie

'Tim,' I muttered at the receptionist in the mental-health centre. 'Tim Furniss, Tim, where is Tim . . .'

'I'm sorry? How can I help you?' The woman looked resigned behind her glass window.

'Tim,' I repeated, starting to cry.

'Are you his patient?' the woman asked. There was a sign by her desk, saying, *A smile costs you nothing!*

I tried to smile, but it was impossible. Stephen's plane had landed and he was on his way to Hackney. *I'm coming to find you*, said a message he'd sent five minutes ago. *Stop running away, Annie. You're making things so much worse.*

'I'm not Tim's patient, no. It's a personal matter. I'm so sorry, I know you're all very busy here. But please could you call him? And tell him Annie's here and it's urgent?'

The woman sighed. 'Take a seat,' she said. 'I'll see what I can do.'

It was here. The time I'd rehearsed mentally for as long as I could remember. The time when a man was chasing me.

At first, the calls that came thundering into my phone – relentlessly, repeatedly, like storm-boiled waves – were from America. Even when I'd landed at Heathrow at nine o'clock last night he was still calling me from the hotel on Broadway.

But by the time night had fallen over New York it must finally have dawned on him that I had left the country. The calls started coming only from his mobile. I'd imagined him speeding furiously through the Queens–Midtown Tunnel in a taxi, seething at having been outwitted.

For seven eerie hours the calls had stopped as Stephen had flown through the night, but they'd started again this morning. The first message had said, *I'm at Heathrow and I'm coming to help you. We need to get you to a doctor and we need to do it quickly. I'm your best friend, Pumpkin. I want to look after you. I know you better than anyone else. Please trust me. xxx*

I had almost laughed. *I know you better than anyone else?* If he thought that I would stay in the same town – the same *continent* – as a man who'd had me up against a wall and threatened me, he did not know me at all.

Stephen had had no idea how hyper-prepared I was, every moment of every day, to disappear without a moment's notice. He had no idea that I'd spent my life working out what I'd do if something like this happened. Negative fantasy, my therapist called it, but I'd always thought that was unfair. It was self-preservation, and if recent events were anything to go by, it was entirely reasonable.

You can never truly know the person you love, someone had once said to me. How true! How dismally, horribly true. But I knew my boyfriend now. Thirty hours had passed since I'd left that hotel room, and in that time I'd learned a great deal about Stephen Flint. It was amazing what you could find out, when you knew where to look.

I'd spoken to Lizzy on my way over there. She was beside herself. 'I thought he was lovely,' she had wailed. 'I just can't believe it. Please, please, *please* come to mine as soon as you're done with Timmy. Get him to bring you here. I'll leave work as soon as you want me to.'

I pressed my hands down into my legs, as if perhaps that might stop them shaking. I had no idea how Tim was going to react to this mess. To me. If he appeared at all it would be a miracle, but I had to see him. I needed information and I needed it fast.

Oh, how I hated myself for having doubted Tim Furniss! For being so easily led! I still didn't know what had actually gone on that day when I'd sprinted off down the street away from him, convinced he was going to assault me (or worse), but the more I had read about Stephen in the last thirty hours the more certain I was that Tim was not in love with me. Or darkly obsessed with me, or any of the other awful things Stephen had said. I was certain now that Tim had never turned up in the middle of the night, like Stephen had told me, and the terror I'd felt when he turned up at Stephen's house that morning had been brilliantly orchestrated by none other than my loving boyfriend.

I'm so sorry, Tim, I thought, as my legs hammered uncontrollably up and down.

'Annie?'

Tim looked solid and dependable, an NHS lanyard round his neck and his shirtsleeves rolled up.

The guilt steamrollered me.

'Are you okay?' he asked.

'I'm so sorry,' I whispered. Tim glanced at his watch, then held the door open for me, pointing me through

342

with an armful of cardboard folders. Someone in a room to the left was shouting. There was a lot of swearing and mentions of someone called Chesney. Just for a moment, I smiled. That was a name. That really was a name.

We walked through benign corridors, peppered with euphemistic signs that reminded me of being a post-suicide-attempt teenager, and eventually arrived in a hot little administrative office with Tim's name on the door. Tim pointed me towards a chair crammed into a corner and shut the door behind us. My phone was ringing again.

I crawled into the chair and started sobbing.

'Oh, Annie.' Tim handed me a box of tissues and waited for me to cry it out, a hand on my knee.

'Are we safe?'

Tim smiled. 'If Stephen comes here for you I'll have him locked away before you can say, er, I dunno. Security.'

'How did you know this was about Stephen?'

Tim politely declined to comment. 'Do you need some chocolate?' he asked instead. 'Some ice cream? Some heroin?'

I couldn't even smile. 'Stephen's after me. I found out that he'd been cheating on me, several times over, and when I tried to talk about it he rammed me up against the wall.'

Tim's face fell. 'Oh, God . . .'

'He's on his way to Hackney right now. From Heathrow. He said he's coming to find me. I've had, what, a hundred calls? More? And probably just as many text messages. He's crazy, Tim.'

'Okay. Before we do anything else, we need to call the police.' His phone was already in his hand.

343

'No!'

'Yes. I'm no lawyer, Annie, but it sounds like he pretty much assaulted you, and the calls and messages are harassment. As is his threat to "find" you. We need the police at your house if he's heading there.'

You fool, I chastised myself. *You idiot!*

I had a plan. The plan was already in action. And it was a pretty good plan, all things considered, one that I'd spent years firming up, but it depended on the police not being involved.

'Tim,' I said, as steadily as I could, 'we can and will call the police. But not yet. Please will you trust me?'

Tim sighed. 'You're asking a lot of me,' he said quietly. 'An awful lot, Annie, after the last few months.'

'I know. But there are some things I need to work out before I get the law involved. Stephen's clever. He could outwit me very easily if I don't have my story firmed up.'

Tim nodded reluctantly. *A few minutes.*

I took a deep breath. 'Tim, why haven't we talked in nearly three months?'

He frowned. 'What do you mean?'

'I mean, why have we not talked in nearly three months?'

Tim was at a loss. 'You *know* why we haven't talked. You sent me a text message in October, saying that you were having a rough time and that you didn't want to see me for a while.'

'Really?'

'Yes, really. Do you not remember?' He was beginning to look at me as if I were his patient.

I ignored his expression. 'Let me get this absolutely straight. You got a text message, from my phone number, saying, *Hi Tim, I need some time off from our friendship for a while?*'

Tim nodded. 'Yes.'

'And you just thought, Oh, okay, fine?'

'No,' Tim said firmly. 'Of course not. I called you back straight away. And when you didn't answer, I called you again, then again, and then again.'

Yes. The phone ringing on the chair while Stephen and I sat in the bath.

The dull weight of truth was now pressing hard upon me. 'I didn't send that text,' I said. 'It was Stephen.'

He was astonished. 'What? Why?'

'Let me tell you what *I* have spent the last three months believing,' I said, feeling my colour rise. This was not going to be easy. 'In my infinite wisdom, Timmy, I decided that you were talking about me that night in the tube station when you said you'd been in love with someone for years who didn't feel the same.'

Tim looked slightly amazed. 'Er, really?'

'It was Stephen's fault. He was convinced from the very beginning that you had feelings for me. He used to talk about it all the time, pointing out things you'd said and done. I ignored it for ages but in the end it got under my skin and I started to believe him. Sadly, as you know, it doesn't take much for me to distrust men.' I exhaled. 'I'm still horribly ashamed that I doubted you. Of all people. That part makes me very sad.' I looked at him, at his kind, trustworthy face.

'I am really, truly not in love with you, Annie.'

'No need to sound quite so disgusted.'

'Oh, Annie, come *on*! It'd be like being in love with my

sister!' He began to blush. 'I was talking about —' He stopped. His cheeks were roasting red. 'I was talking about Lizzy. Not you.'

Just for a second, I forgot that a man with a severe personality disorder was on his way to my house. '*Lizzy?*'

'Lizzy. I'm sorry, I can imagine that might be slightly weird for you to hear. If not abhorrent.' His voice had dipped almost to a whisper.

I tried to take this in. Tim was in love with my sister? He *what?*

I could remember, clear as day, the first time I'd introduced him to Lizzy back in the nineties. He was wearing an Ocean Colour Scene T-shirt and he had curtain hair and big Vans trainers. Lizzy was listening to Soul II Soul and wearing cropped jumpers and lipstick called Heatherberry. She'd barely acknowledged him, and when he and I had sat out in the garden, drinking ginger beer and talking about bereavement, Tim asked me if Lizzy had a boyfriend and went crimson for two hours. I'd ignored it, because everyone fancied my big sister, and he'd never mentioned her again. All those years, all those girlfriends. Poor Tim!

'I know it's hopeless, and that I'd never stand a chance with her. So you needn't say anything. And, anyway, this isn't the time to talk about it.' His voice was all cracked and wonky.

I just stared at him. 'Why did you never say anything?'

Tim was crimson. 'What would have been the point? You'd have been grossed out — you'd have told her and she'd have rejected me.'

'No, Timmy! Lizzy adores you, she —'

'Lizzy adores me in the same way that you do, Annie. I went a bit mad for twenty-four hours, decided I was going to tell you – that's why I asked if we could meet to talk. I couldn't bear it any longer. But for obvious reasons that didn't happen. Look, can we drop this, please? We've got more important things to talk about.'

My phone rang, as if to prove his point. Stephen. For the millionth time, my insides spasmed with fear. I cancelled the call and almost as soon as I did it rang again. Lizzy this time. 'I'm with Tim,' I said. 'I'll be on my way soon.'

'Thank God.' She sighed. 'If anyone's able to make sense of this mess, it's Timmy.'

Tim could clearly hear her voice. He blushed, and I wondered how I could possibly have failed to notice this before.

'Come on, Pumpkin,' he said. 'Carry on with the story.'

I shuddered.

'Annie?'

'He calls me Pumpkin too. Has done for ages. I think it was some weird brainwashy thing, deliberately planting you in my mind all the time. He . . .' my voice quaked but I forged on '. . . he got me a little silver P on a chain for Christmas, and said it was P for Pumpkin. Only I've since realized that he messed up and gave me the wrong necklace. My P was almost certainly for Petra, that girl in the restaurant in the summer – he's been fucking her all along.'

Tim just stared at me. 'Petra his *niece*?'

'No, nice, trusting Tim. Nice, trusting Annie bought that nonsense too. In reality she was just some girl off the internet. I want to call her a slag but I'm sure she's

347

perfectly nice. Although theirs seems to be quite a sex-based relationship, from the few emails I've seen.'

'Wow.' Tim rubbed his face. 'Wow, Annie. I'm so sorry. You poor, poor thing.'

I shook my head. There was no time for betrayals and broken hearts. Stephen could arrive at my house in as little as ten minutes now.

'How strange that Stephen felt the need to come between us,' he mused, 'when all along *he* was being unfaithful. I wonder what his motives were.'

'I have no idea,' I lied. 'Let's get back to that day, just for now. Stephen called you and said I had food poisoning. I was running a bath. I could hear him talking to you, so I guess he must have been talking to the dialling tone. His only real communication with you was a message that he sent from my phone to yours, saying I didn't want to see you.'

'Bloody hell.'

'Indeed. So, you called me as soon as you got the text message. You called three times, then Stephen answered. What did he say? He didn't tell you I had food poisoning?'

Tim rolled his eyes to the ceiling, trying to remember the details.

'Nope. He echoed what you'd said in the text message, really – that you were really upset about some stuff, and that you were finding it particularly hard to be around men at the moment. Except him. He . . .' Tim scratched his head, looking baffled. 'He was actually *really* nice. He talked about your mum, said he thought this was happening because you'd agreed to move in with him, and that that had probably triggered old feelings.' A pause. 'It was really quite plausible. Very sociopathic behaviour.'

'So, the café? The bakery? When you turned up later?'

'Oh, God!' Tim said, realizing he'd been had again. 'God, he's good!'

I nodded, impatient for him to continue.

'I was early for work,' Tim said, 'And I thought I'd check on you, because if you were in a traumatized state I thought you might need proper help.'

Lovely Tim.

'I was heading to your house when Stephen came out of the bakery. I hadn't seen you two in there so I was taken by surprise. Stephen got quite shirty, asking why I couldn't respect your wishes. I said I was very familiar with your past and felt that you might need some specialized support. Then he got all personal and insulting. I lost my rag a bit, because I was stressed, and he loved that. I actually shouted at him! That's when you appeared. And then I saw you sprint off and . . .' Tim's voice caught. 'Poor Annie,' he said softly. 'I thought you were having an episode. Maybe you were. To run that fast from me . . .'

My phone started ringing.

Stephen again. Was he outside my house?

'Go on,' I begged Tim. I had to know.

'I saw you run and in that moment I completely believed what Stephen had told me.' Tim's eyes became watery, and for a brief, bittersweet moment he became sixteen-year-old Tim again. So young and bruised, yet so determined not to cry, rolling his tatty copy of *On the Road* round and round in his hands, nails bitten down to sore crescents. 'Just so you know, Annie, I did send you a final email, the next day. Said I wouldn't be in contact unless you wanted it but that I was there for you any time. I got a reply saying could I please not email again.'

I put my head into my hands and slowly folded down into my lap. 'Oh, God. He's been accessing my emails. Oh, God, Tim.'

'Whoa,' Tim whispered, visibly shocked. 'What a mess. I had an awful feeling something like this could be happening, but I've been in my own shit about Lizzy and failing to get over it and I guess I just . . . I guess I just chose to believe you. I should have fought harder, though. Carried on contacting you, irrespective of what you said.'

He rubbed his hands over his face. He looked awful. 'I've let you down,' he said sadly. 'I should have trusted my gut.'

No, I thought. I've let you down. And I'm going to do it again. You'll never know how much I hate myself for this.

'I think Stephen's been using my phone to read my messages and emails constantly,' I said flatly. 'He's always known so much, Tim. Things that he claimed I'd told him, but I was sure I hadn't.' My mouth made a sound distantly related to a laugh. 'He'd say, "God, you forget everything, don't you?"'

Tim shook his head. 'This is bloody awful.'

'It's not the best. I'm pretty sure I missed out on some Le Cloob meetings because he simply read and deleted the texts. I'm convinced I wasn't that useless.'

'Bloody hell.'

'He's so good, though, Tim. He accused me several times of stalking him and I ended up really paranoid that he was right! That I was, like, some shady stalker who should feel ashamed of herself!'

'I don't understand.'

'Well, for example, one day he found a photo on my phone of him that I'd Google-imaged at the beginning of our relationship and he was all, like, "Ha-ha! My little stalker!" He said it more than once. I died of shame every time. And all the time there he was, poking around in my phone, my email, my life.'

Tim, who was looking increasingly pale, checked his watch. 'Look, I've got an admin afternoon so I can spare a few hours if I make it up tonight. I suggest we go to your house now and pack some stuff so you can come and stay with me. Or Lizzy. Or Claudine, if you're feeling brave.'

I couldn't smile.

'And I think we should call the police.'

'Not yet.'

'Why?'

'Because I don't want to, Tim. I don't think you understand how clever Stephen is, how easily he can talk his way out of trouble. He's got the very best lawyers, and the very best brain. Unless I have an *overwhelming* body of evidence against him, he'll be out of the police station and at my front door within the hour. I need a couple more days to put it together. Will you give me that?'

Tim looked wary.

My phone started ringing again. 'Hello, Claudie.'

'Oh, my little pepper pot,' Claudine said sadly. 'Lizzy just told me you are back. I am so desperately sorry, Annabel. I am going to come to Lizzy's tonight. We can talk then. Or, if you prefer, we do not talk about it. But I will be there.'

'Thanks.'

'Have you heard from Stephen?'

'Repeatedly.'

Claudine made a worried sound. 'Be careful, my little piglet. I think Stephen is very clever.'

'I completely agree. I'm being very careful indeed.'

I ended the call. 'Claudie just said the same thing. "Stephen's very clever." I beg you, Timmy, don't call the police. Not yet.'

'Okay. But first sign of trouble and I'm calling them,' he muttered.

I felt no relief at all when we got back to my house and found the doorstep empty. If he wasn't there now, he would be soon. He would be there soon and I would have to act on my plan, and I would hurt not only Tim but Lizzy and Claudine. And – worst of all – my dad. My lovely, sweet daddy.

Tim held my hand while he walked around my little house, checking every cupboard. 'I want to call the police,' he kept saying, but I wouldn't let him.

After packing a bag of things we went down to my kitchen to turn off the heating.

And then my heart stopped.

There he was.

In my back garden.

'Annie!' Stephen called, striding towards my French windows, and I heard Tim shouting something.

At first, as my arms, then my legs started to shake, and

I felt breathless and floaty, I didn't realize what was happening.

'Police,' I heard Tim say into his phone, and then shout, 'I've dialled nine nine nine!' at Stephen. I was dimly aware of Stephen yelling something through my back door and Tim pushing me out of the room. Then my chest started tightening and it all came back to me. The sensation of being unable to breathe, hearing myself gasping for air. Sweat breaking thickly across me, like oil, while I scrabbled hopelessly at the threads of my existence to stop myself dying.

And then the bit where it all stopped, when I thought, That's it. I've died.

WHATSAPP GROUP MESSAGE

> LE CLOOB
> Tim, Lizzy, Claudie, You

Annie:

HELLO FROM THAILAND! SURPRISE! And sorry . . ! This is the view from my hut ☺ Guys, I'm so sorry to do a runner on you, but I felt like I had no choice. I couldn't wait around doing paperwork for a restraining order, I just had to go. Please try to understand, and please know that I love you and that I'm sorry. Lizzy, I called Dad and said I wasn't sure about Stephen and had decided to take a nice holiday. Please DO NOT tell him what's really happened. It'll set him right back, and I can't do that to him. Anyway, I'll only be away two or three months; it'll soon pass and by the time I'm back, Stephen'll have forgotten about me. I'm not insane, by the way, I'm FINE. Just sorry if I've made you worry. I love you all. X 6.52am ✓✓

Lizzy:

Oh God, Annie! Please answer your phone. Please tell us where you are. You can send a letter if you think that's safer. Pleeeeeeease, little sister. Or just come back where the police can protect you. Love you so much. Xxxxxxxxx 7.11am ✓✓

Claudine:

Oh dear, Annie. I am so sorry to have been part of the cause of this. I echo your sister. Please do tell us where you are, it is important that somebody knows. Stay safe, my little flip-flop. I also love you. 7.12am ✓✓

Tim:

ANNIE! Please come home. And tell us where you are in the meantime. Please, sweetheart. X 8.00am ✓✓

Annie:

Better not tell you where I am, just in case. Please don't worry about me! I think Stephen's unhinged but I also think he'll give up as soon as he realizes I've gone. By the time I'm back it'll just be a blip in the distant past for him. And, anyway, you know I'm happiest abroad. Especially in Asia. I am eating spicy soup and listening to the birds in the trees. I should split up with mad stalky boyfriends more often! Honestly, I'm FINE. It's utterly gorgeous here, and I feel relaxed for the first time in ages. xxx 8.57am ✓✓

Chapter Twenty-eight

Annie

I was not in Thailand eating spicy soup and listening to the birds in the trees. Neither was I relaxed. 'Can this just go away?' I was saying to myself, sitting on a smooth, cold floor in a windowless building. 'Can this just *stop*?'

It did nothing of the sort.

I had bought a flight to Bangkok with a changeover at Abu Dhabi Airport – where I was waiting now – but I had no intention of completing the remaining leg. Stephen had been accessing my email account. That much was now clear. What I didn't know, however, was whether he'd just been snooping at my emails using my phone or if he'd actually hacked them. This was my test.

If Stephen was hacking my emails, he would know about this flight. And if he was as twisted as I now suspected he was, he wouldn't simply turn up at Heathrow to persuade me to come back: he'd fly out here to find me during my long layover. To stage a proper 'rescue'. Show me *just how much* he cared; how desperately he wanted me back. *I'd follow you to the ends of the earth, Pumpkin. I'd spend every penny I had. We belong together.*

Money was no object to Stephen Flint. And where would be the triumph, the prestige, in snaring me at Heathrow? No. This airport, with its vast eastern mosaics stretching out across the ceiling, four thousand miles away from London, would be far more exciting. A grand gesture befitting a grand man.

'I am the Leader of the People!' he used to say. 'I am God! You don't catch God having a day off!' How I'd giggled.

How I would not have giggled if I'd the faintest clue that he actually meant it.

You crossed the line when you let Tim call the police, he'd been texting. *I'm giving you forty-eight hours to call me and explain yourself. Don't think I won't find you.* Other texts would bang on about how much he loved me, and couldn't live without me. Then some shouted things, like, 'DO YOU HAVE ANY FEELINGS AT ALL? ARE YOU EMOTIONALLY DEAD? FUCKING WELL CALL ME. I AM HAVING THE WORST WEEK OF MY LIFE, YOU COLD-HEARTED BITCH. REMEMBER I HAVE EVIDENCE THAT YOU'RE A STALKER. AND REMEMBER I HAVE EVIDENCE THAT YOU'RE FUCKING MAD.'

Every time a message arrived, another part of me seemed to fall away. There was so little of me left now. What remained was just shrapnel, mismatching scraps of the innocent little hippie I'd once been.

'Are you all right, madam?' asked a lady with a smart Etihad uniform and a soft Arabic accent. She smiled at me as if I were an important first-class passenger rather than some freak in an old trilby, crouching at the edge of the balcony like a stray dog. 'Madam? You do not look very comfortable there!'

'Oh, I'm sorry,' I said, as my brain started working

357

again. 'Jetlag! I'm fine, thank you. Just waiting for my husband. He's coming in from London and we're flying on to Bangkok together. I'll spot him better from up here!'

'Ah, of course, madam,' she said. 'Good luck finding him!' She walked off smartly, her spotless shoes click-clacking away into the low murmur of the terminal.

How effortless it was to lie, I thought. How easy it was, if you had the right accent, spoke the right language, to convince the world that you were doing something perfectly innocent when you were doing quite the opposite.

I wondered at what age Stephen had stopped noticing or caring about his lies. If, in fact, that time had ever come, or if he had just been lying since he could talk.

Did you have a nice day at school, darling?

Yes, said five-year-old Stephen. *I came top in maths homework, Mum!* When in fact he had badly beaten up one of his classmates and spent the afternoon in the headmaster's office. *I got a gold star!*

There was still no sign of him. I wondered if I needed to eat something.

I dragged myself off to a coffee shop where a woman in a hijab was pulling coffees and chatting to a male customer about his fungal toe infection. U2 was playing in the background, that song about the city of blinding lights, and a tiny little girl who looked like she was maybe from Libya was teaching her even tinier brother the Gangnam Style dance. The world had never felt so strange.

I ordered a pastry that I knew I wouldn't be able to eat, and a coffee that would probably send me through the roof, and got out the notebook I'd had close to my body since finding out three days ago that Stephen had not only been cheating on me but was almost certainly in possession of a dangerous personality disorder.

Psychopath, I'd written at the top of the first page, swirling the leg of the H round and round until it rolled off the page.

I knew Claudine would be cursing herself for using that word in her email. She'd have used it to add emphasis to her accusations against Stephen but later regretted it, knowing that the mention of anything like that would throw me over the edge. She was quite right. As soon as my taxi had cleared Holland Tunnel and started zipping along towards Newark Airport I'd been on Google. *What is a psychopath?* I'd written, feeling horribly certain that the answer would describe my boyfriend.

I'd found surprising stuff about how psychopaths often played important roles in society, rather than just running around with axes, and then some less surprising stuff about how they were remorseless and pathologically unempathetic individuals, devoid of the moral compass on which society depends. Lacking impulse control, narcissistic, overly confident, afraid of nothing and no one.

But then had come the real shock: *Psychopaths are often extraordinarily charming, and will go out of their way to appear humble, pleasant and highly entertaining. They rarely struggle to form new relationships, although they have great difficulty maintaining them.*

In two hours I'd made ten pages of notes from the internet and I'd started to plot my escape.

I didn't care if I was being over the top. All I cared about – more, almost, than breathing – was getting Stephen off my tail. I couldn't exist while a man was chasing me. Especially one with a bloody personality disorder.

'. . . to London Heathrow,' said a voice on the Tannoy, and for a second I froze.

In and out, I reminded myself. *Breathe in, then out, Annie.* If Stephen did what I thought he would, he wouldn't be here for another forty-five minutes.

I returned to my notes.

Psychopath, said my notebook. It didn't feel like the sort of word you used for people you met in real life, whom you chatted to in your treatment room, then ended up having sex with in a vineyard. 'Psychopath' felt like a film word. A university-research-department word. An old word, with connections to Victorian dungeons and mad, screaming people. And yet, apparently, psychopaths were everywhere. They were quite frequently your CEO, but they could be your doctor, your hotel concierge – even your teacher. One in every two hundred people, claimed one source. One in every *twenty-five*! claimed another.

Stephen Flint. My knight in shining bloody armour.

My psychopath in shining armour. It would be quite funny, really, if it wasn't the unfunniest thing that had ever happened.

I attempted to eat my pastry while re-reading the observations I'd made from a psychopath 'checklist' invented by a Canadian psychiatrist.

– <u>*Extreme grandiosity: check*</u>. *Stephen calls himself God,* I'd written in trembly blue letters. *He says he is the best in the business. He calls himself Leader of the People. He calls himself God, Jesus, the King. He reminds everyone all the time – even me – of how powerful he is, and he finds it funny.*

- *Superficial charm*. He spent the first month making all these grand gestures to show me how lovely and charming he was. The kindness, the self-deprecation. Ha-ha, look at me, taking twatty photos in Hackney. Ha-ha, look at me, having my scruffy breakfast in the French château. I'm SO NOR-MAL. Ha-ha, look at me, chatting to Le Cloob, showing them all how lovely and attentive I am. How could Annie resist me? Ha-ha! And all the while I'm fucking other women!

At this point the wobbly letters had been blurred by tears.

- *Proneness to boredom*. The man cannot sit still. It's no wonder he's been conducting more than one relationship behind my back. No danger or excitement in monogamy. No fun in being real for five bloody minutes.
- *Pathological lying*. Er, where to start?
- *Lack of empathy and remorse*. Look at the way he talked about the people he's fired! And then how he was all, like, 'Annie, I'm JOKING,' when I looked upset! I'm quite sure that poor Australian girl I used to massage left Flint-Spark because of Stephen. She'd be right up his street. Another victim gone, dispatched, destroyed. And he *just doesn't care*.

It went on and on. The excessive libido, the underhand business tactics, even that framed picture of him cutting up a frog. The signs had been everywhere but, of course, I hadn't been looking. *My boyfriend was a psychopath*. One of the successful ones who managed to go undetected. Rather than the unsuccessful ones who couldn't keep themselves under control and popped off on killing sprees all the time. Stephen was a man whose brain was fundamentally different from that of other human beings; a man who could never be 'cured'.

'Ideal!' I said hysterically, to my coffee. 'Absolutely ideal!' It was horrifying, reading all of this again, but it was a pretty good reminder that I was not being crazy at all.

Besides, I knew enough now to understand that if I was questioning my own sanity, I was probably under the influence of a skilled manipulator. Psychopaths, I'd learned, were fabulous at making their victims think *they* were mad. Look how cleverly he'd turned me against Tim. It had been a devastatingly brilliant campaign: he'd known my precise weak spots and played clever little remarks about Tim right into them. 'I really don't think you should be unduly concerned,' he'd say, 'but . . .' I had run off down the street screaming when my oldest and dearest friend had turned up at my house. I'd even agreed to Stephen's suggestion that I get some medication!

In fact, thinking about it, he'd done a pretty good job of trying to turn me against all of my friends, not just Tim. I felt sick as I remembered the tears he'd forced into his eyes when he'd told me how sick he was of Le Cloob disliking him. God, he was disgusting. And, God, he was good.

'Gaslighting', the websites had called this. *To cause a person to doubt their sanity through the use of psychological manipulation.* In many ways the gaslighting thing was the worst. Going back through the last four months, thinking of all the times Stephen had told me that I had a memory like a sieve. 'Do you even remember telling me your *own* name?' He'd laughed once, when I'd asked how he knew what Lizzy did for a living.

I was pretty sure I hadn't lost my passport in France. That Stephen had nicked it to reduce my confidence in myself. I'd turned my room upside-down searching for it. I'd turned the bloody *château* upside-down. 'You're hopeless.' He'd smiled, handing it back to me.

Jesus, he was clever. One little slip-up, right there at the beginning, and he'd grabbed it. All those 'lost' phones, mistakes and oversights I'd apparently made over the last few months. The horrible suspicion I'd felt that I was somehow unravelling, falling apart, losing it. Even that first day at FlintSpark when I thought I'd lost my client list. He'd been at it even then! Forcing me to doubt myself!

I put my pastry down. It had begun to taste like cardboard.

'I've been shacked up with a psychopath,' I muttered, trying it out for size. The little girl teaching Gangnam moves to her brother on the other side of the café smiled at me, then waved shyly. I waved back. I wanted to cry. Please may you stay safe and protected your whole life, I thought. Please may you never meet a Stephen Flint, you lovely little thing.

I had read that it often took a long time for partners of psychopaths to come to terms with the truth. Even when faced with evidence of multiple infidelities and lies, women would hold on to their original beliefs about their men for months, sometimes years, rather than stare reality in the face. Needless to say, it had taken me about five minutes to get on board with the whole idea. I guessed that was one of the few bonuses attached to extreme paranoia and emotional scarring. You didn't hang around fooling yourself when you were shacked up with Freddy Krueger. You just got the fuck out of there.

I forced myself to finish my pastry. It would all be okay. I had my plan. Dad would hopefully be none the wiser and I'd be safe.

I turned back to my notebook.

One of the blogs I'd read had been written by a woman whose partner had combed the internet for every tiny scrap of information he could possibly find about her. *Google yourself*, she'd written. *You might be surprised at what you find.*

The first thing that had come up under my name, aside from my massage website, was the blog I'd written for a short time a couple of years ago when I was miserable about my crappy work situation. It had been Tim's suggestion: a journal of things I loved to keep me tapped into positivity. When I started to re-read the posts I'd realized that all of them — *every bloody one* — had been raided by Stephen.

There was the blog about flat whites. Stephen had been all over that! The day I met him he had been drinking a double espresso. And the morning he called to offer me a job, I'd heard him order — once again — a double espresso. But by the time I started work at FlintSpark it was all flat whites. And Australian coffee. And specialist milk steaming. He just couldn't believe that we shared the same geeky love of Antipodean coffee!

And I was too *stupid* to notice!

Then there was the story of Stephen having gone to Tresaith as a child for beach holidays. Eating caramel waffles from the post office. That had been *my* story, a blog of warm reminiscence I'd written one particularly dark evening. As if a posh bloke from West Sussex would have gone to a tiny caravan park in a secret corner of Wales for his holidays! For God's sake!

That was assuming Stephen was even from West Sussex.

Another day I'd done a sweet little blog about how desperately I'd longed for a boyfriend when I was a teenager. How I dreamed of a man who'd send me flowers and Milk Tray and mix tapes. Stephen had repeated that verbatim the day I started at FlintSpark! And the piece I'd written about the Counter at Hackney Wick, how Tim and I loved to go there for breakfast. Who had we found wandering the towpath outside?

Jesus.

Then had come the sadder, even more repugnant discovery that Stephen had found and plundered my dad's blog too. He'd even befriended him on Facebook, and sweet, lovely Dad had just accepted the request. It made me blind with rage to think of Stephen infiltrating and infecting my father, just at the time that Dad had turned a corner and started trying to engage with the world again.

All that stuff Stephen had known, he'd stolen from Dad's Facebook page and blog: Dad's love of Rioja wine and Borges the writer; Lizzy's name, Le Clooh's name; my announcement, aged twenty-one, that I was going gluten-, sugar- and dairy-free (and had been hopeless at sticking to ever since). It was all there. Every time Stephen had dropped one of those little nuggets of information into the conversation, he'd convinced me I'd told him myself.

The dropped phone calls whenever I'd visited Dad, too. Of course they weren't Dad's new girlfriend. What sort of middle-aged woman would put the phone down just because her boyfriend's grown-up daughter happened to answer the phone? No, of course it had been Stephen. The predator, just checking in on his prey. Taking a little risk, having some fun.

The worst thing about all of these risks that Stephen had taken, however, was that they had all paid off. I'd heard only the things I'd wanted to hear and interpreted everything the way I'd wanted to. It was funny how your mind could do that. Hi, Annie, here's sign after sign that your man is crazy, but because you like him I'll make every sign invisible. How's that, eh?

The little girl and her brother left the café with their mother and the girl turned to wave at me again. Don't leave me, I thought. Don't go.

They went.

I pushed my coffee to one side. Any more stimulation and I'd take off through the roof, lost for ever in the hot smog of Abu Dhabi city.

Poor, deluded me. I'd thought I'd been in love: deep, cartwheeling love; the kind of love I'd barely allowed myself to dream of. But it turned out that I was not. *Dear Annie, We regret to inform you that, due to unforeseen circumstances, you are not in fact in love. As you will gather from the enclosed literature, you are instead in a 'psychopathic bond'.*

How much longer would it have gone on, I wondered, if Claudine hadn't found him out? How much longer until he started abusing me openly, rather than behind my back? And how could someone like me, who was so endemically terrified of men, have let it happen?

'Stop it,' I said quietly to myself. It had happened

because Stephen had decided to go after me, and that was that. Nobody, not even a highly anxious and paranoid woman like me, would have questioned someone as humble, as self-deprecating, as all-round lovely as the Stephen Flint laid out in front of me. And look at Claudine! Look how she had been fooled by Sylvester!

Poor Claudine. After we'd found Stephen in my back garden, and I'd had a panic attack, and Tim had called the police, and I'd had to answer endless questions and eventually begged to be allowed to go home, and pleaded with Tim to prescribe something to calm me down, we'd all convened at Lizzy's house. I'd been so horrified by everything that had happened that I'd implored Le Cloob not to make me talk about it. Instead I'd spent most of the evening watching Tim and Lizzy, and asking Claudine what in God's name was going on with her marriage.

The answer had been shocking.

'I 'ate Sylvester,' Claudine had said in a tiny voice. 'He is a fat, lazy slob and 'e treats me like his slave. I 'ave earned all the money in that 'ouse for the last five years. He is involved in some stupid sex cult, which pretends to be some sort of therapeutic community. They make out that it is all about "awakening" and "dealing with trauma" and . . .' her slim, manicured hand was shaking '. . . and yet it is nothing more than a group of unwell people fucking each other and using words like "spiritual" to excuse themselves. Sylvester defends it to the 'ilt. He says I do not understand. He says terrible things to me, frequently. 'E would never 'it me but he 'as abused me for years. I am deeply miserable.'

She had clasped her hands until her knuckles were sad

white points. 'And I am a stupid, proud woman, as you know, so rather than talk to my friends, I sign myself up for some dating.'

Lizzy had smiled sympathetically. 'That sounds like my kind of solution,' she said. And I'd watched Tim flinch.

Stephen, she told me, had asked her out on an internet site a few days before I had met him. She had instantly disliked his profile. 'He called himself LeaderOfPeople,' she said disparagingly. 'I mean, come *on*.'

He was still online after he and I had started going out, so she had emailed him, making clear she was a friend of mine, and asking what the hell he was doing. He had replied a few days later to say that he'd thought he'd cancelled the account and hadn't logged on in weeks. His account had been deleted the same day so she had given him the benefit of the doubt. But recently she had joined another site, after Sylvester had gone off for one of his sex 'retreats', and, not recognizing her from her photo – she had again tried to keep her identity fairly hidden – Stephen had emailed her once more asking her out.

Stephen had actually been pestering Claudine for a date on New Year's Eve, while dealing with all of the shit at his New York office.

It was mindblowing. 'We were both taken in,' she had said softly. 'And this does not make us stupid women. Well, it makes me a stupid woman, because I 'ave not yet left my 'usband. But I will. I need time.'

Claudine was not stupid. Neither was I.

I scanned the terminal again, wondering how much longer I had. People continued to swarm past, pulling trolley bags, dragging children, checking phones, scanning departure boards. The coffee shop was playing Paul Weller now. My hands had stopped shaking; they looked shrunken and old.

I didn't care.

I thought tiredly about the number of gaps in my understanding of what had happened, the mysteries I hadn't yet solved. There were still several things that could not be explained by Stephen Googling me, hacking my emails or reading my texts. I wondered how I would cope when I worked out what he'd done and I wondered, most of all, why. Why me? Why had he decided to make me a victim?

Then, as I scanned yet again across the terminal below me, my hat jammed down over my eyes, I saw him. He, too, was scanning, quietly and unobtrusively, from the outskirts. Tall, tanned, eyes like headlights. Ice-blue. Ice-cold. I turned in one movement, sliding out of sight before those eyes swivelled upwards towards the balcony.

I got my ticket out of my wallet, the other ticket I'd bought with cash at Heathrow earlier. No emails attached to this one. No paper trail. No possibility of Stephen finding me.

Because right now he fully expected me to be here, waiting nervously for my connection to Thailand. It wouldn't occur to him that – for the first time – I was one step ahead. He'd wait here for me, and if he couldn't see me anywhere he'd simply board the connection to Bangkok and wait for me there. It was a plan of chilling genius.

But mine was even better.

'Because I won't be there,' I said to myself. 'I'll be thousands of miles away from Bangkok. I'll be somewhere Stephen will never, ever think to look.'

With a pleasant fuzzy calm I walked on with my old woven little handbag, the only possession I'd taken, and began to smile. Stephen had turned up here, proving that he had hacked my email, proving that he was — *at very best* — deeply unstable. He had proved that I was not going mad, that I had every reason to run.

I had doubted myself again and again since meeting Stephen. Questioned my sanity, agreed to see a therapist, to dull my brain with medication.

Enough. I would never again allow anyone to tell me I was mad.

I turned off my phone and threw it into the bin.

Chapter Twenty-nine

Kate

A girl lies awake, watching night slowly leach into morning. Above her the ceiling still seems grey and pitted, darkening to black at the edges.

As if she has been struck, she rolls suddenly on to her side, clutching the striped quilt to her with knuckles whitened by happiness. She breathes in and out, slowly and steadily, marvelling at her body's ability to regulate itself when it feels like it's been injected with sunlight, music, the purest oxygen. She watches the rise and fall of the man's chest beside her and feels seismic joy shifting in her chest.

She wants more than anything to lean in and kiss him, hold him, watch him wake, but she won't. She wants him to rest. She worries that what finally happened last night might have put a strain on his still-fragile bones, even though they were the gentlest, sweetest few hours of her life.

So she lets him sleep, planting the softest kiss on the pillow near to where his head lies.

She drops her feet cautiously to the floor, perhaps fearing that what is inside her might rush out into the floorboards and disappear, like earthed electricity, into the ground. It does not. It has been a week since they first kissed and the feelings have as yet made no attempt to escape. She is beginning to think that they might actually stay, and with this little hope comes an entirely different future: one of which she should never have dreamed.

She has her fears, of course, some of which grip her with an iron fist, but now she knows what it feels like to sleep in his arms she is certain that there is a solution to them all.

A sleepy arm slides out from under the duvet – like a paw – and hooks around her waist, just as she prepares to rise. A muffled sound comes from behind her and smiling, laughing, she folds back down towards its source. There is life! 'You're not allowed to go anywhere without kissing me,' says the muffled voice. He's like a sleepy bear; her heart is bursting. 'It's a new rule. Kissing and cuddling before you start work, even if I'm asleep.'

She curls around him, kissing the side of his head, his ear, his hair, until a face slides into view. It may be barely awake but it is lit up with a smile that melts her bones.

'Hello,' says the face, and slides across the pillow to kiss her. 'You're my favourite,' he mumbles, running his nose through her hair. 'My favourite of all things.'

'Hello, Bear.' She kisses the bear's paws all over.

And she thinks, I love you.

She dresses fast and effortlessly and within minutes is in cold air that carries the sharp promise of rain. The light is thick purple and grey; the day is drawing near.

She jumps in fright as a car pulls into the driveway but manages to hold steady when she sees that it's just the postman's van. She'll have to talk to Mark. To her bear. Today. She can't leave it any longer. He has noticed how jumpy she is; how she watches the driveway whenever she's outside.

She heads off to the postbox and her stomach twists uneasily as she tries to imagine what he might say.

The hedgerow is heavy with sloes, rosehips, bryony vine. 'It'll be okay,' she tells herself, as swallows fly in a silent clump overhead. 'It'll be okay.'

She reaches into the postbox and imagines the people who will have written to her lover today. Computers reporting his financial affairs. A man hoping for a signature on his wife's birthday card. A farrier needing to be paid.

Her hands hold the small bundle of letters for maybe twenty seconds before she glances down and sees what is on the top. And then she stops, and the cameras pull sharply away from her: a girl standing alone in a silent corner of Somerset at seven in the morning. The other letters have fallen lightly around her; one rests loyally against her ankle.

The girl's face is white as she stares down at the envelope in her hand. She feels the universe cracking around her. I was so happy, she thinks, as she stares at the handwriting she has seen in her dreams a hundred times over. I was so happy.

Annie Mulholland
Hythe Farm
Near Wootton Courtenay
Somerset
TA24 0ZX

'Stephen,' I said into the restless morning. 'Stephen found me.' And at that moment the world, in which everything had started to seem possible, slammed shut like a guillotine.

I sat down in the wet grass. I stared at the envelope with blood pounding in my ears. Stephen Flint had found me. It had taken him a while — nearly ten months — but he'd got there eventually.

It was the documentary, of course. *Why didn't you go?* I whispered hopelessly to myself. *Why didn't you leave when you still could?*

Of course he'd written to me. How much more satisfying this would be, I thought, picturing myself crumpled on the ground by the postbox, my heart pounding and my body shaking like a thin autumn leaf. How much more satisfying than the obvious drama of his sudden arrival in the yard, in a sleek, anonymous car, me screaming and the horses skittering around.

Almost as soon as I'd sat down I sprang back up. He's been here, I realized. He'll have driven down and looked around, so he can picture me right here, having this moment. His prey.

I started to walk along the hedge back to the farm on legs that didn't really work. Somewhere near me a solitary wood pigeon sighed. Oo-oooo, oo-oo-oo, it said. I wondered if Stephen was actually watching me now.

I bent double, suddenly, and threw up into the grass under the hedge, clutching wildly at the twisted branches for support but finding only the thorns of a blackberry bush.

It took me what seemed like a lifetime to get to my safe place. But as I approached it, I backed away. Blood from my fingertips had smudged all over the envelope and my breathing was ragged. I couldn't inflict this on Stumpy.

I doubled back to the other stable block, which was still empty, and crouched in what was once Madge's stable.

Annie. Dearest little Annie, who stood by and watched while her friend reported me to the police.

So here you are, my sweet lover. My girl. Here you are, hiding out on a farm like some rural rat in a shed. An interesting choice, Pumpkin. What took you down there? Was it the idea of another wealthy man you could fleece? Another unsuspecting bloke trying to make an honest living from whom you could leech money and affection and maybe free rent?

Oh, Annie. I believed you. I believed you were a genuine girl who loved me for who I was, rather than what I had. I honestly thought you didn't care less about my money or my position. But of course you did. They always do! You wanted somewhere to live, someone to protect you, someone to fund your holidays, someone to buy you expensive dinners. You wanted someone to make your broken life feel easy.

You rinsed me, Annie, and then you ran off, fuelled by some ridiculous accusation cooked up by a mentally unstable friend who'd found out her husband was a bloody <u>sex cult leader</u> and wanted to punish all men. It blows my mind that you didn't allow me to tell you what really happened. To show you how amateurishly and spitefully your 'friend' had set me up. Instead you just assumed the worst and – zoom! Gone!

In spite of everything, I never gave up. I couldn't stop loving you, even if you could me. And so when I saw you on a late-night repeat of some television programme, Annie, I cried. I sat there and cried, and thought, That's my girl. How moved I was by your concern for a complete stranger injuring himself at Badminton.

And then how surprised I was when I called the idiotic woman at this 'stranger's' eventing yard only to discover that the girl who'd been pictured running screaming towards Mark Waverley was 'his lovely Irish groom, Kate'. She told me she had high hopes for you and Mark. Said you laughed him back to good health. How touching! How very nice!

You owe me, Annabel. You owe me big-time. You walked out on your contract mid-term and thus you owe me just shy of twenty thousand pounds to buy yourself out for the rest of the year. You owe me for all the breaks we went on and you owe me for the many, many things I bought you while you shamelessly used me. You owe me rent and dinners and most of all you owe me for the grief I suffered at your sudden disappearance.

Whatever your friends may have led you to think, though, I'm a decent bloke. I know you don't have that kind of money so I'm willing to make a trade. In spite of all of the awful things you've done to me – the police, the insulting lack of trust, the willingness to just walk out of my life without any thought for me and my feelings, not to mention the vast amount of money you owe me – I'm willing to take you back. Because underneath it all, I'm just a normal guy who loves you. If you come back, move back in, I will forgive it all.

Remember, Annie. You owe me.

I'll pop down to chat this through with you, very soon.

Your Stephen xxxx

I scrunched the letter up and sat perfectly still on my heels. The stable was still. It smelt of Jeyes Fluid; Joe and I had scrubbed it down only yesterday. Halfway through the job Mark had texted me and told me to meet him in the hay barn in the top field. I'd run there with my heart pounding happily, thinking, Jilly Cooper would totally have written a scene like this. Except we hadn't had rampant sex and nobody had invited us to an orgy by a pool. There had been no damp bushes or kohled eyes or women emptying bottles of Je Reviens all over themselves.

It had really been very tame, me and Mark just lying in a little hay cave, kissing and holding hands and laughing guiltily about our messed-up childhoods. I'd told him about Mum dying, and it had been the easiest thing. Mark had not tried to stop me crying, or to fix me. Neither had he pretended that his own mother had died.

I was certain Stephen had made up his mother's death. It was quite a common tool in the psychopath's infidelity repertoire, apparently: 'My family are too raw to meet you right now,' they told their girlfriends. 'Another time . . .' While they ran off to have sex with their other victims.

I'd often wondered who Stephen's grieving father really was. Petra? Someone else? And that conversation on Christmas Day when he'd told me he was walking down the street in his father's supposedly chocolate-box village and seen a dog crapping on the pavement. Where had he actually been? Whose Christmas had he actually been sharing?

A gust of wind blew past the stables, carrying the smell of damp turf and wet heather from the moor. I had to get out of there. He could be literally minutes away.

I ran inside, managing to dodge Joe who was already out filling water buckets. I locked myself into my room and started throwing things into my wheelie case, pausing every few seconds to check out of the window. My phone beeped suddenly with an incoming message and I gasped with shock.

Morning, you very nice thing, said the text. Mark. *No sign of you in Stumpy's stable or the yard. I would pay good money for another cuddle. Please come out of hiding. Mum just asked me why I'm smiling so much. xx*

I began to cry. I was right back where I'd started: a fugitive in my own life, looking over my shoulder, petrified by the sound of a creaking floorboard. Only now I had the guilt of abandoning my family and the heartache of losing Mark. Mark, my lovely warm bear, with the gentle paws and the big kind eyes and the slow, sweet smile.

'Why?' I asked the empty room. 'Why must my life be like this?'

The room shrugged. *That's your lot*, it said. *You couldn't hide for ever.*

That was the worst part, I thought, tipping the contents of my dressing table into a carrier bag. I was back to being Annie Mulholland again, couldn't pretend to be Kate Brady for a moment longer.

But I didn't *want* to be Annie Mulholland! I hated being her! I wanted to carry on being Kate Brady! There'd been laughter in my time being Kate! Fun! Joy! Why was it that, wherever I hid, Annabel bloody Mulholland – with her bereavement and her breakdown and her small, frightened life – *always* found me?

I stuffed the contents of my little chest of drawers into my wheelie case, holey socks, holey gloves, holey jumpers, and with that my life was packed once again.

I called Becca. 'Morning, pet,' she said. I could hear her munching her dry Shreddies. 'How's things?'

'He found me,' I said. 'Stephen's found me.'

'Okay, pet,' Becca said, without a pause. 'I'll be over in five.'

'I have to get away. Properly. Will you take me to Bristol Airport?'

Becca paused.

'Please, Becca. I beg you.'

'Is that a good idea?' she asked, less certain. 'Would it not be easier to call the police?'

'No. He got out of it in four hours last time, Becca, and now he's angry.'

'Okay,' she said reluctantly. 'I'll square it with the gaffer and jump in the car.'

'Please hurry.'

I sat with my hands circled tightly round my legs. What wouldn't I give for just two more hours as Kate Brady. Two more minutes.

When I had discovered on New Year's Eve ten months ago that my boyfriend was mad and possibly dangerous, I knew I was going to have to put my long-held emergency plan into action. At that stage, however, it had not so much as crossed my mind that I should pretend to be someone else, once I'd snuck back into the UK from Abu Dhabi.

All I'd worked out was that I would take the first train out of Paddington and head west. I'd stay in a B&B wherever the train terminated – somewhere buried deep in the Devon or Cornwall countryside, hopefully – and find myself a job. Some sort of live-in job where I'd be paid cash; a pub, maybe. I would throw away my phone and get a new one with a new number, and I'd close down my email, Facebook and Skype accounts. And everything else Stephen could access.

But once my plane to Abu Dhabi was airborne I'd begun to panic. My online life no longer existed. My phone was soon to be dismantled and thrown away, and once it had gone I would be completely alone. There would be nobody on earth who knew where I was. It was just me, entirely alone in the world, trying to start again. How exactly was I going to find this mythical job? How much would they want to know about me? What if someone recognized me?

I'd found myself in a sort of terrified stupor. I had reached into my little bag for some Rescue Remedy, but before my hand had found it, it had found a fat envelope. Kate! Of course, I'd had a letter from Kate. It had been at the top of the pile on my doormat when Tim and I had gone to my house and found Stephen in the garden. I opened it, praying slightly hopelessly that it might cheer me up. Or at least break me out of this mental paralysis.

And, actually, it had. A little. It was a wonderful Brady ramble, a rude, hilarious and rather moving account of her six months on a 'farm sabbatical' somewhere in Kilkenny.

I've had the time of my LIFE [she'd written]. And now I'm back in my little box of a flat, squeezing myself on the bus every morning to get to Google, wondering what the feck I was thinking of, coming home. I keep whacking myself round the head with one of those trendy copper saucepans that my mam made me buy, shouting, WHAT WERE YOU THINKING?

. . . It was the best thing I ever did [she wrote later, in a more thoughtful passage]. Those earthy smells, and the feeling of having done a hard day's work, and being near those lovely horses. Not having any phone signal. Annie, do you remember what that felt like? I had to use a phone box when I wanted to call someone! It was wonderful! Although I did miss chatting to you all the time.

I'd read the letter again and again, feeling a little less frightened and alone each time.

And then: *A farm?*

The first train out of Paddington had taken me only as far as Exeter, which still felt far too close to London, so I'd taken the next departure and ended up in Barnstaple. I'd checked into a tired B&B, with a thin strip of a sea view and, after a short, fitful sleep, had started scouring the internet for jobs on horse yards or farms. If it had worked for Kate, it could work for me.

After a few weeks a sweet little advert had appeared on the Yard and Groom website, written by Sandra, for a job only twenty miles from where I was now. No pay, said the ad, but all meals and accommodation provided.

Great, I thought. If I wasn't being paid they wouldn't want National Insurance numbers or bank details. I doubted Stephen was up to hacking bank systems but I wasn't going to take any risks. And since he'd hired me I'd been earning stupid money, which I hadn't spent because he'd paid for everything. I could afford not to earn for a while, as long as I was being fed and housed. Stephen, ironically, had funded my escape.

I jotted down the email address – a lady called Sandra Waverley; Mark's wife perhaps? – and sat down to write a letter of application.

At first I'd struggled. Should I pretend to have experience I didn't? Should I spend time researching Mark Waverley first? And what about horses? Should I try to sound knowledgeable?

I read Kate's letter again, in case there was any useful farm vocabulary I could pinch.

Nothing.

What would Kate say? I found myself wondering.

And that was how it began, really. As soon as I started trying to think like Kate Brady might, I began to write. I wrote a short, funny, honest letter to Sandra – no lies, no bullshit, just a nice email that probably made me sound decent and hard-working, rather than desperate and frightened.

My hands hovered above the keyboard before I signed off. I couldn't imagine how Stephen would ever find me there, but Annie Mulholland was quite a distinctive name. And it was a name that many people knew anyway: that poor girl whose mother was raped and murdered up in the Peak District, back in the eighties. Do you remember? Terrible business.

What if this Sandra recognized my name and mentioned it to someone else?

Kate Brady, I signed off, just like that. I gave the K a big long flourish, like Kate probably would, and found myself smiling. Slightly manically, but a smile all the same.

The next day, to my great surprise, I received a lovely reply from Sandra inviting me to come to the farm for 'a cup of tea and a nice chat'. I'd swung into a hairdresser's and had my long blonde hair dyed red, then gone and bought a load of clothes; the sort of clothes that modern people might wear. Normal people. Kate-type people. Toiletries too; normal people spent money on those. I even bought a bottle of Kate's perfume.

Why not?

I arrived back at my B&B feeling happier and more hidden. I was disappearing out of Annabel Mulholland by then, although I hadn't realized it yet.

On my way to the 'interview' with Sandra a few days later, I'd got myself into another terrible panic. What if I wasn't offered the job? What then?

What would Kate do? I interrupted myself. I took a deep breath. Kate would not be flailing around in the Bad Shit, for starters. She'd be sitting on this bus, maybe whistling a tune, or chatting to the mad old guy on the seat behind. Or she might be counting trees-that-looked-like-goats, which was something she used to do during long-haul bus journeys when we were travelling.

By the time I'd arrived at Hythe Farm I'd felt lighter than I had in days. 'You see?' I muttered to myself, in Kate's Irish accent, as I walked up the drive. 'You see how much better life is when you're not sitting in the Bad Shit?'

I paused. Irish accent? Would I do that, too?

Of course not. That'd be insane! Basket-case territory!

Still I paused. Mum was Irish. When I'd stopped being able to remember her face without looking at a photo, I'd still been able to hear her voice when I closed my eyes. Soft and musical, as if someone had filed down all the sharp points of the English accent and left only its rolling hills and rounded valleys. Lizzy and I had been perfecting our Irish accents since we were tiny, and as an adult I found it almost as easy to speak in an Irish accent as I did my native English.

But even so, I thought. That was *mad*.

Then: 'You'll be grand,' I heard Kate Brady say. 'Stop worrying, you great dingbat! Go for it! It's a brilliant ruse!'

I didn't care if it was mad. I didn't care about anything, really, other than being untraceable for the next few months.

So that was that. I cut off Annabel, because I couldn't cope with her, and I became Kate, because in her shoes, life was bearable. The monstrous fear of Stephen had not gone away. Or the mess of my life. But as Kate I'd been able to cope with all of it. What would Kate do? I'd ask myself, day in, day out. How would Kate react? What would Kate *think*? And, after a while, I discovered I'd started to see the world through Kate's eyes without prompting.

As Kate I looked for the humour in everything; I always had a joke to crack or a story to tell. As Kate I trusted and liked people; I found a cheekiness and ease of communication I'd never felt in myself. Above all I felt hope: hope that I would somehow get through all of this Bad Shit and have a decent life again.

Kate Brady had made me the best possible version of myself. She had made me a human being that people liked. Fell in love with, even. She had made me happy.

I yelped as a sudden rap on the door set off panic like a gun.

'Kate?' It was Mark. 'Kate, are you okay?'

'Grand,' I called. A terrible sob came out, strangling the word.

'What's wrong?'

'I'm grand,' I repeated. 'Doing some admin.'

'Really?' Mark asked. 'Admin? With screams and sobs?'

'Yes.'

The floorboards were still creaking: Mark wasn't going anywhere. For a brief second I had a sense that he was smiling – that warm, slow, lovely smile that melted my bones.

'I don't think you're doing admin,' he said. 'Let me in.'

'I will,' I called. 'But later. I need some time to, er . . .'

'To do your admin?'

'Yes.'

'You're being weird and mysterious.' Mark's voice was gentle. 'What was it? *Nescio et mirum*?'

My heart was breaking. I had to get this precious man away from the mess of my life and I had to do it now. Where was Becca? 'I'll catch up with you later,' I called. 'Okay?'

'Now look here . . .' he lowered his voice '. . . look here, you. I've just hauled my crappy legs up two flights of stairs and I'd quite like a little kiss and a cuddle before I go back down. Can I at least have that?'

'Not right now,' I called, and another terrible sob came out.

'Okay, you fruitcake. But I'm reserving you for some kissing and cuddling later, Kate Brady, and that's that. I think you're the very best.'

And I couldn't answer because I was crying so hard. I'm not Kate Brady, I wanted to shout. I'm just a messed-up freak-show of a woman who's about to leave you without saying goodbye. And my heart is completely broken.

I cried silently into my hands, and eventually I heard him go.

I'm outside, Becca texted a little while later. *Parked behind the barn. Mark's teaching some Pony Club kids and Joe's out on one of the horses. Coast's clear.*

I slid my phone into my pocket, and grabbed my things. As I did, it beeped again.

Hello, Pumpkin.

My phone didn't know the number, but I did.

My chest felt no more substantial than air. 'Oh, God,' I whimpered, running down the stairs. 'Oh God, oh God, oh God.'

Chapter Thirty

'I didn't say goodbye to Stumpy,' I muttered, slamming the car door and locking myself in.

'No, pet, you didn't,' Becca replied, starting the car. 'But neither did you say goodbye to Mark, and you've been sleeping with him.' She put a steadying hand on my shoulder. 'I know this feels like the end of your world, pet, but it's not. You will see Stumpy again. And Mark. It'll be all right.'

'Do you really think so?' Becca inched the car forward slowly, leaning forward to check that the coast was clear.

'I do. Can you see Joe anywhere?'

'No.'

'Okay, then. Let's go.'

'Please.'

Becca set off. 'It's bloody weird hearing you speak in an English accent, pet. Are you sure you're not Irish?'

'Certain. Just mad.'

'You're not mad. I ran off to the farm too, remember?'

'Yes, but not while pretending to be in Thailand. And not nicking your friend's identity.'

'True.' We swung out into the driveway. I still couldn't see Mark.

'I've lied to my family all this time,' I said sadly. 'It's killed me, Becca. The guilt's nearly driven me insane. And yet I've carried right on lying.'

'You did it to protect them and protect yourself,' she said softly. 'Stop beating yourself up.'

She turned briefly towards me and I saw her face, softened to white at the sides by the low, bright sun. 'You look so lovely, Becca,' I said, then began to cry. 'I don't want to leave you. You, Mark, Stumpy, Joe, Sandra. I don't want to go back to my shit life.'

Becca stopped the car down the side of the indoor school and held my hand while I cried.

'I can't stand the thought of being Annie Mulholland again. I loved being Kate.'

Becca handed me a dirty old bobbly glove, just like she had on the day we'd met. 'Blow your nose on this filthy thing,' she said soothingly. 'And listen, pet. You were always Annie Mulholland.'

I looked hopelessly at her.

'I know you think you'd sort of "become" your friend Kate, sweetheart, but I'm afraid that's a load of shite. I've not met the girl but I'm pretty damned sure that all you did was to approach life with more of her positivity. You were still you. Still Annie.'

If only! 'No . . . Kate Brady is, like, this funny, mad, beautiful Irishwoman. She's sparkly and hilarious and everyone loves her. Whereas I'm just a depressed, washed-up, frightened old mess. Trust me, Becca, I've lived in this skin for a long time. Mark would never have fallen for the real me. It was Kate he fell for. I should introduce them some time,' I said, and cried even harder.

Becca seemed to be smiling. What was wrong with her? 'Pet,' she said gently. 'As I said, you're talking shite. You never stopped being yourself. You just decided to be happier and more confident. More in control of your feelings, rather than letting them control you, as my mam might say.'

She tucked my hair behind my ear. 'The girl who brightened up our yard was *you*. And the girl Mark fell for was you. Annie Mulholland.' Then: 'Fuckin' hell, that's weird.' She grinned. 'Annie Mulholland!'

'That's my name.' I dabbed Becca's dirty and now snotty glove at my eyes.

Becca watched me kindly. 'Are you sure?' she asked. 'Sure you don't want to say goodbye to everyone?'

I wavered. One last sight of Mark, one final chance to inventory every detail of him. One last hug with Stumpy, his warm breath and round ears and his fail-safe ability to lift my mood. And Joe, and Sandra, and those lovely dogs.

'No,' I said softly. 'Mark's been through too much already. I'll call him tonight once he's back in the house and he's got his mum there.'

Becca seemed unconvinced. 'Right. I'm sure that'll make him feel loads better.'

My phone beeped loudly and I jumped, fear pinching at my stomach. I pulled it out of my pocket and passed it to Becca with shaking hands. 'Is it him? I can't bear to look.'

Becca's face fell. ''Fraid so, pet,' she said quietly. 'The fucking twat. *Soon I'll be waking up with you in my bed, Pumpkin. What a thought. It'll take me a while to forgive you everything but I know I'll get there. S xx PS Isn't the Somerset countryside glorious?*

'Fucker,' she muttered. 'Fucking fucker. Pet, can we *please* call the police? I don't know the first thing about the law but this sounds like stalking to me. I mean, how did he even get this number?'

My eyes were fixed on the drive. 'We need to go. Now.'

Becca sighed, turned her key in the ignition, and it started slipping away from me. The hedgerow along the drive, the barns, the outdoor school, round which trotted some excitable girls who were no doubt as much in love with Mark as I was. The back of Joe, driving the Tank round the side of the muck heap with four bales of straw wobbling precariously on the front. My life, my happy place. I forced my eyes straight ahead.

As soon as I saw a silver car turn into the drive ahead of us I knew it was going to happen again. My breath shortened almost to nothing and I felt a terrible weight on my chest. As my muscles drained of energy I tried to yell, 'Reverse! Get out of here!' but all I could hear were the gasping noises coming from my own mouth.

The car. Nose to nose with ours. My heart racing, screeching, and Becca's voice coming in slow waves.

Then another voice: 'Annie, oh, my God . . .'

A hand coming through the window. A bright flash of blonde hair, a strong waft of perfume. Somehow I was out of the car and in my sister's arms, and she was crying – crying and laughing and telling me how much she loved me and how much she'd missed me.

'I think she just had some sort of a heart attack,' Becca was saying, and then a man's voice – Tim's! – saying, 'It's probably a panic attack,' and then a familiar pair of arms sitting me carefully on the drive.

I stared woozily at Lizzy. Was it really her? My big sister? Beside her a long pair of legs folded down and Tim came into my vision. Tim Furniss, in a navy coat that made him look all handsome and doctorish. Someone was right behind me, supporting my weight. Becca. She was telling them what had just happened. 'Knew we shouldn't go to the airport,' she was saying.

'Quite right,' said another voice, a French voice, full of concern and edged with brutality.

'Claudie,' I whispered.

'Yes,' she said. 'There will be no further running off, my darling. Do you understand?' And then she, too, appeared in my line of vision, and she had tears in her eyes. 'You mad little elf,' she murmured, hugging me. 'You mad little elf with this dyed red hair, pretending to be in Thailand all this time. We have missed you so much.'

After a while I felt well enough to sit up properly. Everyone sat down with me and, sick with shame, I tried to explain the last few months.

'I'm so sorry I lied to you,' I muttered, when it was done. 'I'm so, so sorry.'

'It's okay,' Lizzy said. 'Please stop apologizing. I'm sure I'd have done exactly the same if it were me. Really, darling, it was an amazing plan! Like a film or something! And at least we got to see you on Skype.'

'Every day I looked up at this drive,' I cried. 'Every single day, panicking that the police would turn up, telling me Stephen had harmed you . . . Or that he'd turn up himself and simply throw me into his car . . .'

'Oh, Annie!'

'A police car came here a month or so ago and I thought I was going to faint. All I could think was, Oh, God, they're looking for me because Lizzy's in hospital or something . . .'

Lizzy looked at Tim, as if to say, 'How bad is this?'

Somewhere amid the chaos I registered surprise. It was a very familiar sort of a look. 'You're not going to commit me or anything, are you, Tim?' I tried to blot my tears with my sleeve.

Tim smiled. 'No.'

'Really? Even though I dyed my hair red and spent months speaking in an Irish accent?'

In my peripheral vision I could see Claudine smiling. 'Mad little badger,' she murmured.

'Annie,' Tim said kindly, 'do you not think it's understandable that you look at a police car and fear the worst? After everything you've gone through?'

'I have no idea what's understandable any more.'

'I know. But please listen to me, because I do. Getting into a relationship with Stephen is just about the worst thing that could have happened to someone with your history – of *course* you reacted badly. And you needn't blame yourself, either. Like any sociopath he was irresistible at the start. He fooled us all!'

'He did not fool me,' Claudine said primly, but Tim told her to shut it.

'None of us could have predicted what he'd do,' he said. 'It was awful and completely unexpected, and I am most certainly not going to handcuff you to Becca's steering wheel for taking matters into your own hands. You won't be the first woman to do something like this.'

I was not. I'd read about women starting again on the other side of the world, some without even saying goodbye to their families. Many had changed their names; one had even had plastic surgery. Some had been protected by the police; others felt they could only trust themselves with their own safety so had decided to go it alone.

All those lives cancelled. All those women, just gone, suddenly. Disappeared.

'You felt you had nowhere to go because that was exactly how he *wanted* you to feel,' Tim was saying. 'He spent months whittling you down, cutting you off from your family and friends so that you were entirely dependent on him. That's what they do, Annie. So, no, I don't think you're "mad".'

'All of what he said,' Lizzy said admiringly, squeezing Tim's hand. He squeezed hers back.

They moved apart, but not until they'd exchanged a look.

Eh? I thought. Lizzy was still smiling at Tim as he pushed his hair out of his face.

He caught her looking at him and blushed slightly. And then *she* blushed.

Hang on, I thought. *Hang on a minute . . .*

'You are right,' Claudine suddenly stage-whispered. 'Your suspicions are correct. It is 'orrible, Annie. They are like teenagers.'

I turned to her slowly.

'They are lovers,' she said, less forcefully. She looked guiltily at Tim and Lizzy, who had both gone red. 'Sorry. I just . . . It is so disgusting I 'ad to share it with someone.'

They both smiled, and Lizzy slid her hand into Tim's. 'This isn't the time,' she muttered, with the widest grin I'd ever seen.

'*What?*' I stared at them stupidly. 'How long? How . . .'

'Six months,' they said simultaneously.

'Although, really, it's been going on for seventeen years,' Tim added. 'But neither of us had the nerve to do anything about it.' He looked mad with pride and Lizzy looked mad with love. I felt mad with shock.

'I . . . Oh, my *God*.'

Claudine nodded furiously. 'Agreed, Annabel. I vomit frequently in protest.'

I giggled. Lizzy and Tim. Tim and Lizzy, secretly in love with each other for years. How had I not known? The number of times Lizzy had got drunk and told me she thought Tim was in love with me! And the pain in her face as she'd said it, too! All that time, all those boyfriends, she was thinking about Tim! And he about her. I shook my head, as if to make my brain catch up. Lizzy and Tim. Tim and Lizzy.

The sound of a vehicle in the lane chainsawed through my thoughts and I scrabbled frantically to get into Becca's car. 'Stephen! Oh, my God, it's Stephen, help, I . . .'

Becca and Tim sat me back on the driveway as the car swished past and on towards the moor.

'Sorry,' I said, slumping back against Becca. 'Sorry.'

'It's fine,' Lizzy said. She took my hand. 'Look, darling, we saw you on telly the other day, and it took us a few days to work out what the hell was going on. We, er, obviously thought you were in Thailand.'

'I know. Apologies . . .'

'Don't start that again, sweetheart. You were very clever, all those Skypes with you wearing vest tops, talking about swimming and mountain-hiking and stuff – you should write spy movies or something! You're so devious!'

I smiled hopelessly. I could think of better things to be talented at.

'So, anyway, Claudine saw you on the documentary –'

'I do not 'ave much of a life since I kicked out Sylvester,' Claudine put in ruefully.

'And after a lot of thinking we called Mark's yard in case they'd had any contact with you since the accident and a lovely lady told us there was a groom here called Kate Brady and we thought, Aha!'

'Stephen did exactly the same,' I said. 'He wrote to me. This morning. I'm on my way out of here.'

They were horrified. 'He what? Where is he?'

'In Somerset. He keeps texting me. I don't know where he is, but he's very close.'

'Motherfucker,' Claudine hissed. 'I will kill him. I will kill his stupid English arse.'

I was woozy still from the panic attack but adrenalin was circulating darkly around me. 'I really have to get out of here,' I repeated. 'I have to go to the airport and fly somewhere to stay for a week or so while I decide what to do.'

'No,' said Lizzy.

'No,' said Tim.

'I will kill you before I allow this,' said Claudine.

'I will too,' Becca said guiltily. 'Sorry, pet.'

'Are none of you listening? He's on his way! He is a *lunatic!*'

'Well, it's actually classed as a personality disorder,' Tim began, but Claudine held up a hand to silence us and, as always, we obeyed.

'Annabel,' she said quietly. 'Here is what is actually going to happen. You come back to London with us –'

'Yes,' she insisted, when I wailed, '*No!*'

'You are coming back with us and you are moving in with Lizzy. It is all planned. I have told Tim he is not allowed to stay the night with Lizzy while you are there because if you hear them having sex you might, quite reasonably, throw yourself out of the window.'

I held my head between my hands. It was all too much.

'We take out a restraining order against Stephen, and then –'

'*No!* Never! Claudie, are you *mad*? Do you not understand how dangerous he is?'

Claudine sighed. 'Read this, please,' she said. 'And then we talk.'

It was a letter from a girl called Ros Martin, sent to Lizzy at her work address.

Dear Lizzy,

I'm trying to contact your sister but cannot find any way of getting hold of her. I decided to write to you at your workplace; I really hope that's OK. If you read the enclosed letter to your sister you'll perhaps understand why I went to the lengths of tracking you down.

Please do feel free to read this message in full before deciding if you think she will be up to dealing with this.

I looked nervously at my sister but she gave me a smile of encouragement. 'It's not nice, but it's good,' she said. 'We're all here, Annie.'

I glanced up at the lane, scanning for cars, but everything was still. I started reading.

Dear Annabel,

I thought long and hard about whether or not to send this letter, but it felt wrong not to. I am very sorry if the contents of this message are upsetting.

My name is Ros and I'm an artist, based in Lea Bridge. Until a few months ago I was in a relationship with a man called Stephen Flint, whom I'm afraid I think you know.

Stephen was a really fantastic boyfriend for a while, but I became suspicious when I kept finding my phone in places that I had not left it. I'm not the sort of person to forget where I've put things, and I suspected that he was checking my messages, even though I couldn't imagine why he would.

I blushed. How sharp Ros Martin was, noticing what was happening with her phone. And what a useless fool I had been with mine.

At the same time, he started working extremely late and became a lot more irritable and difficult. I tried to be understanding about it, because relationships are as much about getting through bad times as they are about enjoying the good. Unfortunately, it seems that our 'relationship' was skewed a lot further towards the bad than I could possibly have imagined.

I called the switchboard at FlintSpark once at around eleven p.m., shortly after he'd texted me to say that he was starting a video conference with San Francisco. The night-time guard said that nobody was in the building at all, other than security. But when I called his direct line a few minutes later, he said he was at his desk. I realized he must be diverting his calls to his mobile.

To cut a long story short, I then decided to find out exactly what was going on, as it was clear that he was lying to me frequently, and I had a quick check of his emails one night when he was in the bath. Regrettable behaviour, but it paid off: I found some shocking pieces of information and am now in touch with many of the girls whose lives he's destroyed.

With regard to you, I discovered that he had hired a man to hack your email account and find you in Thailand. I'm very sorry if this is distressing news but I wanted you to know. From what I can tell he even went to Thailand himself but didn't find you, and the email hacking was fruitless as you appeared to have closed the account down.

I hope that you remain safe out there.

When I confronted him about you – you were the first person I found out about – Stephen said that you had run off with a vast sum of his money, and that he was pursuing you for legal reasons. His argument was very convincing and for a few days I believed him. I wish I hadn't. I knew by then he was bad news. The problem is, as you no doubt know, he is incredibly convincing and lovely when he wants you onside. Even though I was in a state of heightened suspicion, he was able to manipulate me.

Because of my investigations I'm now in contact with six women with whom Stephen has been in a 'relationship' in the last two years. Two appear to have been involved with him at the same time as you – a girl called Petra Navarro who I believe you met in a restaurant in Hackney, and a Nancy Stevens who lives in New York.

Nancy broke up with Stephen on New Year's Eve because she had begun to suspect that he was seeing someone else. He flew out to patch things up with her a few days before New Year's Eve but she discovered that he was staying in a hotel with another woman. From what she's managed to work out, that woman was you.

I sat back, stunned. The last-minute decision to take me to New York, rather than Paris. The endless calls from Stephen's 'office' and his cold fury when he finally got back only minutes before midnight. *He had just been dumped.* By another woman. And then asked Claudine out on the internet. You couldn't make it up.

As for Petra, Stephen told her that you had mental-health issues; that you had tried to commit suicide at the age of sixteen and had been mentally unstable ever since. He told her that since he had ended things with you, you had stalked him relentlessly. Petra later discovered that this was wholly untrue, and that you and he were still very much together when they bumped into you in a restaurant in Hackney.

'It's not wholly untrue, though,' I said, now really frightened. I ran a hand over my face. 'Oh, God, what has he done?'

'What do you mean, pet?' Becca asked. She was still sitting next to me, an arm around my shoulder, reading the letter in tandem.

I swallowed. 'I did try to take my life when I was sixteen.'

'Oh, pet,' Becca said.

Lizzy squeezed my foot.

'But that's not the point. The point is that I never told Stephen.' I looked wildly at Tim. 'How does he know? Is there any way of him accessing my NHS records?'

Tim shook his head. 'Impossible. Are you sure you never told him?'

'Positive,' I whispered. 'What has he done? How does he know?'

399

I felt dazed. Stephen was a monster. A monster completely without limits.

'I have to get out,' I said. 'We have to go. Please!'

'Listen,' Tim said firmly. 'If Stephen turns up here right now, I imagine your sister will probably kill him. And if she doesn't, Claudine will. We all will. You are not in danger right now.'

'Keep reading, darling,' Lizzy said. 'It's okay.'

I blew out a long breath. Yes, I could take a little more. Somewhere inside me, amid the terror and the panic, a spark of rage had ignited.

I am also in contact with his PA, Natasha Everidge, who eventually had the courage to resign from FlintSpark six months ago. She was never involved with him herself – I suspect she was too useful to him – but she helped him pretend to be working late repeatedly. She is deeply upset about the whole thing. She has also secured the co-operation of Stephen's ex-chief operating officer, Rory Adamson. Rory had apparently had several arguments with Stephen about his persistent habit of sleeping with his female staff, which frequently led to him missing important meetings and events.

Of course – Rory. The look he had given Stephen in the château, when Stephen said I was joining them for drinks. *Not again, Flint*, he must have been thinking. *Not this one too . . .*

There is one other woman in the equation who I'm going to have to tell you about. Her name is Penny Flint and – as you might already have guessed – she is his estranged wife. They have a son, Sebastian, to whom Stephen does not have access.

'Oh, my God!' I cried. Barnaby, his nephew. Barnaby was called Sebastian, and he was Stephen's *son*?

'Motherfucker,' Claudine muttered.

Penny replied to my letter, saying that she and her little boy had been through enough now, and wouldn't be able to help with our case, but that she wished us luck. 'You'll need it,' she wrote, which I have to say I found somewhat daunting.

To the matter at hand. Of the six of us, three have been physically assaulted by Stephen, he has broken into two of our flats and all of us have received what constitutes sufficient unwanted contact to put him in breach of the Protection from Harassment Act. We have decided to build a case against him together. The charges will include harassment, stalking, GBH and forced entry. On each count our cases are strong.

However, as you know, Stephen is extremely clever and will hire the best lawyers in the country to defeat us. As yet, he does not know that we are building a case against him, but we have all successfully taken out restraining orders against him so he is already very angry. I am worried that he will be redoubling his efforts to find you, given that you currently have no legal protection.

We would like you to join us in our case, Annie, if you feel able to do so. We are working with a brilliant CPS prosecutor who is completely on our side — she is determined to have Stephen put away, and she feels that you could add real weight to the prosecution.

It may be that you've moved permanently to Thailand, but if you're back in the country and willing to join us (or even if you're not willing to join us) I'd strongly advise you to take out a restraining order against Stephen. He has harassed and stalked all of us

relentlessly, and while none of us thinks he is likely to cause us
serious harm, we want to know we can live safely in London.

   We will understand if you decide you can't go through with a
prosecution case. We, too, are deeply shaken by our experiences but
we feel equally strongly that Stephen cannot be allowed to go on
and do this to any more vulnerable women. Because make no
mistake — it's vulnerable women he's going for.

   Here are my contact details, should you wish to talk further
about this letter.

   I wish you the very best, whatever your decision.
Ros

I closed my eyes, taking in great gulps of cold Somerset air. 'That's awful,' Becca said, in the ensuing silence. 'The bit about him targeting only vulnerable women.'

I looked at her absently. A thought was beginning to grow in my mind. It moved slowly, like a Polaroid print developing.

'I was vulnerable,' I said. 'Badly so. He did well to find someone as vulnerable as me.'

The distant sound of giggling Pony Club girls was carried over on a gust of wind. I remembered myself on the day I'd met Stephen. Tired, helpless, carried along by a tide I hadn't the energy to fight. I remembered how kind he'd been, how he'd seemed to switch on a light and see into my soul. That stuff he'd told me about feeling stuck himself, the story about the man who'd hugged himself happy.

I remembered the little glow I'd felt on my way home that night. The sense of not being quite alone in the world.

And then I closed my eyes again. The Polaroid developed and suddenly I knew. *I knew exactly what Stephen had done.*

'I'll join them,' I said slowly. 'I'll fight him.'

Lizzy stared at me. 'Seriously?'

'I'll fight him with everything I've got. Which isn't much, but it's better than nothing at all.' Becca rubbed her hand up and down my back. 'Brilliant, pet,' she muttered. 'Brilliant.'

Claudine was smiling at me. 'You have just made a wonderful decision,' she said. Her voice sounded like thick blankets. 'This is very brave, and very wonderful,' she added, and I saw she was crying.

Tim just squeezed my hand very hard.

'I wasn't expecting that,' Lizzy said. 'I thought we'd have to fight you all the way to the airport.'

'So did I, at the beginning of the letter,' I admitted. 'But what she said at the end. About Stephen going for vulnerable women.'

Lizzy nodded, puzzled.

'He found me,' I said. 'He knew who I was.'

'What do you mean?' Becca asked.

'People often remember my name because Mum's murder was in the papers for months, right up until Neil Derrick was locked up. "The babe in the wood", I was. And Stephen must have been, what, thirteen or fourteen when it happened? He'd definitely have been aware.'

Everyone was listening intently.

'I think he probably did Google for massage therapists near to FlintSpark when his previous one fell through –' I broke off. 'I wonder if she's one of the six. I wonder if Jamilla is one of the six.'

Probably.

'He found someone called Annabel Mulholland

offering massage on Wednesday afternoons right by his building.'

Lizzy's face had begun to crumple. 'Oh, God.'

'But then I reckon he thought, Hang on, I know that name.'

Becca, too, had begun to realize what was coming.

'I think he Googled my name and was reminded pretty damn quickly why I sounded familiar. *Bingo!*' I closed my eyes. 'I was a perfect project. You'd struggle to come across a woman more vulnerable than one whose mother was raped and murdered while they played hide and seek together.'

I gazed up at the moor. 'Stephen was ready for me. That very first night, he was ready. He had all the right questions, all the right thoughts. He was lovely. So understanding. I felt like he was some sort of angel.'

Lizzy's eyes had filled with tears of rage and disgust.

'I walked out of my crappy life and into his arms, just like he'd planned. It was perfect!'

Tim put his arm round Lizzy. I watched my sister cry and felt the anger crackling at my temples. It had been a long, long time since I'd experienced anger, but I rather liked it. With it came a brilliant clarity.

'I'll fight with those girls,' I repeated. 'And, furthermore, I have evidence.' Excitement began to race through me, matching the anger, as I reached into my bag and closed my hands around my old front-door keys. 'I know exactly how Stephen found out about my suicide attempt! I've been holding on to the evidence for months without even knowing it.'

'Evidence,' Claudine hissed gleefully. 'And fighting! NOW YOU ARE TALKING!'

'Now I'm talking,' I agreed.

I held up my shiny keys. 'Look at these,' I said. 'My Hackney front-door keys. Do you notice anything?'

They looked at the keys, confused. 'Well, there's the fact that you probably shouldn't still have them,' Claudine said, 'given that you do not live there now.'

'I know, I know. I meant to send them back to Mr Pegler but I didn't. Which is lucky. Come on, what do you notice?'

'They're shiny?' Lizzy said doubtfully.

'Exactly!'

'Exactly what? Pet, you've lost us,' Becca said.

'I lived in that house for *years*,' I said. Years and years. My keys were ancient – all tarnished and worn. But somehow I ended up with a new set. Stephen's clever, you see, but not clever enough. He must have had a set of keys cut for my house, so he could let himself in and snoop around. Probably while I was massaging his employees. He gave me the wrong set. He kept the old ones. And I never realized!'

'Fuckin' hell,' Becca murmured. 'Are you sure?'

'Positive. Look how new these keys are – I certainly didn't have them cut. There was stuff he knew about me really early on. Like, he was always suspicious of me and Tim – a quick look through my photo albums would've been all he'd need to start down that road. And it was really early on that he started making me worry about the state of my mental health. I think he went into my house before we even got together.'

We all stared at my shiny bunch of keys. 'Psychopaths are predators,' I said bitterly. 'The more they know about their prey, the better they can control them.'

'So you think your old keys will still be in his house?' Lizzy asked.

I nodded.

'Jesus,' she said.

I looked at my beloved friends. 'Will you help me? Will you help me do this? I'm angry now but it won't last. I'm sure I'll try to wimp out a thousand times. Will you be there?'

'Right as rain we will,' Claudine shouted, and I hugged her. 'Right as rain,' repeated my friend, in her heavy French accent.

Becca piled on. 'I'll come down to that London shithole any time you need me,' she said thickly. 'You can always rely on me, pet.'

Lizzy and Tim piled on too.

'Er, sorry,' Tim said politely to Becca. 'I hope I'm not squashing you.'

'We're going to get him,' Lizzy said.

'Oh, my little button box, so we will,' Claudine said. We stayed there for some time, an awkward ball of human beings on the drive next to Becca's car, until I heard Mark's voice.

'Kate?' he asked. 'Kate? What's going on? Are you okay?'

Mark waved to his Pony Club pupils as they rumbled down the driveway with their horse trailer. I watched him struggling to comprehend what I'd just told him. Dirk and Woody, who had followed us out to the fields, were fast losing interest and had started fighting over a fallen branch in the beech coppice.

Mark looked shattered.

My bear, I thought miserably. How the world has let you down. How brave you've been, pushing on through all the shit life has thrown at you, trying relentlessly to find your way. And now you've found a hopeful path I've gone and exploded a bomb on it.

'I'm so sorry,' I whispered. 'So, so sorry, Mark. But I promise nothing about you and me was made up. That bit was real.'

In the distance, my friends talked among themselves and pretended not to watch us.

'If it helps, I tried not to fall for you,' I said. 'When I arrived here I'd decided never to go near another man as long as I lived.'

Mark's face didn't move.

'But then you opened up and I saw who you really were. And your farm, Mark, the horses, the air, Exmoor, the whole bloody lot. I couldn't help myself. I felt happy whenever I was anywhere near you. Why couldn't you have carried on being a wanker?'

Perhaps the faintest hint of a smile crossed Mark's face but it was gone before I had time to catch it. He leaned on the fence rail, picking at a loose thread on his jodhpurs. Mark still wore jodhpurs every day, even though he was far from getting on a horse. Just like me with my long skirts and tie-dye, I thought sadly. Little uniforms that keep us apart from the world.

'I wanted to tell you the truth. In fact, I'd decided to tell you today. But then the letter . . .' I trailed off. Mark still wasn't saying anything.

My eyes stung with tears. I couldn't stand it.

'Is there any hope for us?' I whispered. 'Any at all?'

I looked at him but he didn't look at me.

'Sorry,' he said, after a long pause. He slumped on the fence, as if admitting defeat. 'It's just . . . too much for me. I'm still coming to terms with all the Maria stuff and I . . . I just don't think I can do this too.'

'But we could go on a date, start again . . . I don't have to go back to London. I can help with the prosecution case from down here. I could go and rent somewhere nearby and we could get to know each other properly . . .'

'No, Kate, I – Annie.' He sighed. 'See? I don't even know your name.'

'I know you're hurt, I know you're confused and very probably angry, but can't we at least try to . . .'

'No,' he said. There was a dreadful finality in his voice. 'I'm only getting to know myself at the moment and I can't do this. Not now.'

He turned to me. 'Listen. I'm not angry at all. I'm horrified by what you've been through and I understand entirely why you had to lie.' For a beautiful second he reached out and touched my hand. 'My poor, poor girl,' he said unevenly. He cleared this throat. 'But the truth is, you and I were simple, and now we're a big awkward mess, and I can't climb another mountain.'

'But I love you,' I said, as tears began to fall. 'I fell in love with you.'

'And I fell in love with you,' he said. He took my face in his hands and I ached at the sadness in those dark eyes.

'I wish I could be stronger for us,' he said softly. 'But I can't. Please respect that. Please go and be stronger than me, Annie. You have to go and fight that monster.'

Tears fell silently down my face as the sun slipped out from behind a cloud and bathed us once more in brilliant autumn sun. 'This is your chance,' Mark said. 'Take it. Go and live your life and enjoy it. Be free. Get out of London, spend some time with your dad. Buy a horse. But forget me.'

'I can't.'

Dirk came and dropped his stick at Mark's feet. 'You have to,' Mark said, ignoring the dog. 'I'm not ready. Even before you told me all of this, I knew I wasn't ready. I guess . . . I guess Stephen made the decision for me.'

'*No!* He can't ruin us! He can't!'

Mark ran his thumb down my cheek. 'He didn't,' he whispered. 'My life ruined us. My circumstances.'

Before I realized what was going to happen, he leaned in and kissed me.

'I love you,' he said. 'Goodbye.'

And with that he walked back along the drive and out of my life.

Chapter Thirty-one

Six months later

'Dublin, my princess.' Joe was sniggering. 'Come here to me, Dublin, you gorgeous thing. Let's have our first kiss right here on this nice little grassy knoll. It'll be beautiful. There's only so much a man can take, darling.'

Kate Brady and Joe were flirting. They were flirting heavily. How had I not seen that one coming?

Kate Brady and Joe Keenan. Jesus Christ. 'Your man Joe's *gorgeous*,' Kate had said to me in the beer tent earlier. She was unusually pink-cheeked.

I'd looked at her and said, 'Oh, no . . .'

'Don't go there, pet. Not worth the pubic lice,' Becca had advised, and I'd laughed, remembering her saying the same to me all those months ago.

Kate had thought about it for a while, then said, 'Thanks, but I'll risk it all the same. I could eat that one for breakfast.'

Of course you could, I thought gratefully. You could eat *anyone* for breakfast. You'll never know how much I owe you, Kate Brady.

I'd told her, of course. I'd told her everything about those months when I'd stolen her accent, her hair and – best of all – the very essence of who she was, so I could run off to Exmoor, and she'd loved it. Laughed and cried and told me I was a right old freak-show. To my amazement, she'd remembered the whole thing in such detail that she'd written to me in April stating her intention to take me to Badminton in May. 'I've had a check and your man Mark isn't competing, as you'll probably already know,' she'd said, 'so you're not at risk of seeing him. I'm just thinking it'll be good for you. Put some old demons to rest, Annie.'

'Er, okay,' I'd said. 'Okay, Brady, you're on.'

So here we were at Badminton: one Annie Mulholland and one Kate Brady, picnicking near the cross-country course, and here, too, were Becca Phillips and Joe Keenan. The latter was already lying too close to Kate on a rug in the shimmering heat of the spring heatwave, whispering filthy nothings into her ear, while Becca and I ate Scotch eggs, pieces of mango and thick splodges of Brie on oat cakes. We watched the whole terrible spectacle unfold and exchanged despairing glances, while in the distance competitors thundered round the cross-country course and the crowds oohed and aahed.

I wiggled my toes happily in the grass. It was lovely to see Joe and Becca after all this time. It was especially lovely to introduce them to Kate, having spent so long pretending to be her. And, above everything, it was wonderful to be there, back at Badminton Horse Trials, knowing that Stumpy and Mark had survived.

'I don't want any information about Mark,' I shouted, as soon as Joe and I had hugged. 'But I would like to know that he and Stumpy are okay.'

'They're grand,' Joe said diplomatically. 'Fighting fit. No worries there, Galway, so you can stop the shouting and looking like the mad article.'

411

'I wasn't.'

'Ah, Galway!' He slapped his leg. 'You're plankin' it over there! Except you're not Galway, are you, you little shyster? You're Bakewell!'

'I'm not "plankin'" it! I'm FINE. And please carry on calling me Galway. I like it.'

Joe smiled understandingly. 'Fine, fine. Well, Stumpy and his old man are both in great shape.'

I'd had to turn away so he wouldn't see the relief and sadness in my face.

I had had no contact with Mark since that day on his farm six months ago, and nor would I. Slowly but surely I would stop loving him, although I did despair over how long it was taking. Every day I woke up and scanned hopefully through my body but it was still there. Everywhere. The profound physical ache for a man I could never have. The giddy memory of his warm body sleeping next to mine, still as strong and sweet as it had been six months ago. When would it end?

Patience, I'd told myself. If you can move on from all the Bad Shit – like you've done so beautifully, Annie – you're sure to move on from Mark at some point.

But the same question kept coming up: what if I wasn't *meant* to move on from Mark?

'So how's your head?' Becca asked. 'You seem pretty sane, pet.'

I laughed. 'Getting there.'

'Go on. Tell us about this therapy.'

'Actually, it's not therapy. I kind of gave up on therapy. I wanted a solution, you know. I was fed up with wallowing around in the problem.'

'Interesting! Tell me more!'

When I'd gone back to London and moved in with Lizzy – and Lizzy had banned me from putting extra locks on her door, and we'd got all of my old stuff out of storage, and Claudine had insisted on burning most of it, and we'd all had quite a lot of wine and then I'd had a long cry about how much I loved Mark, and how I would never get over it – I'd sat down and spent several hours looking at potential solutions for my years-old problem with post-traumatic stress.

Eventually I'd stopped Googling 'trauma' and 'post-traumatic stress' and 'therapy' because every website that came up was full of depressing words. Everyone seemed to want to help me manage my broken life, rather than telling me how to change it.

I decided instead to enter search terms like 'How to be happy', 'How to take control of my own life', 'How to get a life I love'.

I didn't have to trawl through too many websites before I began to find the sort of thing I was looking for. Words like 'reprogramming' and 'tools' and 'solutions' started coming up, and I began to smile.

'I'm sick of therapy,' I said on the phone, to a woman called Clare. 'I've done years of it. I've explored the whole thing too many times now. I just want to leave it all behind and be happy. I know I can be, I just need the tools.'

I could hear Clare smile down the phone. 'It sounds like you're more than ready for a change,' she said. 'Which means I can help.'

I tried to explain it to Becca, but didn't do very well.

'I'm just learning to use different bits of my brain,' I said. 'It's hard to explain. But, holy Jesus, Becca, it isn't half working. Honestly, I go into those sessions with the lawyers and they're like, whoa! Annie's on fire!'

Becca chuckled. 'Of course you are. I'm very proud of you, pet.'

I grinned, stretching out in the grass. 'OI!' I shouted at Joe, who was nibbling Kate Brady's ear. 'STOP IT.'

'Feck off, Galway,' he hissed. 'You had your chance.'

'I'm still having my moments,' I told her. 'Stephen broke his restraining order and sent me a letter a few days ago, at Lizzy's house, and I went into freefall for a few seconds, but then I pulled myself together and got on with taking it to the police station. That's massive progress. Before, I'd have locked myself in the bathroom and cried with fear.'

Becca handed me another Scotch egg. 'That makes me very happy,' she said. 'And you've done it so quickly, too.'

'Well, that's the great thing about the brain. It can change fast. Neuroplasticity, that's called.'

'Really?' Becca asked, watching Joe and Kate with mild disgust. 'Everyone's brain can change?'

'Everyone's.' I grinned. Joe was telling Kate dirty limericks.

'Well, maybe you could have a tinker with his over there,' Becca said.

We chinked plastic cups.

'Anyways, what's the latest on Stephen?' she asked.

Joe and Kate sat up to listen. Dappled sunlight danced across their faces, all flushed and excitable from the high of mutual attraction. For a fraction of a second I allowed myself to remember feeling like that around Mark.

Come on, I reminded myself. *That's not helpful.*

'Well, it's going to the Crown Court,' I told them. 'Which is a good sign of how big the case is.'

'Great!' Joe said. 'Let's get the Queen involved. She'll send him down all right.'

Kate giggled. Becca despaired.

'It starts next week,' I said. 'And of course I'm nervous, but proportionately so. I mean, Stephen's already been granted bail in spite of the evidence, so he's shown us how capable his lawyers are. I don't think any of us expect this to be easy.'

I twiddled a blade of grass on my ankle. 'But I think for me the important thing is being okay whatever happens. Stephen may well get away with it, and if that happens I need to be all right. I can't go into this feeling like my life will be over if he doesn't get convicted.'

'That sounds very wise,' Becca said. 'Very wise indeed, pet.'

'Well, Annie, my sweet love, I'm happy to have him killed for you in the interim,' Kate Brady said. 'Just say the word, darling.'

'Oh, stop it, Dublin, you strong warrior, you,' Joe told her. 'I've a great big boner here!'

'Christ, Joe! Will you shut your hole?' I shouted. Then: 'Oh. Sorry.' A mother of a small boy stared at me with the purest disgust.

'You see what happens when you try to get in the path of true love?' Joe said mildly.

Kate gave him a look. 'There's no true love here,' she

told him. 'I'll use you for sex and then I'll be off back to Ranelagh.'

Everyone laughed.

Becca popped a bottle of Prosecco.

'Thank you,' I said to them all. 'Thank you for coming here. It's doing me a lot of good.'

'To Galway,' Joe said, raising his plastic cup of sparkling wine. 'To our little princess, fooling us all with her strange accent and her flame-red hair. To Galway, for being brave enough to make herself come back here to Badminton. Not to mention bringing us this fine Irishwoman, Kate Brady.'

'To Galway,' laughed Kate, and we all clinked cups.

'All right, Joe, you loser!'

I froze, my glass halfway to my mouth.

'Who's your latest?'

I daren't look around. It was impossible. They weren't here today!

'Ana Luisa, you stinking little devil,' Joe said merrily. 'I'd ask you to please mind your mouth in front of my good lady here.'

Oh, God. Oh, holy Jesus in the sky above. Joe's face was smiling at a spot over my shoulder as he stood up. 'Nice to see you there, boss . . .'

Becca winked at me as she stood up too. 'Hiya, Mark,' she said, 'and hiya, An–'

'BECCA!' Suddenly Becca was surrounded by a fiercely hugging little girl, all skinny legs and shiny brown hair. 'I MISS YOU!'

Ana Luisa hugged my lovely Geordie friend with a

ferocity that made her mist up. 'I miss you too, ferret,' she said unsteadily, hugging Mark's daughter right back.

Everything Clare had taught me was forgotten.

My legs went to such total jelly that I couldn't actually get up. I scrabbled round on my hands and knees in a panic. Get the fuck up! I shouted at myself.

We can't fucking move! shouted my legs.

Eventually I got up and turned to Mark, who was being introduced to Kate. He smiled politely at me, holding out his hand to shake mine.

When he saw me properly, his hand stopped. Everything stopped. Mark stared at me and I stared at him, and all I could think of was how much I loved him. I'm so proud of you! I wanted to shout. You're so brave, coming back here! I love you!

Then, as Mark realized who Kate was, he turned slowly to look at her.

'Kate,' he said. He was amazed.

At that moment Kate worked it out too. 'Oh!' she said, then trailed off.

'Oh,' Ana Luisa echoed, recognizing me. 'Nice hair, Kate. The red never suited you.' I turned to her, uncertain as to whether to hug her. Ana Luisa gave me a polite hug, then stood back, her little hands on her little hips. 'Do you still fancy my dad?' she asked casually.

I made a strange croaking noise. Ana Luisa sniggered. 'Do you still fancy Kate, Dad?'

We both looked helplessly at her. Seven years old and better able to communicate what was going on than either me, aged thirty-five, or Mark, aged thirty-seven.

'Ana Luisa,' Becca said. 'You're a little rat. Kate's name is actually Annie, as I'm pretty sure I've told you on more than one occasion. Now, listen. I'm going to sit you down here, and if you're lucky I'll give you a little glass of Prosecco —'

'No Prosecco,' Mark said weakly.

'Okay. I won't give you a glass of Prosecco but I will give you a pork pie and some strawberries.'

'While Dad and Annie go off to have a snog behind that tree?' Ana Luisa asked. 'Jesus. This is sooooooo school-yard.'

Mark, whose eyes kept flickering back to mine, started to laugh. 'I love you,' he told his daughter. 'But, just for once, will you shut up? I am not going to snog anyone behind a tree.'

'Whatever.' Ana Luisa sat down next to Becca.

Kate Brady was staring at Mark with absolute wonder. 'He's a RIDE,' she mouthed at me, flabbergasted. He was. He was tanned. His hair was shorter. He was so sexy it made my head wobble.

And, before I knew it, we were walking away.

'Um, so, this is a surprise,' Mark said, after what felt like three hours. He sounded as nervous as I was. 'Of all the places on earth I thought I might bump into you, this was not one of them. Ha-ha.'

'Ha-ha-HA. Ha-ha. Ha. Er, same. I thought you weren't coming.'

'I'm not competing.'

'But you came to watch. Ha-ha!' I sounded totally insane. 'So, how are you?'

'Good.' He turned briefly towards me, but I couldn't

418

look at him. I just concentrated on putting one foot in front of the other. There were daisies in the grass.

I hated daisies but, these days, I could deal with them. I could even smell them, and it was okay.

I took a deep breath. I made my heart slow down. My fists unclench. If I could cope with daisies, I could cope with Mark.

We were walking further away from the cross-country course into the lush parkland. Behind us the Tannoy was fading and the sound of the TV helicopter overhead disappeared into birdsong and rustling leaves.

I felt giddy with longing. I could smell Mark's olive soap, and if I squinted sideways I could see the tanned skin of his forearms. 'You look really well,' I told him. 'Nice tan . . . '

Mark chuckled. 'You're not going to believe this, but I went on holiday. A proper one with a swimming pool and big umbrellas and people making my food.'

'No way!'

'Yes way. I took Ana Luisa and her best friend to Morocco and we stayed in a luxury *riad*. I put it on a credit card and didn't worry about money once. It was bloody spectacular.' He paused. '*I* was spectacular. I sat by the pool all week and, apart from keeping an eye on the girls, I didn't do a thing. Who knew?'

Who knew indeed?

He ran his hand along the arm that had been broken. 'It's all working,' he said. 'I'm back up on horseback and everything's still fine. I'm lucky.'

'Wow. I'm so happy to hear you're riding again, Mark, that's fantastic news.' I sounded like a distant acquaintance.

I LOVE YOU, my head bellowed. I'VE BEEN TRYING NOT TO LOVE YOU FOR SIX MONTHS NOW BUT IT'S NOT WORKING. I LOVE YOU SO MUCH IT HURTS MY FACE, MY CHEST, MY LIFE. EVERYTHING HURTS BECAUSE OF HOW MUCH I LOVE YOU.

'The physio says I should be able to start gently competing by midsummer,' Mark said, 'which was a surprise.'

'Surprise. Yes. Um, shall we sit down?'

We sat down and I regretted it immediately. In spite of the heat, the longer grass was still wet and I felt the water seep straight into my shorts.

'This is nice,' I said, as the dew seeped through to my knickers. For God's sake, get up! I told myself. But I didn't want to. Mark's knee was inches from mine. One of his surgery scars was poking out of his shorts, a timid little pink line among the dark hairs on his leg. I wanted to kiss away all the pain it had caused him.

'My arse is wet,' he said politely. 'Maybe we could stand up.'

'Yes. Great idea.' We stood up and started walking again, because to stand facing each other would have been a nightmare.

'So will you start competing this season, do you think?'

Mark shook his head. 'No . . . I've actually retired.'

Now I stared at him. 'You've *what*?'

Mark's eyes were on the cross-country course where someone was galloping up a glossy stretch of grass towards a fence. Even from this distance we could see the sweat lathered up the horse's side.

'I've retired. The press don't know, yet, but I decided last week.'

'Blimey!'

'It's the toughest decision I've ever made. But people started sending me horses they wanted me to try out, and they were all such sweet animals. I love horses,' he said, blushing. 'And that's the trouble. Every horse I tried I just thought, How could I put you through this? What if you broke your leg too?'

Stop being so nice, I thought. It's not helping at all.

'And then I started having the same thoughts about myself. Did I really want to risk getting myself smashed to pieces again? Did I want to risk Ana Luisa losing her dad?' He grinned. 'Did I really want to get up at six thirty for the rest of my life? So I retired. And I'm selling the farm.'

'You're WHAT?'

Mark shrugged. 'I just want a clean slate,' he said. 'I want a house that has nothing to do with alcoholism, or evil wives, or broken bones. Not to mention broken hearts. I'm moving on with my life.'

'But – but it's your family home! For generations!' I ignored the bit about broken hearts.

'Actually it only goes back to my grandfather. But even if it went back to an early caveman named Waverley, I've got to sell it. There are no new starts in ghost houses.'

'Wow.'

Selfish little voices piped up in my head: *But I want you to still be at the farm! What about all my lovely memories? It can't belong to someone else!*

'I don't believe it,' I managed to say. 'This is huge.'

'Isn't it?' He was watching me now, so I tried to look

encouraging. 'I'll probably buy somewhere in Oxfordshire, nearer to Ana Luisa, so she doesn't have to spend her weekends on the motorway. I'll run a livery yard for now. Carry on training other riders, while I plot my next move. Oh, and I'm going to work part-time. Thought I'd, you know . . . get out in the world a bit more.'

'Wow,' I mumbled. There was no disguising the sadness in my voice.

Mark had moved on. Not just from his Bad Shit, but from me.

'My crotch is still wet,' was all I could say.

'Listen, Kate,' Mark began. 'Annie. Sorry.'

'It's fine. Honestly.'

Mark smiled, but I couldn't look at him.

'DAD!'

Ana Luisa was striding towards us, like a little tiger. She was going to be every bit as gorgeous as her father. 'DAD, we have to go, we're meant to be meeting Bea.'

'Okay, coming.' He turned to me but, once again, I couldn't meet his eye. 'Bea's her friend. Listen, I haven't even asked how you're doing. Joe said you'd all gone ahead with the prosecution but I have no idea when it starts, or what –'

'*DAAAAD!*'

'Coming! Look, I'll be in touch,' Mark said apologetically, even though we both knew he would not.

I wanted to cry. 'Nice to see you,' I muttered. 'I'm so happy to hear all your positive news.'

'Good luck with the wet crotch,' he said, as his daughter dragged him away.

'Bye,' I whispered.

'She looks much better with blonde hair,' I heard Ana Luisa say. 'But you need someone more reliable, Dad.'

Chapter Thirty-two

'Are you sure you don't want me to come?' Lizzy asked, as she got ready for work. 'Because it's not too late for me to bunk off. I don't want you going there alone and having a panic attack or anything . . .'

'I'm not going to have a panic attack. I'm going to be absolutely fine.'

Lizzy and Tim went off to work and I giggled as I heard them doing a face-clutchy kiss at the front door. It had taken quite a while to get used to this business. Sometimes Tim wouldn't be able to control himself and would clutch Lizzy's face, mouthing, I LOVE YOU SO MUCH. I think he thought that by mouthing it, rather than saying it, he would somehow stop me noticing. I actually enjoyed how fiercely he loved my big sister. She was so happy. She sang in the shower. She'd stopped drinking and spending so much. She radiated joy.

After they'd both gone I sat on a shiny white stool and drank tea at Lizzy's shiny white island in her shiny white kitchen. The island had one of those taps that gave out instant boiling water, and plug sockets that slid out of nowhere, and in the middle of it was a bowl of peaches that was changed every few days but never eaten. Lizzy was insane when it came to her kitchen and refitted it approximately every two years – she couldn't live with last season's exposed brickwork and filament bulbs when there existed this season's shiny white units and polished concrete floors. 'Don't question me,' she always shouted, when I asked how she afforded it. 'This kitchen is my temple.'

It was nothing of the sort. Lizzy was shit even at frying eggs.

Rain pattered lightly on the windows. It was one of those ambiguous days, all sharp, needling sunlight, then grey carpets of rain. It didn't have the look of the Day of Judgment. I finished my crumpet, remembering with fondness how fanatical and guilt-ridden I'd spent most of my life being around food. Thank God that was done with. Like so many other things.

I sat silently in Lizzy's vast kitchen like something from an Edward Hopper painting, watching the May showers wash clean the streets of Chelsea. It was time to go. The trial began today.

I didn't need to be there, of course. It would be at least a week before I was called by the prosecution, and none of the other girls wanted to be there. But it felt important to me. I wanted to be a part of it. No more hiding.

'I can do this,' I said. 'And I can deal with anything that arises from it.'

The skies were clearing as I left Lizzy's swanky building. I left my leather jacket in her hallway. The weather would work out, and so would the next few hours.

I felt my breath quicken as I passed under the railway bridge and saw the grim façade of Southwark Crown Court ahead. This was it. Just me, alone. Taking part in all aspects of my life, good and bad.

Only I wasn't alone.

Mark was standing on the steps outside the court.

I stopped walking. Mark was standing on the steps outside the court?

I went to take off my sunglasses, but I wasn't wearing any. Mark?

Mark?

Mark. He was walking towards me, and he was smiling, and he was so sexy and lovely that I nearly fainted right there on the street.

'Ah,' was what I managed to say. Ah?

'Hello.' He had stopped in front of me and he was perfect. 'Um . . . So, hi. My name's Mark, and apparently your name is Annie. I wondered if you fancied going for a drink with me some time?'

'Ah . . .'

'I'd really like to get to know you.'

'Ah,' I said, for the third time. Great.

He glanced up at the unprepossessing building above us. 'I know you've got some business here first, but perhaps we could go on a date afterwards. You can pick the venue. In fact, *please* pick a venue, because I was brought here from Paddington and I have no idea where I am.' He grinned. 'On that note, you may have to pay for the date as that taxi cost me a week's income.'

I was still staring at him. Unfortunately I didn't seem able to do anything else.

'Um, I'm joking,' he tried.

Nothing. My brain was in a freeze.

'I'm going to try again. Annie, please can I take you on a date?'

'Aaaah . . .'

He shook his head despairingly. 'Now listen here,' he began. There was a bit of haylage on the collar of his polo-neck. 'I've never asked anyone out in my life and I'm bricking it. Will you help me out here? Say something? Anything?'

If you say 'ah' again, I told myself, I will literally kill you. And just like that, the freeze thawed and sunshine poured in. 'Mark Waverley.' I smiled. 'I would love to go on a date with you. I would love that more than anything else.'

Mark sighed. 'Well, thank God for that. This date is going to be appalling if the asking-out is anything to go by.' He ran his hand through his hair, which was all clean and shiny and nice. I wanted to smell it.

'We're going on a date.' He grinned suddenly. 'A date! I'm excited! I've been wanting to go on a date with you for a very long time.'

A huge tidal swell of joy surged through me. 'Me too!'

Mark had come here for me! He had driven up from Exmoor at the crack of dawn to navigate a city he didn't know or like!

'So.' He jammed his hands back in the pockets of his jeans. 'Date sorted, back to the matter in hand,' he said. 'You.' He gave me another of those huge smiles and I melted just a little bit more. 'I thought I'd come and offer you some moral support. This is a big day, isn't it?'

'How did you know I was doing this today?' was the best I could come up with.

Mark looked shifty. 'I received a tip-off.'

'One of my friends?'

'Pretty much all of your friends.'

I felt myself relax. I love you, I thought. I love you, and I love my friends. 'This is the nicest surprise,' I said, smiling up at him. 'Probably the nicest surprise I've ever had.'

Life was a miracle! There was so much happiness, if you let yourself reach out and take it.

'How are you feeling? Are you doing okay?' He was smiling right back at me. Not just his shy half-smile, but the big beautiful one.

'I'm going to go in and watch, if that's what you mean.'

He nodded. 'Of course you are.' He reached over and squeezed my hand, then withdrew. 'Sorry. We should go on that date before I start grabbing you.'

Grab me any time, always, for ever, I thought giddily.

'Well, I just want to say that I think you're being incredibly brave and brilliant. When I consider what you've been through, I just sort of want to explode with pride.' His cheeks reddened, but he held firm. 'You're totally capable of doing this on your own,' he said, 'but I wanted you to know I cared. And that I'm so very proud of you.'

There was a long pause, during which we just gazed at each other and I thought I would keel over and die if I didn't get to kiss him.

'Um, how did you know I'd be here at this court?' I asked eventually. I could still barely believe he was there.

'My informants were very clear about which court you'd be at, and at what time.' He looked at something over my shoulder and chuckled. 'If you'd changed your plans I think they might have intervened.'

I looked behind me. Lizzy was leaning casually against a lamppost. Across the road from her Tim happened to be standing under a tree. And right in the middle of

Pocock Street, like a tiny bulldog, Claudine stood with her arms folded across her chest.

I burst out laughing, and Mark joined in.

'Do not speak to 'er,' Claudine instructed the others. 'Annie, listen. We are 'ere for you. We love you. Please go and do this thing, then please go on a date with Mark. The penalty for disobedience will be severe.'

I laughed again. Happiness and strength swelled in my chest. I could do *anything*! 'I'll see you afterwards,' I told them. Then I turned back to Mark.

'Do you want me to come in with you?' he asked.

I stroked a finger down the side of his lovely face, and I didn't care. 'I definitely want you to come in. But I think I should do this alone.'

'I'm here if you need me.'

'Thank you,' I said, taking his hand. I kissed it and the smell of his skin sent tremors through my whole body. 'Thank you so much for coming. You are wonderful.'

I did have to do it alone. For me, and the girls, and all the other women Stephen had tried to destroy. Most of all, I had to do this for Mum.

'Your mother would be very, very proud of you,' Mark said quietly. 'If it helps, my mum is crazy with pride back in Somerset.'

'Oh, Sandra . . .'

'Good luck, my beautiful Annie. Be the strong and fearless woman I know you are.'

And then he took my face in his hands and kissed me on the mouth. 'My sweet girl,' he whispered.

He squeezed my hand one last time and I walked up the steps into the foyer.

I had no idea what would happen. I had no idea if Stephen would be convicted, or what would happen if he was not.

But I was up for the fight. This was my time.

Chapter Thirty-three

Christmas Eve. I'd never been in London on Christmas Eve. It was barmy!

I fought my way through the festival-strength crowds at St Pancras, searching for the Chesterfield train, wondering how anyone was going to fit their luggage on to anything departing from there. People were literally moving house, from what I could tell. Huge yellow Selfridges bags, stripy John Lewis bags, H&M and Topshop, occasional Fortnum & Mason and even a decent smattering of Primark bags, all bulging and torn. Long rolls of wrapping paper, Christmas antlers, fat boxes of baubles, *panettones*, champagne, flowers. I looked down at my trusty Burmese bag – containing almost nothing – and smiled.

Right. Platform five. I braced myself and headed off into the fray. As people and suitcases swarmed past me, I thought about all of the many journeys I'd taken to Dad's over the years. The times I'd walked up this exact same escalator, hoping that something might have changed, that he might have turned a corner. And then arriving back a few days later, happy to have seen him but painfully aware of how much smaller his life had got since I'd seen him last.

I love you, Daddy, I thought. You brave and wonderful man. I love you with all my heart.

And then there he was. My daddy, arriving in London

for the first time in nearly thirty years, his lovely girlfriend holding his hand and her teenage son stomping along, thumping things into his iPhone. Dad saw me almost straight away.

'ANNIE!' he cried. 'MERRY CHRISTMAS!'

And I ran forward to hug him, with tears in my eyes. 'Welcome to London, Daddy. Better late than never.'

'So where's your French friend?' Dad asked later. He was sitting on Lizzy's gigantic sofa, the scale of which he found utterly hilarious, and was drunk on the champagne that a beaming Lizzy was pouring continuously into his glass.

'Have my share,' she kept saying. 'And remember my share was always quite big, Dad.'

'Claudie's in Antigua on a "luxury Christmas holiday",' I said, tucking my slippers under Mark's legs. He slid an arm around me, kissing the side of my forehead. 'She met a guy about three months ago and it's been, er, shall we say, intense? Although in a good way.'

Lizzy grinned. 'She'd have killed us if we'd pulled a stunt like this three months into a relationship!'

Dad looked at her, and then at me. 'Well, forgive me, girls, but you've pulled some major stunts quite early in your own relationships, haven't you?' He looked pointedly at Lizzy's pregnant belly, and at the ring on my finger. 'You haven't really waited around.'

'Old birds,' Lizzy told him. 'We didn't have time on our side, Dad.'

Dad's eyes twinkled. 'Well, I waited nearly thirty years for Linda,' he said, 'so I firmly believe there's nothing like a good old-fashioned dose of caution.' Mark chuckled and got to his feet to top up everyone's glass. I smiled at the sight of my bear in a proper shirt. He'd be getting a hairstyle at this rate. (He would not.)

'I'm just glad Linda was so patient.' Lizzy grinned. 'Anyone else would have given up months before.'

Linda, who was without doubt the nicest person I'd ever met, squeezed Dad's hand. 'I knew I'd crack him in the end,' she said kindly. 'He just needed careful handling.' And without caring what any of us thought, Dad leaned in and kissed her firmly on the mouth.

'Snuggums,' I distinctly heard him say.

Mark squeezed my bottom, which was one of his favourite things.

'And your friends from the stables,' Dad said, 'Mark's old grooms, how are they? You are still in touch, aren't you? They sounded so nice!'

'They are,' I assured him. 'They come to visit us at the new farm as often as they can. But they're . . .' I trailed off. 'Oh, God, Mark, what will we *do*? I hardly dare think about it, in case it gives me a stroke.'

Becca had called me a few days ago and had spent half an hour saying strange things. When I'd eventually asked her what was wrong, she'd taken a deep breath and said: 'Pet, there's no easy way to say this, but I've been having it off with Joe. I'm sorry if this sends you into cardiac arrest.'

I had not actually been able to say a word.

Becca had continued, 'It kind of crept up on us, pet, and we've not been apart for longer than about five minutes in the last three months.' *Three months?* Joe's affairs rarely lasted three days!

433

Becca's voice had suddenly got deeper, and I imagined her blushing a deep, silky red. 'We both think it has legs,' she'd said. 'I'm appalled, pet, but actually very happy.'

Mark, next to me, was laughing. Deep rumbles of amusement and disbelief. 'It's one of the more terrible things I've ever heard,' he admitted, 'but I like it.'

'Oh, me too! Can you imagine if they actually make it? Oh, God!'

I leaned round and kissed him, because I was too madly in love not to, just as Tim, who'd been stroking Lizzy's pregnant belly, nuzzled into her neck and kissed her hair. I WILL ALWAYS LOVE YOU, I saw him mouth into the side of her hair.

Rob the teenager got up. 'I'm leaving,' he said. 'I can't take any more.'

Everyone begged his forgiveness and we all rearranged ourselves so we weren't anywhere near the person we wanted to kiss. Poor Rob: it had been disgusting so far. If I were him I'd have set fire to the flat.

'I think we should make a toast,' Mark said.

'I agree!' I said, casting a sideways glance at Dad. Would he want to drink to Mum? With Linda here?

He would not.

'I think we should toast all of us who are in this room,' Dad said firmly. I hadn't heard him so confident or direct in years. 'Because we're all starting over. We're starting new memories now, together as a new family, and I think we're bloody fantastic. Here's to us.'

'To us,' we all said, getting up to clink glasses.

In spite of Rob I somehow found myself next to my man again, and as he slid his hand down my jeans and scrunched my bum once more, and Lizzy said, 'Oh, fuck it, the baby won't mind a little bit more champagne,' and Tim said, 'Oh, yes, he will,' and Dad blew a kiss at Linda, and Rob stormed off muttering that we were all disgusting, I thought, *I'm here*. Here in my life.

And this is where I'm going to stay.

Acknowledgements

It's only really authors and their mates who read the acknowledgements before starting a book, but – just in case – this page contains spoilers. Turn back!

My thanks, first and foremost, to the women brave enough to talk to me about their experiences at the hands of men like Stephen. You are all extraordinary. To S, my warmest gratitude.

Many thanks to top eventer Izzy Taylor, for allowing me to follow her around and for answering many odd questions. Also to Jessica Pidcock, for getting me started, and to Jane Tuckwell, from Badminton Horse Trials, for showing me around the stunning stableyard.

Clare King, for facilitating all of my eventing research and checking through the entire manuscript.

Dr Mark Cross, for his very useful advice on psychopathy. I also drew on material I'd read in the following books: *The Psychopath Test* by Jon Ronson, *Snakes in Suits: When Psychopaths Go to Work* by Paul Babiak, and *Without Conscience: The Disturbing World of the Psychopaths Among Us* by Robert D. Hare.

Orthopaedic surgeon Alpesh Kothari, for the many emails and phone calls spent devising terrible injuries for Mark.

Specialist horse vet Sally Cobbald, for her above-and-beyond help with Stumpy. And Mike Rayment, who really should be charging me.

David Martin, for his very useful advice on Annie's legal situation.

Special thanks to my publisher at Michael Joseph, Maxine Hitchcock, whose clear vision for the publication of this novel – not to mention wonderful support – has kept me at it, day after day. You have been a rock. Thank you to the brilliant Celine Kelly, who edits my books with such imagination and skill! To my peerless copy-editor Hazel Orme – who really does make me a better writer – and my brilliant publicist Francesca Pearce. Thanks to Sarah Arratoon, for marketing greatness, and Lee Motley, for my very exciting new book jacket. Nick Lowndes, Anna Derkacz, Sophie Overment, Olivia Whitehead and Helen Eka – again, thank you. I'm so lucky to have you all.

Thank you to George, for making me laugh every single day. You are my favourite. Thank you to my friends, who keep on pimping my books to anyone who'll listen. To my fellow writers, without whom I would most definitely go mad, and my readers, without whom I wouldn't have a career! Same to you, tireless bloggers: I can't do it without you.

Thanks to my family for the happy years on horseback. Wasn't it wonderful? Apart from when we had to try to get Wriggle and Ben in a trailer.

Thanks to the crack team of brilliant people at David Higham Associates: Harriet, Laura, Alice, Emma, Emily – I hope you know how much I appreciate you.

And thank you, finally, to Lizzy Kremer, without whom I would resign tomorrow. From everything. You are the finest agent on earth.

Reading Group Questions

Plot spoilers ahead – read at your own risk!

1. Did you find yourself empathizing more with Annie or Kate throughout the book, and if so in what ways?

2. Did you realize Annie and Kate were the same person? Looking back, what signs could you have picked up on while reading the book?

3. When we first meet Kate, she's moved to Somerset to escape 'the incessant noise of [her] old life'. Do you think it's possible to change your life with a change of scenery alone?

4. Annie, Lizzy and their father are all shown to cope in different ways with the death of Annie's mother. What are the similarities and differences in how they grieve? Throughout the book how do we see them transition from victims to survivors?

5. When Annie meets Stephen it all seems too good to be true – do you think that Annie was too quick to trust him? Were there clues in his behavior she could have spotted earlier on?

6. Annie struggles to balance her old friendships with a new relationship – what mistakes did she make? Were the members of Le Cloob responsible too?

7. Both Annie and Kate become romantically involved with their bosses. In what other ways do we see repeating patterns of behaviour throughout the novel?

8. Was Mark wrong to react how he did when he discovered Kate was really Annie? How important is a name to your identity? What makes someone themselves?

9. Why do you think Stephen is so obsessed with Annie, despite having 'relationships' with Ros, Petra and Nancy at the same time?

10. Towards the end of the novel, we learn that Claudine has signed up for a dating website while in an unhappy marriage. Do you condone her behaviour? Is it ever acceptable to cheat on a partner?

Also available

THE GREATEST LOVE STORY OF ALL TIME

In her quest to figure out why her life has suddenly gone down the pan, Fran comes up with a failsafe plan: live like a badger and drink gin every night. But then Fran's friends force a very different plan on her and it's nowhere near as fun. How could eight dates possibly make her feel better?

But eventually she agrees. And so begins the greatest love story of all time . . .

A PASSIONATE LOVE AFFAIR WITH A TOTAL STRANGER

Charley Lambert has put considerable effort into achieving a perfect life. Until the day it spectacularly falls apart.

Forced to make a new start, Charley discovers her talent for helping the lovelorn online. And then William arrives in her nbox. Within hours of his first email, her world starts to change.

But will Charley be brave enough to turn her back on her old life – all for a total stranger?

THE UNFINISHED SYMPHONY OF YOU AND ME

Sally is a woman of many (hidden) talents.

But she made a promise to her cousin Fiona that she would udition for Opera School and for complicated reasons, she can't get out of it – even though she'd rather claw her own eyes out than sing in public.

Sally has a lot to learn, but will she realise that stage fright is about more than forgetting the words? And that perhaps her real problems lie very much closer to home?

Find out
more about Lucy
and her novels by visiting
her online

© Tania Beagley-Brown

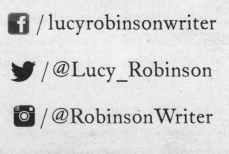